Railroad Ties: The Marmion Grove Murders

by

M. S. Spencer

Railroad Ties: The Marmion Grove Murders

COPYRIGHT © 2025 by Meredith Ellsworth

Cover Art by *Tina Lynn Stout*

The Wild Rose Press, Inc.
PO Box 708
Adams Basin, NY 14410-0708
Visit us at www.thewildrosepress.com

Publishing History
First Edition, 2025
Trade Paperback ISBN 978-1-5092-6128-4
Digital ISBN 978-1-5092-6129-1

Published in the United States of America

Dedication

To the Beer & Marching Society of Garrett Park

Chapter One

It gets laughed at because it is a small town, I know, but nevertheless it is a place where great men may be born any day, for fair winds and foul blow right on over it without distinction.

~ Henry David Thoreau

Vassar Book Sale sorting center, District of Columbia, Tuesday, April 2

"I can't tell you how much I appreciate this, Sophie." The little woman with the sparkly black eyes and bustling air put down a cardboard box and brushed the fringe of hair out of her eyes. "Ginny's baby shower is in Georgetown, and I'd never make it if I had to do a book pickup in Maryland first. I swear it's twenty miles of the worst traffic in America."

"No problem at all, Connie." Sophie untied the pink smock that covered her jeans and denim shirt and hung it up. "Where in Maryland is it?"

"Marmion Grove is between Bethesda and Rockville. Quickest route is to head north on Wisconsin Avenue. Take a right on Strathmore Avenue. You can't miss it—when you hit a wall of old growth forest you've arrived."

"You're kidding, right?"

"Nope. Most of the trees in the town are over a

1

hundred years old." Connie wiped an imaginary drop of perspiration from her brow. "You know how torrid DC summers are, right? Well, Marmion Grove is like a verdant refuge—the air is noticeably cooler the minute you set foot in it."

Sophie drew her sweatshirt over her head. "It's fifty degrees outside. I'd rather be warmed up than cooled down."

Connie looked her friend over. "What are you? Twenty-eight? You're too young to be cold, my dear."

She let that slide. "I read an article in the *Clarion* the other day about Marmion Grove—it sounds like a charming town. This will give me a chance to explore it."

"Well, be careful. It's rumored to be haunted. Tales of unsolved murders, or so I hear. Disappearances. That sort of thing."

Sophie peered at her. "I hope you're joking."

Connie winked. "By all means, do a little sightseeing. Just don't forget to pick up the books. Mr. Pennyman will meet you there. He says he has quite a few boxes."

"Is he an alumnus?"

"No. His mother Vivian was class of '72." Her hand flew to her mouth. "Oh dear, you only have the little Kia, don't you? I'd lend you my station wagon, but I need it for the party supplies. You might have to take two trips." She handed Sophie a slip of paper. "Here's the address."

Sophie kept her chagrin to herself. Connie was the heart and soul of the Vassar Book Sale and was—in Sophie's opinion—run ragged by all the volunteers. *I'm not going to add to her stress by whining about gasoline prices and drive time.* She skimmed the slip of paper.

"Peveril Hall, 4715 Waverley Avenue. Waverley? That's a familiar name… Where have I heard it before?"

Connie grinned. "Good for you. It's from the Sir Walter Scott novel. In the 1880s, a speculator bought land next to the rail line for a summer retreat from the DC swamp. He named the town after a famous Scott poem, and all the streets after his books: Waverley, Kenilworth, Montrose. Like that. Some of the original owners joined in the game. Thus we have Peveril Hall, after *Peveril of the Peak*."

"Haven't heard of that one. Peveril Hall, huh." She pictured a crumbling limestone castle—ramparts, turrets, and all. "Sounds rather grand."

"To us maybe. It was considered a simple 'cottage' in the 1890s. It's a Queen Anne—complete with tower and wrap-around porch. Vivian Pennyman lived in it for over forty years. According to her, it was one of the first houses built in the Grove." She nodded happily. "There are servants' quarters and even a stable and hayloft."

Sophie laughed. "Servants' quarters? Hayloft? Not really so simple then. Did Vivian keep a horse and carriage?"

"Don't be flippant, dear. It doesn't suit you." Connie added with an air of approval, "And none of that new-fangled air conditioning either."

"Really? It must be sweltering in the hot months."

"Not at all. Heat rises, and since Victorian houses have fifteen-foot ceilings, the hot air hovers high over your head."

Sophie resisted the urge to look up and snared her keys from the table. "It'll take me a while to get there. If it gets late, I'll keep the boxes in my car overnight and bring them tomorrow."

Connie pointed at the books stacked around the room and cascading into the hall. "No rush. The book sale is still a month away, but as usual we're way behind on sorting." She shook her head. "I don't know how Eudora and I are going to manage it."

"Eudora tells me you say that every year, m'dear. We have the Mellon Auditorium reserved, and Alison's got a crew of bookkeepers lined up to help her. I've already recruited a hundred volunteers from twenty Vassar classes. Every shift but the first afternoon is covered. If we can't pull it off, no one can."

Connie snorted. "I think we should have a banner made: Seven Days in May."

"Seven Days in May? What does that mean?"

She chortled. "You're so young, Sophie."

Sophie recalled the strand of gray hair she'd found only that morning. "I don't feel young, Connie. Just tell me."

"*Seven Days in May* refers to a 1962 novel about a president who is trying to prevent a nuclear war and the general who mutinies against him. Edge of your seat thriller—just like the book sale."

"Ha-ha. Well, in my experience, Vassar grads can do anything they put their minds to."

"Unless it's fixing a flat."

Sophie decided to take Connie's remark as a kindly jab and not a snide reminder of the time it required five Vassar alumnae and a fellow they roped in from a Seven-Eleven to change her tire. "I'll be off then."

She keyed the address into her GPS and drove out of Northwest Washington to the Maryland suburbs. The blooming cherry trees and azaleas that made Washington the most beautiful city in America in springtime were at their peak. *I'm glad I decided to come back home. It was too lonely in Paris.* A tear welled up. *If only... If only Thomas were here with me, it would be perfect.* But Thomas was gone. Off into the wilds of the Mongolian desert.

She had come to see him off at Orly Airport. He explained for the tenth time why he didn't want to return to the States. "It's not the country I grew up in, Sophie. Americans don't *think* anymore—they just follow. I need a place where the individual is still celebrated, not vilified or forced to abide by the dictates of a decadent elite." He didn't ask her to go with him.

That was the part that hurt the most, but in a way she was grateful. She still held out hope for America. *A staunch preference for liberty is built into our genes. It's non-negotiable. We'll never submit completely to some out-of-touch, deranged global cabal that wants us to eat crickets and live in tall sealed towers without windows.* Wasn't there a book about that? Isaac Asimov. *That's right,* The Caves of Steel. *Nothing new under the sun, I guess.*

She drove through Bethesda and then seemingly endless strip malls and gas stations before turning right at a hill dominated by a glassed-in concert venue. A mile on, a large banner proclaimed the Marmion Grove Estates. Row upon row of perfectly uniform, postage-stamp-sized brick houses marched alongside her. She topped a rise and abruptly hit a bank of tall, mature trees, transforming the road into a shadowed green alley. *Connie was right. I feel like I've entered a primordial paradise.* She half expected to see a brontosaurus lumber by, chewing its cud. She was gazing up at the huge oaks and almost missed the sign—Marmion Grove:

Incorporated 1898. Declared the First Nuclear-Free Zone in the United States in 1982.

She turned down the shady lane and took a right at the fork onto Waverley Avenue. A few houses down she found number 4715. The stately white Victorian with jarringly scarlet shutters stood atop a terraced slope. She squinted at the roof. *Yup, the cupola is red too.* The owner must be either color blind or have revolutionary aspirations. *I'll have to ask Connie if Vivian Pennyman dabbled in communism.*

She parked at the curb, where a hedge of yellow forsythia marked the property line. The front lawn led up to a porch completely engulfed in a reticulated wisteria vine as thick and complex as fine lacework. Halfway up reared an ancient tree, its knobbed and serrated trunk perhaps five feet in diameter. The pendulous branches were the size of fully grown trees and were only kept from falling by a steel chain wrapped around them. Its broad leaves were gigantic. *They must be almost two feet long!*

As she sat gawking, a pleasant male voice said, "It's a swamp magnolia. At least a hundred and fifty years old."

Startled, she knocked her knee on the steering wheel. "Ouch!"

A young man came around the car and peered in her window. "Are you all right?"

She looked up into cornflower blue eyes partially obscured by a shrubbery of sandy hair. "Oh, sorry. I didn't mean to stare. It's just... I've never seen such big leaves before."

"We used to use them as dinner plates, but they're a bitch to wash." He leaned in. "May I help you?"

6

She left off gazing at him and shook herself. "Oh. Oh, yes. Is this"—she checked Connie's directions—"Peveril Hall?"

"It is indeed."

"Do you live here? I'm supposed to collect a load of books for the Vassar Book Sale."

"Ah. No. I mean, no, I don't live here. Anymore. I used to. I grew up here, but I've been away a long time."

"Then you can't help me?"

"Huh? No! I mean, yes, I can help you. This is my house."

"But you just said…"

He pointed to his left. "Head on up the driveway there. I'll meet you out back." And he loped off across the grass.

Okey doke. Sophie followed a lane along the side of the house to a gravel lot fronting a two-story garage. The backyard was dotted with small buildings. She got out and scanned the area. A small octagonal hut stood near a stately sycamore. Next to it crouched a one-room shanty with a chimney. *That must be the servants' quarters.* She looked up at the garage. A huge hook painted green was attached to the wall just under the gable. "I wonder what that's for."

Just then the young man came around the corner of the house. "Hey there. I'm Noah, by the way. Noah Pennyman. My mother was the Vassar grad. And you are?"

She took a moment to admire his mobile, angular features. He seemed always on the verge of speaking…or maybe singing. The shock of blond hair fell negligently across his brow. When he shook her hand, a very masculine aroma of citrus and spice

7

enveloped her. She suppressed the urge to inhale. "Sophie Childress. I'm from the—"

"Vassar Book Sale. So you said." He reached out and flicked her hair. "Nice French braid. I never could figure out how it's done. Come on inside."

She retrieved a dolly from her trunk and followed him. They entered a vast kitchen, bifurcated by a peninsula eight feet long. Along both walls were counters and sinks—enough for a platoon of cooks and scullery maids.

He led her past a breakfast nook to a dining room where dozens of boxes were stacked on and around a long cherry table. Sophie raised her eyes to a distant ceiling, then lowered them to gaze out a tall bow window. "Ooh, I love this house! Connie—she's our chairman—told me it's one of the original ones in the town."

"Yes. It was built in 1894. Marmion Grove was developed as a getaway for DC dwellers during the hot and humid summers. It was a great house to grow up in— except in July." He pretended to pant. "I don't care what Mother said, air conditioning is a necessity even with the high ceilings."

Hear that, Connie? "You said it was your house, but you don't live here?"

"Correct. I have an apartment in the District. My mother died four months ago, and my sister and I inherited the place. Gretchen is happily ensconced in Colorado and transferred the title to me."

"What are you going to do with it?"

"Clean it out, then put it on the market."

Sophie felt a fleeting stab of envy. She'd never lived in such a grand house. "I'd be sorry to give it up." She spun the dolly around. "Well, we'd better get started."

Noah piled the boxes on the dolly, and Sophie hauled them to her car. An hour later, she closed the trunk. "I'm afraid that's all I can carry. I'll have to come back for the rest."

Noah perked up. "That would be great…er… I mean, you have to do what you have to do."

Sophie—who sensed Noah was experiencing the same feelings she was—said quickly, "Oh, I don't mind. How long will you be here?"

His smile faded. "A few weeks. There's a lot of stuff to dispose of besides the books." He waved a hand toward the backyard. "Not only the house, but the stable and the playhouse are filled with junk accumulated over forty years."

"And when you're done, you'll sell the house."

"That's the plan." He cocked an eyebrow. "Of course, it won't be easy. This old house has a lot of history—and its share of ghosts, I'm told."

Sophie gulped. "Really?"

He laughed. "Nah. I was just trying out my sales pitch on you. Should I mention the eerie will o' the wisps and midnight shrieks? Would that attract you or frighten you off?"

She assumed it was a rhetorical question and remarked, "With or without ghosts, it should bring you quite a fortune."

He pursed his lips. "Funny, my parents bought this house for $90,000 in 1983. Today Victorians like this one are going for several million."

She scrutinized the white clapboard mansion and sighed. "You said you have a place downtown. So you'll be going back and forth?"

"I'll see how it goes. I have an apartment near Federal Triangle."

"Have you lived there long?"

"About two years. I'd been in Chicago for five and before that Boston. It was time to come home." His face fell. "I should be glad I was here in Mother's last years, but it's been difficult."

"I'm so sorry." She visualized an elegant, ramrod-straight old lady presiding over the long cherry table, her son at the foot. While the sunbeams poured in through the bay window, bouncing off dust motes, a butler would ladle thin soup from a tureen. *It must have been grim.* "Did you stay here with her?"

"Oh, no. It was too long a commute to work. Plus, I was used to living alone, and so was she." He waved a hand. "I like the house, but it's too big, too old, too…GU."

"GU?"

"Geographically undesirable." He roused himself. "I'll palm it off on some double-income couple as soon as I get it in shape."

She shyly swiveled her eyes to his. "That's a shame."

He held her gaze. "Is it?"

Chapter Two

There is no greater mistake in life than seeing things or hearing them at the wrong time.

~Agatha Christie

Sorting Center, Wednesday, April 3

Sophie finished unloading the car. "This isn't even half of it, Connie. There were at least fifty boxes in Peveril Hall."

"Vivian Pennyman had an extensive library. I believe her husband collected first editions. Eudora is looking forward to appraising them."

"Me too." Sophie was just learning the procedures for pricing rare books, which comprised a large portion of the donations they received. Valuation involved extensive searches through the reference books that lined the shelves in the Rare Books room, not to mention quite a bit of online research. Once the value was established for a book, Eudora—head of the department—would set a price. It was always significantly lower than the market price. At first Sophie protested, but the prim little woman with Ben Franklin glasses perched on a snub nose clucked, "We're a non-profit, Sophie. Our purpose is to swell Vassar's scholarship coffers. Besides, we're famous for asking a modest amount for a fabulous find. You'll see at the sale—booksellers camp out overnight on our doorstep to be the first to snap up our treasures."

Sophie checked her watch. "It's five o'clock. I'm off home."

Connie put the last box on the stack. "When will you be able to pick up the rest of Vivian's books?"

"I'll see if I can squeeze it in tomorrow."

Sophie took back streets, avoiding the heavy boulevard traffic in central DC. Her townhouse on Capitol Hill was just beyond Union Station. She loved it because it was close to everything—the Senate office buildings, the Library of Congress, the Supreme Court, transportation, and restaurants. It was expensive, but as the real estate agent said, "Location, location, location." While her freelance editing business kept her in food and shelter, she planned to spend her free time writing a novel. She hadn't quite settled on mystery or romance but fully expected inspiration would come.

She found a rare parking spot on her street and surveyed the sky for a blue moon. When she opened the passenger side to get her purse, she noticed a cardboard box in the well. "Oops, I forgot one." *Didn't Connie say Mrs. Pennyman owned some first editions?* "I'd better take this inside just in case." She dropped it in the dining room, then went to the kitchen and made herself a sandwich. Twisting the top off a cold beer, she carried her plate and drink back to the box. "Might as well take a look at the contents."

She heaped the books next to her. "*Hmm. The Adventures of Tom Sawyer.* Original artwork. Some foxing." She checked the inside leaf. "First edition, but third printing. May be worth something." She chose another. "Evelyn Waugh, *The Loved One.* Now *that* was a funny book." She continued to sort through the volumes. Nothing jumped out at her until she reached the bottom of the box.

"What's this?" She lifted out a heavy polyethylene bag. She knew from Eudora's instruction that the bag was archival quality. *Now why was this one protected when the others weren't?* She slid the book out. "Agatha Christie. *The Mysterious Affair at Styles*." Christies were a dime a dozen. Most of her works had millions of copies in print. It was unlikely this was valuable, even though it was a hardback. *Maybe it was a gift. There could be an inscription or note inside.* She checked the flyleaf. Nothing. She turned to the copyright page. "First edition, first printing." *Okay.* New York: John Lane Publishing Company, 1920. *Wait a minute.* She set it down, puzzled. *New York?* Christie's books were published in England. *It must be the first American edition.* Still, sometimes those fetched surprisingly good prices. *Another thing to research at the center.* As she reinserted it in its plastic bag, an envelope fell out. Yellowed and stained, it was addressed to Constable Bustwick, Montgomery County Police. *No return address or stamp.* She opened it.

Inside was a scrap of butcher's brown wrapping paper. *It's a letter.* The handwriting was shaky. *An older person? A child?* Though the date was obscured by a streak of dried ink, she could make out "April" and "1920." *The same year the book was published.* She sat down to read.

Dear Constable Bustwick,

I write to you in great distress. I believe I may have witnessed a horrible act. However, I do not know if it was truly a crime, so I am begging you to investigate quietly. If I speak out publicly, I risk my position.

The event occurred two nights ago. The master and

mistress had retired. I had closed up the house and returned to my room when a thunderstorm barreled through. For a time the thunder was quite loud. Lightning struck one of our cherry trees with a great CRACK. I had finally dozed off when a noise outside woke me. It was perhaps an hour past midnight. We have had problems with raccoons in the garbage pit lately, so I took my broom and went out to frighten the creatures off. It was very dark after the storm, with only the feeble light from the hitching post lantern to see by. A figure came around the side of the carriage house. He had a large bundle slung over his shoulder. Mr. Constable, I think it was a body! As I watched, he toppled it into the back seat of an automobile parked on the gravel. When he tried to close the door, a man's hat fell out. He picked the hat up, threw it inside, and drove away.

I was terrified, but the master had left strict orders not to disturb them, so I went back to my quarters. The next morning the master and mistress had breakfast as usual. Neither mentioned a late night visitor. The stable held only their Ford Model T and the carriage. The car in the driveway had been much larger and fancier. I remember the lamplight glinting on a chrome hood ornament that resembled a flying bird.

When the day had almost passed and the master had not altered his normal routine, I began to feel that I'd dreamed the whole thing. Then late that afternoon I was sweeping the carriage house floor and found the glass bottle we keep the rat poison in. It lay in the floor drain, shattered. Constable Bustwick, I do not know if the broken bottle has anything to do with the body, but I fear it does. I beg you to look into it, but please, please don't contact my master or mention my name. I pray there is a simple explanation for all this.

Sincerely, Agnes Reilly.

The letter fell out of Sophie's hand. *My God.* Did this Agnes really witness a murder? And why didn't she mail the letter? Did she mean to hand carry it, or perhaps she couldn't find a stamp? And how did it end up in the book? She sat, fanning herself with the envelope. Hefting the volume, she quickly slipped the letter between its pages and dropped it back in the box.

I have to return to Marmion Grove anyway. I'll ask Noah about the letter. She was ashamed to realize the thought gave her pleasure.

****

Sophie's apartment, Thursday morning

The next morning Sophie called Connie. "I'm going to pick up the rest of the books from the house in Marmion Grove. Do you have a phone number for the man who's staying there?"

"You mean Vivian's son, Noah? Sure, let me get it." Sophie heard rustling, then Connie's voice again. "301-555-2657. That's his cell phone. Was he nice?"

"Oh yes." Sophie broke off, savoring the image of eyes the color of chicory growing beside the highway and hair like a wind-tossed wheat field. "Yes, very."

"Vivian was so proud of him. She was always going on about how thoughtful and helpful he was." She paused. "Her husband Roger walked out on them when Noah was very young, and he had to grow up fast—be the man of the family. Vivian always said she wouldn't know what she and her daughter would have done without him. Although…"

Sophie waited. She had learned from experience that her friend liked to round out her descriptions with a comprehensive picture of her subject.

"Are you there, dear?"

"Yes, Connie. You were saying?"

"Well, I do so hate to cast aspersions, but Vivian also said he was a handful as a child—always getting into trouble. You were at the house, right? Then you know the garage used to be a stable. Well, little Noah liked to jump off the second-floor loft onto the ground. Broke his leg once. And he and his sister… Now, what was her name?"

Sophie listened to the tapping. *At least it's not elevator music.*

"Gretchen. That's it. She was a few years older than Noah. Anyway, they would sneak candy and cookies into the playhouse and leave the crumbs and wrappers all over the floor." She sniffed. "Vivian said it attracted rats. It's a wonder neither child was bitten."

"Playhouse? Do you mean the little cabin in the backyard?"

"Yes. It was converted from accommodations for the domestic staff into a playhouse in the thirties. Most families had to let their help go during the Depression."

"Were the Pennymans wealthy?"

"Oh dear, no. Poor Vivian was a single mother—didn't I mention her husband abandoned them? They got by on her librarian's salary. Anyway, she didn't move into the house until the early eighties. She told me once that it originally belonged to the railroad, although what a railway line would want with a house I can't fathom."

"I'll ask Noah."

"You do that. Bring the rest of the boxes straight here, please. We need them ASAP. Eudora is in one of her moods; you know—antsy."

Sophie hung up and dialed Noah's number.

His phone went to voice mail. She tried a few more times, but the morning passed without getting hold of him. Finally, just before noon, she decided to go anyway. *He may have been busy packing and didn't hear it ring.* She checked herself in the mirror. Her long French braid was still neat, the golden brown hair glossy and warm. It went rather well with her warm brown eyes. She smirked and struck a pose. The pink shirtwaist dress brought out the rose in her cheeks and accentuated her narrow waist nicely. *I may be pushing thirty, but I still got it—at least some of it.*

After a moment's thought, she carried the box with the Christie book to the car, then headed up to Marmion Grove. As she parked on the gravel behind the house, Noah was backing down the rear stairs, a standing lamp in his arms. She got out. "Can I help?"

He yelped and dropped the lamp on his toe. "Ouch, ouch, ouch!" He danced around to face her. "Why did you *do* that?"

She set the fixture upright. "I'm sorry. I thought you heard me drive in."

He pulled out his ear buds. "No, I didn't. What are you doing here?"

"I came to get the other boxes. Remember?"

"Oh, yeah. I didn't know you meant today. You could have called." He gave her a reproachful look. "I'd have showered or made coffee or something."

Sophie took a moment to wonder why those two activities were on the top of the list. And how they related to her arrival. "Coffee sounds nice."

"Come on inside then." As he set up the coffee maker he said casually, "Sorry if I stink—I went rock climbing this morning and just got back."

"Rock climbing! Isn't that dangerous?"

"Not if you know what you're doing. I love to puzzle out where to put my foot next—although I've been known to miss the point and put it in my mouth."

She laughed dutifully. "Connie—my colleague at the sale—knew your mother well. She says you were a hellion when you were young. Always getting into scrapes."

He hung his head. "I blush to confirm. Alas, I've never grown out of it." He showed her a finger twisted into an unnatural shape. "Landed on it when I was sky diving."

"Sky diving? Rock climbing? What other extreme sports are you into?"

Noah eyed her meditatively. Finally he said, "I can't tell if you're interested or mocking me."

"Just curious."

He handed her a mug and turned to make a cup for himself. "I have a scuba diving certificate. I race Harleys." His lips twitched. "I once built a balsa wood raft and sailed it across the Pacific to prove the Americas were settled from Polynesia and not the Bering Strait."

"Really?" Sophie had been listening with growing consternation until his last remark. "Okay, now you're just making things up."

He chuckled. "Sort of. Since Thor Heyerdahl already accomplished that feat, there was no need for me to try." He polished his fingernails. "I like to be unique."

She giggled. "Not to worry."

He took her empty mug and put it in the sink. "Now, shall we move those boxes?"

Sophie clapped a hand to her mouth. "I almost

forgot! I have something to show you." She ran out to her car and retrieved the envelope from the Christie book. She held it out. "Do you know anything about this?"

He slipped the fragment of paper out. His eyes widened as he read. Finally he looked up. "Is this a joke?"

"A joke? That hadn't crossed my mind."

"Where did you find it?"

"Inside a first edition of Agatha Christie's first published book."

"*The Mysterious Affair at Styles.*"

"Yes." She looked at Noah with new eyes. "You're a bibliophile?"

"I read, if that's what you mean. I don't spend all my time under a parachute or clinging for dear life to a cliff face."

"What do you do for a living?"

But he was re-reading the letter. "We need to know more about this. Do you remember which box the book was in?"

"I can do better than that." She led him to her car.

He heaved the box out and set it down on the gravel.

Sophie pointed at the writing on the top. "All it says is 'Roger's.' Do you know who Roger is?"

Noah was quiet for a long minute. Finally he said, "My father."

Chapter Three

Books are a habit-forming drug.

~Agatha Christie

Peveril Hall, Thursday, April 4

"Roger is your father? Oh. Well, perhaps we should send the box to him. He may not have agreed to donate it to the Vassar Book Sale. After all, a first edition Christie is worth a lot. I haven't done the research yet, but—"

"I'm sure he doesn't care." Noah was curt.

Wait a minute—didn't Connie say Vivian's husband took off when Noah was a child? "Is he... Is he..."

"Dead? I have no idea. He could be by now. He skipped out when I was five. We haven't heard from him since." He picked up the box and strode toward the house. "Tell you what, I'll look through my mother's papers. Maybe she listed this one with instructions on what to do with it."

"So you don't know anything about it?"

He shook his head. "I would've set it aside if I did."

"Where did the boxes I took Tuesday come from?"

He spread his hands out. "Who remembers? I gathered books from every case and dumped them in no particular order in the dining room, where I filled the boxes. Mother had already packed some up. This must have been one of hers. I just stuck it with the rest."

"Didn't you check inside any of her boxes?"

"Nah. I didn't think it mattered since they were either going to your sale or to Goodwill." He jutted his chin toward the backyard. "There's more stuff stored in the stable and the playhouse."

"Could you have brought it in from out there?"

"I haven't tackled either place yet."

"You said the playhouse. That's the little house in back, isn't it?"

"Right, the cabin between the garage and the summer house. We used it as a playhouse when we were kids, but it was originally lodging for the servants. It has a fireplace and benches for sleeping."

"Sounds cozy."

He smiled reminiscently. "Me and Gretchen—my sister—would camp out there sometimes. Mom would make up a fire, and we'd eat snacks and tell ghost stories. Gretchen never lasted long—she'd get the wind up and run back inside." He snickered. "Could have been my lurid, spine-chilling stories. Dunno."

Sophie wished he wouldn't meander so much. It would be nice to get back to the sorting center so she could price the Christie book. But then her glance fell on his sinewy hands curled around the coffee mug. *There's no real rush, is there?* "So you have no idea where this box came from?"

"Sorry. I was in a hurry to have everything ready for you." His eyes narrowed in thought. "I did haul some things down from the top floor."

"Huh. Well, there are still a lot of books for me to take. Maybe something will turn up that lends some clarity."

He pinched a corner of the letter. "We should probably hold on to this as well as the Christie, in case there *is* a connection."

She watched with chagrin as the dollar signs floated away. "All right."

"In fact, we might as well leave the whole box here. There could be a clue in it." He took it to the living room and deposited it under the coffee table. "Are you ready to fill up your car again?"

"Yup." She smiled. "We'll take everything you have."

"You got all the books from the dining room last time. Let's start on the garage."

The ground floor of the building consisted of two bays for cars. A sleek, pearlescent white sports car sat in one. Sophie raised an eyebrow. "An Aston Martin? That's a hundred-thousand-dollar car. You neglected to tell me what you do for a living. Stock broker? Or maybe a plumber?"

"I'm not smart enough to be a plumber." He patted the hood. "Magda is my baby. I inherited her from my grandfather. As for me, I'm just a lowly minion at the Smithsonian."

"A janitor?"

"Janitor?" He looked startled. "Nothing quite so glamorous. I work in the collections. There's a huge amount of material stored in vaults. I sort through it and prepare things for exhibits."

Sophie loved museums. "Sounds fascinating."

"It can be." He waved a hand around. "I'm pretty sure it's only housewares and knickknacks down here. Let's try upstairs."

They went up a narrow flight to a large open space.

"This was where they kept the hay. The hook for hauling it up from the wagon is still under the gable."

"Oh, so *that's* what it was for."

Half the room was empty, the other half a jumble of furniture and boxes. "Whew, this may take a while. Do you have time or should I do it myself?"

"No! I want to solve this mystery."

He shrugged. "There may be only the one box. After all, my father's been gone thirty years." At her snuffle of dismay, he added, "I can call you if I find something of note."

Instead of answering, she picked up a large framed picture of a Victorian woman in a lace cap and severe black dress and moved it to the side. "Come on."

Two hours later, Sophie sprawled, panting, on a rocking chair that was missing one arm. "That was the last carton. The only item the book sale might be able to sell is this circus poster." She held up a colorful depiction of a lion tamer. "It looks old."

"Nothing else?"

"Nothing marked Roger."

"As I suspected."

"Damn."

He looked at her curiously. "Why are you so concerned about my father's things?"

"Honestly? If he had one first edition, there might be more."

"Ah. The book sale again. It's nothing to do with the letter?"

Her hand flew to her mouth. "Oh my God, I forgot all about the letter. You know, maybe we should be looking for Agnes's belongings rather than your father's."

"Meaning, the letter and book ended up with Roger's things by accident? Serendipity?"

"I don't know, but it was Agnes who saw the man with the body, not your father."

"Okay." Noah cranked the window open that overlooked the servants' quarters. "We can start on the playhouse if you want."

Fatigue washed over her. "Oh, Noah, I'm tired." She checked her watch. "No wonder! It's six o'clock." She slumped on the seat. "We're right in the middle of rush hour. I'll never get home."

He leaned against an old bureau. "Tell you what: I'll take you to dinner. It'll allow the traffic to wind down."

A fillip of excitement rumbled in Sophie's chest, but she didn't think it proper to accept his offer. "All right, but we'll go Dutch. Do you have a place in mind?"

"There's actually a restaurant in the old P.O., but I've heard it's rather fancy." He looked down at his dirt-spattered sweatshirt and flicked a speck of dust from Sophie's braid. "We are demonstrably not in 'casual business attire.' " He must have heard her gulp, for he gave her a speculative look. "It sounds a bit expensive, too. Tell you what, let's drive up Rockville Pike. There's bound to be a pizza joint."

Sophie felt she should offer to drive but wasn't above giving the Aston Martin a longing glance. Noah said with a twinkle, "How about we take Magda out for a spin?"

"Oh? Okay. If you insist."

"She could use the exercise."

They'd gone a few miles without seeing anything appealing when a blinking neon sign caught Sophie's attention. "Isn't that a belly dancer? Could it be a Middle

Eastern restaurant?"

Noah followed her gaze. "Melina's. It's Greek. Supposed to be very good."

"I love Greek food."

"Well, it's not pizza, but it'll do." Noah swung into the parking lot.

The hostess seated them at a table by the window and handed them menus. Sophie tried and failed to stifle her gasp at the prices. "Um… Everything looks really…good, but I…er…had a big lunch, so maybe I'll just have the soup." She hoped Noah wouldn't point out that they'd worked through lunch without stopping.

Noah ran his eye over the items. "You know what? Let this be my treat. You worked hard today. You deserve it."

"I did, didn't I? I should've just grabbed the books and fled."

"You were intrigued. I admire that in a girl. Please allow me to take care of dinner."

Sigh. "Just this once." She smiled at him.

He sucked in a breath. "Did anyone ever tell you you're beautiful?"

Is that like asking when I stopped beating my husband? "Um…"

"That rich caramel hair, and your perfect little nose. Eyes a toasty brown, like warm hazelnuts." He reached out and touched her cheek. "Don't be embarrassed. I had to justify why I keep staring at you, didn't I?"

Sophie fought to remain cool. Lucky for her, the waiter appeared at that moment. "I am Yiannis. I shall be your server this evening. Do you have any questions?"

"Yes I do. Do you have a bar?"

He drew back, his eyes crinkling. "I take it you had

a bad day?"

"Not bad, just long." Noah ordered a martini.

"A vodka tonic for me."

Once they had their drinks in hand, Noah leaned forward. "Now tell me about yourself. All I know is you pick up books for some book sale."

"Not 'some' book sale. *The* book sale. The Vassar Book Sale has been in existence for forty years. It began in an alumna's basement with donations from their classmates and grew to fill the Mellon Auditorium downtown."

"The Mellon? That's just across the street from my office."

"Then you know how large it is. We take in donations year-round and hold a week-long event in May. Some two hundred alumni volunteer, both to price and at the sale." She straightened proudly. "We regularly net upwards of a hundred thousand dollars, which goes entirely to scholarships."

"It must be a very popular event then."

"Dealers and book lovers from all over the country—and even from abroad—come to our sale."

"Wow. Impressive. What's your part in this enterprise besides collecting donations?"

"That's not my usual schtick. When I was in college, I helped out with sorting during the summers and got involved in earnest when I returned to DC last year. I'm in charge of recruiting and scheduling volunteers. Plus, I'm learning to appraise and price rare books. That part is the most challenging."

"I imagine it is. It's a bit like what I do at the Smithsonian—identify and evaluate things." He finished his cocktail. "Is that how you recognized *The Mysterious*

Affair at Styles as a first edition?"

"Uh-huh."

"About that." He touched the back of her hand lightly. She suppressed a tingle. "The more I think about it, it has to be linked to the mystery. Because of the date."

Sophie felt a little thrill. "Agreed. Agnes's letter was written in 1920—the same year the book was published."

His eyes glinted. "Perhaps something in the story—plot or characters—holds a clue to the identity of the murderer?"

She wasn't prepared to go that far. "I don't see how. Agnes couldn't see the man's face in the dark."

"How about the victim?"

"All she saw was a human shape and a hat. She also said her employers didn't mention a guest the next morning and seemed perfectly composed. That's when she began to doubt whether she'd seen anything at all."

"Right." Noah tapped an only slightly dirty fingernail on his glass. "The question then remains, why did she put the letter in the book?"

"If she did."

"What do you mean?"

"It was a brand new book at the time. It seems clear from the letter that Agnes was a servant. How could she have afforded it?"

"It could have been a gift."

She shook her head. "Who would give a maid a book?"

"Well, aren't you the snob. Perhaps her mistress was teaching her to read."

"With Agatha Christie?"

"Encouraging her anyway. With something more amusing than Dick and Jane."

"Hogwash. And I'm not a snob." Sophie felt unaccountably testy.

"Sorry." Noah didn't seem to be. "Okay. Moving on. We did find it in my father's box of books. Maybe it belonged to him."

"Then how did Agnes's letter end up in it?"

Before Noah could answer, Yiannis brought a tray with several small dishes. "Your mezze." As he placed each plate on the table, he recited the ingredients. "First, we have smoked Manouri cream with parsley pesto and pickled raisins. Next is summer squash with Galotyri cheese, smoked date cream, and crispy quinoa." He pushed the candle aside to place a third appetizer. "Taramasalata with pickled green apples and shaved beets. And finally"—he set the last dish down with a very Hellenic flourish—"grilled calamari swirled in fava puree, caramelized shallots"—he pronounced them "shaaloo"—"and topped with a cumin-vinegar emulsion."

Sophie kept a straight face with some difficulty.

When the waiter had moved to the next table, Noah whispered, "So what he *meant* to say was cheese, beets, squash, and squid."

"It's the new fad to describe every single ingredient that goes into a dish. I'm surprised he didn't add 'sprinkled with salt and pepper.' "

"Please." He imitated Yiannis's raspy voice. "Dusted with Corsican rosemary sea salt and smashed pink peppercorns."

When they'd finished the appetizers, Yiannis replaced the dishes with chicken souvlaki mounded over pilaf and a carafe of wine. They ate quietly for a while, then Noah put down his fork. "Okay, what were we talking about?"

"The book. What we should do about it."

"As I said, keep it for now."

"All right." She was thoughtful. "What about the letter? Should we take it to the authorities?"

"You mean to the police?" He dipped the last piece of bread in the sauce.

He was still chewing on it when the waiter leapt forward and removed the plate. "Would you care for dessert?"

Sophie and Noah exchanged looks. *Must be closing time.* She noticed that the only other couple had left. *I don't really want to go, but all that heavy lifting is beginning to take its toll.* "It *is* getting late."

Noah had been watching her. "No, thanks, Yiannis. Give us five minutes, and we'll get out of your hair." He turned to Sophie. "Coffee?"

She nodded, relieved. "Sure—Greek coffee?"

When Yiannis—a thin sheen of disappointment draped over him—had provided them with tiny cups of foamy delight, Noah resumed. "I say we keep all the evidence we have for now. I want to do a little sleuthing before we involve the police. Once we've finished searching the grounds, we should investigate unsolved murders in 1920 in Marmion Grove."

Sophie's eyelids were drooping. "Okay, but can we talk about it tomorrow?"

"What? Oh, sure. I'm sorry. I'll take you home."

"Um. What about my car? I left it at the house."

"*Hmm.*" He took her hand. "We'll figure it out on the way back."

When they reached the entrance to Marmion Grove, the darkness enveloped them. "No street lights?"

"We try to sustain the Victorian atmosphere. If desired, George—he's our mayor—deploys the fog machines."

"You *are* being funny, right?"

"I hope so." He turned into the driveway. "Okay. I can take you home, and you'll have to take the bus back up in the morning. *Or—*" His eyes flickered.

"I don't think so."

"Hear me out. I've been sleeping in my old room at the top of the house."

"In the tower?"

"No, there's a whole suite up there with its own bathroom. I can put you up in my mother's room on the second floor. It's still made up."

She could tell he was trying not to sound too eager. She was very tempted—her limbs ached and her neck hurt. *But I don't have a toothbrush or clean underwear.* For some reason, that meant a lot. *I want to be attractive, and squid breath won't cut it.* "If you don't mind, I'll just drive myself home. I would feel more comfortable."

He popped his lips. "I understand. Are you sure you'll be okay driving? I insist you call me when you get home. You have my number, don't you?"

"Yes. But will you pick up this time?"

He grinned. "A bad habit left over from my youth. It's easier to text a reply than get stuck on the phone at an inconvenient time. Yes, I promise I will answer. I'll do one better. I'll keep my cell under my pillow." He walked her to her car. "What time will you be back?"

"Oh! I almost forgot. I have an editing job starting tomorrow."

"Is it in an office?"

"No. I can do it at home, but I have to meet the client

tomorrow and discuss the project. I can come up Saturday if you're free."

He bent his head to hers. "I'm free. And Sophie?"

"Yes?"

"If you don't mind." He kissed her quickly, then opened her door. "Thank you. If you'd stayed overnight, I wouldn't have had the nerve to do that."

Chapter Four

One of the saddest things in life, is the things one remembers.

~Agatha Christie

Peveril Hall, Saturday, April 6

"Well, there you are."

"Here I am. I told you I couldn't get here before eleven."

Noah checked his watch. "It's five after."

Sophie laughed. "Miss me?"

"Yes. What kept you?"

"The client I met with yesterday had some more questions this morning. I couldn't get him off the phone."

"Him?" Noah beetled his brows at Sophie. "Is he perchance writing his memoirs? The life of a rake or a scoundrel?"

"Mr. Iverson is no Tom Jones, but he *is* writing an erotic story revolving around a game of chess. He wants to submit it to *Play Around* magazine."

"*Play Around*? Isn't that the publication featuring assorted ladies in unmentionables?"

"Uh-huh." She snickered. "The problem is, he knows a lot more about chess than he does about sex."

"And you're going to instruct him?" The eyebrows

32

remained beetled.

"It may be too late for that. He's eighty-five. No, I'm going to suggest he send it to *Chess Illustrated* instead."

"Huh. You'd better come inside." Once in the kitchen, he handed her a mug of coffee.

Sophie sipped. "Okay, what would you like to tackle first?"

"I think we should go about this methodically. After all, this is my area of expertise."

"What is?"

"Research. Identifying obscure objects."

Sophie was amused. "Such as?"

"I was once given the task of cataloguing a truckload of specimen jars that this intrepid amateur explorer brought back from China in 1910. He left it to others to do the actual identification and didn't bother to label anything. There were a lot of plant fibers and birds' nests and seeds. All brown."

"Were you successful?"

Noah didn't immediately answer. Finally he muttered, "No. But it gave me a lot of helpful experience. Finding a body should be a breeze after that."

Sophie dropped the mug onto the table. "Finding a body! I thought we were only looking for proof that Agnes was right."

"And that proof would entail the actual corpse, would it not?"

"I… I suppose." Sophie felt a little queasy.

He gawked at her. "Were you mayhap dozing when I talked about unsolved murders of 1920?"

Sophie racked her brain. All she remembered was a kiss. After that, everything else had evaporated into the night sky. "Might've been."

"Well, Agnes wrote that she saw a man carrying a body, didn't she? The body had to be ditched somewhere. Find the body and we're halfway to clearing up the mystery."

"That would be nice, but all she saw was a man carrying a bundle."

"A human-shaped bundle."

Sophie had to grant the distinction. She rallied. "For all we know, he was helping a drunk friend home."

Noah pounced. "In that case, wouldn't the master of the house have said something about an inebriated guest?" When Sophie's mouth opened and shut again without responding, he continued, "And what about the rat poison?"

"Someone in the house broke it by accident. Agnes didn't find it until the next day."

"Well, she wouldn't, would she?" Noah got up and retrieved the carafe. "More coffee?"

She held her cup out.

He filled both mugs, then started up again with renewed energy. "Then there's this. Agnes said the man threw the body—"

"The bundle."

"The bundle. He threw it into a car and drove off." Noah slapped a palm on the table. "So what happened to the car?"

"How would I know?"

"I say we find the car, we find the body. Okay, strike that. Reverse it."

Sophie looked down a tunnel of endless speculation and retreated. "Okay. We've finished with the garage. Where to next?"

"The playhouse, by which I mean the servants'

quarters. I've been thinking. In 1920, the building was still used as lodging for the staff. Agnes was obviously a maid. If she left any other notes, they might be there."

"Wait a minute. What if the book *did* belong to your father?"

"Nah. It looks hardly used—no dog-ears or jelly stains. That makes it more likely that Agnes acquired it in 1920 or shortly thereafter."

"Not necessarily. Like any collectible, a first edition is often kept pristine to maintain its value. Roger could have bought it from a collector or a rare book emporium."

This only stopped Noah for a second. "The issue is not the book; it's the letter. We need a starting point of some kind. I say we search all the premises. We look for anything to do with Agnes. Then we move on to archival research."

Sophie felt increasingly cross. "What do you mean by archival research? Missing persons from the twenties? Servants in Marmion Grove named Agnes? Cold cases?"

"All of the above."

As she cast about for an escape route, a thought struck Sophie. "We're going on the assumption this was an unsolved murder. Maybe the mystery was quickly cleared up and—"

"And that's why she didn't mail the letter? Possible." He rubbed his chin. "All the more reason to keep looking for information. Are you finished?" He took the cup out of Sophie's hands.

"I guess I am now."

"Let's go."

The little structure consisted of one large room and

a tiny kitchen. The living space boasted a fireplace and built-in benches. A rickety card table was set up by the door.

"No bathroom?"

"An outhouse. Grace E. D. Sprigg's influence hadn't extended to the servants."

"Grace—"

He spoke over her. "The servants laid mattresses on these benches for sleeping, then stored them underneath during the day."

Sophie examined the room. "It's really quite snug, isn't it? Big for a playhouse though."

"Not at all. Luckily we had the summer house to expand into."

"Luckily." She lifted the cover of one bench. "Aha! Boxes."

Noah chose one, laid it on the card table, and opened it. "Seems to be old toys. Oh look, here's my slingshot! And this"—he extracted a rifle with a rusted trigger and splintered stock—"is my sister's Daisy Red Ryder BB gun." He sighted down the barrel. "She let me hold it when Mom wasn't looking."

Sophie tittered. "Looks like your mother hid all your weapons out here."

"I wouldn't put it past her." He held up the slingshot. "I forgot all about this when my dad…" He paused. "When Dad bought me the tricycle."

Unable to come up with a comforting reply, Sophie let him continue to sift through the contents, exclaiming happily whenever he rooted out another favorite plaything. She laid a second box on the table, this one wooden instead of cardboard. It had two letters painted on the lid: A. R. "This looks promising."

Noah read over her shoulder. "A. R. The letter writer? Agnes... Did she give her last name?"

"I don't recall. Where's the letter?"

"I put it in the living room."

"Go get it."

"How about I just go look at it?"

Sophie heaved a sigh. "I'll wait here."

In a minute, Noah was back. He waved the letter. "It was easier to bring it out," he said cheerily. "Her name was Reilly. Agnes Reilly."

"A. R. This must be hers then. Open it up."

He pointed. "It's nailed shut."

Sophie waited him out.

"Okay, okay." He skipped back to the house, returning with a crowbar, and pried the top off.

She carefully removed several miniature porcelain animals wrapped in burlap, then a pair of worn woolen gloves, a scarf, and a maid's cap. At the bottom lay a small, pink notebook tied with a ribbon. "Her diary?"

"I think the ribbon's a dead giveaway."

They sat down together on the bench. Sophie untied the bow and turned to the first page. "It's the same handwriting as on the letter."

"Good. So it does belong to our Agnes."

Sophie read the first few pages. "She talks of what it's like being in service." She looked up. "Do you suppose she was the only servant?"

"What difference would that make?"

"She might have shared what she saw with another staff member."

"Good point." Noah picked up the crowbar. "Hang on. I want to make a list of topics to explore." He went back to the house and returned with a pad and pen.

Sophie had continued to read the diary.

"She sounds quite young. And poorly educated. Her grammar and spelling are atrocious. Here she talks about writing to her mother about her job. She doesn't seem very happy."

"Well, would *you* be if you worked for a murderer?"

"We don't know that. I forget—was there a date on the letter?"

Noah unfolded the paper. "It says, Sunday, April…*hmm*…" He squinted at the writing. "The date is smudged."

"Oh right. Well, that at least gives us something to go on. Let's see if she has any entries for April."

"The diary might not be from the same year."

"It's all we've got." She riffled the pages. "Aha." She read aloud. " 'April 17. I'm so excited! I can't believe he'll be here.' "

"Be where? Who is he?"

"She doesn't say. The ink has run, and the writing is very crabbed."

"What's next?"

"Nothing. Just the two sentences. The next passage is dated April 19… Odd. She seems to start up in the middle of a sentence. 'Momma says I should keep quiet, that I don't really know what I saw. She says I could lose my position if I even hint at foul play. The master hasn't said a word about their guest. Momma always says my imagination will be my downfall someday." Sophie fanned through the rest of the pages. "That's the last entry."

"That settles it. Something did happen that night."

"I don't know—she seems to have doubts. It might account for why she changed her mind and didn't send the letter. Maybe there are other diaries. Look over in that bench."

Noah rummaged through the compartment. "Here's an old newspaper." He looked up, a gleam in his eye. "Wouldn't it be cool if it were dated April 1920 and the headline screamed about the disappearance of the mayor of Marmion Grove—missing and presumed slain by his political rival?"

"Yes, it would." She pointed at the headline. "O. J. Simpson Not Guilty." When he laid it aside, she bent down. "Wait, here's another box marked ROGER."

He snatched it from her. On top lay a folder. He took a sheet out and read. His face crumpled. "It's the receipt from their honeymoon hotel in St. Maarten. And here are some photos of my parents."

Sophie beheld two people obviously in love, standing in front of a thatched-roof building. Another showed a woman in a bikini mugging for the camera.

Something dislodged from the folder and dinged on the floor. Noah picked it up. "Well, well. It's mother's engagement ring. She took it off when it finally became clear he was gone for good."

Sophie admired the stunning blue-green stone set in a circle of diamonds. "It's an emerald, isn't it?"

"Yes. Dad brought it back from a trip to Colombia." He let a sunbeam play with the colors, then absently stuck it in his pocket.

"She never remarried?"

"No."

He didn't seem inclined to elaborate, so Sophie went back to the box. "What's this?"

He took it. "Another circus poster." He inspected it. "This one is more recent. The Royal Hanneford Circus still tours on the east coast. They set up by the public library only last year."

"Is it new?"

"What? No. The date says August, 1989." He tapped his lip. "I wonder…"

Sophie pulled more pamphlets out. "And these?"

"Playbills from the Kensington Players—our local amateur theatrical group. My mother and father were active in it."

"What year did your father leave?"

"Let's see. I was five, so 1990." He touched the flyers. "These are from the eighties." He gazed at Sophie. "I don't think this was Roger's box. These are mementos my mother saved after he left. To remember him by." He closed the flaps.

To fill the mournful silence, Sophie said, "I don't think we're going to find anything else here. I'm famished. Can we get some lunch?"

"Oh, cripes. It's one o'clock! I don't have anything but breakfast food in the house. How about we try the eatery down at the P.O.—I mean Dane Circle? My neighbor says its food is more casual than the dress code."

Sophie had been in such a hurry to get up to the Park to see Noah she'd forgotten to eat breakfast. She was too hungry to quibble. "I'll just freshen up a bit."

The day was warm, so they strolled down the avenue to the restaurant. A bubbly woman in black greeted them. "The patio is open. Would you like to sit outside?"

"Yes, thanks."

They found a table for two in the shade of a towering tulip magnolia in full bloom. The restaurant was crowded. "Oh look, they have pizza. Want to split one?"

"Sounds good. Sausage?"

"Let's see what toppings they have." Sophie read the menu. "You're in luck. The house special is sausage and jalapeños. How…er…inventive."

"Can't be any worse than smoked cheese and pickled raisins."

"If you say so."

After the waitress had filled their glasses from a decanter of red wine, Sophie leaned on the table. "You called this the P.O. How come?"

"That's how we referred to the building when I was growing up. It still houses the mailboxes for town residents. The front part of the building used to be a butcher." He stopped. "Louie, that was his name. My mother refused to buy meat from him. She swore it had nothing to do with Mr. Chisholm's horse vanishing right before Louie ran a special on pot roast, but the neighborhood kids knew better."

"He left?"

"Louie? Uh-huh. Then a general store moved in. It had a whole wall with barrels of penny candy. After school we'd come down to get our mail and buy candy lipstick and those little wax soda bottles filled with sugar water." He sipped his wine. "A classmate of mine, Rusty Dane, lived in the apartment above the store."

"That must have been fun."

"He didn't think so. Everybody expected him to dole out free candy. His mother's still here. She's the postmistress."

As they were eating, a train rumbled past. Sophie jumped when it blew its whistle. "I didn't know the trains still ran."

"Marmion Grove is on the commuter route from

DC. That's why it was built—to accommodate people who wanted to get out of the swamp in the summer." He chuckled. "Still true after a hundred and fifty years."

She craned her neck. "I don't see a station. Where does it stop?"

"There's only a shelter now." He grew pensive. "When the B&O Railroad came through in the 1880s, they built a traditional wooden station here with a ticket counter and waiting room. It had already been abandoned for years when I was a kid. Once my sister and her friends climbed in through a broken window. She found all these circus posters from the twenties in the attic."

"Like the ones we found?" She didn't wait for an answer. "Can I have dessert?"

"Wow. You *were* hungry!"

After Noah paid the bill, they walked back to the house. They had arrived at the front porch before Sophie spoke. "Okay, where do we go from here?"

"I say to the mattresses."

"The what?"

"Just kidding—we can save that for when the Gambino family moves into the territory. I meant to the internet. The town records. Maybe the tax rolls. We need to find out who owned the house in 1920."

"We should also figure out who Agnes was and what happened to her."

"Why?"

"Well, for one thing, the letter. Was it Agnes who hid it in the book? Or did the murderer? Did she simply lose her nerve…or—" She wavered as a horrible thought struck her. "Was *she* done in?"

Chapter Five

People should be interested in books, not their authors.
~Agatha Christie

Peveril Hall, Saturday, April 6

Noah stopped short, his hand on the front door knob. "Agnes? Done in? You have quite the vivid imagination."

"She *did* witness a murder—"

"We don't know that."

Sophie regrouped. "Well, she *did* write a letter in which she stated she *might* have witnessed a murder. It's perfectly possible that the killer thought he had to dispose of her."

"A valid point. All right, we'll concentrate on Agnes. We still have to search the property records as well. Otherwise we have no place to start."

"Agreed." She checked her watch. "I don't think we can do anything until Monday anyway. I have to go home and feed the fish."

"Fish?"

"A goldfish. My niece won it at her school fair and her father—my brother—claims he's allergic to fish, so I had to adopt it."

"I've never heard of an allergy to goldfish."

She winked. "I'm not the only one in my family with

a vivid imagination."

"Ah."

"It seems the school assumed it was common knowledge that these are 'feeder fish'—bred as food for more exotic species, and die very quickly. Which is why they're so popular as prizes. Since I missed the memo, I went out and bought a fifty-gallon tank with all the trimmings."

"I take it the fish died the minute you set it up in its palatial residence?"

"Au contraire! In fact, Jelly—that's his name—thrived and is now four inches long. I'm thinking of breeding him."

It took several minutes for Noah's guffaws to subside. Finally he spluttered, "B…b…breed him?"

Sophie said huffily, "It's not *that* funny. Goldfish are carp. Given enough room and proper nutrition, they can grow up to eighteen inches long. You know those ornamental pond fish? Name begins with a 'k'?"

"Koi."

"Yeah, that's it. Koi are just fancy carp. I'm thinking I could breed Jelly with a koi and sell the offspring. They go for hundreds of dollars."

"You, my child, need a real job."

****

Sophie's apartment, Monday morning

"I can't come, Noah. I promised to work at the sorting center today." She switched her phone to her other ear so she could feed Jelly.

"Sorting center… You mean for the book sale?"

"Uh-huh. Eudora is educating me on rare books, and has promised to give me a lesson in evaluating first American editions."

"As opposed to regular first editions? Does a first edition *have* to be published in England?"

"No, no, but if a book is first published in England, and then *republished* in the US, it's considered a separate edition. Sometimes it actually becomes *more* valuable, especially if there are editorial changes." She wrinkled her nose. "Although oftentimes—notably in children's books—the American version is dumbed down from the English."

"Really? In what way?"

"For example, the first Harry Potter book was originally entitled *Harry Potter and the Philosopher's Stone*. The US publishers thought that was too esoteric for backward American children so they renamed it *Harry Potter and the Sorcerer's Stone*."

"Huh. As I recall, the philosopher's stone was a substance that could turn base metals into gold."

"And was also supposed to be the elixir of life. Yes." She scoffed. "Any school child knows that."

"Or should. So, how does the pricing process work?"

"We consult a lot of different guides—some that tell us what the book has sold for before; some that give us the current market value. We try to reconcile the differing opinions, determine a price, then cut that in half."

"In half! That doesn't sound like good business."

"We're not in this for profit. We're raising funds for our school. And we've become famous not only for our expertise in pricing, but for the great deals buyers can get."

Noah rustled some papers. "While you're at it, why don't you do the Christie book?"

"What a good idea! Oh, but shoot! I forgot—it's at your house, isn't it?"

"Right, along with the letter."

"Darn. Eudora's at the center today. She could help me."

"How about if I bring it to you? I have to drop by my apartment anyway to get some clean clothes."

"Okay, but leave the letter at Peveril Hall. I don't want to misplace it."

"Got it. Address?"

"We're in the basement of 2809 Connecticut Avenue in Woodley Park. You know the area?"

"Sure. It's a straight shot down Connecticut."

"Yup. Come around the back of the building and look for our sign."

"Sign?"

"Vassar Book Sale Sorting Center."

"When will you be there?"

"Noon to five."

"I'll drop it off and come back later. I have some errands to run."

****

Sorting center, Monday afternoon

"Have you been able to price the Christie?"

"I'm working on it."

Noah looked over Sophie's shoulder at the large volume open before her. The other volunteers had gone home, and the two of them were alone in the rare books room. She sat at a makeshift wooden table. Reference works lined the shelf in front of her. Books that Eudora had singled out for appraisal were stacked in a five-foot pile beside her on the floor.

Sophie was acutely conscious of Noah's aftershave

as he leaned over her. *Dark rum and lime*. It made her think of a pirate swashing his buckle while chugging from a frothing tankard.

He sniffed. "What's that perfume you're wearing? It's um…appetizing." He sniffed again.

"African violet and cocoa butter. It's just soap."

"Ah. I was wondering why I was craving something sweet." He stuck his tongue out and pretended to lick her cheek.

"Stop that!"

Noah held up his hands. "Okay, okay. So what have you found? Is our book sale-worthy?"

"Eudora was not helpful."

"What does that mean?"

"She decided the Christie book would be good practice for me and gave me full responsibility." Her brow furrowed in concentration. "The *Rare Book Price Guide* only lists the London edition, not the one I have in hand… Wait." She looked up at the computer monitor. "Whoa Nellie. Abe Books has a first *Canadian* edition, also published in 1920, priced at—are you ready?"

"Hit me."

"Forty-five hundred dollars!" Sophie read on for a bit. "Here's the order of provenance. *The Mysterious Affair at Styles* was first published in New York by John Lane, a year *before* it was released in London." She referred back to the publishing page of her book. "My gosh, that makes this the true first edition." She gazed at Noah. "It must be worth a *lot* of money."

"The question is, was it worth a lot in 1920?"

"Couldn't have been. It was the first novel by a then-unknown author—and a woman to boot. I'll have to research what books cost then. Agnes might have picked it up for a nickel."

Noah said reluctantly, "Roger kept it in a plastic bag, so he must have determined it was valuable."

"The question is, did he know about Agnes's letter? Have you had any contact with him since he left?"

Noah's face froze. "No. And as far as I know, neither did my mother."

Oops. She went on quickly. "You were five years old, right? What, if anything, do you remember about him?"

He was silent for a minute, then said slowly, "Not much. He was tall—at least to me. He had blue eyes like mine. He read a lot—his study had heaps of books everywhere, just like here." He patted a pile. "They even spilled out into the hall that led to my bedroom."

"Was he a writer?"

"No idea. Gretchen told me he taught American history at Rockville High School. He may have done some writing on the side." Noah's eyes grew sorrowful. "He'd been gone a year when Mother finally acknowledged that he wasn't coming back. After that she never spoke of him. My sister might have clearer memories—she's five years older than I."

Sophie scanned his face. "Are you okay?"

Instead of answering, he straightened. "Look, let's go get a drink. I've had enough speculation for one day."

"Okay, I just have to lock up." She held up the book. "What do you want me to do with this?"

"Keep it for now. We may need your expertise with rare books again."

"All right, but I'm going to take it home. Otherwise Eudora will appropriate it."

Sophie ran into the bathroom for a quick checkup.

Not too bad. Not too good either. Sigh. She found Noah standing in the parking lot. "Shall I follow you?"

"How about I follow *you* back to your apartment, then we'll take my car. I know a great place."

She eyed the Aston Martin. "That'll work." *Plus I can change my dress and put on a little mascara.*

She lucked into a space near her apartment. When Noah pulled up next to her she leaned in his window. "You'll have to wait in the car—you won't find parking around here."

"Okay, don't be too long then."

Sophie zipped up her steps. She put the Christie book on the kitchen counter, sprinkled food for Jelly, then tore her clothes off as she hurtled down the hall. She was back at the car in ten minutes. "How's that?"

"Good timing. A cop has gone around the block twice now, and he's been giving me the fish eye. I think he's salivating over filling his ticket quota early."

Sophie strapped herself into the passenger seat, and Noah drove through a series of back streets to a building on D Street. She looked at the blank brick wall and windows that had been filled in with concrete. "It looks like it's closed."

"It's not." He rapped on the door.

A voice from the other side said, "Password?"

Sophie nudged him. "They *do* know Prohibition is over, right?"

"*Shh.*" Noah spoke loudly. "Zookeeper."

The door swung open onto a foyer. Beyond it was a large dining area. A mahogany bar ran the length of the room, its polished brass rail brilliant in the light of shaded sconces. The walls were studded with the mounted heads of various exotic animals. "What is this place?"

"The Wayfarers Club. A place to relax and drink after you return from safari. Or from climbing Everest. Or from paddling down the Amazon. We're pretty flexible."

"And you're a member. Are you a great white hunter?"

"Me? No. You don't actually have to kill animals to be accepted. You just have to have a taste for adventure. Phineas Fogg was a founding member."

"I see." Sophie wasn't sure what else besides the reference to Jules Verne's Phineas Fogg was fiction but wanted to get a stiff drink before she tackled the subject.

Noah led her to the bar. "How about something unusual? Eldridge is very creative."

"As long as it's not too sweet."

"Eldridge, my man, this is Sophie Childress. Do your magic."

The bartender, a young man with a wispy goatee and a tiny head precariously balanced on a thickset frame, grinned. "I have just the thing."

They watched as he expertly poured a tot of green liquid, a tot of blue liquid, then jiggers of gin, vodka, and rum into a highball glass. He popped a little paper umbrella into the drink. "I call it the Titanic."

"Oh dear, I hope that doesn't mean one swig and I sink to the floor." She sipped. "Delicious!"

Eldridge turned to Noah. "Your usual, Mr. Pennyman?"

"Right-o."

He poured a tall mug of lemonade and shunted it across the counter.

Sophie tilted her head. "Lemonade?"

"It's what Lawrence of Arabia ordered from the bar after he trekked a hundred and fifty miles across the Sinai desert to arrive, exhausted but triumphant, in Cairo. I figure if he could take it, so can I."

The maître d' approached. "Will you be having dinner with us, Mr. Pennyman?"

Noah smiled at Sophie. "Would you like to stay?"

She drained her glass. "I think I'd better. After that drink I need some food in my stomach."

The host led them to a corner table and handed them leather-bound menus. "We do have a special today. One of our members recently returned from South Africa and generously donated the wildebeest she shot. We have marinated the steaks. They are accompanied by chakalaka—a vegetable ragout—and pap."

Noah whispered, "Cornmeal mush."

"Sounds…tempting." Sophie thanked her stars that she had an open-minded palate.

"We'll have that. And a bottle of shiraz-cabernet."

When he'd gone, Noah took Sophie's hand. "Now, the last time I asked this question, you distracted me with tales of rare books and scholarship drives. Pray tell me something *personal* about yourself."

"All right." She described her time teaching English in France, hopping neatly over her relationship with Thomas. "I decided to return home to the States last year. I'm freelancing as an editor now, but I hope to land a full-time job with a publisher." She dropped her eyes. "I'm also thinking of writing a novel."

"Oh?" Noah put down his wine. "A murder mystery perchance?"

"I don't know yet."

"Well, you have the makings of one already." He

was thoughtful. "Does this mean you're through traveling?" His gaze wandered to the African masks and outlandish weapons mounted on the walls.

"Oh no! I love to travel. I'm just flat broke at the moment."

"*Hmm.* Well, then. I shall take you on a safari through the halls of the Smithsonian. That's free and almost as thrilling as galloping across the Sahara on a stallion, or stalking the elusive giant pitta in Borneo."

"Speaking of, how are you able to take time off to deal with your mother's house?"

He looked momentarily nonplussed. "I…um…" He petered out, then, just when Sophie was going to give him an excuse, he burst out, "I took a leave of absence. Had some…er…vacation coming and took advantage. I have to look in now and then, but otherwise my time is my own."

Sophie hoped her pleasure at the news wasn't too obvious. *With luck he'll attribute my silly grin to the Titanic.*

The wildebeest was pronounced delectable, and the chakalaka a suitable accompaniment. By the end, Sophie was dreaming of far-off lands and elephant herds trundling across the savanna. Noah said rather abruptly, "I'll take you home."

"What?" *Think, Sophie.* "We…uh…haven't decided what's next on the agenda."

"I thought we were going to check tax records. Are you free tomorrow?"

"I just have to do a little editing in the morning, then I'm all yours." *Gulp—did I just say that?*

"All right. Shall I pick you up at your apartment?"

"Sure."

Noah left her on her doorstep, and Sophie watched the Aston Martin's rear lights blink out of sight. *Damn. I should have kissed him. I should have dragged him to my bed and ravished him.* She giggled. *That's the alcohol talking.* She closed her eyes and envisioned his sky blue eyes riveted on hers as his fingers unbuttoned her blouse. A delightful shiver coursed through her.

On the way to her bedroom, her stride slackened. *On the other hand, except for that one kiss, he's made no move toward me. Maybe he doesn't like me. Or didn't like the kiss. Maybe he just needs a friend to help him solve the mystery. Maybe I need another Titanic.*

She went to the kitchen and pulled out the rum.

Chapter Six

A small town has as many eyes as a fly.

~*Sonya Hartnett*

Sophie's apartment, Tuesday, April 9

"That's done." Sophie minimized the page and checked the clock. "Noon. Now, when did Noah say he was going to call?"

Her phone buzzed. "Hey, I'm on my way over."

"I hope the traffic isn't too bad. You think half an hour, forty minutes?"

"Huh? Not unless I get stuck behind a parade. I'm in my apartment. It's only a few blocks from yours."

"Really? Where are you?"

"Penn Quarter. H Street."

"That's a pretty nice area."

"Yeah, I really lucked out—cheap places are hard to find in this neighborhood. Plus I can walk to work."

Sophie caught sight of the clock. *Not much time to get myself decent then.* "Okay. Bye." She ran to her bathroom, spritzed on some cologne, brushed her hair, and checked her teeth. Then she flew to the bedroom and threw on the outfit it had taken her three hours to pick out the night before. She started to drop her toothbrush into her purse, but reconsidered. *Now I think about it, last week's kiss was really rather brotherly. He was just showing me the door. A courtesy.* She put the brush back on the sink.

She had reached the sidewalk when the Aston Martin rounded the corner. "Hop in."

Traffic was heavy, and it took an hour to get to Marmion Grove. Noah stopped in front of a gray and white building. Sophie admired the square bell tower. "This looks like a chapel."

"It was—until the town bought it and converted it into the town hall. They keep the archives here."

"Is it open?"

"I called ahead. Mr. Oglethorpe—he's the town clerk—said he'd come over to help us."

A short man wearing suspenders and a beret met them at the door. "Well, well. Vivian's boy. I don't think I've seen you in twenty years!"

"How do you do, Mr. Oglethorpe. May I present Sophie Childress?"

The old man winked at her. "Oh, yes, Miss Vivian would have liked you. You're perfect for our Noah."

Sophie's jaw dropped and stayed down. Noah cleared his throat. "As I told you on the phone, we'd like to do a search of the archives."

"Sure, come through here. What are you interested in? We have several collections."

"I'm trying to find out who owned my house in 1920."

"Oh? That would be in the tax rolls. You'll need to check the county records."

"Their online database doesn't go back that far. Before we traipsed all the way to Rockville, I hoped there might be something here that could give us a lead. You know, something like a group photo of a Fourth of

July potluck. It's such a small town after all."

"*Hmm.*" Mr. Oglethorpe hooked his thumbs in his suspenders. "You should start with the Appleton files then. Lowell Appleton was mayor for twenty years, and a Marmion Grove history buff."

He led them to a back room filled with file cabinets and tapped one. "It takes up the top three drawers."

Two hours later, Noah sat back and let a sheet of paper drift from his lifeless hand. He gave a languid nod in Sophie's direction. "Did *you* find anything?"

"Only a letter complaining about a neighbor's rooster. Oh, and some visitor was outraged that the speed limit was five miles per hour when in this day and age— he says—cars are capable of *at least* ten."

"No reports of wild parties at 4715 Waverley Avenue?" When she shook her head, he added, "How about cars with suspicious bundles in the back seat?" He must have noticed her expression turning mulish, for he said hastily, "Okay, that's enough paper pushing for now. What'll we do next?"

"I'm hungry. Do you have anything at the house to eat?"

"As a matter of fact, I do. I've been camping out there off and on while I go through Mother's things."

At the house Noah set out bread, cheese, grapes, and wine. He handed Sophie a glass. "A jug of wine, a loaf of bread, and thou." He toasted her.

The kitchen suddenly darkened. "What's going on?"

He looked out the back door. "It looks like a storm is in the offing." At that moment, thunder crashed overhead. Sophie jumped. Noah flipped a switch. "Damn. Power's out." He pushed open the swinging door to the dining room. "I'm sure Mother left candles in the pantry."

He came back a minute later. "Even better. I found an LED lantern."

The rain slashed against the windows. Sophie shivered. Noah kneaded her arm. "You don't like thunderstorms?"

"No, I love them. I'm just thinking of the mystery. Didn't Agnes say something in the letter about a storm that night?"

"I believe so, but, as I recall, she said it had passed. Otherwise, she wouldn't have ventured out to shoo raccoons away. Also, the man with the body was outside. Not in the house." He scrutinized her face. "Come on, let's go up to my room."

She held back. "Aren't we safer here?"

"My laptop's up there. We can watch the weather channel." As they climbed the narrow staircase to the third floor, the downpour stopped abruptly. A weak sun shone through the skylight. "There, see? It's all fine now."

Sophie found herself in a large room, split into two sections by a bathroom. The first alcove held a couch and a desk. Noah's things were strewn about. He opened a computer and began typing. She moseyed past the bathroom to the sleeping area, and looked out the dormer window. Across the driveway stood a row of cherry trees in full bloom. On the ground beneath them a carpet of pink blossoms was strewn, ripped from the branches by the wind. The carriage house lay on her right, and Waverley Avenue on her left. She imagined herself in 1920. A Ford Model T might rumble past. Children trotted down the hill toward the P.O. clutching their pennies in soon-to-be sticky hands. Perhaps a horse would canter by. She sighed. "This is such a lovely house, Noah. I'll bet it has a lot of history."

He dropped the laptop's cover. Coming up behind her, he put his hands on her shoulders. "It does. I know I said I was planning to sell it once I cleaned it out, but now I'm not so certain."

She turned. "You want to live here? How wonderful!"

They stood inches apart. Noah whispered, "You'd like that?"

"I…uh…"

Before she could figure out what to say that would be both positive and not imply anything more than she meant, he took her in his arms and kissed her. When they broke apart, he said huskily, "I've been wanting to do that again for days."

Her heart thumped. Just then thunder boomed, and the rain returned, falling down in sheets. Noah gazed into her eyes. She glanced down at the bed. Slowly his hands went to her blouse.

****

Peveril Hall, Wednesday morning

Sophie opened her eyes. "Where the heck am I?" The room was dark. A warm arm held her crushed against a warm chest. "Noah?"

"*Mmph.*"

"My God, we must have fallen asleep. Noah! Wake up! What time is it?"

Noah sat up and checked his watch. "Five." He peered out the window. "But is it five in the morning or in the afternoon?"

"It's got to be morning. The storm hit about 4:30 p.m."

Noah tested the bedside lamp. "Power's back on."

They looked at each other. What they had done suddenly came home to Sophie. *It's the first time I've...well...since Thomas left me in Paris.* Thomas had claimed he loved her, but that he couldn't live in America. He didn't even like Europe any more—"too desiccated, too debased, too decadent, Sophie." He'd waxed poetic over arid landscapes and wide open spaces where he could spread his wings. "Mongolia, Sophie. It's the last bastion of freedom in the world. They shook off the Soviet yoke in 1991 and now are among the most enlightened societies in the world. I shall write you."

But he never did. She felt around in her heart. No guilt. *Whaddya know?* She snuggled back under Noah's arm.

After a few minutes, he stirred. "We'd better get up. I think I left the food out."

Sophie rose and wrapped the quilt around her bare shoulders. She peeped around the corner. A long hall, lined with bookcases, led to the front of the house. "What's down there?"

"The tower. It was my father's study."

"What's it used for now?"

"Nothing." His lips set in a thin line. "After he left, Mother locked it and threw away the key."

"Can I see it?"

He hesitated, then nodded. "I guess it doesn't matter now. Mother won't care."

"Let me get dressed."

Noah peeked under the covers. "Oops. Me too."

When they were both respectable, they trooped down the hall to a small door. It reminded Sophie of Alice in Wonderland. Noah fiddled with the lock. "Hang on." He slipped a credit card from his wallet and ran it up and down between the jamb and the door. *Click.* "Ah."

They entered a twelve-foot-square room. Windows ran around three sides, affording a glorious view of heirloom trees and peaked roofs. Taking up most of the space was an oak desk, covered in jumbled papers and uncapped pens. Two of the desk drawers had been yanked out and their contents scattered. Boxes had been opened, then piled up willy-nilly by a filing cabinet. The books from a small case were strewn on the wooden floor.

Sophie surveyed the scene. "What a mess! Why would Roger leave it like this?"

Noah said gruffly, "He was in a hurry before he split—looking for cash. Or a passport."

"You'd think your mother would have cleaned it up."

"Like I said, she shut it up and never came here again."

"What's this?" Sophie tugged a cardboard box from under a pile of 78-rpm records. Written in magic marker across the top was the name Agnes. She looked at Noah. "Do you think this is more of Agnes the maid's effects?"

"No idea." He put it on the desk.

"Let's open it up."

He obliged. The top flaps had been folded to form a pinwheel. When he wiggled one flap, it came away in his hands. "The cardboard's rotten." He carefully unfolded the other flaps.

An apron lay on top. Sophie lifted it out. "There are stains on it." She gazed at Noah, half in apprehension, half in anticipation. "Blood?"

He studied it. "*Hmm*. It's blackish. I'm pretty sure old blood would be brown. It's more likely a grease stain. This is a maid's apron, after all."

"Why is it here and not with the cap we found in the playhouse?"

"Who knows?" He sniffed it and scrunched his nose. "Smells foul." He set it aside. "What else?"

"Some letters." Sophie perused a couple. "Addressed to a Mrs. Reilly. Her mother?" She lay them on top of the apron.

He pointed. "Something shiny is wedged in the corner."

She drew out a gold ring set with three opals. "Why, it's beautiful! What do you suppose a young girl was doing with such an expensive ring?"

Noah took it from her and tipped the band. "There's an inscription inside." He squinted and read, "H to A. And a tiny heart. Huh. A gift from her boyfriend?"

"If it's an engagement ring—or even a friendship ring—why wouldn't she take it with her?"

"Simple. He broke off the engagement."

"Or she did. Maybe after the murder she went to pieces."

Noah said crossly, "We know nothing of the sort. At this point, we don't know *what* happened to her. All we have is a dirty apron, a diary, a ring, letters to her mother, and a draft missive about a fishy event. On top of that, we don't even know who Agnes was; we don't know who the master or mistress were; and we don't know for sure a crime was committed."

"Well, she did see a man put a body in a car. That's not normal. And if it was something totally innocent, why didn't her employers mention it?"

"Because—as she opines—it was just a bad dream."

"Okay." Sophie had kept the zinger for last. "Then why did your father keep her stuff?"

Chapter Seven

Never tell all you know—not even to the person you know best.

~Agatha Christie

Peveril Hall, Wednesday, April 10

"What makes you think my dad was collecting Agnes's possessions?"

Sophie pointed at the items on the desk. "If he wasn't, how did a box marked Agnes end up in his study?"

"Maybe my mother cleaned out the playhouse and threw it in here."

"But Agnes's other things were still there. Why bother to put this *particular* box in here?"

Noah lifted an eyebrow. "Happenstance? When I arrived during Mom's last illness, the house was in a shocking jumble. She'd been trying to pack everything up between bouts of chemo. There wasn't any rhyme or reason to placement."

"But why lug it up three stories? Anyway, you told me she locked the tower after Roger left."

"Not until a year after he abandoned us. It took her that long to accept it."

"Okay…" Sophie wasn't finished. "Who put the book and Agnes's letter in the box marked Roger?"

"Same answer. After I left, my mother consolidated a lot of junk." He smirked. "I remember when my sister went off to college, Mom took half of the thousand-and-one stuffed animals Gretchen had amassed and gave them to Goodwill. Sis never noticed."

Sophie was beginning to tire of the discussion. It had been a long night. *Long, yes, but not without its diversions.* She allowed a secret smile to cross her face. "Noah? I have to go home. I have work to do, and I promised to put in a couple of hours at the sorting center."

"Oh? Oh, sure." He tried to hide his disappointment, which she found endearing. "I guess I was getting used to you being here." He held her face in his hands and kissed her. "When can you come back?"

"I…uh…don't know. I need to get my schedule in order." She went to the bedroom and picked up her sweater. "I also need to brush my teeth."

He brightened. "I'll get a new toothbrush for you today."

She looked at him. "Noah, I… I'm not sure. I—"

"Never mind. It's okay. I'm sensing that this is going too fast." He didn't look at her. "It's just that I'm captivated by this mystery. I don't want any interruptions. See?"

Yeah, right. The moment she'd dreaded had come. *I'm going to have to tell him.* "Noah, I left Paris because my boyfriend and I broke up. I'm… I'm a little skittish right now."

"He's still in France?" His eyes sparked with hope.

"Uh, no. He…uh…went to Mongolia."

"Mongolia! Interesting choice. I presume it wasn't to get as far away from you as possible." When she

64

bristled, he said hastily, "Is he French?"

"What? No. He's American."

Noah clapped his hands. "That's good. I wouldn't stand a chance if he were French."

She was forced to laugh. "I'd better go."

He followed her downstairs. The kitchen was in shambles, the counter awash in dirty dishes, rogue grapes, and soggy cheese. "Damn, it's worse than I thought. You're getting off easy. Flee while you can."

Sophie was staring out the back door. "Actually, I can't." She pivoted toward him. "I don't have my car here."

"Fancy that! I forgot as well. Okay, let me clear this away and I'll take you home."

When he dropped her off at her apartment, she asked, "What are you going to do today?"

"I think I'll tackle the letters Agnes wrote to her mother. Maybe she mentions something noteworthy. And I might go back to the town hall. We only got through about half of the archives."

As he left, she whispered, "I'll see you when I see you then." She headed toward the goldfish tank.

****

Sophie's apartment, Thursday, wee hours

Sophie spent the rest of the day trying not to think about a lanky, sandy-haired dynamo with intense blue eyes, and failing.

She gave up about ten o'clock and went to bed. She was asleep when the phone rang, rousing her from a delicious dream in which she and Noah sat at the edge of the tide and let the warm ocean waters flow over them. "*Mmm*. 'Lo?"

"It's Noah. Are you sitting down?"

Her eyes flew open. "No, I'm *lying* down. I'm in *bed*, Noah."

"Miss me that much, huh?" Before she could retort he said, "Can you come up? I have news."

She was wide awake now. "What news?"

"It's better to show you. Can you drive up?" He gave a little hiccup. "That way you'll have your car."

She checked the clock. "You mean *now*? It's one in the morning!"

"Is it that late? I lost track of time. Yes, yes, now. ASAP."

She longed to say yes, but held herself in check. *He's right. I do feel we're moving too fast. I need time.* "I'm busy today. How about Friday? The sorting center is closed, and I'll be finished with my editing project by then."

There was a short pregnant silence. "All right, but we are dealing with a potential homicide here."

"A cold case."

"Nonetheless. Listen, Sophie, you and me—we'll take it slow, but I feel in my bones that this is important."

She wasn't sure if he meant their relationship or the mystery. *Take the plunge, Sophie.* "I can come up around noon."

"Perfect. Now relax, don't let me interrupt your nap."

"It's—" But he'd hung up.

****

Peveril Hall, Friday, April 12, noon

"There you are. I'd about given up hope." Noah opened Sophie's car door.

"Traffic was brutal. Everyone must be out Easter shopping."

"It *is* a fine day. The folder's inside."

"What folder?"

"I mean the letters from Agnes's box. I put them in a folder."

She began to follow him but he held up a hand. "Wait, let me bring it out. We can sit in the summer house."

Her glance went from the little octagonal building, its walls latticed to allow the breeze to flow, to a nearby double swing hanging from the sycamore tree. "Why don't we sit there instead?"

"Whatever. I'll be right back."

She sat down, slightly deflated at the revelation that Noah's news consisted of a bunch of papers instead of a bloody shirt or an andiron covered in gore. When he joined her, she pushed off from the ground. They swung gently.

He extracted a sheaf of cheap foolscap from a manila file. "Okay, these are Agnes's letters to her mother."

"Wait…they're *to* her mother? Why would Agnes still have them?"

"Good question. No matter, they've given us a leg up on the investigation."

"Okay. Go on."

"The first ones are mainly Agnes griping about the work. Apparently, the mistress was very demanding. She seems to admire the master though. She mentions his job. He was an executive with the B&O Railroad." He looked up. "Since the train was the lifeblood of the community and the principal form of transportation for the first twenty-odd years of the town, he was assuredly a very prominent citizen."

"Does she give his name?"

"Yes! That's one of the new bits of information. I think it was in the fifth or sixth letter." He shuffled the pages. "Here we go: Northcutt. Mr. Northcutt. No first name."

"She was a servant; she wouldn't have used his first name."

"We're lucky she didn't just refer to him as 'the Master.' At least it's something to go on when we tackle the county property records."

The swing had gradually slowed while they talked, and Sophie pushed off again. "Is that it?"

"Nope. I now have a theory as to why Agnes never sent the letter to the constable."

"Aha."

"She was fired."

"Why would that stop her from writing to the police?"

"She was fired for theft. It stands to reason she didn't want to draw attention to herself."

"Theft! How do you know? Did she confess to her mother?"

"Not exactly." He skimmed the pages. "Here it is. The date on the letter is April 20. She whines she was unfairly let go for stealing a ring. She sounds distraught. I gather her salary was keeping her whole family afloat, and she was heartsick at the loss of income." He paused. "She makes what might be an oblique reference to our mysterious sighting." He read, "You were right, Mama, about the other night. I'm sure now it was nothing."

"The ring. Do you think it was the one we found in the box?"

"Yes. She described it. Gold with three opals. Agnes

says it was a gift. She tearfully tells her mother that Mrs. Northcutt claimed it belonged to her."

"How do you know she was tearful?"

"Splotches on the paper. Elementary, my dear Watson. There's more. 'Harry *gave* me the ring, Mother! How could it be Mrs. Northcutt's when Harry told me he bought it himself out of his first paycheck? As for the wedding, we'll go to the magistrate's office, so you don't have to worry about coming all this way. I hope you're happy for me, Mother.' There are a lot more blotches around here, making it illegible, and then 'please forgive me, your loving daughter, Agnes.' " He put the papers back in the folder. "That's as far as I got. Our next move should be to learn more about the Northcutts."

"Why?"

"Why? Because I find it strange that Agnes would be dispensed with on spurious grounds right after she may have been privy to a murder."

"Spurious? How can you be sure? Can you prove the ring belonged to Agnes?"

"Remember the inscription? 'H to A'. It could only be Harry to Agnes."

Sophie wasn't entirely convinced. "Okay. We might as well visit the county offices. They're in Rockville. I looked up the address." She jumped off the swing. "But first, let's eat."

"Hungry *again*?"

"It seems to happen every four or five hours. Go figure."

After a lunch of grilled cheese sandwiches, they headed up Rockville Pike to the huge government complex in Rockville Center. They parked and made their way to the public records office.

A woman with flabby jowls and improbable red hair cropped close sat behind a high desk. She wore thick glasses, through which she glared forbiddingly at the couple. "Can I help you?"

"We want to look up property records from 1920."

Without a word, she pushed a clipboard toward Noah. "Fill this out. Search fee is a dollar per search." When he brought the form back, she took it without looking up. "You got ID?"

He showed her his license and snaked a dollar out his wallet. "Here you go."

She just stared at him, making no move to take the bill. "We only take credit cards."

Noah's brows went up. "For one measly buck?"

"We can't keep cash." She glanced around furtively, then leaned forward. "Confidentially? The council wants to go digital. They're talking about using only crypto—as soon as there's a government-controlled one." She nodded with satisfaction. "It'll be so much easier then."

"Why not go full *Nineteen Eighty-Four* and install microchips in us? That way you can just tap a phone on our foreheads and transfer all our income to the treasury."

The woman lit up and was about to say something when it dawned on her that Noah was not on board the totalitarian train. She scowled and pointed at a computer table. "You can use that monitor."

Noah slapped Sophie on the back. "Did I rain on her communist utopia?"

Sophie grinned. "In my experience, the minute a person is employed by a government of any size, they acquire delusions of grandeur and seek to gather all power unto themselves."

"The life cycle of the North American apparatchik." Noah sat down on the chair, and Sophie hovered behind him. "Okay, let's start with 1920, then narrow it down to Marmion Grove."

It took a few minutes to find the screen. "I'll plug in Northcutt. *Hmm*. Don't see it."

"Try the address."

"Says here 4715 Waverley Avenue is owned by the Baltimore and Ohio Railroad Association."

"Didn't you tell me Northcutt was a railroad executive?"

"Right." He swiped his phone. "Let me see if I can find a list of executives from 1920."

Sophie was looking for a seat when he crowed. "Hah. B&O Vice President for Development in 1920 was—drum roll—Hiram Northcutt."

"Huh. Does it give his wife's name?"

He did some more searching. "Here it is. Audrey."

"Now we're getting somewhere. What else does it say?"

He read on. "Not much. Hiram was originally based at the headquarters in Baltimore before he was promoted to the vice president position and transferred to Washington, DC. One of the perks of the job was free lodging."

"Peveril Hall is not a bad perk."

"Well, I suppose what we consider a mansion was factory housing in 1920."

Sophie straightened. "All righty. Can we go now?"

"Not yet." Noah continued to scroll down on his phone. "Says here he was promoted to vice president in 1918, the same year he married Audrey." He looked up. "So they would have only lived in Marmion Grove for two years."

Audrey... Married... "What were the Northcutts' names again?"

"Audrey and Hiram. Why?"

"I was just thinking. Audrey and Hiram—A and H. Just like the ring."

Noah turned to stare at her. "So Agnes might have stolen the ring after all?"

Chapter Eight

One of the important things about being a small-town reporter is knowing what not to put in the paper.
~Terry Pratchett

Public records office, Friday, April 12

Sophie nodded. "Audrey and Hiram have the same initials as Agnes and Harry: A and H. It's not that much of a stretch to conclude she stole the ring from Mrs. Northcutt and the initials are a fluke." She frowned. "But didn't you say Agnes was adamant in her letter to her mother that Harry had given it to her?"

"Yes. And so far Agnes hasn't exhibited any felonious tendencies. Trouble is, she's our only source of information on Harry. He may not be the saint she claims he is. Perhaps *he* purloined the ring from Mrs. Northcutt's jewelry box to give to his sweetheart." He rose and shut the computer off.

"She told her mother he'd bought it with his first paycheck."

"Well, he's hardly going to admit he spent *that* on cheap liquor."

She folded her arms. "I refuse to impugn his character without further verification. On the other hand, Mrs. Northcutt could have been mistaken."

"She'd recognize her own ring, wouldn't she?"

Sophie had no answer to that. "The ring's ownership may not have much bearing on the mystery anyway. I'm betting it was simply a matter of Mrs. Northcutt not liking Agnes's work and looking for an excuse to let her go."

Noah tugged on his ear. "This seems to be getting murkier rather than clearer. More research is definitely called for."

"So what do we do now?"

Noah took her hand and led her to the door, waving breezily at the apparatchik. "Cocktail time."

****

Peveril Hall, Saturday morning

I should have put that toothbrush in my purse after all. Sophie licked her teeth. Her tongue almost stuck to them. She slipped out of bed. Noah snored on. She caught a glimpse through the window of rose-colored azaleas in the side yard, attesting to the inherent charm of this house. *Will he miss it when he sells it?*

She padded to the bathroom. There was nothing but Noah's Dopp kit sitting on the back of the toilet—no aspirin, no shampoo, nothing. *Right—he's only staying here temporarily. I'll try the second floor—there must be another bathroom.*

Narrow stairs led down to a short hall. The first door she poked her head through held a twin bed, a dollhouse, and a shelf of delicate porcelain animals. *This must have been his sister's room.* She ran a finger across the shelf. Caked with dust. She recalled the porcelain figurines in Agnes's wood box. *Gretchen must have taken some of them.* That meant she knew about Agnes's box. *Then why didn't she tell her brother about it? Why nail it shut again?*

Across the hall lay the master bedroom. From it a side door opened into a bay-windowed space that mirrored the dining room on the ground floor. A couch and several easy chairs formed a circle around an old cathode-ray tube television. *I bet they called this the "tv room."*

She finally came to the bathroom. *Aha.* Towels and a box of travel toiletries were stored in a small cabinet. She checked her face in the mirror. Smeared mascara and a dab of something that looked like spinach dip was stuck on her chin. *Shower time.*

An hour later she entered the kitchen. Noah turned at her cough. "Good morning, sunshine. Flapjack?"

"A full stack please." She slid into the small nook inhabited by two pine benches. "I'm starved. I didn't get any dinner."

"Ah, but we did partake of sustenance." He kissed the top of Sophie's head.

"Yes, well, the only roughage I digested was the paper from the little umbrella in my planter's punch."

Noah busied himself around the stove. "I'm glad I haven't packed up the kitchen yet. Mother left it quite well stocked."

Sophie realized she hadn't shown any sympathy for his loss, caught up as they were in the mystery. "I'm so sorry about your mother."

His face fell. "Yes." He was quiet for a minute. "It was a release for her, poor old thing. After my father… After he left us, she never quite recovered."

"Did they have a happy marriage?"

"I thought so, but then I was only five when he left. Much later she confided to me that life hadn't been all that hunky dory with him."

"Oh dear." Sophie poured syrup over her pancakes. "He wasn't…abusive, was he?"

"Oh, no, just difficult. She said he had one of those obsessive-compulsive personalities. He'd get a bee in his bonnet about, say, the public school curriculum, and write reams of caustic letters-to-the-editor on the benefits of using primary sources." He chuckled. "Marmion Grove is chock full of characters like him. I imagine there's an entire file cabinet somewhere in the county council's office simply for communications with the curmudgeonly Grove residents."

"What did you do after he left?"

"We muddled through. Mother worked at the public library. When I left for college, I had no real interest in returning to Marmion Grove. Ten years and assorted degrees later, I was flying into DC to visit Mother and it hit me."

"What hit you?"

"Not a Canada goose as you might suspect. No, it was just how resplendent Washington is. And it can be exciting, fulfilling, alluring…even lucrative. I landed the job at the Smithsonian, which has been a dream come true. There's something about museums—and libraries. They're so cozy, yet at the same time filled with worlds upon worlds and ideas upon ideas." He halted. "Does that make any sense?"

"So much." Sophie felt the same but had never met another person who shared her affinity for rooms walled in heavy tomes and lit only by green-shaded lamps. "What about your sister?"

"Gretchen? She went to American University in order to spend her weekends with Mother, but then she got married and moved to Denver. We exchange

Christmas cards, but we've pretty much drifted apart."

"And your mother was alone—in this house—all that time?"

"Well, Marmion Grove is a very sociable place. She had many friends." He closed his eyes. "Someone would come by daily and check on her all the way to the end. She told me she was blessed."

They ate silently for a while. When Noah took their plates to the sink, Sophie thought it would be okay to change the subject. "So what's next?"

"Now that we have the Northcutts' first names, I'm going to do some on-line searching. We'll see if Hiram shows up in any links."

"Okay. I'll dive into unexplained disappearances."

"It's a plan."

She rose. "I think I'll do it at home, though."

His face fell. "You mean you don't want to work side by side—like Pierre and Marie Curie, or Abelard and Eloise? Oh wait, those two weren't allowed to work together, were they? Anyway." He grinned. "We could become a famous duo of amateur sleuths—called upon by celebrities and governments to solve cold cases and diplomatic snafus."

"You mean like Tommy and Tuppence?"

"Who?"

"They were a pair of Agatha Christie's amateur spies. You haven't read their stories?"

"To be honest, I've never read an Agatha Christie." He said impishly, "I should start with *The Mysterious Affair at Styles*, eh? Now where did I put that book?"

"It's at my apartment. When this is all cleared up, I plan to donate it to the Vassar Book Sale. We should make a tidy sum on it." She considered. "I have a whole shelf of Christie's paperbacks. I can lend you some of them."

He settled down. "I suppose that'll work. I've nothing to read around here. Mother gave what books she didn't set aside for Vassar to the Marmion Grove Ladies' Auxiliary rummage sale." He tried on a puppy dog face. "Perhaps you could come back later today and bring some?"

Sophie would have liked nothing more than to come back. *But it's better to maintain some distance. For now.* "Um, maybe tomorrow afternoon. I'm going to church in the morning."

He slapped his forehead. "Oh my God, I forgot it's Easter! Tell you what: we'll go together. Do you have a new frock? Bring it this afternoon. Then we can go to the church I grew up in."

"Oh? Didn't you grow up in Peveril Hall?" She thought facetious was a nice touch.

"Silly woman. No, we were devoted parishioners. Afterward we'd always go to this little bistro and have steak frites and mousse au chocolat." He smacked his lips. "I can still taste the bearnaise sauce."

"What is it?"

"A sauce made with eggs and tarragon and…*hmm*. I don't what else."

She said patiently, "I meant, what is the denomination of your church?"

"Episcopalian. Rather high. Heavy on the incense and ritual. Gothic arches, flying buttresses, stained glass windows." He sighed dramatically. "The perfect venue for Easter services."

If it will make him happy. "See you anon."

****

78

Peveril Hall, Saturday afternoon

"All right, this one's my favorite." Sophie handed Noah a copy of *The Murder at the Vicarage*. "It's Christie's first book in the Miss Marple series. Most people like the Poirot ones best, but I always found his friend Hudson tiresomely naïve."

"You didn't bring the Styles book back?"

She said defensively, "No. I want to ask Eudora to examine it first."

"We really should keep it with the letter."

"It'll be fine. I won't let her price it."

Noah took the paperback. "Looks kinda short."

"Her books aren't long, but they're perfectly crafted. A practicable number of suspects with just enough character development so you care about them. Plus you can always count on an unexpected denouement."

He pointed. "What about that one?"

"*Partners in Crime*? That's Tommy and Tuppence. I told you about them. You'll love it." She watched Noah thumb through the pages. "By the way, I didn't spend all my time mustering books for you. I did some research. Would you like to hear what I nosed out?"

"Okay." He put the book down.

"As you recall, I was investigating disappearances."

"And what did you find?"

"Nothing. Well, nothing that jumped out at me. So far I've only checked the local paper, the Marmion *Bugle*. It wasn't founded until 1953, but it has a section on historical events."

"And?"

"No accounts of anyone vanishing in 1920. The only instance listed was in June of 1990. A railway worker named Miguel Vasquez."

"1990, eh?" Noah sucked in a breath. "Apparently my father decamping didn't merit a mention."

Sophie's jaw dropped. "Gee, I hadn't... There wasn't..." She petered out.

He hunched his shoulders. "That's okay. It was hardly something my mother would want in the papers." After a minute he said, "So what was the deal with Miguel?"

"He didn't show up for work for two days, but his landlady found a letter on his dresser from his mother indicating that his brother was ill. The supposition was that he went back to Guatemala to tend to him."

"All right. So no joy from 1920 at all?"

She checked her notes. "This may be relevant. A woman reported a pearl brooch missing sometime in January. The owners had employed Agnes Reilly before she was hired by the Northcutts. They alleged she was the culprit."

"Was she arrested?"

"No. The owners had no real basis for their claim. According to the article, they were miffed that Agnes had jumped ship to work for the rich B&O executive." She tapped a lip. "That means Agnes was only with the Northcutts for a few months."

"But it does suggest she had light fingers. First the brooch and then the ring."

"True. Do you suppose she lied to her mother? Could the whole Harry thing be a fabrication? The ring? The wedding?"

"It's a thought..." Noah shook himself. "Then why write the letter to the constable? Why would she make something like that up?"

"I don't know, but as I opined before, it would

resolve the issue of why she didn't send it."

"It was all fiction? Or she *was* a thief and she was afraid she'd find herself under the microscope."

"Either way."

Noah paced restlessly. "No other police reports? Enigmatic absences?"

She smothered a giggle. "Well, there *was* the post in the Pet Corner column about a fugitive hamster named Lucky."

"I presume he wasn't. Lucky I mean."

"On the contrary. After a frantic search, he was found hiding in a closet. However, while he was er…mislaid, the family acquired a replacement hamster, whom they named Cat Food."

Noah waited. "Well?"

"He was." She tittered. "I know it shouldn't crack me up but…"

"That's it?"

She turned a page. "Only one other felony perpetrated in Marmion Grove between 1920 and now. The postmistress reported her apartment was broken into. Among the items stolen were a sack of silver dollars and some books. Most of the books were later found in a heap by the railroad tracks, but the silver was never recovered." Sophie went to the refrigerator. "Ooh, I see you've stocked up. Are you planning to stay here while you clean the house out?"

"Pretty much. I'm on leave, but I need to check in at the office now and then. They'd miss me there."

"Do you have Easter Monday off?"

"Yes. And tomorrow I propose we cloak ourselves in finery and, after the service, march in the annual Marmion Grove Easter parade. Are you so inclined?"

She blushed. "I did bring a dress for tomorrow. The forecast is warm and sunny."

"Then that's settled. Now, did you remember a toothbrush?"

She blushed even harder. "Uh-huh. And underwear."

Before she could react, he took her in his arms and kissed her. His voice was husky when he mumbled, "I'm glad you're here."

To her relief, the prickly feeling along her spine was not due to arousal but to the cold emanating from the open refrigerator. "Do you…do you want something to drink?"

"Yeah, pull me out a beer. Thanks." He went to sit in the nook. "Now, do you want to hear my news?"

"Weren't you searching for press articles about the Northcutts?"

"And Hiram's business. Yes. I found something that could be important."

"*Mmm?*"

Noah took a sip of beer. "Hiram Northcutt was in charge of development. That meant he interacted with every business, landowner, and town that bordered the rail line. B&O owned a wide corridor, and people were always trying to buy buildable parcels next to the line. I gather it could be quite cutthroat."

Sophie felt it was time to goose the messenger. "Okay. Something happened in 1920?"

"Don't rush me. I worked hard for this moment in the limelight." When she didn't respond, he said grudgingly, "I scrolled through the local Kensington papers."

"And?"

"There was a bit of a dustup at a town council meeting."

"*Hmm.* Hostilities in small towns are hardly out of the ordinary. Was Northcutt involved?"

"I don't know. The lady came in and told me they were closing, and I would have to come back."

"That's *it*?"

He didn't seem to notice her disgruntlement. "Sorry. I'll go back when they're open. They have limited hours. For now, I want to show you something."

"Oh?"

"Come upstairs."

She pursed her lips. "Noah…"

He drew back. "My, my, what a naughty mind you have." He grinned. "I'll have to take advantage of that in the near future." When she didn't react, he added, "No, really. I found it in the tower."

He led her upstairs. A tube box about a yard long lay on the desk.

Sophie raised an eyebrow. "How did we miss this one?"

"It was behind the bookcase." Noah plucked out some colored prints and unrolled them. "These are the circus posters I told you about—the ones Gretchen found in the attic of the old railway station. She and I hid them in the playhouse."

Sophie sifted through them. She held up one depicting a girl in a sparkly blue leotard riding a white stallion. The words Greatest Show on Earth were painted in bold, red letters across the top. "Ooh, they're marvelous! I wonder if they're worth anything. I could ask Miriam. She's in charge of art for the book sale. She—"

"Sophie? The point is…how did they get *here*?"

Chapter Nine

One of the luckiest things that can happen to you in life is, I think, to have a happy childhood.

~Agatha Christie

Peveril Hall, Saturday, April 13

"Maybe your father found the circus posters in the playhouse and confiscated them." Sophie unrolled a second poster, this one portraying an even more scantily clad nymphette riding an elephant. "Perhaps he thought they were too risqué for little children."

"At five years old I was too young to know risqué even if it sat in my lap." Noah lifted out another one, this one of a bare-chested man hugging two snarling tigers. "Gretchen had this notion that we could sell them. Being kids, it didn't take long before we forgot about them." He frowned. "The point is, they were never in the house."

"Well, if he were looking for illicit contraband, the first place he'd try would be the playhouse."

"As I said, we were kids. That didn't occur to us."

"So, he brought the posters up to his study in the tower. Why?"

Noah shrugged. "Maybe he thought they were worth something too?"

"Was he a collector?"

"No idea. I don't think he was the kind of man looking to make a quick buck, though." He stroked his chin. "He could have been interested in them for their historic value."

"I can understand that." She touched the picture of the elephant rider. "They might fetch a good price at our sale."

Noah hastily moved it out of her reach. "*Or* maybe he figured out where they came from and planned to punish us for trespassing in the old station."

Sophie stood up and stretched. "It's not really worth speculating on." She shivered. "It's chilly up here. Let's go downstairs."

Noah made up a fire in the living room, and they cuddled on the couch in front of it. After a few minutes, Noah rose and idly stoked the logs. "Christmases in this house were the best."

"It's the perfect house for it." Sophie noted the French doors. "Do those lead to the dining room?"

"Yes." He sat back down. "On Christmas morning, they'd be closed. We'd troop into the living room and empty the stockings that we'd hung on the mantelpiece the night before."

"Then you'd open the doors to the tree?"

"Nope. This is sacrament I'm talking about. No deviations. Once we finished with the stockings, Mother made us go out to the hall and down to the kitchen for breakfast. She'd make this huge meal—eggs, bacon, and her fabulous Swedish coffeebread. Gretchen and I were always too excited to eat much. Then we'd follow my father back down the hall to the living room where, with great fanfare, he would fling open the doors. Behold! This wonderland of gifts would be piled up next to the fifteen-foot tree." He smiled reminiscently. "To my five-year-old eyes, it looked like the North Pole had sent everything they had just to our house."

Sophie thought of the apartment she shared with her mother and brother after her father died. His collapse had been totally unexpected, due to an undiagnosed heart ailment. He was between jobs at the time, and they lost everything—the house, the furniture, the car. They were destitute—barely making ends meet—for two years. When the second December arrived without relief, her mother announced that she had had enough of being miserable. "Sophie, my darling, we shall have an old-fashioned Christmas." They made paper chains to decorate the house plant and sprang for a single string of lights, which they tacked to the front door. The neighbors were invited for cookies and wine, and they sang carols until after midnight. Sophie remembered it as one of her happiest Christmases ever.

Noah had been watching her. "How about you? How were your holidays?"

"Oh, we had…some dandy ones too."

Noah squeezed her shoulders and leaned close. "Sophie, I want to know everything about you. Everything. Your childhood. Your wayward youth. Your favorite song and movie and poem and—"

"Whoa! How about if we space the revelations out a bit?"

Noah's face fell. She couldn't help herself. "Well, maybe I could confess a few things now." She kissed his cheek. That was enough.

Five minutes later, she found herself in his arms and in his bed.

****

Christ Church, Easter Sunday morning

"Wow." Sophie scoped out the paintings in gilded frames that lined the stone walls. She gazed upward, where the soaring arches of the cathedral faded into the gloom. Stained glass clerestory windows shed only a feeble light. "Why is it so dark in here?"

"*Shh*. Wait for it."

The organ played doleful music. A lone soprano stood at the lectern and sang "Were You There When They Crucified My Lord" a cappella. Sophie was mystified. She'd always thought of Easter as the most joyous part of the Christian year. *After all, the Resurrection is what it's all about.* She turned to Noah and whispered, "They're not very jolly in this church, are they?"

He put a finger to his lips. "I said to wait for it."

Suddenly, a chorus of voices swelled from the back of the sanctuary while the organ music built to a great crescendo. The choir came marching two by two down the center aisle, singing "Jesus Christ is Risen Today, Alleluia!" Everyone joined in. The ushers dashed along the walls and yanked down black curtains, allowing the sun to pour through the lower windows in a great flood of color and light. She gulped and wiped a tear away with a shaking hand.

Noah kissed her hand. "It's always darkest…"

****

Marmion Grove, Sunday afternoon

"Marmion Grovers take this Easter parade thing awfully seriously, don't they?" Sophie's feet hurt. "How much farther do we have to walk?"

Noah waved at an acquaintance. "Just to the bottom of the hill. Everyone gathers at the P.O. for cookies and elderberry wine. Come on, step it up, will you?"

She plodded behind him, grumbling. "You try marching in three-inch heels."

He looked back. "I *told* you we were going to the Easter parade."

"I thought that meant we'd sit at the rope line and cheer for the children and dogs in bunny costumes."

"No, *sir*. The entire town turns out in their spring regalia. It's like New York's Fifth Avenue parade, only more eclectic. See the old lady over there? That's Clara Gardiner. She always gets her grandmother's mink stole out of mothballs for the occasion. Doesn't matter if it's hot or cold, rainy or sunny."

"Who's the old geezer with the cane?"

"That, my dear, is the world-famous author of *Ferdinand the Bull*, one of the most beloved children's stories of all time." He gave the man a thumbs-up. "The king of Spain gave him that cane. It has a sword hidden inside."

Sophie thought it best not to ask for an autograph.

They reached the plaza in front of the post office building called Dane Circle. People milled around a long, folding banquet table, munching on sweets and chattering. Noah fetched Sophie a Dixie cup of dark purple liquid. She took it with some trepidation. "Elderberry wine reminds me of *Arsenic and Old Lace*. Do you happen to know where it came from?"

"No idea who makes it now. Here, I'll taste it first. If I keel over, you'll know to throw yours out."

"Ha-ha." She sipped tentatively. "*Mmm.* It's not as bad as I expected."

Noah's attention had shifted. "Oh look, there's George Weatherby, the mayor." He pointed at a man of about fifty, as wide as he was tall, wearing a scruffy tweed jacket with patches on the elbows, and a stained Oxford cloth shirt. "He's a mine of lore about the town. Let's go talk to him."

George noticed them and touched the shoulder of his companion. "Excuse me a minute, Ian."

Ian—gaunt, with a slight stoop—turned toward them, and Sophie realized he was younger than his gray hair implied. *On the cusp of forty?* His dark gray eyes glinted with momentary annoyance. "Sure, sure, George." He pantomimed chugging a glass and headed toward the drinks table.

George hailed Noah. "Why, if it isn't Vivian Pennyman's son! What's it been? Ten years?" He paused. "Oh, I guess you're here because Viv…"

"Yes." Noah was brusque. "Thank you. May I present Sophie Childress? She's helping me with…Mother's things."

George smiled at Sophie. "It's a pleasure. I hope you'll stay for a while. It's a great little town." He turned to Noah. "Speaking of, do you intend to keep the house? It would be grand to still have Pennymans there." He winked at Sophie. "Especially if there are little Pennymans running around."

Sophie was thankful she didn't have to respond so she could concentrate on quelling the hot flush that threatened to consume her whole head.

Noah didn't seem to notice her discomposure. "I'll eventually put it on the market, but it needs a lot of work." He regarded the people ambling under the towering oaks in their gaudy Easter frocks. "Mr. Weatherby is right, Sophie. It *was* a nifty town to grow up in."

George slapped him heartily on the shoulder. "Call me George. You know you're always welcome here, Noah."

When he'd gotten his breath back, Noah sputtered, "Actually, I want to bend your ear on something."

"Eh?"

Noah cast an eye at Sophie. "We're trying to clear up a mystery about a family who lived in my house in 1920—the Northcutts? I thought you might have come across something about them. The husband's name was Hiram."

"Hiram Northcutt… Let me see." He rubbed his temple. "Oh yeah. He was an executive with the railroad. He and his wife were members of the Whistlers Club. That was the precursor to our Beer and Marching Society."

"Beer and Marching Society?" Sophie pictured the rotund gentleman before her in a band uniform blowing strenuously on a tuba, his cheeks like pumpkins and his brow dripping. She pressed her lips tightly together.

"Well, the beer part's accurate. The marching part is more in the realm of fantasy. We drink and play bridge. The Whistlers played whist. I suppose that was their idea of a good pun." He rolled his eyes. "But we were talking about the Northcutts." He wiped his neck with a handkerchief. "Wife's name was…Audrey. That's right. They're still on our member rolls." He tapped his lip. "Doris has been promising to clean those up for years—the rolls, that is—but if I so much as mention—"

Noah brought him back around. "You were saying about the Northcutts?"

"Oh, eh? They only belonged a couple of years. Moved to Baltimore, I believe. Don't know if he resigned or was transferred. The house belonged to the railroad at the time, and they used it to lodge VIPs. B&O sold it in the sixties to the Goldsmiths. They were the ones who lived in it before Roger and Vivian."

"Were the Northcutts active in the community?"

"Besides the whist club? I'm told Hiram was instrumental in getting B&O to contribute to the beautification of the railroad station."

"You mean the old wooden one that was here when I was a kid?"

"Yup." He sighed. "We used to hold our community parties there, before we converted the chapel into the town hall."

"When did they tear it down?"

"I don't remember. Hey, Will Minor, come over here!" He beckoned to a very tall, very thin man dressed in a frock coat and cravat. He jogged over to them. "Will, you remember Vivian Pennyman's boy, Noah, don't you?"

Will peered at Noah from under salt-and-pepper eyebrows. "Indeed I do. You're the one who kept falling out of my crabapple tree."

Noah bowed his head. "That was me, yes."

"And the one who tried to ride a unicycle down Donley's Hill. Crashed into my prize heirloom tomatoes." He shook his head sadly. "Grew them from seed I scrounged from a farmer in west Texas."

"I apologize for my childish peccadillos." Noah turned to Sophie. "This is Mr. Minor. He is famous for his fruit and vegetable gardens."

Will eyed her. "And who is this? Another daredevil come to knock my greenhouse down?" His smile was genial, and Sophie relaxed.

"This is Sophie Childress. She's very well-behaved."

George hooked Will's sleeve. "We were talking about the old wooden station. Do you recall when it was torn down?"

"*Hmm.* That'd be the late 1980s I think. Unfortunate decision. If we'd kept it, it would have been eligible for historic designation—like the Kensington station is now. Be a good tourist draw."

"Yeah, well, a lot of town residents thought it was a fire trap." George nodded at Ian, who had just returned, plastic cup in hand. "Wasn't it a relative of yours who led the charge for replacement, Ian?"

"Replacement of what?"

"The old railroad station. He had a steel construction business. Talked us into the shelter. Prefab. Cheap."

Will wagged a finger. "So cheap."

Ian shook his head. "The old building may have been historic, but it was in pretty bad shape. My cousin was right." He pointed at a small lean-to that looked more like a beach cabana than a train station. "After all, the shelter's still standing after thirty years."

George brushed this off. "Yeah, yeah. Actually, the last straw was when Florence Crockett's kid cut himself on broken glass climbing through a window."

"You mean Matthew? He went to school with my sister, Gretchen."

"Yeah, he was a little rascal." George shook his head indulgently. "That gang got into all kinds of trouble. I remember Gretchen was caught too. She was the lookout."

Ian wasn't as amused. "Those kids did a lot of damage to an already fragile building."

93

"They were just horsing around."

"They vandalized the place." Ian's face showed his disgust.

"Not on purpose." George was placating. "Matthew swore he saw something moving inside. The children were convinced the place was haunted."

"It's a good thing the women got together and forced the town council to raze it."

"Haunted, huh?" Noah was fascinated. "Has anyone else seen anything…er…spectral?"

"Oh, there have been sightings over the years. Every fifty years or so someone claims they see shapes wafting around and hear noises. Why, just a few weeks ago, Clara Gardiner was adamant she saw the figure of a man floating a foot above the ground there. Translucent, she said. But huge."

Sophie cleared her throat. "Um…if it was the old station that was haunted, what would ghosts be doing there now?"

Chapter Ten

A woman who doesn't lie is a woman without imagination and without sympathy.

~Agatha Christie

Marmion Grove, Sunday, April 14

The men stared at Sophie. Finally, the mayor muttered, " 'Course there aren't any actual *ghosts*. They're just fumes emanating from the old foundations. You know, from the concrete."

Ian nodded sagely. "I wouldn't be surprised if the fumes were toxic—asbestos or whatever they used for building materials at the turn of the century."

Will added eagerly, "We should probably have the air and soil tested there."

Sophie looked over at the shelter. It was surrounded by flowering shrubs. "Those plants wouldn't survive if the soil were poisoned, would they?"

No one had an answer to that, although Sophie caught a fleeting look of frustration on Will's face.

A young girl came over and tugged George's sleeve. "Mr. Weatherby, Mrs. Weatherby says to come help clear the tables." He left with her, and the party began to disperse, some heading down Rokeby Avenue and others up Waverley.

Sophie and Noah followed a noisy group up the hill.

"The old railway station is where you found the posters, right?"

"Gretchen found them, but yes. If it was torn down in the late eighties, it must have been soon after she and her gang broke in."

"Did Gretchen say anything about seeing ghosts?"

"Uh-uh, but her friend Matthew Crockett insisted he saw lights winking on and off and a filmy apparition near the tracks one night when he was out with his dog."

"Huh."

They turned onto the pathway leading to the house. A voice called from the street. "Hey there, you're Vivian Pennyman's son, right?"

Noah looked over his shoulder. "Ian, isn't it? Yes, I am."

"George told me who you were. Sorry about your loss. She was a good woman."

"Thanks."

The man walked on.

Sophie climbed the steps to the porch. "I don't know about you, but those cookies weren't enough."

"Agreed. That's why I started the lamb before we left."

"Is that what you were doing so early in the morning!"

He grinned. "In my youth, we considered roast lamb a luxury. Should my sister or I bring a date home who met with Mom's approval, she'd roast a leg. It got to be pretty funny, although to this day I'm not sure she even realized she was showing her hand."

Sophie set the table in the dining room, and they settled down to a lovely feast of crusty brown lamb with mint jelly, potatoes, steamed asparagus, and corn pudding.

"The jelly is delicious—not too sweet and very minty. What's the brand?"

Noah went to the kitchen and returned with a small crock. "It's home-made. Gretchen has a huge garden with lots of herbs. She puts up jellies and pickles every year and sends me a few jars at Christmas." He took a sip of claret. "She got the bug from my mother. Mom used to make elderberry wine and root beer. She would joke that we were survivalists."

"Elderberry wine? Was it by chance hers that we drank at the festivities?"

"Nope. Hers was infinitely better than the schlock they buy now." He took their plates to the kitchen and came back with dessert. "Lemon curd tarts with fresh strawberries and Devonshire cream."

Sophie finished hers. While she was carving out half of Noah's and dropping it on her plate, he poured coffee. "So what did you think about George's information?"

Sophie sat back and rubbed her stomach. "You know what? I say we set the mystery aside for today and just decompress."

"I'm amenable. Let's finish the dishes, and then go for a ride in the horse and buggy."

"The buggy?"

"Magda. I like to think of her as buggy and horse rolled into one. Only with a lot more horsepower."

****

Peveril Hall, Sunday, midnight

"What was that?"

"Waa?"

"I heard something outside." Noah rose. "I'm going to go check it out."

"Want me to go with you?" Sophie didn't really mean it.

"Nah. If it's raccoons in the garbage, I'll just send them packing."

Just like Agnes that night. "Maybe I *should* go with you."

"*Shh.* I'll just be a minute." He slipped into his shoes and went downstairs in the dark.

Sophie waited, wide awake. Five minutes went by. Then ten. By fifteen minutes she was out of bed and searching for Noah's bathrobe. *Something's not right. My spidey sense is tingling.*

She stood at the top of the stairs, listening. All was quiet. Too quiet. She decided to go with her gut and see for herself. She made her way to the kitchen. Empty. She rummaged through several drawers for a flashlight without success. The yard was pitch black. *Should I call out? That might spook the raccoons. But what if it's an intruder—a human? Would that draw attention to me? Or worse, give away Noah's position? Where the hell is he?* She opened the screen door. Nothing. Not even a foraging squirrel broke the stillness.

Okay, I'm going outside, intruder be damned. She stepped down the stairs. The outbuildings loomed in the darkness—the summer house on the right; the playhouse in front of her; the garage on the left, its two-story bulk shutting out the moonlight. Just then a car went by on the road, and its headlights flashed across the courtyard. Sophie saw a shape by the side of the garage. *Oh dear, is it...?*

She ran across the grass. Noah lay crumpled on the ground, out cold. She tried to lift him, but something resisted her efforts. *Wait, didn't I see floodlights under the gables?* She left Noah, who hadn't moved, and opened the door. The switch was easy to find, and soon the whole backyard was bathed in light. When she returned to him, he was stirring. "Thank God, you're not dead." She felt for her phone. *Darn—I left it upstairs!*

"Sophie?" His voice was weak but clear.

"Noah! Are you all right?"

"I think so... I seem to be attached to something. It's holding me down."

She turned him over. A thick rope was tied around his waist and trailed along the ground. "What the hell?" She picked at it, but the knot was too tight. "Hang on a sec."

Back in the kitchen, she selected a meat fork from a stoneware crock filled with kitchen tools. She carried it outside and worked the knot back and forth until it loosened up enough to untie.

Noah sat up, wide awake now. "Ooph. I must have fallen out the window."

She coiled up the rope. "How did it happen?"

"I don't know. The last thing I remember seeing was a light flickering in the carriage house. I went to investigate. It's all a blank after that." He massaged his rump. "I must've hit the ground hard."

"You don't remember going up to the hayloft?"

He shook his head.

She examined the rest of him. "There's a big lump on the back of your head, too." She leaned back on her haunches. "Someone clubbed you."

"Then how did I hurt my arm?" He rotated it, revealing a dark bruise.

"Who knows?" She looked up. "The window's closed." Just below it the hook protruded from the wall.

She picked up the end of the rope. "This is just about long enough."

"Long enough for what?"

"To toss over the hook, hoist you up, and then drop you." Goose bumps bristled on her arms. "You were supposed to die, Noah."

****

Emergency clinic, Monday morning

The nurse removed the cold compress. "Doctor says to alternate hot and cold for at least a day to keep the swelling down. Nothing is broken, but your coccyx is badly bruised. How far did you fall anyway?"

Sophie caught Noah's glance and sliced a finger across her throat.

"About fifteen feet. I…uh…was fooling around in my hayloft and slipped."

Sophie went into full schoolmarm mode. "I told you time and again to stop doing that. You're not a kid anymore, young man."

The nurse growled, "True. He's very lucky he didn't do more damage. He could have landed on his head."

Sophie couldn't help it. "In that case, he'd be just fine."

"*Hmph.*" The nurse left it at that.

Sophie drove Noah back to Peveril Hall. She made him lie down on the living room sofa. "Where do you suppose the guy got the rope?"

"It's mine. When I went to college, I stashed all my climbing gear in the garage."

"And the killer found it and employed it to further his evil intent."

"Killer? Why are you so sure someone wants to kill me?"

"Have you got any other explanation for a person breaking into the garage, hitting you over the head, stringing you up, and dropping you like a bale of hay?"

"A prank?"

She just looked at him.

"Okay, but why would anyone want to kill *me*?"

She shrugged. "Ya got me. Maybe you bullied some kid when you were young, and they saw the opportunity for revenge now you're back."

"Impossible! I was extremely popular at Marmion Grove Elementary. Why, the students voted me friendliest boy in the sixth grade."

"Well, then, it could have been a burglar. He panicked when he heard you."

"Seems kind of an elaborate way to liquidate an inconvenient person."

"Not really. Say he was making off with your gear when you came rooting around. He knocked you out, then decided to use the rope to make it look as though you'd jumped."

"In the middle of the night?"

She shrugged.

"Okay, we'll pretend for now that's the 'how.' What about the who? Who would do this?"

She held her phone up. "I say we call the police."

"Isn't it too late?"

"It's been less than twelve hours. There are bound to be fingerprints or something."

"Okay."

****

Peveril Hall, Monday, late afternoon

"We recovered the print of a man's shoe in the mud behind the garage. No fingerprints other than yours anywhere inside or out." The policeman held his pen over his clipboard. "You didn't see your attacker?"

"Sorry, Sergeant Kent. I don't remember anything until I woke up to find Sophie hovering over me."

"I bet it was a burglar. It's well known in the neighborhood that your mother passed. The guy probably figured he could take advantage of an empty house. Any idea what was stolen?"

"I haven't had a chance to look. Mother used the hayloft for storage after Gretchen and I left home. I've been slowly going through it."

"What for?"

"I have to empty the house if I'm going to sell it."

Sophie watched Noah. He didn't look happy. *Is he itching to get away from here now?* She felt a tug. It had only been a few days, but she already loved the house. *Not that I'd be living in it...but I could visit.* And the town. There was something special about the town. *Yeah: there's a murderer on the loose.* She woke up to hear the officer wrapping up.

"We'll take the print back to the lab. It looks like the only lead we have. Call this number when you have a complete inventory of what's missing. We can be on the lookout if something turns up in a pawn shop or on eBay." He glanced at the donut pillow on which Noah gingerly rested. "Don't forget to notify your insurance company."

Noah took the card. "Thanks."

Sophie saw the sergeant off, then joined Noah on the couch. "Doctor said to rest. You don't have a concussion, but that's a nasty contusion."

He tried to stand. "Later. First I want to check out the hayloft."

She pushed him back down. "Not now." When he started to grouse, she compromised. "I'll go."

"You don't know what was up there before."

"Yes, I do. We went through it looking for Agnes's things."

"Right, but we weren't focused on valuables."

"*Hmm*. Then we'll just have to wait till you're feeling better. He won't come back tonight."

"How do you know?"

"I'm leaving the floodlights on all night. Plus that nice Officer Kent promised to keep watch in his squad car until morning."

Noah gave up. "All right." He lay back. "I think I'll just grab a little shuteye. You might want to take the good sergeant some coffee and cookies."

"Will do."

Once she was sure Noah was asleep, Sophie climbed the stairs to the tower room. She took the posters from the box and rolled them up, securing them with a rubber band. She returned to the kitchen, scooped up some Oreos, and filled a thermos with coffee. *Might as well get the posters we found in the garage and the playhouse, too*. She added them to the roll and went out to the squad car. She gave Officer Kent his snack and dropped her plunder in the back seat of her car.

"Where are you going, miss?"

"Home."

He peered at her. "You didn't remove anything from the crime scene, did you?"

Her heart gave a lurch. "Um, no. Those are only some pictures that I…that I brought to show Noah. They're…mine. Just some old pictures." She jumped in the car and, without bothering to turn around, backed down the driveway as fast as she could.

Chapter Eleven

The nice thing about living in a small town is that when you don't know what you're doing, someone else does.
~Immanuel Kant

Sorting center, Tuesday, April 16

"So, Miriam, what do you think? Are they worth anything?"

The art specialist studied one of the circus posters with a magnifying glass. "They seem to be first-run—not modern reproductions. No *P* in the margin, and I don't see any sign of pixelation." She put the glass down. "By the way, circus people don't call them posters; they're lithos or bills."

"Bills?"

"Short for handbills." She tapped the paper. "They are technically works of art, but I think Eudora should take a peek. She might have a better handle on their worth."

"Why?"

"Because they're copyrighted. An original painting won't have copyright language printed on it, so the valuation process is less precise. These might show up in your reference works."

"Okay. Eudora will be here this afternoon—I'll leave her a message. Meanwhile, I'm going to search the timetables of these circuses. If they came through Marmion Grove in 1920, it would affirm the bills' authenticity."

Miriam shrugged. "They might have been dropped off at the station to be parceled out to neighboring towns."

Sophie considered that. "According to Noah's sister, they were scattered on the floor."

"Oh? So these could be extras, leftovers from the packets."

"Making it harder to track the shows' schedules. Shoot."

Miriam continued to peruse the picture. Her magnifier moved to the top. "*Hmm*. There's a brown stain on this one."

Sophie looked closer. "Clyde Beatty-Cole Brothers. You don't think it's part of the image? I mean, it could be the lion tamer's blood."

"No. See here, the stain spreads to the white border. Too bad. That will lower the value considerably."

Sophie laughed. "Maybe it's a drop of very rare, expensive red wine—a Lafitte-Rothschild 1920 perhaps. We could price it even higher."

"Ha-ha. How about we throw in that the wine was spilled by Ernest Hemingway or Dorothy Parker." Miriam took a pen knife and scraped up a tiny bit of the stain. She sniffed it. Her eyes concerned, she held it out to Sophie. "Smell that coppery scent? It's not wine, Sophie. If I were to hazard a guess, I'd say this was blood."

"Blood!" *Agnes's victim*? "Real blood? Not paint?"

Miriam stared at Sophie. "You look scared. What aren't you telling me?"

Sophie sighed. "I'd better start from the beginning. Noah's sister snitched these posters—I mean, handbills—from the town's old railroad station. We found them in a box in Noah's father's study."

"Okay, but why are you frightened?"

She told Miriam about Agnes and the letter, their subsequent research, and finally, Noah's misadventure of the night before. "We're going on the presumption that the incident is a response to our investigations. Someone wants us to stop."

"How long ago were the bills…er…acquired?"

Sophie did a quick calculation. "It would have been in the eighties—the 1980s, that is. Noah's mother died recently, and he's been clearing out the house in Maryland. We think Roger—Noah's father—stumbled on the children's cache and kept them. If Agnes was right and a murder took place in 1920, maybe it was near this poster."

"But why would that be important?"

"Why save it otherwise?"

If Sophie thought that would convince Miriam, she was in error. "But he kept *all* of them. They couldn't *all* be connected to the event. Which, by the way, happened a hundred years ago!"

There's no point in arguing with her. "Listen, I'm going to take this poster to the police. They can test it."

"Fine with me, but leave the other ones for Eudora." Miriam caught Sophie's elbow. "You're sure you're not jumping to conclusions because the mystery is on your mind?"

"There's only one way to get the mystery *off* my mind."

****

Gaithersburg, Tuesday afternoon

The police dispatcher directed Sophie to the Montgomery County Public Safety Headquarters in Gaithersburg. She only persuaded the technician on duty to test the handbill after she concocted a farrago about a long-lost cousin who had just returned from Beijing to contest her grandfather's will. When he suggested buying a commercial testing kit, she confided her concerns about Chinese data theft—"You know…with my family connections and all." She left him grumbling about precious police time.

As Sophie was leaving the parking lot, her phone buzzed. "Where'd you go? *Why* did you go? What are you doing? Why aren't you here? Are you coming back?"

She cut in. "Hi, Noah. How are you feeling?"

"Much improved. Officer Kent kept me company through the endless hours of pain and loneliness. He made me a friendship bracelet and dropped a hint about the policeman's ball. I'm tempted…but what'll I *wear*?"

"Look through your mother's closet."

"I repeat: are you coming back? We've been invited to dine with the Weatherbys. I plan to shake George down for more scuttlebutt on the Marmion Grove of the 1920s. I'm thinking we should expand our inquiries to include the community. Feuds between neighbors, that sort of thing."

"Fine, but we haven't really delved into the Northcutts themselves yet. And we should try to find Agnes."

"Oh! Speaking of. After a refreshing nap I searched the garage. I came across something of interest in the hayloft."

"A milkmaid?"

"Alas, no. What I *did* blunder upon was a shovel."

"Well, that's nice. Now you can dig yourself a hole."

"Ah, but this is an especially beguiling shovel, a singular shovel, one with whom you'll want to acquaint yourself. I reiterate—and I certainly hope I'm not boring you—when are you coming back?"

"I'm pulling into your driveway now." She heard a click.

Noah stood in the doorway, tapping a foot. "Took your sweet time." He consented to being kissed and allowed Sophie to enter the kitchen. "So why did you light out so precipitously—by which I mean without telling me—last night?"

Do I have to tell him about the posters? "I…uh… You were asleep. I needed to go home."

"All right, then what have you been doing all day today?"

Bite the bullet? Nah. Might as well wait until the police lab has the results on the stain. "I went to the sorting center."

"Huh. Okay."

"So, where's this wretched shovel?"

He went to a side counter and picked up an object wrapped in a blanket. "I didn't want to touch it—fingerprints, you know."

"What makes you think it's special?"

"Number one: it was hidden behind a loose panel. Number two: it has dirt on it."

"Oh wow. Who'da thunk you'd find dirt on a tool used for moving earth?"

Noah showed incipient signs of irritation. "Can you

work with me just a little? Why would anyone hide a shovel? And why wouldn't the person clean it first? *Hmm*? Perhaps because they'd used it to bury a corpse?"

Sophie's interest was piqued. "Could you tell how long it's been there?"

"I don't know, but those panels were put in after the stable was converted to a garage sometime in the twenties."

"Do you think it might have blood on it that could be dated? Like on the poster?" Her hand flew to her mouth. "Oops, I mean…"

"What are you talking about? What poster? Oh… The circus posters?" His eyes narrowed. "You filched them, didn't you? That's why you took off yesterday." He was angry. "You had no right, Sophie."

"I'm sorry. I truly didn't think they had anything to do with our mystery. I gave them to Miriam to examine. I didn't *steal* them."

He took a deep breath. "What did she say?"

"That they could be originals and quite valuable. But Noah?"

"What?"

"There was one dated 1920—a Clyde Beatty-Cole Brothers circus litho. It had a brown stain on it. Miriam thought it might be blood."

"Blood? You're suggesting that it has the victim's blood on it? The mysterious dead man? That's a huge stretch. The posters came from the railroad station, blocks from this house."

"Maybe the stained one was here all along."

Noah thought this over. "It's something to go on, flimsy as it is. Okay. What shall we do with it?"

"I took it to the police lab this morning."

He looked like he was about to remonstrate, but then sighed. "That was one way to deal with it. When did they estimate they'd have results?"

"Not until tomorrow."

"All right, we'll bring the shovel with us and ask the lab to examine it too." He tapped a finger on the counter. "Why don't we take Agnes's apron while we're at it? Maybe it has blood on it as well and they can compare it to the other specimens."

Sophie recalled the bad-tempered tech. "We can only try."

"Better yet, call them now. Give 'em a heads-up."

She extracted a card from her purse. "This is the number for the crime lab." She dialed and talked to the receptionist. "She says they're not busy and to bring it in now."

****

Peveril Hall, Tuesday afternoon

"The lab technician said we'd get test results for all three items tomorrow. Who's he going to call—you or me?" Noah turned the Aston Martin into his driveway.

Sophie said, "Me. I put my name and number on the forms."

"Okay." Noah checked his watch. "We'd better get ready for dinner."

"Oh right, dinner. It's with the mayor? Is it black tie?"

"Only if you tie it around your waist and pretend to be a karate expert." He squeezed his collar. "Bolo ties are always in good taste."

After a pleasant interlude in which the conversation revolved around what felt good and what felt even better, they dressed for the affair and drove across town to the

Weatherbys.

George met them at the door, sporting a smoking jacket and flannel trousers. "Welcome. Sophie, isn't it? We met at the Easter parade. I'm so glad you were available." He took her arm and led her down the hall. Noah followed, his jaws flapping soundlessly. George spoke in her ear. "Tell me, my dear, how did you come to be acquainted with this young lug?"

"We met over a box."

George took the statement in stride. "I see. Ah, here's Doris. Allow me to introduce you to my wife. Doris? This is Sophie Childress, a new friend of little Noah Pennyman."

Sophie shook hands with a petite woman as slight as George was substantial. She wore a pink cashmere twinset with a gray and pink houndstooth skirt, and pearls. Sophie was reminded of her mother's high school photo.

"We do so miss Vivian. I don't know if George told you she was a charter member of our Beer and Marching Society." Doris led them to the living room.

A familiar stick-like figure rose to greet them. "How do you do? You were at the Easter parade, weren't you? Will Minor, and this is my wife Lola."

Sophie and Noah shook hands all around.

Another man came in from the kitchen. "I brought more ice, Doris." He caught sight of the newcomers. "Noah Pennyman and Sophie Childress, correct? Ian Surry, at your service."

George said heartily, "Well, all present and accounted for. Now, do sit down." He spoke to Sophie. "What's your poison?"

"Um... White wine?"

"An old-fashioned it is. Doris?"

"My usual, dear."

"A pink lady coming up." He went off to the kitchen to mix the drinks.

Sophie inspected the room. It evoked memories of her grandfather's house—comfortable chairs paired with reading lamps, overflowing bookshelves, and antique travel prints on the walls. A fire crackled merrily in the grate.

George came in with a tray. "Here you go!"

The evening was a lively one. George was a consummate storyteller, and Doris turned out to have a wry, but piercing sense of humor. She had made a Moroccan chicken tagine—"I bought the damn pot and had to use it sometime"—which was roundly praised, as was her homemade harissa sauce. "You'll all be relieved to hear I went with conventional for dessert."

Ian excused himself. "I have to take the dog for a walk. Thanks for another memorable evening, Doris."

While they savored brandy along with the soufflé au Grand Marnier, George spoke up. "You haven't said how you're getting along in the old manse. When are you going to put it on the market?"

Noah hesitated. Sophie watched him. *Second thoughts?*

"Not yet." He touched Sophie's elbow. "We want to solve the mystery first."

"Mystery? Is Peveril Hall haunted?" George grinned at Will. "That would make at least three in Marmion Grove."

"Not that I know of, although foul play may have occurred there." Noah told them about Agnes's letter and their search for any mysterious vanishings. "We've uncovered quite a bit about Hiram and Audrey Northcutt, but there's nothing implying any scandal attached to them."

He didn't mention the shovel or the poster, for which Sophie was grateful. She felt an obscure territoriality about their clues. She wanted to hold them close for the time being.

George's curiosity was clearly piqued. "I'll check my files. I might have something useful. Are you staying in the house?"

"Temporarily. I have an apartment in DC, but it's easier to camp out here."

"Don't you work in the Smithsonian? That's a bit of a commute."

"They gave me a couple of months off to get Mother's affairs in order."

"Ah. Well, then, I'll pop by the Hall if I come across anything worthy of scrutiny."

They said their goodbyes. Just as they reached the Aston Martin, Ian hailed them.

Noah turned. "*Mmm*?"

"Glad I caught you. George called and asked me to give you this." He took a slip of paper from his pocket. "I think I know how to reach Agnes."

Chapter Twelve

The art of living in a small town is one of the most difficult to acquire.

~*Doris Lessing*

Marmion Grove, Tuesday, April 16

"You know where the Northcutts' maid is, Ian?" Noah frowned. "She's gotta be getting up there in years. We assumed she was dead and were only hoping to find out what became of her."

"She *has* passed, but I still get Christmas cards from her daughter Blanche."

"You were acquainted?"

"Only with Blanche. My mother went to school with her, and they stayed in touch."

"Did your mother ever mention how Agnes fared after she left the Northcutts' employ?"

"Uh-huh. She stuck around the Grove—I got the impression she didn't want to go back to her family. She became kind of a fixture in the neighborhood—lived in this rundown house on the old convent property."

Noah blinked. "Oh yeah, the convent. We used to sled down their hill. The nuns were forever complaining to the town that we'd destroyed their lawn."

Ian laughed. "Yeah. They finally gave up and left. It's now the Strathmore Music Center."

Sophie thought she'd better move things along. "So did Agnes live with her daughter?"

"Yes. They moved to a neighborhood called Montgomery Village in Gaithersburg some twenty-five years ago."

"*Hmm*. Well, it would be constructive to talk to Blanche—maybe she can clear up a few things. Do you have the address?"

"Sure, hang on." He took his phone out. "The place is called Shiny Acres, 202 Watkins Mill Road. It's an assisted living facility, so Blanche was able to move in with her mother. Even though Agnes is no longer alive, her daughter was allowed to stay."

Move in? "Is Blanche single?"

"Yes."

"Is her last name Reilly too?"

"No, it's Prine. In her thirties, Agnes married a man named Prine and had Blanche."

Noah wrote the information down. "That's super helpful, Ian. Thanks so much."

"No problem." He headed toward his car. In the darkness, Sophie could make out the impressive lines of a Mercedes.

She slid into Noah's Aston Martin and crowed, "Isn't this great? Now maybe we'll be able to get some answers."

"Yeah." Noah was quiet. "It's funny. I remember that house. The sisters rented it to people down on their luck. By which I mean, young ladies who were in the family way and had to stay *out* of the way of their families."

"You think Agnes…?"

He crossed Strathmore and took the right onto

Waverley. "We'll see if Blanche is willing to talk."

****

Shiny Acres, Wednesday morning

"Blanche Prine? She's in the Maple Vale section. Here, let me mark the map for you." The receptionist drew a red line in marker from the main office to a building overlooking a lake and rotated it so Noah and Sophie could see. "She's in Building 8B." The woman shook her head. "She may be in her eighties, but she's not ready to give up her own place. Tough old biddy." Her eyes filled with tears. "Her mother passed a few years ago. We all miss her."

Sophie and Noah followed the map to a red brick, ranch-style house and rang the doorbell. "I hope she's home."

"If we can go by the receptionist, she's probably chained herself to her sofa."

They heard shuffling, and a woman opened the door. Stocky and large-breasted, she had curled her white hair to within an inch of its life. She looked them up and down. "No soliciting."

"We're not trying to sell anything—not even spiritual salvation. We'd just like to talk to you, Miss Prine." Noah indicated Sophie. "This is Sophie Childress, and I'm Noah Pennyman. I grew up in Marmion Grove."

"Oh! *Hmm.* Well, all right. Come on in."

A short hall led to a living room heavily stocked with knickknacks. The room had that smell too often associated with old people—musty and a bit sour. The curtains were closed despite the sunny day, and the room was dark. "I apologize for the gloom. I suffer from migraines." Blanche indicated the couch. Sophie sat on a cushion so soft she sank in it up to her waist. Noah parked on the arm. Blanche lowered herself into a Windsor rocking chair and smiled expectantly at Noah. "So you're from the Grove?"

"Yes, ma'am. I grew up at 4715 Waverley Avenue—Peveril Hall. I believe your mother worked there when she was young…for the Northcutts?"

This produced an instantaneous response. Blanche—her rubbery cheeks rippling—let loose with a string of decidedly unladylike epithets. When she had subsided, Sophie leaned forward. "I'm so sorry if we dredged up painful memories."

Blanche took a deep breath and patted her hand. "No, my dear, it felt good to get that out. I've kept it bottled up for years. You see, I could never say what I thought while Mum was alive. She wouldn't countenance a critical word from me—at least about Mr. Northcutt. She always maintained that it was just a misunderstanding."

"What was a misunderstanding?"

"About the ring. Mrs. Northcutt accused my mother of stealing her opal ring, but she was mistaken. Harry Quayle gave it to her. It was a ring of engagement. He wished to marry her. He proposed." She said the last almost defiantly.

"Ah, so she *was* fired. We didn't have confirmation before this."

"Yes."

"Do you happen to know the date?"

Blanche stared at the ceiling. "It was in April of 1920, I know that. Let me see… Yes, April 20."

Sophie nodded in satisfaction.

Noah coughed. "Could Mrs. Northcutt have

sacked…er…let your mother go for a different cause?"

Blanche stiffened, then slumped. "I suppose it's all right to admit it now. She was pregnant with my brother."

Sophie had a feeling this wouldn't have been news to anyone in Marmion Grove.

"The sisters at Holy Mary offered her the bungalow at the bottom of the hill. She gave birth to little Harry Junior there."

"Did the…er…wedding fall through?"

"Yes. No. Well, to be clear, Mother's fiancé disappeared just before they planned to elope. He was a bartender in the city. He left his job late on April 17 and was never seen again."

"Did he run away?"

"Don't ask me." Blanche got up and went to a sideboard. Her back to them, she picked up a small bone china statue of a woman carrying a carpetbag and fiddled with it. She said quietly, "Mum was sure he'd been mugged and left for dead." She put the sculpture down and returned to her seat.

"So she was on her own." Noah moved to an upholstered chair. A tiny dust cloud rose around him, along with the smell of spot remover and stale coffee. "How did she cope? What about her family?"

"They would have nothing to do with her." Blanche scowled. "She had started working at fourteen to help out, but her mother cut her off completely."

Sophie glanced at Noah. "That's why Agnes had the letters. Her mother must have sent them back." She turned back to Blanche. "How awful! Did she have any savings? Means of support?"

"Nothing. She had sent all but a tiny portion of her

wages back home. After she left the Northcutts, she was able to find odd jobs with various residents in Marmion Grove. Took in washing. Alterations." Blanche smoothed her gingham dress. "She was a good seamstress."

Sophie said, "I understand she remarried…or rather, did finally marry."

Blanche nodded and said dreamily, "One day a man who had just moved into the old Donley house called at the bungalow and asked if she would clean for him." Blanche's lip trembled, and a tear edged out of her faded blue eye. "Stanley Prine. My father."

Her two guests listened raptly.

"He welcomed Harry Junior as part of the family. For a while all was peaceful, but a few years before I was born, Harry began to act out."

"Act out? You mean rebel?"

"Uh-huh. He felt he didn't belong. He wanted to go find his real father. No matter what my parents said or did, he grew more and more morose and finally took to the road when he turned sixteen. They didn't hear from him again."

Just like his father. Chances are Agnes was better off without either of them. Noting the pinched look on Blanche's face, Sophie kept her mouth shut.

Noah said gently, "So you never met your half-brother?"

She wiped away the tear. "No."

Time to get to the point. Noah cleared his throat. "Miss Prine? We found a book—an Agatha Christie novel. There was a letter tucked inside, signed by your mother. Do you know anything about it?"

"Book? No. Mum wasn't much of a reader. She only

had a sixth-grade education. Sharp as a tack though. Her handwriting was terrible, so when cell phones were invented she was one of the first to buy one. Even taught herself how to use the computer." She squinted at her visitors. "You found a letter? What did it say?"

Noah said carefully, "It was about her life with the Northcutts."

"Well, it must have been important to goad her into writing. I'd love to see it. Did you bring it with you?"

"No! Er, I can bring it round if you like."

"Thank you. It would be nice to see something of hers. This place is so empty without her."

It appeared that Noah wasn't going to mention the contents of the letter. *All well and good, but I'm going to toss a lure out and see what bites.* "Miss Prine, did your mother ever mention witnessing a crime? Perhaps a murder?"

Blanche's expression turned dodgy. "Heavens, no."

Noah rose. "Well, I think we've taken up enough of your time."

"Not at all!" She escorted them to the door. She said wistfully, "I miss the old town. It was a great place to grow up in."

"When did you leave?"

"I went away to college, but came back a few years later to take care of Mum after Dad died. Not that she needed it. She was active and independent into her nineties, when we moved here."

"How long ago did you lose her?"

"Two thousand and two. She was ninety-eight." Blanche beamed with pride.

As they headed to the car, Sophie poked Noah. "Why didn't you tell her what was in the letter? Did you think it would upset her?"

"Yes. There seemed no need to distress her unnecessarily since we don't yet know if it's true. Did Agnes in fact see a corpse? Did a murder even occur?"

She sighed. "Agreed—for now. So where to?"

"Let's drop by the police lab—they may have the results on our bequests."

Sophie was quiet until they reached the lab's parking lot. "Noah? Blanche said Agnes had a sixth-grade education."

"Uh-huh. Street smart but not book smart. She must have used the Christie to balance a table or something."

"Which means she didn't have much experience in composition."

"Yeah. So?"

"I remember Agnes's handwriting was pretty sketchy, but the mechanics—the syntax and spelling—of the letter were unremarkable."

"By which you mean?"

"They weren't bad enough to notice. As opposed to her diary, which was dreadful."

"Okay. What about it?"

"Someone must have helped her with the letter." She turned to Noah with a troubled face. "But who?"

Chapter Thirteen

Assumptions are dangerous things.

~Agatha Christie

Police lab, Wednesday, April 17

After twiddling their thumbs for an hour while they waited for the technician, Noah was still stumped by Sophie's question. "You're positing that Agnes had help with the letter, which could only mean there was another witness."

"Not necessarily. It could have been a friend—or another maid—she confided in."

"But wouldn't she have mentioned a name? No, it's just your editorial persnicketiness kicking in."

Sophie decided not to pick this battle. *Yet.*

It was getting on to two o'clock when the sergeant returned with their request forms. "*Hmm.* DNA check. Blood check." He looked at the couple. "I'll have to certify that we're authorized to release this information."

"What's the problem"—Noah read the policeman's nameplate—"Sergeant O'Toole? We didn't take the items from a crime scene or anything. *We* brought them to *you* for analysis."

The sergeant was unmoved. "You brought them in because you thought they might be related to a crime, though, didn't you?"

Sophie caught the remains of a spiteful grin on O'Toole's face as he turned away. She whispered, "You've no call to antagonize him, Noah."

"I can't help it; I'm hungry. It's been a long time since breakfast."

A minute later the officer returned. He set three objects wrapped in thick plastic on the counter. "Here you go."

"Well?"

He looked at the tags. "Okay, first, the poster… It's really awesome, by the way. I took my kids to a Cole Brothers circus only last year. Would you be interested in selling it?"

Noah just glared at him.

The sergeant blew out his cheeks. "*Anyhoo*, the material *is* blood—"

"Aha!"

"But the tech says it's too old to accurately date. Doesn't match anything in our records either. He figures it's from some circus memorabilia fan with a paper cut."

"Circus fan? But my sister and I found it when we were kids. Nobody else touched it but us."

"Are you sure of that?"

That shut Noah up.

Sophie asked, "Can you tell us *anything* about the blood?"

"It's from a male, Caucasian, slightly anemic. We don't have the means to determine the age of the person." He raised his brows at Noah. "You said you were the only one to handle it. Could be you."

"Hey!" Noah jumped up and pushed his chair back. "I'll have you both know I have regular physicals. It's a necessity with my—shall we say—active lifestyle." He dropped to the floor and executed a quick push-up. "I am not, I repeat not, anemic."

At Sergeant O'Toole's questioning glance, Sophie warbled, "Noah's into extreme sports."

"Ah."

Best to change the subject. "What did they find on the shovel?"

"A few scrapings of blood we haven't yet identified. Most of the residue was dirt and gravel, but the sample contained quite a few toxic substances."

"Toxic? As in poison?" Sophie leaned forward eagerly. "*Rat poison?*"

He shook his head. "Asbestos, formaldehyde, creosote. Best bet is it was used at a construction site. Or a demolition site. You find tons of the material in old buildings."

"So he couldn't pinpoint where the dirt came from?"

"God no."

"How about dating? Do they still use asbestos in buildings?"

"You'd have to ask a contractor. Considering it's such big business for lawyers, I wouldn't discount it. You've seen those ads." He droned, "All we do at Tort Brothers is asbestos claims." He snorted. "Tells you how much profit these parasites make off gullible blue-collar guys."

Noah was glum. "Removing old asbestos isn't recommended. There are plenty of buildings still around that have it as insulation. Trying to pin down the specific one would be futile."

Sophie was more sanguine. "You said the paneling was installed in the twenties, so the shovel had to be put there before that."

"You're proposing someone left it leaning against the wall and the carpenter paneled *over* it? Ridiculous."

Sergeant O'Toole had been reading the file. "Lookee here. Forensics says the shovel was sold circa 1918."

"How could they tell?"

"By the age of the wooden shaft and the amount of rust on the metal. That, and the fact it still has the manufacturer's sticker on it."

"All right!" Noah almost cheered. "We take 1918, and research construction sites in the area for a few years on either side."

The sergeant handed Noah the items and smirked. "Good luck with that. You know how many buildings were knocked down in Montgomery County after the war?"

Sophie added, "Just because it was made in 1918 doesn't mean it wasn't used recently. Hand tools aren't like appliances—they don't become obsolete."

"*Hmph*. We haven't used flint axes in some twenty-six thousand years."

She brushed the comment aside. "And anyway, if the shovel were used by a construction worker, how did it end up in your garage?"

"You're saying it could have belonged to a gardener or a local handyman?"

"Doesn't it seem more plausible?"

"But the asbestos!" Noah's voice spiraled into a wail.

"Easy now." O'Toole looked at Sophie. "You'd better take him home before he bursts a blood vessel."

"Thank you, Officer. Will do." She grabbed Noah's hand, but paused. "I almost forgot. What about the apron? Did you identify the stain?"

He turned a page. "Ah, here's your rat poison."

Noah swallowed hard. "Rat poison...on Agnes's *apron*?"

"Yeah. I—" Just then the cop's phone rang. He clicked Talk and turned away from them.

"But...but..."

Sophie hissed, "Pax! We'll discuss it later." As she led a gibbering Noah out the door, the cop called after them.

"Oh, miss. We got the results on that footprint Sergeant Kent found after your boyfriend was strung up."

She halted. "Was it distinctive? Could you match it?"

The man couldn't keep the mirth out of his voice. "Yup. The tech identified it as a Converse high-top, but the commissioner wasn't satisfied, so we brought in an expert. He pegged it as belonging to a left-handed animal with a limp. Our staff primatologist believes it's a chimpanzee. We have an APB out for him."

She marched out to snorts and whinnies.

****

Peveril Hall, Wednesday afternoon

Noah rolled to a stop in the courtyard and banged his palms on the steering wheel. "We're left with too many questions and no answers."

Sophie demurred. "We've been assuming that our so-called 'clues' are tied to Agnes's vision. There's no real indication that they are."

"What about the rat poison on the apron?"

"She said she cleaned up the broken bottle. Naturally, she spilled some."

"Tampering with the evidence?"

"What for? She's already shown she had no loyalty to the Northcutts. And anyway, why write the letter then?" She said firmly, "I think we should set the apron and poster aside for now and concentrate on the shovel."

He sighed. "Agreed on the apron, but why the poster?"

"First off: there's precious little linking it to the letter. And second, the shovel was hidden, implying someone didn't want it found."

"True. All right, I shall investigate when, where, and which buildings in Marmion Grove have been demolished since…since what date?"

"Since 1920, although the lab technician said he couldn't identify the blood on the shovel."

"That's all right; the dirt might be enough. After all, Agnes didn't say anything about seeing blood. If we locate the dirt, we might locate the body." Noah turned off the engine. He glanced sideways at Sophie. "You wouldn't by chance be angling to take the poster to the book sale, would you?"

"I hadn't thought of that," she said primly. *Well, not a lot.* "Speaking of, we're a little more than two weeks from the sale. I need to spend some time pricing books and organizing the schedule."

He got out and opened her door. "Actually, that's fine. I heard from my office. They've laid their hands on a bevy of Javanese shadow puppets which has been languishing in a storage cage for a decade. I have to…er… They want me to help sort through them. See you later?"

She stepped into her car. "Maybe this weekend if I can manage it. This is a frantic time of year for the sale, and I have responsibilities."

His smile dipped. "Oh. Well. Do let me know what they think the posters are worth."

****

Sorting Center, Thursday morning

"Eudora is super excited, Sophie."

Sophie set down the first edition of Douglas Adams' *Hitchhiker's Guide to the Galaxy*. "Has she found something special, Miriam?"

"Your circus handbills."

She gulped. "Oh?"

Miriam smiled happily. "Some are from the twenties and some from the 1940s, but they are all originals. Eudora says that since lithos were usually printed on cheap paper, they didn't last long. These are in excellent condition, and therefore quite rare. She thinks we're going to make a bundle on them."

Sophie felt a little shiver. *I should bring the other one back.* She was fairly sure Noah would object, though. He'd agreed to set it aside, yet still seemed wedded to the idea that it had something to do with the alleged murder. "What is she going to price them at?"

"At least $300 each. According to WorthPoint, they range in value from $675 to $1000. A nice find, Sophie."

****

Peveril Hall, Saturday morning

"Oh, there you are. I can't find it."

Sophie took her time getting out of the car. When she finally straightened, Noah was tapping his foot impatiently and muttering under his breath.

"What can't you find?"

"The shovel. It's the weirdest thing. I left it on the front porch—"

129

"Why?"

"Why? Because I got distracted, that's why. The wisteria vine is completely out of control, so I set the shovel down and went into the house to get a pair of pruners. When I came back it was gone."

"Why did you have it on the front porch in the first place?"

Noah looked blank. "I went to see if the newspaper had been delivered."

"And you took the shovel with you?"

"It was in my hand." He seemed to think that was sufficient explanation.

Sigh. "You didn't see anyone? The paper boy maybe?"

"No. The paper was already there. Whoever did it swooped in during the couple of minutes I was inside." He tapped his chin. "There was a big black car up the street in front of the Crockett house. I noticed it idling as I came down the front steps."

"A delivery van?"

"No, a sedan—Buick? Mercedes? Cadillac?" He shook his head. "I wasn't really paying attention."

"Amazon uses private drivers to deliver packages now and then. Did you find a package at the door?"

"Why yes." He held up a cardboard box. "My drone. So it could've been an Amazon deliveryman. But why would he steal the shovel?"

"It was wrapped in plastic. Maybe he thought it was a pickup."

"*Hmph*." He looked her over. "You might as well come inside."

"Why, thank you. Most kind."

He set the package down by the sink, made Sophie

a cup of coffee, and sat down across from her. "So how's the sale going?"

She took a sip. "It's rushed. Eudora is frantically pricing the rare books, driving everyone bananas. The rest of us are stacking the boxes that are ready to be taken to the sale site."

"It's held in the Mellon Auditorium?"

"Yes. They used to have to scramble to find venues each year, until Eudora's husband snagged the Mellon. They've been able to rent it for several years now. It's a huge space—"

"I know."

"—which will be packed with tables and artwork. There's a smaller room behind where we display the rare books." She sighed. "This is what we've worked for all year, but the next two weeks will be very stressful."

"Can I help?"

"Don't you have to work?"

"I'm still on leave, but I said I'd look in on their progress with the shadow puppets. I'll be right across the street at the Smithsonian. You can send up a smoke signal if you're desperate."

"I may just do that."

He stirred his coffee. "Are you going to sell my posters?"

"If you don't mind. Eudora says they're worth several hundred dollars each. We won't include the one with the bloodstain, of course."

"I don't know. If you can rake in big bucks from it, why not?"

Sophie felt curiously resistant to the idea. "Let's just keep it here for now, okay?"

"Oh? Sure. No problem."

"So what's on for today?"

"We still need to find out who Agnes's victim was."

Sophie put her mug down. "Can't we just leave it for a while? Do something non-murder-related?" She batted her eyes at him.

"Thanks for the reminder—I should be packing." He paused. "You know, now you mention it, I did have something else down on my calendar."

"What's that?"

"Better to show than tell." He took her hand and led her upstairs.

****

Peveril Hall, Saturday afternoon

Sophie, a sheet wrapped around her, called from the top of the stairs. "Noah! What's the holdup? I've been waiting for a glass of water for ten minutes." She listened. All was quiet below. "Noah?"

She went back to the bed and, slipping Noah's T-shirt over her head, went down the stairs. "Noah?"

The hairs on the back of her neck tickled. *Not again.* "Noah! Where are you?"

She ran into the empty kitchen. Her voice rose another octave. "Noah!" She opened the back door to a vacant backyard. Both garage and playhouse were clear of unconscious Noahs. *Back to the house!* She ran down the hall to the living room. No Noah. *The front porch?* The pruning shears still sat on the bench by the wisteria. She spun around. "Where's my phone?" She had a hand on the banister when she wavered. *Maybe he went somewhere.* There could be a note. She looked around wildly. Nothing jumped out at her, no paper stuck to the door or on the desk. Hysteria curled its gnarly hands around her throat. "Oh my God, *Noah!*"

Chapter Fourteen

It is a curious thought, but it is only when you see people looking ridiculous that you realize just how much you love them.

~Agatha Christie

Peveril Hall, Saturday, April 20

Sophie halted in the middle of the living room and closed her eyes. *You're all in a dither for nothing, Sophie. Noah is off chasing butterflies. He is not, I repeat, not strung up like a side of beef. Stop. Listen.* She held her breath. *What's that?* A creaking sound, like a door swinging on its hinges. It was coming from the dining room. She threw open the French doors and was greeted by yet another unpopulated room. Her gaze hopped from the bow window to the dining table. *I know it came from in here.* A movement caught her eye. She twisted her head, hoping to see what it was without moving her feet. *If I have to hoof it, I don't want to waste any time.*

A door in the far wall she hadn't noticed before hung slightly ajar. *A closet?* The house was built in the 1890s—perhaps a cubby for the telephone? She approached and peered in. Built-in shelves held crockery and serving platters. A bottle of bourbon lay out of reach on the top shelf. *Aha! A butler's pantry.* Her eyes dropped to a counter on which sat a cake stand and an ice bucket. A Mason jar filled with a dark red liquid stood next to the bucket. She reached out to pick it up and stubbed her toe on something.

A body lay huddled on the floor, curled into a fetal position. Low groans emanated from it. "*Noah*?" She bent down and shook his shoulder. "Are you all right?"

He raised his head. His face was ashen. "Do I look like I am?"

She knelt beside him. "What's the matter?"

"Sick."

"I can see that."

"*Mmph mmph.*"

"What did you say?"

"9-1-1. Call 9-1-1."

It took her a moment before it hit home. *This is serious!* "I'll be right back. My phone's up in your room."

She took the two sets of stairs three steps at a time, but the phone was nowhere in sight. She scrabbled among the bed clothes. It fell to the floor with a clunk. She went down on her knees and picked it up. *Click.* "Hello? 9-1-1? I have an emergency!"

****

Peveril Hall, Saturday evening

"He's going to be all right, miss. We've given him a dose of ipecac. He'll expel most of his stomach contents, but to be on the safe side we should take him to the hospital."

"You're saying it was something he ate?"

"He's not coherent enough to give us a straight answer, but yes. You weren't with him?"

"No. He came downstairs to get a glass of water. I

don't know why he went in the pantry."

A second EMT emerged holding a slice of fruitcake on a napkin. A jagged semicircle had been carved out of it. "I found this behind the cake stand. Could be moldy."

The first medic dropped the slice into a glassine envelope with a gloved hand. "We'll be able to tell when the doctor examines him." He smiled at Sophie. "Can you find some clothes for him?"

"I'll be right back."

He took the sweatshirt and jeans from her and stuffed them in a zip-lock bag along with Noah's shoes. "Do you want to follow us?"

She nodded, distracted. "I have to get dressed first. Where are you going?"

"City Hospital. It's on Rockville Pike. When you get to the end of Strathmore Avenue, go left. Hospital's on your right."

"I'll meet you at the ER." As they trundled the gurney out to the waiting ambulance, she inspected the pantry one last time. "Wait a minute. What's that?" She bent down. A smear of red on the floor. *Oh my God, is that blood?* Something glistened in a dark corner. She picked up a chunk of greenish glass. The color and shape were familiar. *A Picardie tumbler.* The kind French workmen quaffed their *vin ordinaire* from. A fruity aroma assailed her nostrils. She raised her eyes to the shelf. A yellowing label on the mason jar was partly torn off. She could just make out the faded cursive. *Elderberry Wine, Vivian Pennyman, 1989.* "Oh, my God." She ran out in time to see the ambulance turn the corner on Waverley Avenue and drive out of sight.

****

City Hospital, Sunday morning

Sophie stood, her mind in an anxious whirl, in front of the doctor. The ER nurse had sent her home the night before. "There's no advantage in you hanging around while we're working on him. Come back tomorrow."

"So it *was* poison, Doctor Tumulty?"

The doctor—a youthful, bushy-haired man in a white coat and cross trainers—nodded. "Yes. We found a high enough level of arsenic in his gastrointestinal tract to make Mr. Pennyman very ill—but luckily not enough to kill him." He held up a clipboard. "We're doing a course of chelation therapy to clean the toxin from his system."

"Do you think it was the fruitcake?"

"Questionable. He only had a bite—maybe a tablespoonful. And anyway, it wouldn't be easy to inject arsenic into an impermeable hunk of ancient fruitcake."

One down. She handed him a paper bag. "I forgot to bring this along with me last night. It's a container of elderberry wine and a broken glass. It might provide a clue—or even be what the poison was in. Shall I take it to the police?"

He took the bag and peeked inside. "It would be better if it goes through official channels."

"You mean, they won't like me touching the evidence? I already have."

"Still. I'll give them a call." He waved an orderly over. "Take this to the lab, please." The doctor marked something on the clipboard. "I'll add that to the request for testing the cake."

"When will you get results?"

"Not for a few hours." He scratched his cheek thoughtfully. "Most wine contains a certain amount of arsenic already. It's present in the groundwater used in its production."

"Would that be enough to make a man sick?"

"I certainly hope not." He grinned.

She felt a chill. "Then if the offender turns out to be the wine, someone had to have deliberately added *more* arsenic to the bottle?"

The doctor thought this over. "I can't say for sure. It's best to have the lab figure it out." His phone rang. "You do? She does? Okay. She's right here. I'll tell her." He hung up. "That was Captain Hinckley of the Montgomery County Police Major Crimes Division. He's asked that you come up to the police station and give them a statement."

Sophie was not thrilled with the idea of dealing with the police again, but it couldn't be helped. At least now—after a second incident—they'd treat her with more respect. "All right. Would you please give the lab my phone number and have them call me?"

"Are you related to the patient?"

"Um, no. Is that a problem?"

Tumulty glanced over his shoulder. "Let's just say I didn't hear your response. Give me your card, and I'll see that you're informed."

Sophie returned to Noah's room. He was rocking back and forth on the bed, clutching his middle. "Ooh, my tummy is *so* sore. What the heck did they do to me?"

"Dr. Tumulty said they irrigated your GI tract. Noah? They found arsenic in it."

"Arsenic!" His eyes widened. "Excuse me." He sprinted to the bathroom, dragging the IV stand with him, and slammed the door shut.

She shouted through it. "The doctor is sending the bottle to the police, but—"

His voice was muffled. "Bottle? What bottle? What was I doing with a bottle?" He came out and flopped on the bed. "Where did you find me anyhow? It's all such a blur."

She sat down next to him. "You were in the pantry. There was a slice of fruitcake on the counter and a jug of elderberry wine next to it. I found a broken tumbler and a puddle of wine on the floor."

"Elderberry? Oh, yeah, now I remember. I found it next to the bourbon on the top shelf. I thought I'd take a nip while I was in there." He gave an embarrassed smile. "Actually, I'd eaten a forkful of the fruitcake and too late remembered my great aunt sent it to Mother five years ago. It was like solidified lava. I had to wash it down with something quick."

"Someone may have dosed the wine with arsenic."

He looked shocked. "My mother made that wine."

Sophie kept her eyes averted. "I know."

"But… It's been there for decades. That was the last of a batch she put up thirty years ago." His eyes filled with tears. "It was just after my father left. She told Gretchen she needed to do something to keep her mind occupied."

Sophie didn't know what to say.

He tapped his lip. "I wonder—does elderberry wine go bad—as in toxic—after a certain time?"

Relief swept her. "It's definitely something to check into."

Noah fell back and let out a deep breath, then groaned. "Ooh, it still hurts."

Sophie kissed his forehead. "I have to go give a statement to the police. The doctor said he'll release you soon, but he wants to make sure the poison has been completely flushed out."

Noah groaned again. "Tell him not to worry. I won't try to escape."

****

City Hospital, Sunday afternoon

Sophie found Noah sitting on his hospital bed, one shoe on his foot and one shoe in his hand. His sweatshirt lay crumpled by his side. She looked around. "Well? I'm here. Why aren't you ready? Are they insisting you leave in a wheelchair? I hate that. You end up waiting an hour for a damn chair you don't really need. I—"

Noah interrupted brusquely. "Where's the car?"

"It's in the visitors lot. I was going to bring it round once you're released. I repeat, are you ready?"

"Well, I hope it's free parking." His face was a mask of gloom. "Doc Tumulty was just in here. He has decided to keep me one more night in case I have a relapse. Blast."

"Why are you putting your shoes on then?"

"I'm trying to take them off, but bending is excruciating." He held up a shoe by the lace. "Can you help me?"

She was trying to shimmy the sneaker over his heel while he moaned piteously when her phone buzzed. The shoe made a last attempt to hang on, then fell with a plop. Noah flipped backwards and yelped.

"Hello?" She put her hand over the microphone. "It's the police."

"Ask them about the fruitcake."

"*Shh*. The doctor sent it to them for testing… Yes? Yes? Oh dear. The wine? I see. Yes, it was homemade." She listened. "I'll ask him." She looked at Noah. "They want to know who made it. Shall I tell them?"

"Uh-huh. No use trying to hide it."

She told the technician. "He also wants to know the source of the berries."

"Our backyard. Mother used to harvest the elderberries from these shrubs that grew rampant along the back fence." He licked his lips. "She made cherry pies from the trees by the driveway, too. They were the best." He choked up. "She called it free food."

Sophie went back to the phone. "Mr. Pennyman says the berries were local. From Marmion Grove. Right. The date? The label said 1989. Um…Officer? Do you know if fruit wine lasts that long? Could it have turned deadly just by sitting there for three decades? Oh." She whispered to Noah, "He says the wine could last that long…but so could arsenic."

"Arsenic! So they *did* find arsenic in the wine?" Noah had gone pale.

She nodded and turned back to the phone. "Yes, certainly. I'm at the hospital now, but I'll be back at the house in twenty minutes." She clicked off. "The police want to examine the pantry."

"Did they find any fingerprints on the bottle?"

"Yours and mine." She rose. "I have to go let them in. Are you going to be okay?"

He managed a tired grin. "I think my charms are working on Nurse Deborah, so yes."

Chapter Fifteen

Any coincidence is worth noticing. You can throw it away later if it is only a coincidence.

~Agatha Christie

Peveril Hall, Sunday, April 21

Sophie sat at the dining table while the technician worked the pantry, taking samples and field testing the substances he found. Finally, he came out, introduced himself as Ethan, and sat down across from Sophie. "We found no arsenic anywhere except in the wine. The label said 1989. Do you know if it's that old? Was it perhaps decanted into the jar?"

"I'm not sure, but Noah—he's the victim—says his mother made it, so it's probably been in the same container since the day of its production." *I'll give it another shot.* "Could the wine itself become poisonous after thirty years?"

"I don't believe so—the fermentation process acts as a preservative. Depending on how it's stored, it could turn to vinegar, which might irritate his intestinal lining, but it won't kill him."

"How about the ingredients? The berries, for example?"

"Arsenic is a metalloid. It's not present in plants, at least not naturally."

Sophie remembered Dr. Tumulty's comment. "Maybe not, but the doctor said it leaches from the soil into the groundwater and can be sucked up through the vines into the fruit."

"True, but in very small quantities. It… Hold on a minute." He called to the other CSI agent. "Hey Pete! Did you happen to find any rat poison in the basement?"

Pete came in from the kitchen. "Nope, but there's a whole bottling apparatus for home-made root beer down there." He nodded happily. "Love these prepper types. They probably have a closetful of pickles and dried meat somewhere."

"Should we test the root beer?"

"There wasn't any."

"Too bad. Did you finish with the garage?"

"Yeah." Pete looked through the window. "I've never seen a two-story garage before. What's with that?"

Sophie answered. "It was originally a stable."

"Huh." He smirked. "That explains the smell."

Ethan tapped a finger on the table. "So? Was there rat poison in the garage?"

"As a matter of fact, yes. There was a bottle on a shelf in one of the bays."

"Open?"

"Seal was off. If any was used, it wasn't much."

Agnes's bottle? No, that was a hundred years ago. And it was broken. Sophie touched Ethan's elbow. "What are you getting at?"

"Historically, rat poison was manufactured from arsenic, barium, or other noxious substances. If the perpetrator poured it into the wine, it might show up on the scans as arsenic."

"How…how long does rat poison last?"

"Oh God, forever."

"As long as a century?"

Pete answered. "Sure, but the bottle I found was modern. KittiKat Bait was established in 1980, so it couldn't be more than forty years old."

Sophie's head was beginning to swim. "Then when would it have been added to the wine?"

"An apt question. Our quandary is this: both arsenic and elderberry wine can remain stable for at least twenty years. So if the arsenic came from that bottle, it could have been added anytime from 1989 to the present."

"Great." She gazed at the tech. "You didn't find anything else?"

"No." He started to pack up his gear. "There's nothing more we can do here. We'll take the evidence to the lab."

"You'll get back to me if you figure it out?"

"Sure." Ethan wrote her number down. "And the victim? What's his number?"

Sophie gave it to them and stood in the courtyard watching the CSI van leave. *I'm going to fix a stiff drink and read a book.* She headed to the living room and opened a box at random. On top was a beat-up old Agatha Christie paperback. She smiled to herself. *Perfect.*

****

City Hospital, Monday noon

Noah was slurping Jell-O from a minuscule cup when she arrived at the hospital the next morning. He looked up. "My favorite, red." He held it out. "Want some?"

"No, thank you." She repeated what Ethan had told her. "The police have finished searching the premises.

143

There doesn't seem to be anything problematic except for the bottle."

"I've been thinking. What if I wasn't the intended victim?"

"Surely you don't think someone is after *me*?"

"No, of course not. The wine's been there since 1989. My father left us in 1990." His eyes were troubled as he gazed at Sophie. "Could he have tried to kill Mother?"

Sophie felt suddenly light-headed. "Was your father capable of such an act?"

He put the Jell-O down. "I have no idea. My most vivid memory of him is being bounced on his knee."

"What did you say he did for a living?"

"He taught eleventh-grade history, but his hobby was cold-case crime. He would spend hours at the library searching through back issues of police bulletins and crime magazines."

"Did he ever solve any?"

"I'm not sure, but he sent innumerable letters with lots of attachments to the FBI." He was quiet a minute. "He also loved Agatha Christie's novels."

Sophie drank from his water cup. "Christie, huh. *The Mysterious Affair at Styles* was in a box of his books. Could he have been the one who put Agnes's letter inside it?"

He followed her train of thought. "You're suggesting he found the letter and buried himself in an old mystery, this one close to home. That's why he stockpiled Agnes's things?"

"Could be."

"Then why did he leave them behind?"

An orderly bustled in. "You finished with your

meal?"

Noah snorted. "Yes, and please send my compliments to the chef. The aspic was both attractive and inspired. He must give me the recipe before I depart this fine establishment."

The orderly was unimpressed. "Will do. So can I take the tray?"

"Yes, thank you. I presume since I ate lunch at ten in the morning I can count on dinner before I leave?"

"Ha-ha."

The orderly backed out, and Sophie asked, "Did the doctor say when you'd be released?"

"Oh my! I was so engrossed by the cuisine—and I do mean en*grossed*—that it slipped my mind. I can go any time."

"Let me get the discharge nurse in then, and I'll take you home."

He looked nervous. "Um, Sophie? Do you think we should go back to Peveril Hall?"

At first she thought she'd put on a brave front, but instinctively knew she couldn't hold to it. "Maybe not tonight. I'll take you back to your apartment."

He said diffidently, "Or to yours? Just in case—you know—I have a relapse. It would be good to have someone nearby. In case."

She toyed with keeping him on tenterhooks, but relented. "That sounds very sensible."

He gave her a wary look but allowed himself to be wheeled down to the curb.

"I can drive you back to Marmion Grove tomorrow morning, but I have to get down to the sorting center by noon."

They were settled in her apartment on Capitol Hill

when the telephone rang. She held her palm over the receiver. "It's the police. They forgot to tell me that a man came to the house asking for you. He said he'd come back tomorrow."

"Who was it?"

"He said you don't know him, but he thought you might have heard of his grandmother."

"Did he give a name?"

"Harry. Harry Quayle."

He considered. "I don't think I know any Quayles."

"That's technically true."

The truth dawned. "You're talking about Agnes's boyfriend, aren't you? Blanche called him Harry Quayle."

"Yup. This is his grandson. And he's looking for you." Sophie clicked the phone off.

Noah stared at her. "What on earth would Agnes's grandson want with me?"

"You got me." She pondered. "Do you suppose Blanche gave him your name?"

"Does that worry you?"

"It depends on what his intent is."

"Nefarious?" His eyes sparkled. "Ooh, the plot thickens. Is he holding Blanche for ransom? Does he have libelous information about the Northcutts? Or did he hear I inherited a castle in Spain from Agnes and wants a piece of the action? A veritable plethora of story lines. I—"

Sophie didn't like where he was going. "So a long-lost relative turns up on the doorstep of a woman who has no connection to any of our players. It doesn't mean it's tethered to our mystery."

Noah raised a cynical eyebrow. "Run-on sentences?

That's not like you. Are you perchance losing focus? Tired? Hungry?" He leered. "Horny?"

Sophie went with her signature withering expression.

He shivered at the look but continued doggedly. "Because it seems to me that Harry and Blanche are indeed integral parts of our mystery. Grandson of the alleged fiancé and the fiancé's son's sister—"

"Half sister. Who never met him."

"Anyhoo, I intend to follow through even while you're slacking off."

"And do what?"

"I shall interrogate Mr. Quayle, delve deeply into his secrets, and reveal the truth of what happened that night in April of 1920." With that, Noah tossed an invisible cape over his shoulder and bowed.

****

Peveril Hall, Tuesday morning

Noah looked around and said briskly, "Well, it doesn't look the worse for having police crawling all over it."

Sophie surveyed the rolls of wrapping paper and open boxes littering the living room. "How can you tell?"

Someone knocked on the front door. Sophie went out in the hall. She called back, "It's a stranger."

"Maybe it's Harry Quayle. Open the door."

Not until I'm darn sure he's trustworthy. There've been too many incidents. She opened the door a crack. "Hello?"

The man who presented himself was heavyset and balding. About sixty, he wore a mauve plaid jacket and polyester slacks, putting her in mind of a racetrack tout. Adding to the effect was a battered pork pie hat lodged

147

on the crown of his head. He held up a pudgy hand. "Hello, is Mr. Noah Pennyman at home?"

"And you are?"

"My name is Harry Quayle. I came by yesterday, but the police told me he wasn't available. May I come in?"

Sophie looked him up and down. "Okay." She led the way to the living room. Quayle stood on the threshold, staring at Noah.

"Can I help you?"

"What? Oh, yes. But first, if you don't mind my asking, why were the police here?"

The question seemed to vex Noah. "I really don't think it's any of your business."

Quayle shook himself. "Let me backtrack a bit. That way you'll understand why it may well be my business."

Sophie said, "Why don't you sit down?" When he glanced around the cluttered room, she said quickly, "I'll just get these boxes out of your way." She cleared the sofa and chairs and indicated the recliner for Harry.

"Thank you." He let out a little whoosh of air as he sat down. "I told you I'm Harry Quayle. To be precise, I am Harry Quayle the Third. And I'm here to tell you about Agnes Reilly."

Chapter Sixteen

Crime is terribly revealing. Try and vary your methods as you will, your tastes, your habits, your attitude of mind, and your soul is revealed by your actions.

~Agatha Christie

Peveril Hall, Tuesday, April 23

Sophie nodded. "We figured. You're Agnes's grandson, right?"

"Right. My grandfather, the first Harry Quayle, was engaged to be married to Agnes Reilly in 1920. Agnes was employed as a maid by Hiram and Audrey Northcutt in this house."

He may know the answer. "Were there other servants?"

"A cook, but she didn't board here. Agnes lodged in the little house in the back. Harry had just landed a job in the city tending bar, and the two were finally in a position to tie the knot."

Noah snorted. "Huh. That about sums up what we've already uncovered."

It would have been nice to find Harry before we expended all that effort though. We could've been... She caught Noah's eye and blushed.

Harry frowned. "If I may continue. Three days before they were set to go before the justice of the peace,

Harry went to work as usual. He was never seen again. Poor Agnes was left in the family way and was summarily dismissed by the Northcutts." He wiped his forehead. "She was only sixteen!"

"Knew that. Anything else?"

Sophie couldn't understand why Noah was acting so obnoxious. She could see it was starting to aggravate Harry. She asked mildly, "What happened to her after that?"

"She stayed in the area, taking in work from other families in Marmion Grove. She gave birth to my father, Harry Junior, in September of 1920."

Noah said archly, "Before you go any further, I think we should tell you that we located your aunt."

"Aunt? Oh, you mean Blanche Prine. She's only my half aunt. My grandmother married Stanley Prine when my father was fourteen. He ran away before Blanche was born."

"You never met your grandmother either?"

He shook his head regretfully. "No, and after my parents were divorced, my mother and I had no dealings with my father."

"Then how did you know about Blanche?" Noah gave Sophie a canny look.

"I knew of her existence, and this past week I tracked her down. She gave me your name and said you were living in this house."

"I'm not—"

Sophie touched Noah's arm. She wanted a few things cleared up, and the man seemed to be the type who took forever to get a story out. "Blanche told us Agnes was discharged for pilfering. Do you know anything about that?"

"The ring. Yes. That's something else I'm trying to unravel. Before he ran away, my grandmother often told my father the saga of her opal ring. Agnes contended she hadn't nicked it, that Harry had given it to her. She was crushed to have to leave it behind when she was sent away from Peveril Hall. Mrs. Northcutt told all the neighbors she had kicked her maid out because of the theft, but my hunch is she was actually trying to preserve Agnes's reputation."

"Because of the pregnancy?"

"Uh-huh."

Sophie was skeptical. "Did Agnes ever intimate she believed that?"

"Not that I know of. She insisted that Mrs. Northcutt was a horrible person who coveted the ring for herself. According to her, Audrey would crawl over broken glass before she'd do anything nice for Agnes." He stopped. "Although she didn't have a bad word to say about Hiram. *Hmm.*"

Sophie prompted, "So was Mrs. Northcutt a harpy or not?"

"According to Agnes, yes, but I have been unable to corroborate that opinion."

"And since everyone who knows the answer is dead, chances are you'll never be able to."

"Not at all. I—"

Noah interrupted him. "Thanks for dropping by." He stood up.

Sophie gave him a hard look. *Why is he cutting him off?* "If you'd like to see Agnes's old room, I'll be glad to show it to you."

Harry waved a hand at her. "That's not why I came. I need your help."

Noah sat down again. "Oh?"

"Yes. See, I'm a private investigator. I was working on a case and came across a news item about a raid on a speakeasy called the Lion's Paw in downtown DC in 1920. The blurry photo of the bartender looks remarkably like the photo my father kept of his father. I was able to verify that Harry Quayle Senior was employed there part-time. Which means he did go to his job in DC that day, just like Agnes said."

"Not necessarily." Noah seemed inclined to be recalcitrant. "Do you have any employment records that would show he was there on that day? You say the photo was blurry. You could be mistaken."

Sophie stirred. "Blanche also told us Harry worked at a bar. She didn't mention anything about a police raid, though."

Her intervention seemed to grate on Noah. "Yeah, so, he might or might not have been there the night before he disappeared." He regarded Harry belligerently.

Harry was silent.

Noah shrugged. "So what's your goal here?"

The man grew animated. "My aim is to prove he didn't run away, that he didn't leave Agnes high and dry."

"You want to exonerate your grandfather? Is that it?"

Harry said it simply. "Yes, I do."

Noah leapt up again and began to pace. "What do you think happened to him?"

"The only credible explanation is my grandmother's—that he was ambushed and murdered on his way home."

Noah stopped in front of Harry. "What about the

raid? He might have been taken into custody."

Harry shook his head. "The article doesn't mention any arrests."

"In that case, he could have been dumped anywhere between DC and here."

"Actually, I found one informant whose father was the train conductor. He liked to regale his family with stories about the midnight run out of Union Station and the quirky characters who rode it regularly. He spoke of one young man who was drinking bootleg whiskey out of a flask. When the conductor confiscated the flask and reminded him that alcohol was illegal, he burst into song."

"Song? What song?"

"Some old ditty about getting married—'For Me and My Gal.' The conductor let him celebrate. That was the last time anyone saw him."

"What was the date?"

"April 17, 1920."

"We found a letter written by Agnes about the same time, stating that she thought she witnessed a murder."

His eyes bulged. "You don't suppose she saw her own *fiancé* done in?"

"Maybe. If it was he, the Northcutts may have been a party to it."

He wiped his forehead. "And you're speculating that that was the true pretext for canning Agnes?"

"Could be. We're still looking for answers."

Sophie studied Harry. "Is it possible your grandfather was killed here—in this house?"

He looked dismayed. "No, no—but it could have been on his way to the Hall. That is, if he got off the train at Dane Circle. It's why I hoped we could join forces.

See, I know you took the shovel to the police lab. If that shovel was last used in 1920…"

Noah stopped and put his hands on his hips. "It was *you*! You stole the shovel."

"I didn't steal it—I just borrowed it for a spell. I saw you leave it on the porch and go inside—"

"Wait—do you happen to drive a black Mercedes?"

"Me? A Mercedes? In my dreams. No, but I *have* been surveilling you. I wasn't sure if you were friend or foe. I overheard you saying you found it behind a panel in the garage. What did the lab say?"

"They didn't find any prints—just dirt."

"Ah." He gestured toward the street. "It's in my car."

Sophie looked out the window. A battered black Cadillac of indeterminate age sat at the end of the drive.

Noah rose on his toes. "Oh really. I—"

Sophie held a hand out to stop Noah. "So what kind of help do you need, Harry?"

"You're trying to clear up the mystery of Agnes's letter to the constable, aren't you? I'd like to do the same. And if it turns out it was my grandfather who was iced, I want to solve the case."

Sophie crossed her arms. "First we have to find out if there was a murder *at all*—then we can deal with who, what, when, where, and how."

Noah had been gazing into the fireplace. "I think there's someone out there who's afraid we're getting close to the answers."

"Oh?"

He turned back and stared hard at Harry. "Yes. Since we started investigating there have been two attempts on my life."

"Huh." Harry seemed no more than mildly intrigued. He must have caught sight of Sophie's indignant expression, for he said quickly, "You seem to be all right. What sort of attempts?"

Noah told him.

"Wow. Rat poison?" He paused. "You tell me that Agnes opined in the letter that the broken bottle of poison was connected to the murder—"

"Yes, but she chalked that up to fancy too."

"Anyway, that doesn't jibe with stringing you up from the hayloft. Two different M.O.s."

M.O.? Oh yeah, he's a detective. "Are you suggesting that two separate people tried to knock Noah off? Or it's a conspiracy?"

"I have no idea. You're positive it's related to your looking into the letter?"

Noah pursed his lips. "I'm not in the habit of being targeted by assassins, if that's what you mean."

Harry rubbed his chin. "It couldn't be the shovel, could it? Or have you unearthed something else that would attract someone's interest?"

"If we have, we don't know what it is." Noah and Sophie took turns telling Harry about their activities.

He listened carefully. "So your father abandoned you in 1990. Did you ever hear from him again?"

"No."

"And the elderberry wine was made in 1989?"

"Yes." Noah bowed his head. "He…he may have tried to poison my mother."

Sophie put in, "And then fled when she survived."

Harry thought this over. "Did they hate each other? Fight?"

"I don't remember ever hearing raised voices, but I

was only five when he left. They seemed happy—although they might have put on a brave front for me." Noah raised a forlorn face.

"What was your mother like after he left? Depressed? Vengeful? Calm?"

"Again, I was too young to notice. Although as I grew up she always seemed very content. Whenever I asked her if she expected to remarry, she'd say, 'Once was enough, thank you very much.' "

"*Hmm*. That could have several meanings." Harry looked gravely at Noah. "Could it have been the other way around? Could your mother have tried—or succeeded—in killing your father?"

Chapter Seventeen

From now on, it is our task to suspect each and every one amongst us.

~Agatha Christie

Peveril Hall, Tuesday, April 23

Dead silence greeted this remark. Finally Noah said, "No way. No. My mother was incapable of such an act."

"Poison is a woman's method." Harry tried to look solemn, but Sophie picked up on the veiled smirk. "If your father had doctored the wine, she could have drunk it any time after he left, but she didn't."

Noah stood up and took a step toward Harry. "Quayle—"

"Wait." Sophie intervened before the bickering devolved into open conflict. "If Vivian was responsible, she would have thrown the jar away after…after…" She choked. "Has it been sitting in the pantry since 1989, Noah?"

Noah made an obvious effort to calm himself. "I don't know. Mother bottled a whole case that year. We had had a bumper crop of elderberries, and she wanted to preserve them."

A terrible thought reared its ugly head. "Um, Noah. Your father assembled materials on cold case crimes, didn't he? Could he have come across something incriminating?"

"Incriminating to my mother? Not on your life! She was born and raised in Maryland and only moved from Kensington to Marmion Grove when she married my father. Her life was an open book."

She sat back. "Oh, well. I'm merely tossing out different scenarios. It would be comforting to know your…er…mishap was merely accidental, that's all."

Noah stared at her. "Excuse me?"

Harry mumbled something.

"What's that?"

"It *is* worth looking into."

"Well, don't." Noah's face had grown progressively darker. "My father deserted us in 1990. He's probably remarried and living in Mount Airy. If Mother had killed him, I can't see her simply going on as if nothing had happened. Either my sister or I would have sensed something."

"Okay, okay! It's the private dick in me—always looking for different angles."

Noah barked, "What angles? What do my parents have to do with a 1920 maid? This is ridiculous."

Harry glared accusingly at Sophie. "*She* started it."

A quick look at Noah's face and Sophie decided to change the subject. "Would you like some coffee, Harry?"

"Sure."

She put cups on a tray and brought them back to the living room. Noah continued to glower at Harry, so she said lightly, "We were discussing our mutual cooperation. What did you want us to do?"

"Keep working on Agnes's role. See if you can glean any more clues from the letter. Who was

Bustwick? That sort of thing."

Sophie had the feeling he was giving them busy work. *But why?* "And you? What's your contribution?"

"Huh? Oh. Um, I'd like to run to ground any descendants of the Northcutts. They may have information on Agnes's firing."

Noah remarked, "The Northcutts didn't live here very long—only about two years."

"Hiram was a B&O executive, wasn't he?"

"Yes, and this house belonged to the company."

"So first we find out where the Northcutts went."

Sophie checked her watch. "I'm sorry, but I have to get to the sorting center." She made no move to leave. "Are we finished here?" *I don't want to miss anything.*

Harry put his cup down and rose. "Yes. I—"

Noah held up a finger. "Not so fast. What about my attacker, Harry? I think we should start there instead. After all, I may still be in jeopardy."

"Sorry. First things first." Harry headed to the front hall, but stopped and turned. "I still have a hard time believing the attempts are related to Agnes's letter. The three of us are the only ones who know about it." He scratched his chin. "You're planning to sell the house, right? It could be a real estate agent who wants to knock the price down. Maybe a buyer."

He walked out before they could point out how absurd the idea was. Sophie turned to Noah. "Why were you behaving that way?"

"What way?"

"Hostile and dismissive? We're all on the same page. Aren't we?"

"Oh that." Noah smiled mischievously. "Psych 101. If he thought I didn't care he might cough up something new." He preened. "I think it worked."

"That's just silly. He came here to tell us what he knew. He didn't need to be tricked into it."

"So *you* say."

It's not worth arguing over. As Sophie was getting ready, she noticed that Noah seemed preoccupied. "What is it?"

"It's just that… Harry said only the three of us knew about the letter, but there was one other person."

"Who?"

"Blanche." Consternation furrowed his brow. "Agnes suffered dearly at the hands of the occupants of this house. In some twisted way, could she be exacting revenge for her mother?"

"Don't be ridiculous, Noah. Why would Blanche try to kill you?" Sophie stood, her purse in her hand.

"I don't know, but she was very defensive of her mother and strongly resented the Northcutts."

Sophie tapped a foot. "Seems awful far-fetched."

He kissed her. "Everything about this seems far-fetched. We're trying to solve a hundred-year-old mystery and our only reference is a letter written by a functionally illiterate teenager."

She kissed him back. "You'll figure it out."

"Are you coming back tomorrow?"

"No, I'll be madly sorting all day. Wednesday?"

"It's a date."

He followed her out to the courtyard. As she started the car, she looked up to see Noah staring down the driveway. "What is it? A rabbit?"

"No." Annoyance and apprehension battled for dominance in his expression. "It's Harry."

"Oh dear. Is he coming back?"

"I wish." He turned his gaze on Sophie. "He still has the shovel."

****

All-you-can-eat Indian buffet, Wednesday noon

"How's the sorting going?"

"Well, Connie is hysterical, and Eudora is implacable. Connie wants everything packed up and ready to move, and Eudora wants to price every last rare book in the place. According to the seasoned volunteers, it happens every year."

Noah chortled. "Do they ever come to blows?"

"No, but Connie has been known to hide books that Eudora set aside for evaluation. She puts them in the back of her station wagon and covers them with blankets. Sometimes it works." Sophie spread thick, red stew over basmati rice and topped it with a mound of chutney. "Even with Eudora's obstructionism, the sorting center's almost clear. The movers are coming next Friday."

"Does that mean the deluge is about to begin?"

"Not yet. The sale opens Saturday, May 4. I'll have to go set up on Friday, but there's not much to do until then, so I have a little breathing room." She added a samosa to her plate alongside a dollop of the cucumber yogurt sauce called *raita*. "Have you heard from Harry?"

"Last night. He said he's located the company librarian at the CSX headquarters in Florida. Turns out the B&O was incorporated into the Chessie system in 1971, and that was absorbed by CSX in 1980." He frowned. "It didn't occur to me that the trusty old B&O was no more. Anyway, she's going to help him track down the Northcutts. He said he'd get back to us."

Sophie could tell that Noah was completely recovered from his bout with arsenic by the mountain of food on his plate. "You do realize you can go back for seconds."

"I intend to. Can you grab us a couple of beers from the cooler? I'll find a table."

They sat in a corner of what Noah pronounced was already his favorite Indian all-you-can-eat buffet.

"Lucky for them it's the *only* Indian all-you-can-eat buffet in the greater Washington area."

Noah was unfazed. "It reminds me of this hole-in-the-wall I used to frequent in Nepal. What that cook could do with yak defies description."

Sophie stopped, the forkful of brown meat halfway to her mouth. "This is yak?"

"Dunno. Taste it."

She put it down. "You go first, Mikey."

He scooped up a morsel, added yogurt, and slurped the whole thing down. "Yum." He waited until she started tapping an impatient finger on the table. "It's not yak."

"Okay." Sophie summoned her courage. Her fork had touched her lips when Noah chirped, "It's goat."

She carefully put the fork down and instead took a spoonful from the dish of green puree with white cubes floating in it. "*Mmm, this* is good! What is it?"

"Spinach with paneer—farmer's cheese. Try the lamb biryani. Oh, and the little cauliflower fritters are fabulous."

"They're the ones labeled 'pakora'?" Sophie had gobbled down almost everything before she realized that Noah hadn't touched his food. "What's the matter?"

"I don't know which to eat first."

"Try whatever's closest to you."

"Nah." He rose and went to the buffet table,

returning with one of the large serving ladles. He held it up. "This way I can get a bit of everything at the same time."

An hour later they rolled out to the car. Sophie leaned back on the seat. "I have to admit that was very good. I hope I don't regret it."

"You won't." He closed her door and went round to the driver's side. "You would if you had tried the pork vindaloo. That's too hot even for me."

"So… Nepal. I gather you visited. Did you go for the food?"

"Nope, although that was a perk. I went for the vista."

"Vista?"

"The view from the summit." He grinned at her.

She straightened. "You climbed Mount Everest?"

"That's a bridge too far even for me. I tackled a few of the lesser peaks—Bokta, Chekigo. Pretty mild stuff. Climbing mountains is more or less hiking vertically. I prefer cliff climbing. That way I can avoid freezing my buns off in below-zero weather."

"So you're only semi-extreme." When he didn't laugh, she asked, "What's the most difficult climb you've done?"

A faraway look came into his eyes. "Let's see. I think my greatest feat was Yosemite, although Devil's Tower was more fun."

"Fun." Sophie sized him up. "What do you suppose makes you want to risk your life for nothing?"

"The answer is usually 'because it's there' or 'for the kudos,' but I actually think my brain needs a shot of adrenaline now and then. I get sluggish unless I've cheated death at least once every six months." He touched his shoulder, and then his stomach. "Considering the events of the last ten days, I should be good for a year."

Sophie was about to concur wholeheartedly when his phone buzzed.

"Hi, Harry. What? Great. Sure—at my—the house in Marmion Grove. Seven o'clock. See you then." He hung up. "He's come up with something."

Chapter Eighteen

Every murderer is probably somebody's old friend.
~Agatha Christie

Peveril Hall, Wednesday, April 24

"Don't mind if I do." Harry accepted the gin and tonic Sophie offered. "It's been a busy few days."

"Let's go sit in the living room." Noah led the way.

Harry lugged the gin bottle with him. "No sense in schlepping back to the kitchen."

Once they were settled, Sophie prodded Harry. "You told Noah you have something for us."

"I have tracked down a Northcutt." He beamed.

"Capital! Where?"

"In Glen Echo."

"Glen Echo!" Noah gave a delighted whinny. "There used to be an old amusement park there. I wonder if it still exists?"

Harry shrugged. "Haven't heard of it. The town is in Maryland, right on the border with DC."

Noah pulled out his phone and started clicking. He waved a hand. "Go on, I'm listening."

Harry took a swig of his drink, then resumed. "Anyway… His name is Oscar Northcutt. He's the grandson of Audrey and Hiram."

"Good work!" Sophie felt a little encouragement

was in order.

"Yes, well, that's my profession after all. It wasn't too hard."

"As I recall, you were working with the railroad librarian. Is that who gave you the scoop?"

"The CSX gal? No, she was a bust, so I toddled up to the B&O museum in Baltimore. They have a small library with archived human relations records. Hiram was transferred from Marmion Grove to the B&O headquarters in Baltimore on May 1, 1920. He remained with the company until his retirement, rising to executive vice president. He and Audrey produced a son—Richard, who in turn sired Oscar, now in his seventies."

"Did you talk to this Oscar?"

"By phone, yes. He told me his grandparents were happily married for fifty years. He himself was employed by B&O as a structural engineer. In fact, he supervised the demolition of the old station here in Marmion Grove and the construction of the shelter that replaced it."

"The old station!" Noah looked at Sophie. "Did he mention finding anything of interest in it? Posters? Playbills?"

"He said the station roof had fallen in after a big snowstorm, and the interior was completely wrecked. Nothing was salvageable."

"Darn."

Harry put down his glass. "Actually, he joked that he was a little disappointed. He said there were persistent rumors of treasure buried under it."

"Treasure? As in pirate gold?"

"He didn't specify. He said the local munchkins kept nagging the demolition crew, asking if they'd found 'the buried treasure' yet. Kids were just yanking their chain."

"Treasure… Money…"

Sophie glanced at Noah. "What are you thinking?"

"Nothing. It's just… They always say there are only three motives for murder: love, power, and money. If Agnes *did* see something, could it have to do with money?"

Harry leaned forward. "In the past, trains carried mail and bank transfers. I could check if there were any robberies around that time."

Sophie said glumly, "Aren't we getting ahead of ourselves? You're skipping from children's gossip to a great train robbery. Even if there *was* a heist, it couldn't have anything to do with the Northcutts or Harry."

Noah refused to be reined in. "But say for a minute a train *was* robbed that night—was it April 17? 18? What Agnes saw could have been the robber, carrying a sack of bills over his shoulder."

"And nobody was actually killed—including my grandfather? Suits me." Harry poured himself more gin without asking.

Sophie clicked her tongue. "One teensy problem with that."

"Oh?"

"If it was nothing to do with the Northcutts, what would the robber be doing at this house?"

****

Sorting center, Thursday afternoon

Sophie put the box down and sniggled her phone out of her pocket. "Hello?"

"Are you busy? It's me, Noah."

She sighed. "I know it's you. Yes, I am. The man who comes and takes our discards is late. And Eudora fell and twisted her ankle, so I have to finish pricing the last pallet of rare books myself."

"Oh. Well. I guess it can wait."

She sighed again. "Tell me."

"I chanced on another link to the Northcutts."

"Spill." She hoped he could hear her tapping her foot. To make certain, she tapped louder.

"I was down at the P.O. chatting with Peggy Dane—she's the postmistress. She told me there's a relative of Audrey Northcutt still living right here in Marmion Grove. A nephew or something." He paused. "Funny that George didn't mention him."

"Who is it?"

"Well, that's the issue. She was called away by a customer and never told me."

"Do you think George would know who it is?"

"Worth a try. I'll go ask him. You get on with your work."

"Why, thank you. I'll get right on it." She clicked Off, wishing she was on an old-fashioned land-line phone so she could slam it down.

****

Sophie's apartment, Saturday morning

"Noah? Are you ill?" Sophie felt a frisson of alarm at hearing Noah gasping at the other end of the line. "You didn't drink anything iffy again, did you?"

His voice came in short bursts. "Just…moving furniture… Wait a sec." She heard a series of thumps and groans, then he came back on. "Sophie? I didn't think I'd hear from you. Aren't you going berserk with the sale?"

"I was… I am. But Connie and Eudora have decreed a day of rest, to refresh ourselves before the big push next week."

"Where are you?"

"At my apartment. I have the whole day off and—"

"Well, that's swell. You can come supervise the moving van."

She sucked in a breath. "Moving van?" Her voice was faint. "So you've found a buyer for the Hall?"

"What? No. I haven't put it on the market yet. I'm just getting rid of some of the old furniture and kitchenware. I swear Mother kept every pot and pan she ever owned—and every kitchen gadget. Did you know she had a tortilla maker? And an industrial-sized juicer. I don't think I ever saw her use either one… Where was I?"

"The moving van?" She couldn't help it—her voice wobbled on the words.

"Oh, that. I'm giving a bunch of it to Habitat for Humanity. They're sending a truck." He stopped. "You don't sound happy. Was there some item you coveted? The ravioli maker perhaps? The panini grill?"

"No. It's just that…that…"

"You don't think I should sell the house?"

"Me?" She gulped. "It's nothing to do with me." When he didn't immediately reply, she took the plunge. "It's such a beautiful old house though. I'd hate to see someone buy it only to tear it down."

"Ah. I see." She couldn't tell from his tone if she'd said the right thing or the wrong thing. "Well, fortunately, that can't happen. We're on the National Register of Historical Places. You can't even add a bathroom, much less demolish the building."

"The whole town? Or just Peveril Hall?"

"The old part of the town. Some fifty-four acres, including Waverley Avenue, are protected. Peveril Hall was one of thirty-three Victorian houses built here between 1891 and 1898."

"Huh. And what happened in 1898?"

"The town incorporated. That's why we celebrate Grace E. D. Sprigg Day every June." He waited.

"You mentioned her before. Who was Grace Sprigg?"

"Grace *E. D.* Sprigg. A very modern lady. She moved into town and proceeded to install—ready?—indoor plumbing in her house. The neighbors were appalled."

"As indeed they should have been."

"They asserted—correctly—that her cesspool would be a breeding ground for typhoid and cholera. The town fathers convened and decided to incorporate Marmion Grove. First order of business: shut down Mrs. Sprigg's crapper."

"Oh dear. What did she do?"

"Like any good litigious American, she took them to court. She lost, and with the cheers and jeers of the townsfolk ringing in her ears, left for more salubrious climes."

Sophie shivered. "Are you saying your house still has an outdoor latrine?"

"No, no. At least I don't think so. Mother may have preserved one in case one of her children was locked out. No, Peveril Hall is suitably plumbed."

"Well, that's good." She stifled the domestic image that rose, of Noah tinkering on his car in the garage—or should it be currying the horse in the carriage house?—while she made cherry preserves from the fruit of their trees. *Those elderberry bushes by the back fence are still there. I could… Urp. No, maybe not.*

Noah was mumbling.

"What was that?"

"It *has* been nice living here. Brings back such fond memories. My sister and I would hide in this big storage closet in the basement and watch Mother making root beer. We'd jump out and nip a bottle when she went up to the kitchen." He smacked his lips. "Nothing tastes as good as homemade root beer."

"Maybe we should try it. Didn't one of the forensics guys—Pete?—say there was still bottling equipment down there?"

Noah didn't respond immediately. His tone nostalgic, he crooned, "In the fall we used to jump from the hayloft into the leaf pile. Gretchen was ascared, but I loved it. That is," he said wryly, "until I broke my leg. Mom sealed the hatch, closing the loft off."

"Yes. Connie told me—"

"Back then kids roamed all over town. When it was time for our supper, Mother would ring this iron triangle on the back porch." Sophie heard a door open and close. "Yup, it's still there. A little rusty."

She swallowed hard. "Er… Anyway… Noah? Can I get a word in?"

"What? Oh, sure."

"I wondered if you'd like to play hooky too—just for a few hours?"

"Absolutely. We both deserve it. Say, I have a great idea. When can you get up here?"

"I'll be on the next Conestoga wagon."

"All right. Or—you could drive your car. Then you wouldn't have to stop to water the horses."

Chapter Nineteen

You gave too much rein to your imagination. Imagination is a good servant, and a bad master.

~*Agatha Christie*

Glen Echo, Saturday, May 27

"Where are we?" Sophie surveyed what looked like an old movie set as Noah drove through the front gates.

"Glen Echo Park."

"Oh right, Harry mentioned it. Oscar Northcutt lives *here*?"

"No, no. He lives nearby. I thought we'd swing by here first, then go seek out Master Northcutt."

Sophie admired the old growth trees and meandering paths. Swatches of brightly colored awnings pranced between the leaves. "So what kind of place is this?"

"An amusement park."

"It reminds me of the sidewalk chalk painting scene in Mary Poppins."

"A jolly holiday with Mary? Yes, it does." Noah whistled the tune. "When my mom was a kid Glen Echo was *the* place to go. There was a big swimming pool, and bumper cars, and other rides."

"So…a mini theme park?"

"Big for the time. It went out of business in 1968.

The National Park Service took it over and closed most of the rides and the pool but renovated the Spanish Ballroom and the carousel."

He parked next to an elaborate merry-go-round in full spin. Children sat astride the splendidly carved and painted wooden animals, joyously shrieking at their parents, whose worried cries nearly drowned them out. "Mom used to bring Gretchen and me here. Oh, look— there's the brass ring!" Noah vibrated with excitement. They watched as a tall boy leaned precariously from his horse, his hand snatching fruitlessly at a large metal hoop just out of reach.

Sophie watched the next child try his luck. "I've only read about the brass ring in children's books. How does it work?"

"A little machine dispenses rings automatically. Most of them are iron—or nowadays plastic—but every once in a while the machine spits out a brass ring. If you get hold of it, they give you a free ride."

"Did you ever catch it?"

Noah's mouth turned down. "No. You have to be riding in the outside row, and only Gretchen was allowed to sit there. Mother made me choose an inside horse because she said I wouldn't have as far to fall."

Sophie patted his arm. "I daresay you made up for the early coddling later, huh?"

He lifted his chin. "I presume you refer to my history of audacious feats of derring-do."

She read the placard. "The Dentzel carousel has been operating continually since 1921. The music's from a band organ, one of twelve in the nation. It's called a 'menagerie carousel' because it has several kinds of animals, not just horses."

Noah craned his neck. "Right. I see rabbits, ostriches. Ooh, there's a giraffe and a lion."

The music gradually slowed, and the carousel came to a stop. The children leapt from their steeds and ran out to their parents. "Was it always an amusement park?"

"No. Glen Echo was founded in 1891 as a Chautauqua assembly—you know, for cultural and educational enlightenment. It became an amusement park in 1911. Nowadays the Park Service rents it out for art shows and open-air markets."

They headed back to the main thoroughfare. Noah pointed at an ornate building. "That's the Spanish Ballroom. Let's go check it out."

The vast room at first appeared empty, but as they were about to leave, a trumpet sounded. Sophie jumped. "What was that?"

There followed in quick succession the beat of drums, the clacking of castanets, and finally, a fluting pipe.

Noah shaded his eyes. "I don't see an orchestra anywhere."

"The music's coming out of those loudspeakers." She pointed at black boxes mounted near the ceiling.

"Yeah, but human musicians have to be making it. Wait. There, at the far end of the hall. Come on."

They halted halfway down, at a spot where light from a window cut through the gloom. A man sat on a raised stage with his back to them. Before him rose a huge wooden instrument, painted with pastoral scenes and flowering garlands. Sophie nudged Noah. "I don't see his hands moving. He's not really playing it, is he?"

"Could be a mannequin—part of a tableau."

At that moment, the music stopped and the man

swung around on his stool. Wisps of white hair stuck out all over his head, and keen brown eyes peeked out of a rutted desert of wrinkles. He called in a high, tremulous voice, "You there. Come closer. Would you like to know about the Wurlitzer?"

"You mean the calliope?"

The old man's face flushed purple. "This is *not* a calliope, young man. That cacophonous monstrosity is used to herald the arrival of the circus in town. It's nothing but a bunch of whistles on wheels. This, *this* is a band organ." He stood up and came down the steps to the main floor. "It's a Wurlitzer band organ 165, built in 1926. We've completely renovated it and reinstalled the pierced barrel to use paper rolls."

"Rolls?"

"Yes. A band organ is a different animal from a church organ. It's entirely automatic."

"You mean, like a player piano?"

"Exactly. You insert a paper roll that is perforated in a pattern that plays popular tunes."

"Why is it called a band organ?"

"Because it's capable of simulating many of the instruments in an orchestra—from cymbals to horns to a violin. This baby is configured to replicate the sound of a marching band."

Sophie ventured, "You pipe the music to the carousel?"

"Yes. I can recreate merry-go-round music, parade music—even big band music." He looked the two over. "You should come back this evening—we're holding a 1950s sock hop."

"Oh, I'd love that! My father taught me to jitterbug when I was a little girl."

Noah stiffened. He turned to the man. "Are we allowed to drink before we dance? A *lot*?"

"Well, we have punch." He grinned, pretending to draw a flask from his pocket.

Sophie waved at the vast array of pipes and valves. "And you're in charge of maintaining it."

"Yup." He patted the keyboard. "Been patching her up for twenty years." He held out his hand. "Oscar Northcutt, general factotum and music man, at your service."

"Northcutt!" Noah glanced at Sophie. "We actually came to Glen Echo to see you! Were your grandparents Hiram and Audrey Northcutt?"

He jerked back, eyeing them suspiciously. "You're the second person in two days to ask me that."

"You may have talked to Harry Quayle."

"Harry Quayle?" His expression went blank. "Who's he?"

"Oh. Um." Noah shut his mouth.

Either someone else is looking into the Northcutts or Harry gave him a false name.

The man's eyes narrowed. "So what are you after?"

Noah kept his face straight. "I grew up in the house they lived in in Marmion Grove. I'm collecting stories of the town, and Mr. Quayle has been helping me track down former residents."

His ability to lie well concerned Sophie. *What other past statements merit a review?*

"Oh. That was before my time. They left Marmion Grove in 1920. My father was born in Baltimore in 1925, and he had me in 1950. Spent most of my adult life in the city before I retired down here."

"Do you remember them at all? Did they ever talk

176

about Marmion Grove?"

"Sure. That's why my son decided to move back."

"You have a son?" Something clicked in Sophie's brain.

"Kendrick. Yes." He pressed his lips together. "We…uh…stopped communicating several years ago. He had succumbed to a family frailty—gambling. Dropped a chunk of change. We had a parting of the ways."

Noah looked at Sophie. "That must be the relative Peggy Dane told me about. I hadn't gotten around to asking George who it was."

Sophie cast her mind back. "You said it was a nephew, but Kendrick would be Audrey's…" She ticked off her fingers. "Great-grandson?"

"Then who—?"

Oscar interrupted him. "So…um…how is he? Kendrick, I mean." The old man seemed torn between curiosity and the desire to appear indifferent.

Sophie said gently, "We haven't met him. Would you like us to get in touch with him for you?"

He drew back, his lips in a snarl. "Not on your life." With a noticeable effort, he pulled himself together. "I'd rather you didn't. There's a good reason we haven't been in contact." He sighed. "Thank you anyway."

Noah said abruptly, "You said you worked for the railroad. You didn't live in Marmion Grove, but did you ever visit?"

"As a matter of fact, I supervised the demolition of the old station and the construction of the new shelter."

That's right—Harry told us that. "When was that?"

He rolled his eyes upward. "Late eighties, early nineties. It was the last thing I did before I retired in

1995."

Noah said casually, "We've heard tales of buried treasure there. Do you know anything about it?"

He made a face. "It's just a yarn the kids made up. They were sure a hoard of Spanish doubloons was buried under the building. If there was anything there, we'd have found it."

"Well, thanks for your time."

As they left Oscar called, "Be sure to come back to dance—the music starts at seven!"

They wandered around the grounds, checking out the pottery displays and tchotchke booths. Sophie planned to talk Noah into returning to the Spanish Ballroom that evening but discarded the idea after he tripped over his feet for the fourth time. "How about some lunch?"

"Already flagged. There's a tavern near here—the Irish Inn." He rubbed his hands together and blew on them. "I don't know about you, but I'm in need of some medicinal brandy."

The restaurant was a short drive from the park. The hostess seated them before a roaring fire and took their order for two Jamesons. Noah accepted the tumbler and wrapped his palms around it. "So, what did you think of Mr. Northcutt?"

"He was a nice man, but he really didn't give us any leads."

"No leads? What about the whopper—one Kendrick Northcutt living among us?"

"I suppose… If Oscar didn't know anything about his grandparents, Kendrick can hardly be expected to. Anyway, it sounds as though his son is a bit of a loser."

"Do you think he's telling the truth that he didn't

talk to Harry?"

"That struck me too." She sipped her drink. "Harry's a PI—maybe he always uses aliases."

"But why in this instance? He's pursuing an investigation of his own family. Giving a false name would only confuse the issue."

"Could it be he's afraid there's still bad blood because of Agnes?"

"There's one way to find out." Noah grinned. "I wonder when Mr. Quayle the Third will grace us with his presence again?"

"When he does, we can ask him what he knows—or doesn't know—about Hiram's great-grandson." Sophie skimmed the menu. "What, no bangers and mash? No shepherd's pie? Duck confit and smoked salmon carpaccio are hardly down home fare."

Noah rattled his menu. "They list the Irish dishes on the other side."

The waitress came over and stood expectantly before Sophie. "The duck confit with mushrooms and spinach, please."

Noah shook his head disapprovingly. "When in Rome, my dear. Corned beef and cabbage for me."

They spent an hour discussing food etiquette. Sophie pronounced the duck divine, and Noah averred that the corned beef was very authentic. "Exactly how I imagined it." As he handed the waitress his card, he said, "To get back to Oscar. It appears that the Northcutts lived a very uneventful life after Marmion Grove."

"Maybe we should cross them off our list of suspects."

"You mean for the murder that never happened?"

****

Peveril Hall, Saturday afternoon

Harry had left a voice message for them on the answering machine. "Good news! There *was* a train robbery in 1920. Thieves boarded the train in Kensington and made off with the mail run—thousands of dollars in bonds and payroll checks."

Noah put the machine on pause. "Aha!" He pressed the button again.

"Bad news is they recovered every penny of it."

"Damn. There goes my theory of murder for profit."

Sophie felt a pang. "And our chance at getting our hands on buried treasure." She looked at Noah. "Have we hit a blank wall?"

"Maybe we were right—there's no there there. This all started with Agnes's letter, but our searches have turned up nothing—no bodies, no motives, nada. She must have dreamed it after all."

"What about Harry's absence on the eve of his wedding?"

"Cold feet."

"The broken rat poison bottle? The stain on Agnes's apron?"

"Rats."

She wouldn't give up. "The shovel?"

"Incompetent carpenters boarded it up by mistake. Look…" Noah slung an arm over Sophie's shoulder. "Agnes was only sixteen after all. Teenagers tend to overdramatize." He picked up a paperback from the coffee table. "Especially after reading pulp fiction."

"Or…" Sophie hated to say it. "Maybe she made it all up to take the heat off her boyfriend's theft of the ring."

"Blanche insists Harry didn't steal it."

"Blanche is going by what her mother told her. Agnes wasn't about to snitch on Harry."

"She loved him." Noah said it as though he considered the conversation over. He was misinformed.

"Even though he bolted?"

"She didn't know that. I'm confident she expected him to turn up some day. She waited, what? Ten years to get hitched?"

Sophie wasn't convinced. "All right. If she was so sure Harry would return, why did she leave the ring behind?"

"Because Mrs. Northcutt confiscated it from her."

"Okay. Then why did *Audrey* leave it behind?"

****

Peveril Hall, Sunday morning

"Oh my God, look at the time! I have to get down to the sorting center. We're having a planning meeting and all the heads of departments will be there." Sophie scrambled out of bed.

"On a Sunday?"

"You forget. The sale opens next Saturday. Starting on Thursday, book dealers and collectors will be camped out in front of the Mellon auditorium. It's a madhouse. We have to make sure we have everything in order. I still have some slots to fill."

"Slots?"

"Shifts. We divide each day into two-hour shifts. It's all volunteer, so we don't want to ask too much of any one person."

"What kind of positions do you have?"

"Table packer, cashier, snacks, treasurer. Gofer."

"Could I help?"

"Don't you have to work?"

"I'm still on leave, but I'll be dropping by to check on the progress of the shadow puppet exhibit. My office is right across the street in the Natural History Museum. I could do a lunch shift or something. Or help you set up?"

"That would be splendid! Saturday afternoon is still a bit sparse. We really need good, strong men—they're in short supply even though Vassar is co-ed now." She grimaced. "With everybody working, people don't have the free time to volunteer anymore."

Noah gazed at her a minute, a speculative gleam in his eye. "Well, my job is very flexible. My bosses encourage me to take time off." He gazed heavenward. "Why do you suppose that is?"

Sophie kissed him. "I'm sure it's because you're twice as productive as anyone else when you *are* there."

His face cleared. "That must be it."

Driving home, a sudden, unexpected euphoria gripped Sophie's soul. She wasn't sure what it meant, but she couldn't keep the huge grin off her face.

Chapter Twenty

All these here are linked together…by death.
~*Agatha Christie*

Sophie's apartment, Sunday, April 28

"Okay, I've signed you up for the afternoon shift on Saturday, Noah. That's the first day of the sale, so it's really hectic. Think you can manage it?"

The voice that came through the phone line sounded artificially timorous. "As long as you don't expect me to cashier. I can't give change to save my life."

"No, no. We need your manly muscles to carry boxes back and forth to the tables. We still don't have enough men." She grumbled, "What I say is, what's the point in going co-ed if you can't take advantage of the Martians?"

"As in, men are from Mars?"

"Right. We need more yin, less yang."

"I'm game. Oh, by the way, while I was whiling away the hours before I see you again—"

"I'm warning you—it could be days. This is loco time."

"We'll find a way," he said comfortably. "We'll meet behind the barn or by the old oak tree."

"You are aware the Mellon is in the middle of the Federal Triangle?"

"Ulp. Perhaps there's a family restroom we can slip into for a cuddle."

She saw no reason to discourage him.

After a minute, he said, "Anyhoo, I found something interesting."

"Buried treasure? A skeleton dating to 1920 with a knife between its ribs? A letter from the Pope absolving Agnes of her sins?"

"Nah—they would mess up the script. I ran across a bit of controversy to do with the railroad."

"Concerning the Northcutts?"

"In a way. I think I told you that once the line opened up between DC and Point of Rocks, the land along the corridor shot up in value. B&O owned the right-of-way extending a hundred feet on either side of the tracks. Naturally, developers clamored to buy property as close as possible to them. It's like the Metro corridors in Maryland and Virginia. Commerce and housing followed the line like children after the Pied Piper." He paused. "When I was a kid, they cut down a whole stand of timber on the other side of the tracks and put up tract houses. Those woods were our forest primeval—we built forts there and pretended to hunt squirrels with our BB guns. My best friend and I were outraged, so one day we snuck over and rolled logs down onto the construction site."

"Were you caught?"

"Luckily, no. We didn't do any damage anyway— the logs only made it a few feet before exhausting their momentum."

Noah seemed to be lapsing into childhood memories, so she prompted, "You were saying about the Northcutts?"

"Oh, yeah. I finally got a chance to go back to the local Kensington papers and reread the item about an altercation at the town council. Turns out there was a shouting match between a developer and an executive of the B&O."

"Hiram Northcutt?"

"Bingo. According to the article, a guy name of Charles Filou wanted to buy twenty-five acres between the Kensington and Marmion Grove stations. The council was all in favor, but it required consent from the railroad line. Northcutt, as vice president of development, raised an objection. He announced he had had a run-in with Filou before. The man had tried to bilk shareholders out of their profits at a project in upstate New York. Hiram was hired to audit the project and blew the lid off his scheme. There was no way he would approve the sale. Evidently Filou went apoplectic. When he hurled an oblique threat at Northcutt, security was called to remove him."

"What kind of oblique threat?"

"Didn't say."

"So Northcutt was an honest businessman." Sophie pondered this. "What does that tell us?"

"I'm not finished. A few days later, the developer's Hispano-Suiza H6—that was a super luxury sedan of the period—was found ditched near White's Ferry thirty miles away. No sign of Filou."

"You don't think…"

"The man menaces Northcutt and a few days later disappears."

"So Hiram was maybe not so honest after all? Maybe even homicidal?"

"If he was involved, that would account for his

sudden request for a transfer."

"Sudden?"

"Harry told us he was transferred on May 1, 1920. That's less than a fortnight after Agnes wrote the letter."

Sophie didn't think this qualified as sudden. "The transfer could have been in the works for months."

Noah conceded the point. "Mebbe… On a more hopeful note, Harry might have the answer to that."

She considered Noah's story. "How about we look at it another way? This man—what was his name?"

"Charles Filou."

"He's the one with a crooked history. Say he realized Northcutt had the goods on him and simply decamped."

"Then why did he abandon his very expensive car?"

"He drowned in the river."

Noah snorted. "Why didn't they find his body?"

"*Hmm.* Perhaps we should revisit our hypothesis."

"Perhaps."

"*After* the book sale."

Noah sighed. "All right, but that doesn't mean I can't task Harry with looking into it, does it?"

The suggestion did not appeal to Sophie. "I don't want him to solve the mystery while we're tied up."

"He'll keep us posted, I'm sure. We still don't have any grounds to affirm a crime was committed. It'll keep him occupied and out of our hair."

****

Mellon Auditorium, Saturday, May 4, afternoon

"Hurry, Noah! The cookbook table needs replenishing *now*." Sophie wiped a wet forehead. The crowds hadn't died down even after the lunch break. She consoled herself that they were making money hand over fist for the scholarship fund.

Connie scuttled up to Sophie. "This is going to be the best sale ever!"

At that moment, a scruffy-looking man in a ragged sweatshirt and board shorts passed. The box he was carrying rammed into Sophie's back. "Ouch!" The man went on, impervious to her yelp. Sophie turned to her companion. "Sheesh, Connie. Some of these dealers are real jerks."

"Jerks willing and able to spend oodles of dough, Sophie." Connie brushed past her. "I'm taking the morning's spoils to the treasurer's office."

Noah came back. "What now?"

"Refill the paperback fiction—that always empties fast. I'm going to Rare Books to see how Eudora is doing."

She wended her way through the vast hall, past tables crammed with books, readers circling them like starving jackals. The back room was much calmer, as only serious dealers scanned the rows of first editions and folios. Eudora held court at one end. "Yes, Philip, that's the Dodd, Mead edition of Charles Kingsley's *The Water Babies*, released in 1916. The illustrations by Jessie Wilcox Smith make it the most famous edition of the book. Signed? Not by the author, but if you'll look on the flyleaf, it was presented to her daughter by Lady Charles Darwin. See? We've authenticated it as Lady Darwin's autograph. Quite unique."

The dealer groused, "I suppose that's why you're charging so much. I won't be able to make any profit on the resale, Eudora."

"You know as well as I do, Philip, that that book is worth three times what we're asking."

Philip shrugged and headed back to the children's literature section. Sophie sat down beside Eudora. "I have something to show you." She handed her the copy of *The Mysterious Affair at Styles* they had found in Roger's box. "What do you think?"

Eudora looked it over and fanned the pages. "Prime condition. Why haven't I seen this before?"

"You palmed it off on me as a training exercise."

Eudora studied the copyright page for several minutes. "It's a first printing all right. But it's published by John Lane in New York. Weren't all Christie's books first released in London?" She regarded Sophie quizzically.

"Interestingly enough, no. There were several with first printings in the US, usually published by Dodd, Mead."

Eudora nodded. "Right. I'd forgotten. Dodd, Mead bought out John Lane."

"However, the Bodley Head editions are still the most sought after."

"So the UK print would fetch a higher price than this one?"

Sophie demurred. "Its *current* market value is higher, yes, but only because people are unaware of the US edition. *The Mysterious Affair* was Christie's first book. She wasn't established yet, and evidently gave John Lane first crack at it. Lane's UK branch, Bodley Head, didn't release it until the following year." She tapped the book. "It was also published in Toronto a few months before the UK edition, by the Ryerson Press."

Eudora whistled. "Then this little book could potentially be worth a packet."

"How much would you say?"

"You know I never like to pass judgement until I've at least consulted *Antique Trader Book Collector* and the *Rare Book Hub*. We'll have to save it for next year's sale." She said it reluctantly.

"Oh, no! I don't want to sell it—at least not yet."

Eudora showed signs of temper, a rare occurrence in the rigorously proper lady. "Would you mind clarifying?"

"First off, it's not mine to sell. I—we found it in a box of donations."

"If they're donations, they belong to us. And who's 'we'?"

"We is me and the donor. We think the book might have been put in the box inadvertently."

"Oh?"

Sophie glanced over her shoulder. "Tucked inside it was a letter written by the eyewitness to a murder."

"A murder! Are you sure?"

Not for the first time Sophie hesitated. "Well, not a hundred percent sure. The writer talks about seeing a man carrying a body."

Eudora allowed herself a discreet titter. "You *are* aware that this book is a murder mystery?"

"I'm aware of the irony." Sophie stopped. It hadn't entered her mind that the letter could actually be *affiliated* with the Christie novel. *An attempt at creative writing*? "Would you mind holding onto it for a minute?"

"But Sophie… All right."

"Promise me you won't sell it." When Eudora resorted to a sphinxlike expression, she began to worry. "Eudora…"

"No, I won't sell it. I told you, I'd have to price it first."

"Okay." Sophie crossed the hall in five strides and found Noah hefting a cardboard box marked Biography. "I just showed the Christie book to Eudora."

"Oh yeah? What did she say?"

"She pointed out that it's a murder mystery." She waited.

"So? This is hardly news."

"No, no! I mean, what if Agnes were simply trying her hand at fiction? What if she made the whole thing up?"

Noah thought this over. "Doesn't fit what we know about her. Blanche told us Agnes wasn't much of a reader. And she wasn't well educated. I can't see her as an aspiring author."

"Agreed, but that begs the question: if she wasn't reading it, why did she have the book?"

"She must have borrowed it from one of the Northcutts."

"Perhaps, but she couldn't have intended to give it back if she stuck the letter in it."

"It was a spur of the moment thing—she had to hide the letter quickly."

"Yes…but again, how did she come by the book?"

He balanced his box on the table's edge. "I've no idea. Someone nearby was watching her so she picked up the nearest thing at hand."

"At least we know Agnes survived. If the culprit suspected she had observed him, there's no chance he'd have let her live." Sophie gasped. "Oh my God. You don't think we're stirring up a hornet's nest with our inquiries?"

Noah shook his head. "It happened a hundred years ago. Could *anyone* involved still be alive? Agnes isn't. I wouldn't get all het up about it." He hiked the box onto his shoulder. "Now, where's the table for Biography?"

"Over there." She checked her watch. "Your shift is over in ten minutes."

"Oh my! Two hours sure do go by quickly. Do you want to get something to eat?"

"I can't leave until the sale closes at six."

His face fell. "Will you be late all week?"

Sophie was amused. "It's not like I have to go all the way up to Marmion Grove. I live fifteen minutes away."

His mouth twisted in chagrin. "Right you are. I was getting used to you being in the house. So you'll be staying in your apartment this week?"

"Uh-huh. I have to be at the sale every day."

"Does that mean you won't even have evenings free?"

So that's what a hang dog expression looks like. She took pity on him. "No, it doesn't. Tomorrow our hours are eight to two."

"Oh." He started to walk away, then stopped. "Tell you what. After I drop this box, I have to go back to the Smithsonian. I'll meet you here at six and we'll get dinner."

"Sounds good."

He looked over her shoulder. "By the way, you might want to get the Christie book back from Eudora. We haven't had the police check it for prints."

She ran all the way back to the rare books room.

****

Old Ebbitt Grill, Saturday evening

Noah guided Sophie up the narrow stairs to a magnificently dark bar. An offbeat assortment of people lined the mahogany counter—from Armani-clad lobbyists to tourists in Hawaiian shirts and Birkenstocks. He boomed, "This is the Old Ebbitt Grill, Washington DC's oldest saloon. Several presidents—including Grant, Cleveland, McKinley, and Teddy Roosevelt—patronized the place."

"Let's sit at the bar."

A recumbent nude in oils greeted them as they slipped onto stools. The bartender, who—with his white shirt and bow tie—could have come from the pages of *Saturday Evening Post,* sallied over. "Sir? Ma'am? What's your pleasure?"

"Um…" Sophie let the Roaring Twenties atmosphere soak in. "A sazerac?"

He nodded with approval. Noah ordered a beer, then swiveled on the stool to Sophie. "So, I take it you recaptured our Exhibit A?"

"I literally snatched it out of the buyer's hand. I can't believe Eudora left it sitting on the table like that."

"She knew you didn't want to sell it, right?"

"Yes, but these dealers are unscrupulous. They'll even steal boxes away from their competitors. We don't have much control."

Noah nodded. "I saw them camped out last Friday on my way to the museum. Mangy bunch."

"Mangy maybe, but they know books, and they know bargains."

"Did Eudora certify that it's a first printing?"

"Yes. She was very excited. I had to promise her that when we were finished with it she could have it."

The waiter slid menus in front of them. "It's still happy hour, folks, if you want something from our raw bar."

"Ooh, oysters. Lots of them." Sophie rubbed her

stomach.

"A dozen each of the Pemaquid and the Wellfleet, my good man."

When Sophie had slurped down four of the tasty sea-washed mollusks, she resumed. "What was all that about checking the book for prints?"

"Just giving you more ammunition to wrest it from Eudora's clinging arms. Any usable fingerprints would have been overridden by now." He sipped his beer. "The puzzle remains how Agnes got her hands on it."

"She was a maid. She picked it up while dusting."

"I suppose." He put the glass down. "You'll be off tomorrow at two, correct?"

"Uh-huh." Sophie was concentrating on her food. "These oysters are superb."

"Yes, yes, Sophie? Marmion Grove is having a Cinco de Mayo celebration tomorrow. Fireworks, a mariachi band, margaritas."

"Another one? I haven't recovered from the Easter parade."

"Well, buckle up. Grovers love an excuse to party, although we usually wait till *after* a holiday so we can buy the supplies at a discount. Fireworks are half price on July 5 and May 6."

"So why not hold it on Monday?"

"There was some rather heated discussion along those lines, but the fact that the actual holiday lands on a Sunday won out. They're passing the hat to cover the extra cost of fresh fireworks. The mayor's promoting it by highlighting that this time over fifty percent of the rockets are guaranteed to work."

"Sounds fun."

"Would you like to go?"

Sophie knew she'd be exhausted after the long day, but if it was a way to see Noah… "Sure."

"I'll pick you up."

"No, I may need my car. I'll meet you at the hall." She was about to ask if costumes were expected when Noah's phone buzzed.

"Uh-huh. Uh-huh. Why can't you tell me?" Noah frowned. "All right, tomorrow then." He hung up. "Harry's found something."

Chapter Twenty-One

Very few of us are what we seem.

~Agatha Christie

Peveril Hall, Sunday, May 5

"Okay, before we go down to Dane Circle for the festivities, I have to tell you what Harry had to say." Noah put down his coffee mug. "It's big."

"Oh?" Sophie was busy watching a blue jay chase a cardinal off the bird feeder and could lend only half an ear to his monologue.

"His father."

She turned at that. "Whose father? What about him?"

"Harry's father. Harry Junior. He found him."

"Agnes's son?"

"The very one. Remember, Blanche told us that Harry Junior ran away from home when he was sixteen. By the time he was thirty-one, he had settled down in Ohio and produced a family. Our Harry was born in 1960..." He stopped. "That makes him the same age as my father. Huh."

Sophie thought back. "Harry said he had had no contact with his father since his parents divorced. Was he trying to locate him as well as his grandfather?"

"Not at first. He didn't have much interest in

tracking him down until this Northcutt thing came up. Harry Junior retired thirty years ago and moved to Florida. He moved again several times, and ten years ago he went off the radar. Harry Three found him in a nursing home in Sebring. He's nearing a hundred, and Harry says he's going downhill fast. His memory's still good, but he fades in and out."

"I'm glad they reconnected. Family is so important." Sophie thought of her own mother. She had moved to the west coast to be near Sophie's brother, who was awaiting his second baby. She sighed. *They're all so far away.*

"Indeed. Well, Harry spent an hour probing him about his grandparents. He wanted to see how the old man's recollections squared with the stories he'd heard as a child—stories about Agnes, Harry Senior, the Northcutts, etc."

"And?"

"He had little to impart about Harry Senior since he'd never known him. He did remember how heartbroken his mother was that his father split before the wedding." Sophie noticed a spasm cross Noah's face.

"Wasn't she livid that he'd deserted her and their child?"

"According to Harry Junior, she always alleged that something bad had happened to him."

An idea suggested itself. "Say, did Harry Junior know anything about the opal ring?"

"Only that Agnes insisted Harry Senior hadn't stolen it."

"Uh-huh. That confirms what Blanche told us."

"Right, but Harry Junior added a twist: Agnes once let slip that Harry found the ring on the ground."

Sophie was instantly awake. "He did? Did he

specify where? Peveril Hall? Somewhere else?"

"He didn't say, but it means he didn't steal it from Audrey."

She blew her cheeks out. "It seems we're getting rather far afield here. We don't know that the ring had anything to do with the murder—if there was one."

"It must have some significance, since Roger included it in his box of Agnes's things."

"Which begs the question: after all her huffing and puffing, why didn't Audrey take it with her? Did Roger find it? If so, where?"

"Maybe he had tumbled to the fact that Agnes told the truth—that Harry had given it to her."

"Or maybe he just scooped up everything linked to Agnes and the Northcutts. We have no way of knowing if he'd reached any conclusions." She stopped. "Scooped up everything... Why wasn't Agnes's letter and the Christie book in Roger's box of Agnes's stuff? How did it end up in a *separate* box of books marked Roger?"

Noah rose. "Talk about getting far afield. This isn't a mystery about my father. It's about a 1920 murder case. Rather, a theoretical murder case. Let's stick with that, shall we?'

Sophie didn't want to let it go. "But—"

"It's time to go down to the party. Are you ready?"

"All right." She picked up her sombrero. "You didn't say whether costumes were required, so I brought this just in case."

He looked dubiously at it. "In this day and age, who knows if it'll offend someone."

She thrust it on her head. "Tough. I am celebrating Mexican history today, and in their honor I will proudly wear this hat."

"*Vaya con Dios, señorita.*"

****

Dane Circle, Sunday evening

By five o'clock, Sophie had had enough tequila to feel no compunction about twirling around the makeshift dance floor with a perspiring gentleman in a checked shirt. The mariachi band was going full blast, and people were swaying and singing along with them. As dusk rolled in, someone switched on the strings of green, red, and white lights that wreathed the circle. She had just reeled away from the gentleman's clutching hand when someone grabbed her. "Ouch!"

Noah whispered fiercely, "I think you'd better eat something, Sophie."

"What? Oh, okay."

She bobbed her head at her partner, who bowed in return. His plump face red with exertion, he said breathlessly, "Thank you for allowing me to trip the light fantastic with you. 'Tis time I bid a fond farewell." He made his way through the guests toward the parked cars.

Noah led her to the buffet table. "Having fun?"

"Oh, yes!" She was still panting. "Thanks for bringing me."

"Have some guacamole." He plopped a spoonful onto a paper plate, stuck a tortilla chip in it, and handed it to her.

At the sight of the tomato-flecked green glop, her face took on a similar hue. "How about I just eat the chip?" Noah threw the plate away and filled another with chips.

As she was munching on them, George Weatherby came up to the table. "Whew, Doris and Lola really pulled it off, didn't they?" He scanned the crowd. "I think the whole town turned out."

Sophie cried happily, "It's a wonderful party!"

"I even saw Kendrick Northcutt cutting a rug." He sniggered. "Swinging his weight around as usual."

Noah stopped, a chip halfway to his mouth. "Kendrick Northcutt is here?"

"Oh right, you were asking about the Northcutts, weren't you? Kendrick is Hiram's great-grandson. He moved back here a year ago. Sorry, it slipped my mind."

Sophie elbowed Noah. "Oscar told us his son lived here."

Noah put his plate down. "Would he be a good subject for interrogation?"

George shook his head. "Kendrick isn't really keen on family history. He's more interested in horses." When they looked mystified, he said, "By which I mean racing. He bets. Now, if you want the skinny on Northcutt family history, you should ask Ian Surry."

"Ian Surry? We met him at your dinner party."

Sophie remembered the gray-eyed man. "Are you saying *Ian Surry* is related to the Northcutts?"

George didn't seem to hear her. He shaded his eyes. "He's around here somewhere. Oh, there he is. Hey, Ian!" He waved at a familiar figure.

Ian saw them and came over. "Hi, George. Hello, Sophie. Are you enjoying yourself?"

"Yes." Sophie's eyelashes fluttered. Noah put a hand out to steady her.

Ian turned his gaze to Noah. "I forgot to mention that I was a classmate of your sister Gretchen's. We were about five years ahead of you in school."

Noah grinned. "Yeah, I was the bratty little brother she complained so much about."

Ian said nothing but his eyes twinkled.

"So you grew up in Marmion Grove as well?"

"Uh-huh. Third generation." Ian dipped a tortilla chip into the bowl of salsa he held. "You're getting Peveril Hall ready to sell, aren't you?" He chewed thoughtfully. "I may have a buyer for you—a colleague at the State Department. He's eager to live in the Grove and has been asking me to notify him if anything comes up." He smiled. "He's the deputy secretary and a former ambassador, so I'm sure he can make a substantial offer."

"Oh. Um." Noah looked uncomfortable. "I'm not really ready to sell yet. I…I want to go through all the family heirlooms carefully." He stopped. "It's such a great house."

Sophie watched him, her heart flip-flopping. *Oh, I hope he decides to keep it!* She refused to dwell on why she felt that way. *Like he says, it's a great house. That's all. It would be a shame to have strangers move in. That's all.*

Ian frowned. "I heard you planned to sell it quickly. This fellow is very enthusiastic. You don't want him to get away."

Noah shrugged. "I'm sure there will be others. But thanks for thinking of me."

Ian gave him a long look, then turned to the mayor. "Why did you call me over, George?"

"I saw Kendrick Northcutt leaving the Circle. He's your cousin, isn't he?"

"Second cousin. Yup."

"What was the connection?"

He raised his eyes to the sky. "Let's see. He's my great-aunt Audrey's great-grandson. Her maiden name was Surry."

Noah did a double-take. "Really? Why didn't you mention you were related?"

He cocked his head at George. "I assumed George had."

Sophie poked Noah. "*He's* the nephew Peggy told you about."

"Ah."

Ian hesitated. "To tell you the truth, Kendrick and I aren't close." His eyes drifted across the crowd. "He's a bit of a black sheep."

Every family has its share of scapegraces. Sophie made an effort to wake up.

George interjected, "Ian's the genealogist of the clan."

Ian said modestly, "It's just a hobby."

"Your mother Lillian still lives in Bethesda, doesn't she? Would she have any memorabilia of the Northcutts? Noah is trying to find out more about them."

Ian turned to Noah, his eyebrows high. "Really? Are you still on about that mystery of yours? The ghost?"

"No, no." Noah stopped short. Sophie wondered if he were a little ashamed of their obsession. "I'm…er…writing a book."

"I see." The guarded look on Ian's face faded. "I'm afraid my mother had to go into a senior care facility a couple of months ago. Advanced Parkinson's." At their crestfallen faces, he added, "However, before she moved, I packed up all her family papers. I've been slowly sifting through and cataloguing them. Is there something specific you were interested in? You're welcome to come by my house and have a look."

"That would be much appreciated. What time is

convenient?"

Ian pointed at the crew setting up for the fireworks. "No time tonight. How about tomorrow?"

Sophie sobered. "Oh dear, I can't. The Vassar Book Sale is all this week. I have to be there."

"And I still have a lot of packing to do." Noah appealed to Ian. "Would next weekend work? Saturday?"

Ian stifled an irritated sigh. "Sure, whatever. Give me a call. Here's my number."

****

Mellon Auditorium, Friday, May 10, afternoon

For Sophie, the week following the Cinco di Mayo party was a blur of packing and unpacking books, placating volunteers unused to aggressive book dealers, and soothing book dealers impatient with inefficient volunteers. Friday—the final day of the sale—saw Connie, Eudora, and Sophie shooing the last customers out through the massive doors of the Mellon Auditorium. Connie paid off the fey little man who always appeared in the last hour to take the remainders. Once he'd clumped off, she spun around and flung her arms wide. "And we're done!"

The treasurer came out of her cave and announced that this year's net was upwards of $110,000 for scholarships. "This sale is the most successful one in our forty-year history."

A tired cheer went up. The staff scattered, unable to pump the wattage up enough even to congratulate each other.

A day later, Sophie lay on the sofa in her living room, head on a pillow, and stared at the ceiling. "I'm just going to veg for a few hours, Noah, okay? I don't want to think, to talk, to move… Although I could use a bite to eat. Could you check the fridge for me?"

"This is not okay." Noah paced the room. "Perhaps you've forgotten, but we promised Ian Surry we'd go to Marmion Grove today. He didn't seem thrilled with the idea. I don't want him to renege."

"I'm sure it's an inconvenience. He was very gracious to offer."

"I'm going to call and let him know we're coming."

She struggled to her feet. "All right, if you make me some coffee, I'll put on clean underwear."

He sniffed delicately. "Very gracious of *you*."

Chapter Twenty-Two

Nobody knows what another person is thinking. They may imagine they do, but they are nearly always wrong.
~Agatha Christie

Marmion Grove, Saturday, May 11

An hour later, they were on the road to Marmion Grove. Sophie read the directions Ian had given them. "Turn right on Kenilworth."

They passed the town hall. "Ooh, there's Mr. Oglethorpe." Noah waved at the town clerk.

"Go left here, then right. Is this Montrose Avenue? Okay, it's at the end of the street. Number nine-nine-eight."

They stopped at the curb in front of a light blue cottage with a front porch covered by a portico. Noah pointed at the garage. "Whaddya know? It's a Chevy house."

"Chevy? As in the car?"

"Uh-huh. A company called Maddux Marshall built some thirty-nine small, low-cost homes here in the 1920s. Each came with a Murphy bed and a fancy new radio. The purchaser could roll a new Chevrolet into the mortgage." He pressed his lips together. "They were the precursors to the post-war Levittown houses—a simple plan, tiny, and affordable. The embodiment of the

American dream of individual home ownership."

"And a clever marketing ploy." Sophie regarded the small garden and plain, square front. It lacked the grandeur of Peveril Hall but looked comfortable enough.

Ian stood on the front stoop. "Welcome."

Noah shook his hand. "So how long have you lived in Marmion Grove?"

"Me? Most of my life, but my family was originally from Bethesda. Audrey Surry met and married Hiram Northcutt in Baltimore. When they were transferred here, the families were close enough to socialize, albeit for a short time. Audrey's brother James—my grandfather—bought this house when he married. He willed it to his son Devon, my father."

Sophie stopped at the bottom step. "Didn't you say your mother lives in Bethesda?"

Ian smiled. "I did. When Devon died, my mother and I moved back to Bethesda, but she held on to the house here, eventually passing the title on to me."

Noah held up a hand. "As I understand it, Hiram and Audrey went back to Baltimore after only a few years. If they were gone, why would James want a place here? Why not remain in Bethesda?"

Ian's mouth twisted. He said shortly, "He spent a lot of time here when his sister lived at Peveril Hall. Fond memories, I suppose." He held out an arm. "Shall we go inside?"

Sophie thought his response a little abrupt, but Noah said heartily, "It's very kind of you to let us look at your archives."

Ian wagged his head. "Archives is a bit of an exaggeration. I just gathered everything up when Mother moved to the nursing home. I've been trying to sort through it ever since."

"Still, we really appreciate your taking the time."

"My pleasure. Let's go into the dining room. I've been using it as a holding area."

Sophie was a little taken aback at the cartons and accordion files piled on every surface. It reminded her painfully of the seven days of hell she'd just endured at the book sale. She looked helplessly at Ian. "Where do you suggest we begin?"

"Well, you're interested in the Northcutts, not the Surrys, so I've divided the papers between those of my family and those of the in-laws. I set aside some scrapbooks that Audrey kept that might be of interest. Here's a rough inventory."

As the two flipped through the list, Ian brought out a tray with a carafe and cups. He swept a box to one side and set it on the buffet. "Coffee?"

"Yes, thanks."

When they were supplied with mugs, he continued. "It's true that Audrey and Hiram only lived here a couple of years, but Audrey found the time to engage in quite a few civic activities. She joined the women's circle and the local card group. As president of the garden club, she directed the landscaping in public areas like the town hall and the post office." He chuckled. "She was also a suffragette. A remarkable and exceptionally independent lady."

Huh. A very different picture from the one Blanche and Harry painted of her. "What about Hiram?"

Ian looked slightly befuddled, as though Hiram were a mere afterthought. "Hiram? He was too busy with his job to participate much. And he had no ties to the area like Audrey did. The Surrys had been in Bethesda for several generations already. Hiram came from somewhere in New England." His brow creased. "I take that back. It was Buffalo, New York."

Noah whispered, "Buffalo…upstate New York. That was where Hiram first encountered Charles Filou."

Ian continued. "When Hiram was occupied with business, James acted as Audrey's escort."

"Is that how he came to love the Grove?"

Ian blinked. "Yes, I suppose so." He opened one scrapbook. "Here he is with Audrey at our Fourth of July parade in—let's see—1919."

Sophie saw a fuzzy picture of two people standing in front of the town hall. "She's a lot taller than he is."

"Oh, James was only fifteen then." He tapped the boy's face. "He very much admired his older sister."

"Fifteen! He must have been quite precocious."

"You had to be back then, right after the war. Boys grew up fast." He turned a page quickly. "Here's a clearer photo of Audrey."

Sophie gazed at the rather buxom woman leaning against a wringer washing machine. She wore a flowered poplin house dress and an exasperated expression. Next to her stood a young girl. Slim, with brown hair peeping out from underneath a white cap, her eyes were demurely cast down. She wore a pinafore over a plain gray dress. "Did Audrey have a daughter?"

"No, they only had the one son, Richard." He read the back of the photo. "Ah, this is Agnes, the maid." He looked at Noah. "By the way, did you get in touch with her daughter Blanche?"

"Yes, we did. Agnes had passed, and Blanche didn't remember much about the Northcutts."

Sophie shot a look at Noah. *He must want to tread*

softly, Ian being kin. "Audrey doesn't seem very happy." She peered closer. "Hey Noah, come here. Isn't that Agnes's ring on Audrey's hand?"

Noah came over and took the photo. "Looks like it. Three opals. They're fairly uncommon nowadays. Aren't they considered bad luck?"

Sophie tapped her nose. "Eudora told me that was a canard invented by the diamond industry to undercut their competition."

Ian nodded. "That's true, but the sinister reputation of opals may have actually begun with Sir Walter Scott."

"Scott? *The* Walter Scott whose book titles grace the street names of our delightful hamlet?" Noah pointed outside. "For instance, Montrose Avenue?"

"Also Peveril Hall. Scott's *Peveril of the Peak* was about the Catholic plot to overthrow Charles II."

Sophie remarked, "Marmion Grove's founder must have been a fan."

"Scott's books were extremely popular around that time, so, yes, I imagine so." He grinned. "He probably thought it would add a bit of 'old country' flavor to his new development."

Noah set the photo down. "You said it was Scott who started the rumor that opals were unlucky. How exactly did he do that?"

Ian settled into a chair and interlaced his fingers. "Let me back up a bit. The Romans believed an opal incorporated the colors of all other gemstones and that it brought the wearer prosperity. However, during the various plagues that struck Europe in the Middle Ages, it came to symbolize disease and famine. Later on, it acquired magical powers—usually of the black kind. It was considered the patron stone of thieves and spies

208

because it could make its owner invisible."

"Wow." Sophie snorted. "It must have been hard to keep up with the superstitions. If I wear an opal, will I drop dead or win the lottery?"

"I would not suggest you take the risk."

Noah enquired, "So where does Scott come in?"

"This is the story as it was told to me. In the early nineteenth century, the diamond merchants De Beers sought to devalue the more popular opals in favor of their own product. The company hired a young novelist named Walter Scott to write a story associating opals with calamity. He obliged with *Anne of Geierstein.* In it, a character named Hermione wears an opal hair clasp imbued with magic. She dies when the clasp is doused with holy water." He leaned forward. "Later in the book we discover she was in fact poisoned, but the damage was done. Opals were stigmatized for decades." He sat back. "Totally apocryphal, of course. The connection to De Beers, I mean."

Sophie was confused. "And yet people still buy and wear opals. How, or when, did the perception change?"

"When Queen Victoria declared them to be her favorite jewel and wore one at her coronation. Despite De Beers' best efforts, by the 1920s and '30s interest in opals revived; in fact, they were the engagement ring of choice."

"It certainly didn't improve Agnes's lot." Noah turned the photo over. "It's dated April 20." His eyes went to Sophie's face. "*Hmm.*"

Sophie didn't notice his meaningful look. "I wonder what pissed Mrs. Northcutt off?"

"She had just reamed Agnes out for stealing the ring?" Noah touched the young girl's head. "Agnes isn't acting the humble servant; she's upset that she was caught."

"*Or* that her engagement ring was confiscated."

"More likely repossessed."

Ian stirred. "What are you two on about?"

Sophie pointed at Audrey's hand. "We found this same ring in a box at Peveril Hall. Do you have any idea why Audrey left it behind?"

Ian shrugged. "No idea. She might have simply misplaced it."

Sophie began leafing through a folder with scraps of paper and pages torn from tablets. She laughed. "What an insight into the normal diet and shopping routines in the twenties. Here's an instruction to the itinerant knife sharpener: 'Please remove stains and hone enclosed butcher knife.' " She arched a brow. "Could they be blood stains?"

"Beef, pork, chicken blood, yes." Ian seemed slightly annoyed.

She went on quickly. "And here's a grocery list for the general store: flour—ten pounds; black tea—one pound loose; one garden shovel; one pickaxe; one jar molasses; three pounds each of walnuts and brown sugar; two twelve-ounce bottles rat poison; and a pound of hard candies." She stopped. "I guess you could get anything you wanted at Alice's general store."

"Rat poison?" Noah looked up from the box he was sorting. "What's the date on that list, Sophie?"

"Um… April 19."

"A day before the photo of Audrey and Agnes was taken."

"Wait a minute." Sophie picked up the picture of the two women again. "Could this photograph have been taken *before* Harry gave Agnes the ring?"

Noah objected. "If Audrey normally wore it, Agnes would have seen it on her hand. She'd know it belonged to Audrey and wouldn't accept it from Harry."

"I seem to remember that Agnes had only been working for the Northcutts a short while. She might not have recognized it."

Noah sat back. "Okay… Here's what we know. Harry skips out on the eighteenth—or rather doesn't show up. On the twentieth, Mrs. Northcutt—in high dudgeon—wrenches the ring from Agnes's trembling hand. Also on April 20, Agnes writes a letter to her mother in which she simultaneously announces her wedding plans and the loss of her job. Does that fit?"

"I think so." Sophie thought it over. "Say she wrote the letter to the constable on April 19, she must have seen…*it*…sometime in the twenty-four hours between early on the eighteenth and the morning of the nineteenth."

Noah took the grocery list from Sophie and rattled it. "If this list includes prep for the deed, then it happened *after* the eighteenth."

"No." Sophie was positive. "They're *replacements* for what was used. It happened *before* the eighteenth."

Ian, who had been strangely quiet during this exchange, looked from one to the other. "What the hell are you two talking about?"

Noah blurted, "Murder. We found a letter from Agnes that claimed to have witnessed one on or about that time. She suspected poison."

Ian leaned forward, a look of total bewilderment on his face. "A poisoning at Peveril Hall?"

"Yes. Agnes wrote that she saw a man carrying a

body over his shoulder to a car, and that she found a broken vial of rat poison the next morning."

"This is Agnes Reilly we're talking about? The sixteen-year-old maid who was discharged?"

"Uh, yes."

"For thievery."

Noah shook his head. "Actually we think she was dismissed because she was pregnant."

Ian relaxed. "Let's set that aside for the moment. Back to this letter. Who did Agnes think was the victim?"

"She had no idea, but Noah has done some research and has a theory."

Noah took the floor. "A developer named Charles Filou wanted to buy land adjacent to the railway line in Marmion Grove. Your great-uncle Hiram thwarted his plans, outing him as a charlatan. According to the news account, the developer took…er…umbrage."

Ian jumped up. "Are you saying he killed Hiram? That's ridiculous." He waved his hand over the boxes. "I have tons of personal effects of Hiram and my aunt. See here—" He picked up a thick manila envelope. "These are his letters to his son Richard. They go through 1950."

Noah jerked. "Hiram the victim? No, no. Agnes couldn't identify the body—or the man carrying it. We haven't been able to uncover any corroborating news items from the time. At this point, we're just looking for any indication that Agnes actually saw *something*. The altercation between Filou and Hiram stood out."

"So you have no proof a murder actually took place."

Sophie didn't care for the smug look on Ian's face. "The developer *did* go missing."

Noah nudged Sophie. "So did Harry Senior."

Ian swung around to Noah. "Harry? Agnes's boyfriend? He disappeared too?"

"Yes."

He slapped his knees with his palms. "Well, that settles it. Harry was a scoundrel—he must be the one who stole my aunt's ring. He fled to avoid facing the music."

"But—"

Ian rose. "I think that's enough conspiracy theories for one day. Let me know if you have any other questions." He showed them out firmly.

Noah started the car. His mouth set in a thin line, he said, "Let's go to Peveril Hall. I want to think about this."

"About what?"

"Too many victims and not enough murderers."

Chapter Twenty-Three

Our weapon is our knowledge. But remember, it may be a knowledge we may not know that we possess.

~Agatha Christie

Peveril Hall, Saturday, May 11

"That hit the spot." Noah put the beer can on the counter. "Now I can think." Instead, he picked up a box and shook it. "Do we have any more of these crackers?"

"You ate the last one. How about a sandwich?"

"That would be great. I'd like a ham and cheese on rye."

"Do you have any ham?"

"No, and before we go through the whole litany, I don't have any cheese. For that matter, I don't have any rye bread. It's just a dream of mine—ham and cheese sandwiches stacked on a plate, with an endless supply of PBR to go with."

Sophie picked up Noah's keys. "I'm hungry, too. Let's go to the grocery store. This house needs stocking up."

"Iffy elderberry wine and fossilized fruitcake not enough for you?"

"That reminds me: we should stop at the liquor store too."

"And that boutique in the mall. You'll need some

clothes."

"I will?"

"Since you'll be staying here, yes."

She didn't argue. This could be an adventure.

****

Peveril Hall, Saturday evening

"Can I top up your drink?" Noah hovered over Sophie's glass with the bottle.

"Just a smidgen, thanks." She put down the pad of paper she'd been writing on. "I think it's time we recapped what we know."

"Agreed. Where shall we start?"

"How about we list what we do know, and next to that write what we still need to find out."

"Starting with Agnes's letter. We don't know the exact date, nor why it wasn't sent."

"The letter had to have been written on April 19. She was sacked the next day." Sophie tapped her lip with the pen. "The question is, why would that stop her from sending a letter to the police?"

Noah stared at her. "Because she was afraid her employers were hiding something?"

Sophie thought this over. "In her letter she stressed that both Audrey and Hiram seemed unperturbed the next day. It doesn't sound like she brought the subject up."

"Well, she wouldn't, would she? She was only a maid. She would just watch and listen." He rubbed his jaw. "They could have been putting on a brave front while she was in the room and discussed it once she was out of earshot."

"I'll write that down. Okay… Agnes observed a man carrying a large bundle over his shoulder coming from

215

the carriage house."

Noah considered this. "No. He was coming around the side of the building, not from it."

"What does the stable back up to?"

"A bit of no-man's land. We built a tree house there when we were kids." He put down his whiskey. "I've got it. And this will clear everything up and we can get back to eating and maybe"—he ogled Sophie—"other pursuits."

"Spill."

"Two guys met in the woods—"

"Is this the beginning of a joke?"

He cocked an eyebrow. "I hope not."

Okay, so he's not in the mood. "You're thinking drug deal?"

"In 1920? Implausible. Burglars. Or maybe a man and his bookie."

"Bookie? But—"

"Whatever. The point is, they got into a fight and one killed the other, then ran through our lot to get to the street." He grinned triumphantly. "Nothing to do with the Northcutts or Agnes or Filou."

Sophie wasn't convinced. "He'd have to have hopped your fence carrying a dead weight. Plus, there were all those elderberry bushes. Don't they have prickers?"

"No." At her look, he conceded, "But they *are* pretty dense."

She pounced. "So, why not go around the other side of the stable—or even through the neighbor's yard?" Before he could speak, she added, "*And* he got into a car in the driveway."

"According to Agnes, who wasn't entirely sure what

she saw."

"Damn. All we have for evidence is her letter, isn't it? Perhaps a dream is the best explanation."

"Works for me." Noah opened a package of cheese-filled crackers and began to munch on them. "So why are we bothering with all this folderol?"

"Because people *did* disappear. Even though Agnes didn't send the letter, it doesn't mean she didn't actually witness something."

"Well, now you're just being a contrarian." Noah sipped his drink. "All right, let's take Harry Senior. We know he planned to visit Agnes on April 17 or 18 but didn't show. Was it his body?"

"It's conceivable, although we have another body that's unaccounted for. To wit: the developer Filou."

"That could have been a coincidence. The news article said Hiram Northcutt accused him of being a crook. He could have just taken off."

"Leaving behind a top-of-the-line luxury sedan that in today's market would cost the equivalent of $75,000?" Sophie shook her head.

"I see you've done your homework. Okay. The rationale for abandoning the car goes in the 'don't yet know' column." He nodded at the paper in front of Sophie. "Make a note."

Her pen poised, she asked, "When was the shouting match between Hiram and Filou?"

"The article only said the car was found a few days later."

"I'm sure there are records of town meetings—that should be easy to look up."

"Okay. Write that down too."

As Sophie was doing so, another thought sprang to

mind. "We should also try to find out if Filou was seen in Marmion Grove after the rumpus at the council."

"Why? The session was in Kensington, and the man left in a huff. What would he be doing in Marmion Grove?" Noah refilled his glass. "Back to Harry Senior. Did he run away or was he mugged?" He stopped. "When exactly did he and Agnes start seeing each other?"

"What difference does it make?"

Noah snickered. "Well, they must have been getting it on for some time before—"

"Noah!" Sophie felt it was in poor taste to dwell on the girl's predicament.

"Delicate little thing, aren't you? Okay, they must have been…*intimate* for months, if Agnes was noticeably pregnant by mid-April." He grunted in disgust. "So did Harry intend to do the right thing or was he pushed into it?"

Sophie thought back to Harry III's statements. "Our Harry didn't specify." She said primly, "I choose to believe he was an honorable man."

"I suppose that's better than thinking Agnes was some shrew who harassed him into marrying her." He opened another packet of crackers. "All right, did the ring come *after* the proposal? Or the other way around?"

"I think they were simultaneous."

"Then did he steal the ring from Audrey? If so, why?"

"Because it was there?"

Noah crunched on an ice cube. "Harry had been recently hired at the speakeasy. Agnes was proud of that. I presume that means he'd been unemployed for a while. Ergo, no money."

"Ergo, sees nice ring and nips it. Doesn't tell his blushing fiancée for obvious reasons. Conveniently absent when said fiancée is confronted by an irate mistress." Sophie swilled her bourbon.

Noah watched her. "I think we're drifting from the topic. Whether Agnes was terminated for theft or pregnancy doesn't really matter, does it?"

"I guess not. It's just that it all started with Agnes's letter. She must be at the center of it somehow."

"Not necessarily. She was merely a bystander, a spectator."

Sophie threw her hands up, knocking Noah's glass over. While he mopped up the spill, mumbling under his breath about wasted nectar of the gods, she said helplessly, "Maybe Eudora was right: Agnes was having a go at fiction and the absent people didn't 'disappear.' They merely…shoved off."

"*Or…*" Noah's eyes lit up. "I have it, and we can kill two birds with one stone. Harry killed the developer and then scarpered."

"Balderdash. My grandfather didn't kill anyone, and I can prove it."

They whirled at the voice. "Harry! Come on in."

"Don't mind if I do." Harry looked even more slovenly than he had the last time they'd seen him. The frayed jacket had an ominous red stain dotting the left side. It was no longer possible to tell if his trousers were brown or gray, and his scuffed shoes were tied with two different colored laces. He looked pointedly at Noah's tumbler. "Got any more of that?"

Sophie poured a tot of whiskey in a juice glass and handed it to him. "So what's this proof of yours?"

He held up a folder. "A record of a reservation made

for the honeymoon suite of the Colton Arms Hotel in Lancaster, Pennsylvania, under the name of Mr. and Mrs. Harry Quayle. Arriving April 21, 1920."

"But Harry vanished three days before that."

"Yes. Something happened to him between the time he left his job in DC on April 17 and when Agnes was fired. This reservation proves he did propose—and give her a ring—just like my grandmother always maintained."

"If the reservation was in the name of Quayle, why did Agnes keep her maiden name?"

"They never got a chance to take their vows. Obviously."

Noah clasped his hands together. "Does that mean Agnes *did* see his corpse?"

"No, no. It couldn't have happened that way. He gave her the ring later in the night."

"How do you know?"

Harry closed his mouth with a snap.

Sophie said slowly, "You don't." She pursed her lips. "Remember the photo we saw at Ian's? It was dated April 20."

"And the ring was on Audrey's finger."

"Agnes looked very downhearted. Did she know by then Harry wasn't coming back?"

"It's more likely she'd just been denounced as a thief."

"Wait a minute! If they were planning to elope, she would have had to quit her job."

"Huh. True." Noah looked at Harry. "Would she have told Audrey? Or did she plan to sneak away?"

He shrugged. "I've no idea."

"Okay. So we're still faced with the main question.

Whose body was it?"

"If it *was* a body." Harry rose heavily. "I really don't care about Agnes's fantasies. I want to know what happened to my grandfather. I think I need to go in a different direction."

"What's that?"

"I'm going back to the son of the conductor who talked to him on the train. He may be able to recall where Harry got off." He put down his cup. "Thanks for the shot. I'll see you around."

"Wait, you can't just leave us in the lurch. We're partners."

His head jerked back. "Partners? Since when?"

Sophie jumped up. Arms akimbo, she spat, "Since you asked for our help."

He seemed amused. "Well, you haven't really lived up to your side of the bargain, have you? I've done the heavy lifting so far. What have *you* discovered? Nada. No body, no treasure. I even found Oscar Northcutt before you did."

Sophie squared her shoulders. "We found Kendrick though."

He stopped. "Kendrick? Who's he?"

Noah's answer was clipped. "Hiram Northcutt's great-grandson. And he lives right here in Marmion Grove." He went to the front door and opened it. "See you round."

Chapter Twenty-Four

To every problem, there is a most simple solution.
~Agatha Christie

Peveril Hall, Sunday, May 12

"Maybe we should go through Roger's things again. He was obviously investigating Agnes." Sophie buttered an English muffin.

Noah flipped a fried egg onto her plate. "You mean the box marked Agnes we found in the tower? It could have been Agnes's *own* box."

"How did it get into Roger's study then?"

"My mother left it there?"

"We've already dismissed that idea. You've said your father dabbled in cold cases. This qualifies."

"Good point." Noah finished his juice. "So we're agreed it was Roger who procured the ring, the apron, and her correspondence."

"And the book and letter."

"We have no evidence that he was aware of the letter to Constable Bustwick."

"Fiddlesticks." When his expression continued mulish, she sighed. "For the sake of argument, let's say he was. After all, we found it in a box marked Roger."

"So what was he doing with it all?"

"He thought it might offer some hint—or even

proof—of his theory."

"What theory?"

"That her story was true."

"The murder?" Noah snorted. "We've been through all this. Anyway, there's a concept in law called *habeas corpus*. It means you have to have the corpse in your hot little hand before you can prove homicide."

Sophie was delighted to disabuse the man who claimed to know everything. "Actually, that's something they always say in bad film noir movies, but it's not true. A writ of habeas corpus requires that a person who is in custody be presented at the court to determine if he was lawfully detained or not. The corpus is a body, not a corpse. So to speak."

"Oh really? I didn't realize you had a law degree." Noah sniffed peevishly.

"I don't, but the book sale received a whole law library from an alumna, and I was assigned to go through it. Picked up a lot of juicy legal terms, like amicus curiae and en banc."

He raised his chin. "Don't bother defining them—I know what they are."

She regarded him critically. "Okay, so—"

He interrupted. "Never mind that—what were we talking about? I forget. Oh right. We don't have a corpse to present."

"Nonetheless." Sophie rose. "I propose we open the box again. Maybe something will jump out at us."

"Hopefully not a silverfish—that box has been sitting there for thirty years."

They trudged up the two flights to the tower. The box still sat on the cluttered desk. Sophie opened it. "Where's the apron? Oh, right, downstairs." She looked up at Noah. "We should follow up on the rat poison."

"Another item for our list. What else is there?"

"The opal ring." She set it aside. "How did it end up in this box?"

Noah considered. "If these items were collected by Roger, he could have found it in the house, or come by it some other way."

Sophie wasn't satisfied. "Audrey wouldn't have left it behind after making such a scene."

"Unless she did in fact sack Agnes because of her wanton ways and the ring was simply an excuse."

She lifted out a packet of pink papers tied with a ribbon. "These are the letters to her mother."

"Yes." He stopped. "I wonder why Agnes's diary isn't here. It's important—if only to undergird what's in her letters."

Sophie shrugged. "A young girl usually hides her diary under her pillow or somewhere safe. I bet Roger never found it."

"We did."

She remembered the little bone china animals on the shelf in Gretchen's room. "I think your sister came across the box with the diary and the figurines, and hid it in the playhouse."

Noah's eyes widened. "So *that's* where she got the little animals. Huh. She refused to tell me—said they were only for girls."

Sophie set the packet aside, and peered in the box. "There's something lying on the bottom." She dove in, coming up with a sheet of heavy ivory stock. She handed it to Noah.

"It's a dinner menu." He tapped the paper. "Dated April 17."

"And?"

He read. "Roast beef, peas, Yorkshire puddings. Huh. Pretty fancy chow for a regular weekday." He unclipped a notecard from the sheet.

"What does the card say?"

"It's an order telling Agnes to set three places." He gulped. " 'Charles Filou will be our guest.' "

Sophie stared at Noah. "So Filou was here. At the house. The day before he disappeared."

He was puzzled. "I don't understand. Why would Hiram invite him to dinner when he'd called him out as a reprobate only a few days earlier?"

"Perhaps Mr. Filou asked to meet with him again. Maybe he had a proposal or wanted to make peace."

"Huh. At least that lets out Hiram as the killer. You don't announce who your dinner guest is if you're planning to take him out."

She held up the sheaf of pink foolscap. "You've read the letters, right?"

"Some. Skimmed the rest." He wrinkled his nose. "The color got to me after a while."

"Let's read them all. They might provide some useful hints you missed the first time. Here, take these."

An hour later, Noah put his pile down and said, "If there's a clue here that Roger found, I don't see it."

"Me neither. A lot of complaints about the weather and long hours. Oh, wait. Here's one about Filou. 'Mr. Filou arrived at six.' Aha." She read on. " 'I don't know why, but the atmosphere seemed very tense. When Mrs. Northcutt came into the kitchen to check with Cook about the roast, her face was like a thundercloud. Cook sent me down cellar to get the rat poison, and the master's voice grew so loud I could hear him from below! It seemed to calm down, but when I was about to serve the dessert, Mr. Filou burst through the kitchen door and left. He seemed to be in a great hurry.' "

"Left. So…not there. That means he couldn't be the body. Or the killer. Is there more?"

She turned the sheet over. " 'Mother, I didn't want to tell you before, but I've been stepping out with a young man. In fact, he's coming by tonight. His name is Harry Quayle, and he's very sweet. Before you go all crackers on me, he has just landed a job. He's promised to save a dollar a week from his tips, so I expect he will soon have enough to marry me. I can quit my post here and be a real housewife. We won't have to worry about money ever again.' "

"Coming by tonight… Hold on! Didn't she write about that in her diary? What's the date on the letter?"

"April 17. You're right; it's the same date. And also the night of Filou's dinner." She looked up. "That tells us that Harry was here at Peveril Hall on the seventeenth or early on the eighteenth."

Noah disagreed. "Not definitively. Harry told us his grandfather was on the train, but doesn't know where or when he got off."

Sophie threw up her hands. "Everyone keeps popping out, and nobody pops back in. This is getting ridiculous."

Noah folded the flaps on the box and set it on the floor. "I propose we rest our tiny brains today—go for a row on the river or a hike in Great Falls."

"I'm inclined to acquiesce to your request."

****

Peveril Hall, Monday, very early morning

Sophie woke with a start. "That's it! Why didn't I

realize it before? Noah? Noah! The rat poison!"

She got no response. "Noah?" She felt the sheet. Still warm. "Noah!" Her call echoed. *Where did he go?* She checked the bathroom. Vacant. *Am I alone in the house?* The thought did not enthrall her. She threw on a wrap and stumbled down the stairs. No lights were on. Quiet reigned. *Oh my God, not again.* "*Noah!*"

She checked the butler's pantry. The tiny room was bare. The garage? *That's where he was attacked the first time... The first time! Damn.* She tamped down the growing panic, snatched up the flashlight she'd bought after the last incident, and went out the back door. She surveyed the yard, then entered the side door of the garage. Their cars were in the bays. She shone the light up the stairs to the loft. "Hello?" Her voice echoed hollowly in the void. *I sure as heck am not going up there without backup.*

Instead, she tried the playhouse and then the gazebo. She circled around the house and tripped up the front steps. A sudden swishing sound startled her before she recognized the angry chitter of a squirrel. The front lawn was clear of extraneous humans. A slight movement caught her eye. *There, in the forsythia.*

She stepped as quietly as she could down to the hedge that bordered the curb. When she got close enough, she shone the flashlight into one bush. Gazing up at her were two blue eyes in the face of a very disheveled Noah. She dropped the light. "Noah! Are you all right? What are you playing at?"

Instead of answering, he said plaintively, "Can you please put the light back on? I'm stuck on something."

She did as he asked. He untangled the sleeve of his bathrobe from a branch and crawled out, dislodging a shower of twigs and flower petals. "Whew."

"Are you hurt?"

"No, just scratched. And I think my tailbone is bruised again." He grinned at her. "I don't know why I bother climbing mountains and bungee jumping when I can stay cozily at home and get banged up without having to spring for airfare."

She put her hands on her hips. "What were you doing inserting yourself into the shrubbery in the middle of the night?"

"A habit I picked up in Army Ranger School." He brushed himself off. "I must say, it was more fun then."

"Well, you scared the living daylights out of me."

"*I* scared *you*! I felt like a deer caught in the headlights. Almost had a heart attack."

"I will decipher what the heck you mean by that inside." Sophie marched back to the house. Noah followed, grumbling. When they reached the kitchen, she switched on the overhead lights and inspected him. "Some scrapes and—" She reached up and snagged a forsythia blossom from his hair. "Floral ornaments. Ready to tell me what happened?"

He sat down heavily. "Someone tried to kill me."

Chapter Twenty-Five

*Women are like that. When they are enraged they have
great strength.*

~Agatha Christie

Peveril Hall, Monday, May 13

"Someone tried to kill you *again*?"

"You needn't sound so skeptical. The perpetrator
obviously hasn't finished the job, so it makes sense he
would take another stab at it." Noah massaged his back.
"I hope he's not being paid for this. So far he's proven to
be pretty incompetent."

"And you'd prefer he succeed?"

"Well, no, of course not. Still, his attempts have
hardly shown the level of professionalism one would
expect from an assassin."

"Assassin! Who do you think you are, the petty
despot of a banana republic?"

He perked up. "Cool. Do I get a throne? A personal
army? Maybe a gem-encrusted crown?"

"How about a tinfoil cap?"

"Huh." He looked at the refrigerator. "Could you get
me a beer?"

"It's four o'clock in the morning!"

He shifted on the hard seat. "Least you could do."

"Tough." Ignoring his grousing, Sophie said firmly,

"Out with it."

"I was in the street and suddenly this big black car tried to run me over."

"Oh, really. Was that part of your army training too? Standing in the middle of the street daring motorists to ram you?" As her anxiety eased, the pique took over.

He shut his mouth.

"Well?"

"If you're just going to make fun, I won't tell you."

She sat, her attentive expression as manifestly fake as she could make it.

"I heard noises outside."

"Aha. That's extraordinary right there. A wild beast? Aliens? Ghosts? Or perhaps—gasp—nosey neighbors?"

Noah soldiered on. "I looked out the window. There was a light moving down the driveway. It bobbled."

"A UFO! Good show!"

"Someone was casing the joint."

"Casing the joint? Sounds more like a burglar than a murderer. Or maybe a man looking for a lost dog." Sophie was enjoying not helping him immensely.

He huffed. "With recent events in mind, I thought it best to follow up."

She nodded wisely. "You went to investigate. Smart."

"Yes. Well. By the time I got downstairs, the light had reached the end of the driveway. It proceeded into the street, but flicked out just as I reached the center of the lane. I stopped and looked around for it, but everything was pitch black. Then all of a sudden an engine started up, and before I could react, this car came out of nowhere."

"Did it have its headlights on?"

"No."

"So how did you know it was going to hit you?"

"When it hit me. Duh."

"All right, then how did you end up in the bush instead of flattened like a pancake on the asphalt?" *These "accidents" are getting more and more outlandish. Could he be doing them to himself?* She regarded Noah. *Could he be sleepwalking?* "Noah, are you sure—"

"If you'll let me finish. I know you disapprove of the exploits of my youth, but they stood me in good stead this time. I rolled over the hood and launched myself into the yard."

That got her attention. "That *is* impressive. Did the car keep going? Did it circle back?"

"I've no idea. I decided to sit it out for a while, hoping he hadn't seen where I landed. After five minutes of unrelenting discomfort, I felt reasonably sure he'd given up. I was trying to break free of the bush when you arrived." He plucked a leaf from his sleeve. "Put pruning hedge on the To Do list, will you?"

Sophie was rummaging around for a pen and paper when she heard rustling from the back door. Before she could open it, Ian Surry barreled through. "What—"

"Sit down."

She was going to object when she noticed the pistol in his hand. She sat on a stool by the counter. "What on earth are you playing at, Ian?"

"This isn't a joke, Sophie. I'm not going to shoot you. Unless I have to. I just want you to listen."

Behind her Noah stirred. "Um, Ian, did you just try to run me over?"

Ian reached over Sophie, took hold of Noah's elbow,

and swung him around to sit next to Sophie. "Stay where I can see you, if you don't mind."

Noah crossed his arms. "Well?"

"Yes. Well, no. I only meant to spook you."

"Did you also drop me from the stable hook?"

Ian evaded their eyes. "I didn't expect you to fall. You were supposed to be stuck up there like a sack of potatoes till someone rescued you."

Noah looked confounded. "You only wanted to *embarrass* me?"

Sophie cried, "But why? You didn't even know us then."

"I overheard you asking George about the Northcutts. I knew I'd have to take care of you quickly, before it got out of hand."

"Take care of me? Take *care* of me?" The recent victim flushed angrily.

Ian shook his head violently. The gun rattled in his hand. "If you'll let me explain—"

Noah, his eyes focused on the weapon, said firmly, "Cards on the table, Surry. Are you or are you not trying to kill me?"

Ian's jaw dropped. "Heavens, no. I just need you to leave this house."

Sophie spoke up. "Why?"

"You're getting too close."

"Too close to what?"

He lowered the gun. "Look, if you promise to hear me out, I'll hold off shooting you. Deal?"

"Under the circumstances, it's a fair trade."

"Okay." He dragged a stool around to the other side of the island and sat down across from them.

Sophie was tempted to offer drinks all around but

wasn't sure if that was in good taste.

Ian cleared his throat. "Um… You got any liquor?"

When she started to jump up, he waved the gun around. "Just tell me."

"It's over in that cupboard. We moved it from the pantry after…after…"

Noah interrupted. "Did you try to poison me as well?"

"Poison you? With what? Where?"

"With my mother's elderberry wine."

"You're kidding. Gawd, what an awful thing to do. Your mother's wine was ambrosial. She used to bring it to potlucks." He looked genuinely upset. "Had it gone bad?"

Noah shook his head. "Someone dosed it with arsenic."

"Arsenic!"

"I'll get the bourbon." Sophie got up slowly and went to the cabinet. She reached for some tumblers, then turned to Ian. "We'll need ice."

He waved her in the direction of the refrigerator, obviously distracted. She poured a drink for each of them.

After finishing it in one big swallow, he poured himself another and tossed it off, too. "Like I said, I want you to vacate the house."

"You used the phrase 'you're getting too close.' What did you mean?"

Ian blew out his cheeks. "To what really happened the night of April 17, 1920."

Noah straightened. "Go on."

He gave Noah a searching look. "This doesn't go beyond these walls, okay?"

"I can't promise that."

"No more than I deserve, I guess." He licked the rim of the glass thirstily, but at a look from Sophie, set it down. "My great-uncle Hiram was an upright man. He was well-known for his irreproachable honesty and integrity. That's why B&O gave him the task of dealing with the hordes of developers pressuring the railroad to allow them to build next to the tracks."

"Developers like Charles Filou."

Sophie added, "We told you Hiram exposed Filou as a shyster."

"It's true." Ian gently laid the gun down in front of him but kept his palms flat on either side of it. "This is the story as told to me by my father Devon Surry, Hiram's nephew. Hiram thought he'd taken care of the problem when he called Filou out at the town meeting. He'd detailed Filou's New York scam to the council, which seemed prepared to deny the man's application. They scheduled a vote for the following week."

"But Filou wasn't ready to give up."

"Right. A few days after the meeting, he contacted Hiram. He said he had a deal Hiram couldn't refuse. He swore he was on the up and up now. Hiram invited him to dinner on April 17 to discuss it."

Sophie recited, "Roast beef, garden peas, Yorkshire pudding."

Ian jerked. "How did you know?"

"We found the menu in a box of Agnes's things." Sophie hoped Noah wouldn't reveal what Agnes wrote about the quarrel that night. *We might be able to use it as leverage if he shoots us*. Even as the thought presented itself, it dawned on her that they'd have no leverage if they were dead. Luckily she didn't have time to worry.

"Ah. It didn't list elderberry pie?" At their collective gasp, Ian chortled. "The recipe without arsenic, naturally."

"It's funny." Noah chewed on his lip. "Now I think of it, Agnes didn't mention Filou's attendance at the dinner in her letter to the constable. I wonder why not?"

Ian looked from one to the other. "Letter?"

"The letter Agnes wrote to the constable about seeing a man with a body. She never sent it though."

Ian's face cleared. "I'd forgotten about that. Filou's name didn't come up?"

"No." Sophie dredged up the letter from memory. "Her words were no one came *after* the master and mistress retired. I think if she suspected either the killer or the victim was Filou she would have said so."

Ian shifted impatiently. "It doesn't matter what the maid said or didn't say. Or what she saw. It's a fact that Filou came to dinner and made a new offer for the land. According to Dad, Hiram rejected the new proposal. He continued to accuse Filou of trying to pull a fast one and announced his intention to report him to the bunco squad. Filou grew enraged and shouted that he would implicate him in one of his fraudulent schemes."

So much for leverage. "What did Hiram do?"

"He threw him out."

"Threw him out?"

"Yes."

"Wait." Noah poured himself more whiskey. "Where was Audrey? Surely Filou wouldn't have conducted business—or tried to intimidate Hiram—in her presence?"

"She was there, yes. Dad says she tried to calm the waters, with no success. Hiram was furious. He wanted to go to the police immediately, but Audrey talked him out of it."

"Then what happened?"

"Filou left. Or they thought he did. Hiram took a while to recover his temper, but eventually they went to bed. Audrey was awakened a little before midnight by the creak of a door opening. She left Hiram sleeping and slipped downstairs. A glimmer led her to the small office next to the kitchen."

"Office? What office?"

"It's now the butler's pantry. Hiram used it when he didn't have time to go up to the tower."

"Ah. Go on."

Ian guzzled the last drop in his glass. After Sophie relented and refilled it, he resumed. "Filou stood before the desk holding a kerosene lantern. He was dressed in black and had blackened his face with charcoal. At his side was a brightly patterned duffle bag. Audrey suspected he meant to carry out his threat and plant incriminating material on Hiram. She confronted him. Filou attacked her." He stopped to take a breath.

"Attacked? With a gun?"

"No." He hesitated. "At least Dad didn't mention one. I think he just lunged at her."

Sophie recalled the photo of Audrey and Agnes. "She was a pretty formidable woman. How did she react?"

"She escaped to the kitchen. When he followed her, she crowned him with a rolling pin."

"Oh my God, *Audrey* killed him?"

Ian sputtered, "It was an accident. She didn't mean to, but she was terrified. She told her brother James she just picked up the nearest thing with a handle and whacked him over the head. How could she know the blow would be fatal?"

Noah was puzzled. "But what about the rat poison? Agnes found a broken bottle of it. She suspected it was the murder weapon."

Ian looked blank. "My father said nothing about poison."

Sophie wiggled her fingers at Ian. "This is what I wanted to tell you, Noah. I'd forgotten until now. It was in one of her letters. The night of the dinner she went to the cellar to fetch rat poison for the cook. It had nothing to do with the murder."

Noah wiped his forehead. "Well, I'll be hornswoggled. It was one of our first clues, and it isn't even a clue." He turned to Ian. "What did Audrey do then? Did she call the police?"

"No. For one thing, they hadn't yet installed a telephone in the house. She would have had to roust out the one neighbor who had one, and he happened to be the mayor."

"Surely the town had a police force, or at least a local cop. Agnes wrote to a Constable Bustwick."

"Marmion Grove was patrolled during the day by officers from the county." He waited, and when no one spoke, went on. "Also, Audrey was sure they'd arrest Hiram."

"Hiram? She was the one who clocked Filou. You said Hiram was asleep."

"According to Audrey, the earlier fracas and subsequent ejection had been loud enough to reach the neighbors' ears. If the police investigated, they would have questioned them. Even if Audrey confessed, she feared they'd claim she was lying to cover for Hiram."

"*Hmph.*"

Sophie didn't think Noah believed Ian's account any more than she did. "So…no police?"

"No. She figured the best approach was to get rid of the body and keep the whole thing a secret from Hiram. After all, they had both seen Filou drive off. Hiram would infer he'd left town, since the deal had fallen through. No one had to know he'd come back."

Noah steepled his fingers. "All right. Let's set the scene. Audrey is trapped in her kitchen with a large dead man on the floor."

"She couldn't deal with the corpse alone, so she drove to Bethesda and woke up James—"

"The boy in the photo?"

"Yes. He came back with her. At first they thought they'd bury Filou behind the carriage house, but then James had the bright idea of putting him in his car, driving it out to the country, and dumping him."

"Wait. You didn't mention this before. Filou's car was at the *house*?"

Chapter Twenty-Six

A weak man in a corner is more dangerous than a strong man.

~Agatha Christie

Peveril Hall, Monday, May 13

"According to Dad, Filou's car was in the courtyard." Ian's face went blank. "*Hmm*. That *is* odd, isn't it?"

Sophie was perplexed. "If Filou was going to sneak into the house, why would he drive all the way up the driveway to the carriage house? Why not leave his car on the street?"

Noah chimed in. "You'd think he'd want to be able to make a quick getaway."

Ian threw up his hands. "Hey! Nobody said Filou was a seasoned breaker and enterer. Maybe he wasn't privy to the protocols."

Noah shook his head. "I don't buy that. Filou was in camouflage and carried a lantern. He knew what he was doing."

"And he may have done it before. He *was* a con man."

Ian folded his arms. "I can only tell you what my father told me."

Sophie was way ahead of them. "Your father heard

it from his father, correct? Audrey's brother and co-conspirator?"

"James. Yes."

"I—"

Noah put a finger to Sophie's lips. "You may be onto something. James was Audrey's devoted brother. Could he have altered the narrative to protect his sister?"

Ian's face suffused with anger. "You're implying my grandfather was a liar?"

"It's something to consider. James would surely want to avoid putting her in jeopardy."

Especially if she actually meant to kill Filou. Sophie reflected on Ian's tale. *Was he shielding someone else? Hiram? Could her husband have been conspiring with Filou and Audrey caught them? Or did Hiram himself do the dirty deed?* Sophie kept the speculation to herself. *I don't want to rile Ian up—not with that gun so handy.* "How about we deal with the veracity of the account later. What did James say they did next?"

"He drove Filou's car to White's Ferry and left it there."

Noah turned to Sophie. "Agnes's letter."

Her hand went to her mouth. "Right! She said the man put the bundle into a fancy car. She mentioned a hood ornament. What was it?"

Noah said grimly, "A flying bird. I looked it up. It's Hispano-Suiza's emblem." He turned to Ian. "Was the car a Hispano-Suiza H6?"

"No idea. Why?"

"According to a news account, Filou's Hispano-Suiza was found abandoned by the side of the road near White's Ferry in April, 1920."

"Well, there you are—that validates James's story

240

then."

Sophie was dismayed at Ian's attitude. *He's so blasé. We're talking about concealing evidence of a crime!* "How did James get home?"

"Hitched. And walked. Thirty miles was not considered much of a hike back then."

"And Filou was written off as a missing person?"

"Actually, everyone assumed he had left for greener pastures after Hiram broadcast his corrupt activities. No one asked any questions. He was just one of a thousand itinerant businessmen who blew in and out of towns in the twenties."

Noah mumbled something.

"What did you say?"

"This all happened in the middle of the night. It's hard to believe Audrey didn't scream when she encountered Filou in the office."

Sophie saw where Noah was going. "And there must have been an awful noise when she banged him over the head. Not to mention the grunts and groans as James manhandled a corpse into the car."

"So what?"

Noah finished it. "Do you still contend that Hiram *slept* through the whole thing?"

Ian was unmoved. "Their bedroom was in the front of the house. He wouldn't have heard anything."

Sophie was skeptical. "Audrey didn't tell him what she'd done?"

"Oh God, no! That would have been insane. Hiram would have insisted on going to the police, and at the very least he'd lose his job. And Audrey would go to jail."

"Was James okay with that? He was vulnerable

too."

"James did anything his big sister told him to." Ian appeared slightly ashamed of the fact.

"So they planned to sweep it under the rug. No harm, no foul."

"Except," said Noah heavily, "a man was dead."

The conversation seemed to be at a standstill. Sophie stirred. "Surely, they felt some cover story was in order."

"I never heard of one." Ian stroked his chin. "Audrey must have been worried though, since she started pressing Hiram to ask for a transfer."

"My, my. She was some tough lady. She never evinced any regrets?"

"None. At least, according to my father." He scowled. "Filou was scum. He would have happily ruined Hiram and his family."

Sophie ran through Ian's revelation in her head. "You said Filou made Hiram an offer. Could that offer have included a bribe?"

Ian looked startled. "Why, yes. According to Audrey, while they were at dinner he made noises about a payoff, but when Hiram wouldn't bite, he moved on to threats."

"So he might have brought cash with him that night."

"If he had, she would have gotten rid of it along with the body. She couldn't risk the police tracing the bills."

Sophie found this hard to accept. "Really? So she'd just jettison what was basically a windfall?"

Ian stiffened. "My great aunt was a virtuous woman. You make her sound like some venal gold digger."

"I'm just saying, if it was cash set aside for an illegal transaction, Filou would hardly mark the notes. He would have made sure the source of funds was masked."

Ian spit out, "So my relative, in self-defense, bonks an evil man, then has the presence of mind to commandeer the jackpot and—what? Deposit it in her checking account?"

Sophie was about to retort when Noah put a hand on her arm. "You said James drove the car to the ferry. Did he throw Filou into the river?"

Ian grimaced. "Actually, we don't—"

A voice came from the back door. "I'm afraid that's another detail the family has not been able to pin down."

The three at the kitchen counter whipped around. A chubby man in a checked shirt stood at the door, hiking a baseball bat aloft. Ian cried, "Kendrick! What the hell are you doing?"

"What do you *think* I'm doing, Ian? Trying to save you from yourself." Kendrick Northcutt lowered the bat.

His audience was momentarily stumped. "Um."

"Um."

"Kendrick, I—"

While Ian stuttered, Noah said, "You're Kendrick Northcutt, aren't you?"

His face is familiar. "We danced on Cinco de Mayo, didn't we?"

He smiled at Sophie. "A delightful foxtrot, yes."

"You're Oscar's son—Hiram's grandson."

"Great-grandson to be precise. Ian here is my second cousin once removed if that helps. You've met my father?"

"Yes." Sophie stared at him, then turned to Ian. "At the party, you made it sound as though you were estranged from your cousin—that you had no dealings with him."

Ian looked down at his hands. "I—"

Noah interrupted. "You hoped we'd never even meet Kendrick, much less compare notes."

"Would've worked if Kenny hadn't stuck his colossal nose in." He swept a scornful glance over his cousin. "How did you know I was here, anyway?"

"I know you invited Noah and Sophie to your house. Whatever happened there put you in a tizzy, so I kept an eye on you. When you showed up here, I watched through the window. I couldn't tell if you were going to confess—or shoot them."

"They were obsessed with the Northcutts and…and…you know." Ian's face reddened. "I thought if I frightened them off, we'd be okay."

His cousin eyeballed him. "This isn't your first attempt, is it?" When Ian remained mum, he yelled, "Damn it, Ian! The entire village is rumbling about attacks on Pennyman here. People are installing alarms and sleeping with billy clubs." He shook the bat at Ian. "They're convinced a criminal gang has invaded the town."

Ian said sulkily, "I only wanted him to clear out." He turned to Noah. "You said you were going to pack up the house and sell it right away. With luck you wouldn't delve too closely and just get rid of…of… Well, we'd be safe."

"Get rid of what?"

When Ian didn't answer, Sophie hazarded, "You believe there are still clues in this house, don't you?" She gasped. "It was you! You searched Roger's study."

He nodded. "Without success. I snuck in after Vivian died. Then Noah began staying over. And you too." His tone implied Noah and Sophie were little better than squatters.

Noah glanced at Sophie. "You missed the box of Agnes's belongings my father had collected."

"No, I didn't. I had no idea her things were relevant."

Sophie added indignantly, "And you left an unholy mess."

"Sorry." He faced Noah. "You didn't seem to be budging, and then at the Cinco de Mayo party, you intimated that maybe you'd keep the house." He patted the pistol. "You forced my hand."

Noah jumped up. "You almost bumped me off...twice!"

"I *told* you it was simply a scare tactic." He turned to Kendrick. "When I got here, I couldn't keep up the charade. I decided a full confession was the only solution."

Kendrick's eyes widened. "You didn't... What did you tell them, Ian?"

Ian bit his lip. "About Audrey and the rolling pin. And James."

Kendrick sat down hard on the remaining stool. "So you admitted that our ancestor Audrey Northcutt killed a man and hid his body? Just how did that go over?"

Sophie interrupted. "We were in the midst of it when you barged in."

He barked, "*Barged in*? I beg your pardon, young lady. I was rescuing you from a man holding you hostage." He brandished the bat. "Hence my truncheon."

While all eyes were on Kendrick, Noah deftly snagged the pistol from the table and held it up. "He's no longer armed."

"In that case"—Kendrick laid the bat on the floor—

"shall we pass the peace pipe around?"

Noah said, with more jollity than Sophie thought appropriate, "No smoking in the house. May I suggest whiskey?"

"Even better."

Sophie got another glass from the cupboard and poured Kendrick a tot.

"Thanks. It's a little early for me, but under the circumstances I could use a bracer." He drained it.

"What do you mean, early?" Sophie looked out the window. Sunlight flooded the backyard. "My God, it's morning!"

Noah leveled his glance at Kendrick. "So how long have *you* known what your great-grandmother did?"

"For a couple of years. I came across a letter from Audrey to James while I was collecting papers for the genealogy Ian's working on. I taxed him with it and he came clean."

"What did her letter say?"

"She referred to the 'tragic event' and advised James to stop stewing over it."

Ian added, "She said, 'They'll never find him.' "

"How did you know she was talking about Filou?"

Kendrick nodded at his cousin. "Because on his death bed, James confessed to his son Devon."

"He may have done, but my father always maintained the story wasn't true—that James made it up."

"Why would he think that?"

"James always wanted to look like a hero. Rescuing his big sister from a bad man fit the bill."

"But Devon was wrong. The letter proved it."

"Yes."

Kendrick cleared his throat. "After some soul searching, we decided to keep it to ourselves." He looked anxiously from Noah to Sophie. "We'd like it to stay that way."

Time to probe. "You said Audrey stated no one would ever find the body. You haven't come across anything indicating what they did with it?"

"Nope." Ian shrugged. "That was the only mention she made of the whole event, at least that we've found."

"Nothing in James's letters to her?"

"I don't have any of his letters." He pursed his lips. "My grandfather wasn't much of a writer."

Where have I heard that before?

Kendrick filled his empty glass with water. "Now comes the tricky part. I don't expect you to forgive my cousin for his atrocious behavior, but can we trust you to keep mum?"

Noah seemed persuaded, but Sophie shook her head. "Why should we? You could have killed Noah. And the ridiculous excuse that you want to hush up your relative's indiscretion is unacceptable."

Ian started to talk, but Kendrick laid a hand on his shoulder. "You're right. Nonetheless, we are at your mercy. My great-grandmother killed a man, yes—but it wasn't deliberate. He was a bad egg—and Hiram meant to inform the authorities of his double-dealing and his bullying. He would have gone to jail for a long time anyway."

"So you're going with 'Audrey did the world a favor' defense? Really?"

Kendrick bowed his head. "Really."

Sophie opened her mouth, ready to rant, but Noah jumped in. "Okay."

"Noah!" Her white-hot glare reflected off what appeared suspiciously like a halo surrounding Noah's head. She gave up. "All right."

Both men sighed. "Thank you."

"Although we might call the cops on a couple of home invaders."

When Ian started backing toward the door, Noah crooked his finger. "A joke, gentlemen. A joke. But I do have a question. It's about your father, Kendrick."

"Oscar? What about him?"

"We met him in Glen Echo."

"Oh, is that where he retired to? We…uh…lost touch." His cherubic features sagged.

"He told us about your pernicious habit."

He barely hid the roguish smile. "My eye for the ladies? By which I mean, my preference for big-boned, long-faced females on four legs?"

Noah gave him an arch look.

"It's true. I was gambling heavily for a while. My father disapproved. Strongly. *But* I have mended my ways." He forced a wry smile. "It helped that I ran out of money. Then I met and married a marvelous woman who distracted me enough that by the time she passed away I had shed the urge." His eyes filled with tears. "Bless her memory."

"Well, your father is doing well. He's busy maintaining the Wurlitzer band organ at Glen Echo amusement park."

"Is he now? That's over by Cabin John, isn't it? I'll have to pay him a visit."

"He told us a tale about a treasure buried near the Marmion Grove railroad station." Noah looked hard, first at Kendrick, then at Ian. "Do either of you know anything about that?"

Chapter Twenty-Seven

My point is that there can be no exceptions allowed on the score of character, position, or probability. What we must now examine is the possibility of eliminating one or more persons on the facts.

~Agatha Christie

Peveril Hall, Monday, May 13

Kendrick was the first to respond. "Ha-ha. Yeah, one of Dad's favorite stories was about plunder from a famous robbery that had been hidden in the old station. He finally admitted—once we were teenagers—that it was just gossip. See, he was the engineer who leveled the old station and built the shelter. If there were any treasure, it would have turned up then."

Ian leaned forward. "Could I have my pistol back now?" When Noah drew back, he said, "Surely you don't believe I'd use it on you?"

"It crossed my mind." He handed it to him but only after he emptied it of the bullets.

"The ammunition too."

"I'll hold onto that for now."

Ian shrugged. "It's your party." He turned to go. Kendrick made as if to follow.

Before Sophie could speak, Noah moved to stand in front of the door. "Hold it. We're not through yet. I have a few more questions."

Ian halted. "Oh? Like what?"

"Please come back and sit down."

The two men slowly returned to their seats. Kendrick said, "We've told you everything we know."

"We'll see." Noah folded his hands together. "How heavily was Agnes involved?"

Kendrick looked blank. "Who's Agnes?"

Ian answered. "She was Audrey's maid. The one who swiped her ring."

Sophie interrupted. "She did no such thing. She—"

Noah signaled for quiet. "Ian?"

Ian shifted on the stool. "You're asking what she knew about the murder? Nothing."

"The letter indicates otherwise."

Kendrick was getting frustrated. "What letter?"

Ian answered, "These two found a letter Agnes wrote to the police saying she thought she'd witnessed a murder."

"But she couldn't have seen anything! The maid slept in the servants' quarters. It all went down in the kitchen."

Sophie interrupted. "She didn't claim to have been present at the actual event. She was awakened late that night and saw someone leave with a body over his shoulder."

"James, with Filou. This isn't good." Kendrick frowned.

Noah volunteered, "But she never sent the letter."

"Why not?"

"We surmise that she lost her nerve. She described the scene but in the end worried it might have been a hallucination."

Kendrick stirred. "Didn't Audrey fire that maid?"

"Yes."

Noah blurted, "But was it for the ring or the pregnancy?"

Ian said firmly, "I still say it was the ring."

"And I say Harry gave it to Agnes fair and square." Sophie was equally firm.

"Agnes. Ring. Audrey. Harry?" Kendrick seemed to be floundering.

Ian patted him sympathetically. "Allow me to recap. Harry Quayle was engaged to Agnes. She claimed he gave her Great-Aunt Audrey's opal ring."

Sophie began, "But—"

"Wait." Noah spread his hands on the counter. "Let's pretend for a minute that the ring *did* belong to Audrey and she lost it during the struggle with Filou. The next day Agnes announces the engagement and excitedly shows the ring to her. Audrey recognizes it. With no way of knowing if Agnes had glimpsed James and the corpse, she can't allow her to keep it. So she uses it as grounds for sacking her. She hopes the girl will be too demoralized—and then too busy finding work—to dwell on what she might have seen."

"But what if Audrey *did* discharge Agnes because she was pregnant?"

"*Agnes* was pregnant?" Kendrick looked shocked.

Noah nodded. "She gave birth to a baby boy—Harry Junior—three months after she was fired."

"Well, I'll be."

Sophie caught Noah's eye and mouthed, *Should we bring up Harry the Third?* He shook his head.

Ian heaved a sigh. "Audrey must have known, although she never mentioned it. I think she just wanted

Agnes to go away. If Hiram found out his maid was in the family way—"

"And that Harry had made himself scarce."

"—Hiram would have insisted on taking care of her."

Sophie cried out, "That's it!"

"What?"

"That's how Audrey's ring ended up in Roger's box. I'll bet my bottom dollar Audrey gave the ring back to Agnes."

"Why would she do that after making such a fuss?"

"Ian has a point, Sophie."

Noah's condescending tone goaded her into responding with the first thing that came into her head. "She hoped it would help the marriage along and keep the girl quiet. Her secret would be safe."

Noah objected. "She didn't count on Harry dumping Agnes."

"And that's why *Agnes* left the ring behind." Sophie was triumphant.

Noah had been tapping a finger on the table. "Harry jilted her… But did he? Or did Audrey kill him too? He disappeared the same night Filou did."

The two cousins went rigid. Ian found his voice first. "Harry was a cad. I'm sure he nicked Audrey's ring and bugged out when he learned his girlfriend was knocked up."

Sophie could tell Noah was tempted to defend Harry. The struggle only lasted a moment. "Or his girlfriend made his life miserable, and he refused to submit to the pressure. It's not always the guy's fault, Ian."

Ian flushed. "Yes, it is. Men have the responsibility

to—"

Sophie could see the conversation devolving into a culture clash and intervened. "We were discussing the hypothesis that Audrey killed Harry as well as Filou."

Kendrick gurgled, "My great-grandmother was *not* a killer. I mean, not a dedicated killer. I mean..." He trailed off.

Ian and Noah passed the time lobbing eye daggers at each other while Sophie entertained this new notion. "Kendrick is right. From what we can gather about Audrey, she was a strong-minded woman but not malevolent."

Noah retorted, "Actually *everything* we know about her personality—remember that photo of her and Agnes?—makes her appear ruthless enough to have no qualms about removing obstacles in her way."

"But that's just it." Ian seemed almost desperate. "Harry wasn't an obstacle. What would she gain by killing him? Audrey would consider Harry her means of getting rid of Agnes, who *was* potentially a problem."

"That's logical." Kendrick nodded. "He'd sweep Agnes off to the marriage bed and presumably out of service."

Ian added, "Besides, Audrey had her ring back."

Sophie whistled. "Wait. Audrey's ring. Agnes maintained that Harry had given it to her. If Audrey lost it during the fight with Filou, and *Harry* found it..."

"He would indeed become an impediment."

"She'd *have* to kill him."

In the shocked silence that followed this statement, the clock's ticking gave way to a chime. Nine o'clock.

"That's preposterous!" Ian had risen. He pounded his fist on the counter.

Sophie demurred. "No, it isn't. Harry would never have admitted to Agnes that he didn't buy the ring. He claimed he'd saved up enough from his job to afford it."

"Agnes believed him. She said so in her letter to her mother."

Kendrick brightened. "Aha. Therefore Audrey would have no incentive to fire Agnes."

"Doesn't wash. See, she couldn't risk it. If Agnes saw her and James moving the body, and somehow Harry weaseled it out of her..."

They seemed to be going round and round. Sophie stifled a yawn. "Are we done here?"

Everyone was of similar mind.

Noah glanced at Ian. "No more attacks on my person, I trust."

Ian crossed his heart. "If you want to keep the house, you have my blessing."

Noah stared at him in mute outrage. Sophie said drily, "Why, thank you. Terribly gracious of you. May I show you out?"

****

Peveril Hall, Monday evening

They slept through Monday, only waking now and then to assure each other that they were okay. Toward four p.m., Noah got up and went to the kitchen for a snack. Sophie trailed sleepily after him. "Peanut butter sandwich okay?"

"Extra crunchy?"

"I will have nothing else in my larder."

"How about some tomato soup to go with?"

"Ah. Childhood memories. Has to be made with milk though." He took a can from the cabinet. "*Mm-mm* good."

She sat down to wait.

Just as Noah was ladling soup into two bowls, his cell phone tinkled. "Hello? Oh, hi, Harry." He listened. "Sure, tomorrow at ten? See you then."

"He's coming over?"

"Tomorrow. He says he has big news."

"Excellent. Shall we give him ours?"

Chapter Twenty-Eight

Everything must be taken into account. If the fact will not fit the theory—let the theory go.

~Agatha Christie

Peveril Hall, Tuesday, May 14

Sophie and Noah were sitting in the tree swing when Harry arrived in his superannuated Cadillac. The car wheezed to a stop in the courtyard. He got out and strolled over to stand in front of them.

"So what's your big news, Harry?"

He dabbed his sweaty forehead with a damp tissue. "I've solved the mystery."

"Oh, that's nice. Where did he go?"

"Huh? What are you talking about?"

Sophie tried. "Where did he end up?"

"Who?"

"Your grandfather."

"Harry Senior? No, that's not what I'm talking about."

Noah straightened. "Forgive me, but isn't that what you've been doing all this time? Ascertaining his fate?"

Harry's eyes wavered. "Yes, uh, I suppose. I hadn't... Well, I dug up something else."

Sophie stopped swinging. "What is it?"

"I have proof that Hiram Northcutt killed Charles

Filou."

Sophie looked at Noah. "Hiram? Does that mean Devon—or James—lied?"

"Wow. All these years—"

"And generations—"

"Thinking their great-aunt—"

"Great-*grandmother*, was responsible." She raised her eyes to the sky. "How do we tell them?"

Noah stuck his chin out. "We don't."

Harry's gaze had been leaping between the two. "What are you on about?"

Noah zipped his lip. "Nothing."

Sophie did likewise. "Never mind."

When it became manifest that further elaboration would not be forthcoming, Harry mumbled, "Well, don't you want to hear what it is?"

"The proof? Sure." Noah gestured. "You have the floor."

"I found Hiram's former assistant's grandson."

"I take it you couldn't find his dog walker's son-in-law's nephew?"

He glowered at Noah. "I do not appreciate the snark. Mr. Jones is a records clerk in the Montgomery County Archives. He was able to look up police bulletins and official hearings in the county going back to the turn of the twentieth century."

"Huh."

"He produced the notice of a confab held between the railroad, the county executive, the planning board, and Mr. Charles Filou, on April 16, 1920."

Noah leaned forward. "Was it the same town council meeting in which Hiram called Filou a swindler?"

"No. That was a public hearing held the week

before. The proposal was on the council's markup agenda. All indications were it would be denied, so Filou tried an end run around Hiram and asked for a private parley with the planning board. Northcutt got wind of it and showed up."

"Did he shut it down?"

"That's not important. It's what came *after that* that was of interest."

"Go on."

"Hiram met with the police on April 19."

Sophie sucked in a breath. "Was he going to turn his wife in?"

Harry reared back. "What? Why would he do that?" When no one answered him, he said, "According to the report, he asked them to investigate Charles Filou for fraud. The police declined to pursue the matter. So, *obviously*, he took it upon himself to rid the world of an unscrupulous character."

"That's *it*? That's what you've got?" Relief flooded Noah's face, but he merely said, "Your conclusion's a tad fanciful."

Sophie looked at Noah. *Harry's deduction is pure conjecture. So why is Noah stringing him along?*

Harry stiffened. "It fits the facts as we know them."

"Does it? Question: if Hiram didn't go to the police until April 19, and you're going on the assumption that he killed Filou after that, whose body did Agnes see two nights earlier?"

"She didn't see anyone."

Noah waited, letting the tension build. "Let's just posit for a moment that she *did* see a body. Could it have been Harry Senior?"

Harry went still. Sophie watched while various

emotions slashed across his features. Finally he rapped out, "No. For one thing, Harry didn't have a car. Whose car was he thrown into?"

"The killer's?"

Harry clearly had no answer to that and just as clearly didn't want to accept it. He shook his head. "I don't see it. Agnes made it up out of whole cloth."

Noah let him off the hook. "Actually we have already identified the person responsible for Filou's disappearance."

"What do you mean?" He contemplated Noah. "You've been hinting at something. What is it?"

"Audrey Northcutt killed Charles Filou."

His face went white with shock. "Audrey? Hiram's *wife*? How is that possible?"

Sophie snapped, "Women are perfectly capable of murder, Harry." She wasn't sure why his remark raised her hackles, but it did.

"I know, I know. But Hiram was dealing with Filou in a business matter. Audrey wouldn't have been concerned. What would induce her to attack him?"

Noah took over. "Filou had contacted Hiram to tender a new proffer. Hiram invited him to the house to hear it, but his so-called proffer turned out to be nothing more than a bribe. When Hiram indignantly refused it, Filou threatened to impugn his reputation by spreading false information about him. Later that night, Audrey discovered Filou attempting to insert phony documentation into Hiram's records. She…took care of the problem."

Harry seemed unconvinced. "Where's your evidence?"

Sophie was about to describe Kendrick's and Ian's

midnight visit, then thought better of it. *We more or less promised to shield them from exposure.* She glanced at Noah, hoping he felt the same way.

He drew a finger across his neck. "We're not at liberty to divulge our sources."

"Oh, really?" Harry turned around and headed back to his car.

"Where are you going?"

"Well, apparently you don't need me."

"Wait! You haven't given us a solid basis for your conclusions. Do you have any?"

He slowed, then came back. "I admit they're mainly circumstantial. Motive, opportunity, means."

"But you're asserting Hiram didn't kill Filou until after the nineteenth."

Harry nodded.

"Why wait? And where was Filou during that time?"

Harry rolled his eyes. "Obviously, Hiram expected the police to react. When they didn't, he took the law into his own hands. The fact that no one had seen Filou since the seventeenth means nothing."

Sophie was curious. "So how did he do it? How did he lure Filou back to Peveril Hall?"

Harry grinned. "That's the beauty of my theory. He didn't have to. He could have killed him anywhere, anytime. No one was looking for the man. He was a complete stranger in the neighborhood." He finished triumphantly. "No one would ask any questions."

"How do you account for Filou's Hispano-Suiza turning up at White's Ferry?"

"Hispano…what?" Harry was bewildered.

"Filou's car. A very fancy car. It was found at White's Ferry on the Potomac a few days later."

Harry didn't miss a beat. "Aha! *That's* where Hiram killed him!" He did a little jig.

Sophie glanced at Noah. *It does sound logical. Could Ian and Kendrick have been hoodwinking us after all?*

Noah seemed to sense what she was thinking. He said cautiously, "We have information indicating Filou's demise was accidental."

Harry scoffed. "From the same anonymous source? Big deal." He slapped a palm on his thigh. "Hiram killed Filou. End of story."

That did it. Sophie cried, "No! That *source* is a close relative who told us Audrey surprised Filou in Peveril Hall. He attacked her, and she smashed his head in. Hiram never knew anything about it."

Harry unexpectedly snickered. "Well, I'll be. At least it wasn't Harry. By the way, I tracked down the Northcutt descendants."

"We know. We met Oscar. He volunteers at Glen Echo park. His son Kendrick lives here in the Grove."

Sophie added, "And Audrey's great-nephew Ian lives here as well."

He threw up his arms in exasperation. "Is there anything you *don't* know?"

"We don't know where Filou's body is."

Something gleamed in Harry's eyes. "Ha. Well, how about we leave that to me. I have to retain an iota of pride. After all, it's my profession."

Noah didn't take this well. "I thought we were all in this together."

"We are. But you've basically done all the grunt work. According to you, Agnes's letter was accurate; there *was* a murder. You say the killer was Audrey, although… Say, which relative was your source? Oscar?"

"I…er…meant relative to the event. We did some digging on our own."

"So you don't actually have the smoking gun?"

"Um…" Noah looked helplessly at Sophie. "We do, but we…uh…swore to keep the informant's name a secret."

"From me? Didn't you just say we were partners?"

"Affirmative, but since—as you say—this exonerates Harry, I think you can move on. Isn't that what you were after?"

"Yes, but it still begs the question of what happened to him that night. Did Audrey kill Harry too? Was he waylaid by a highwayman? I need answers."

"All right. If we find your grandfather, maybe we'll find Filou."

"Or the other way around." Harry drew out his car keys. "That reminds me. I was going to seek out some of Filou's partners in crime. Maybe after all this we'll learn he was spotted in New Mexico a week later."

"A tribute to your eternal optimism."

Harry blinked. "Say, I just had an idea. The Hispano-Suiza turned up at White's Ferry. Why don't you and Sophie go check it out."

"What for?"

"Someone may remember something about the car. After all, it was distinctive. And while you're at it, ask if a body was found in the river around April 19th."

"Good idea." Noah's tone was dry.

"Or the twentieth." Harry left.

Noah went upstairs to change. "I have to go downtown. Are you going to be all right? It must be weird not to have the book sale to worry about."

"I have some editing jobs I've been putting off."

"Can you do the work here?"

"Most of it. I have to meet one client for lunch this week to go over his project."

He pecked her cheek. "Give me a call if you want me to pick up milk and bread on the way home."

She waved him off. *Is this what it's like to be a housewife seeing her commuting husband off?* It felt both surreal and comforting. She went back in to phone the client.

"Oh, you only have today free, Mr. Spofford?" Her spirits sank along with her eyelids. "How about we meet at one o'clock for lunch? Bring your manuscript with you, and we'll look it over. Once I get an idea of what's needed in the way of editing, I'll be able to provide you with a time frame and cost estimate."

"That sounds perfect."

"There's an Olive Garden in White Flint Mall. Is that okay?"

"Oh dear." The man's reedy voice began to tremble.

Sophie knew he suffered from prostate cancer and wished to disgorge the saga of his illness on the world. "Is that too far away? I was thinking it would be easy because there's free parking."

"I forgot to tell you. I'm not driving any more. There's a little Cuban restaurant only a few blocks from me. You can park in my apartment garage and we can walk." He gave her an address in Bethesda.

"All right. I'll be there at one."

****

Peveril Hall, Tuesday afternoon

It was after three o'clock when Sophie dragged

herself out of the car and collapsed on the tree swing. Her phone rang. "Hello, Noah."

"Where are you?"

"Home…er… Your house. I mean Peveril Hall."

"Oh, darn. I was hoping you were still in the District. I wanted to give you a tour of the exhibit we're working on."

"I'm sorry, Noah. I'm exhausted. The traffic was awful, and then Mr. Spofford—well, first he seemed to think this was a date." She raised her voice to drown out Noah's snort. "But when I made it clear our relationship would remain on a professional basis, I almost wished it *was* a date. Noah, his writing is execrable. And he seems totally uninterested in learning even the basic elements of style. I think deep down he wants me to write it for him."

"If he publishes under his own name, that would be plagiarism. Drop the job."

"I can't. He's paying me well. Plus we already signed a contract."

"You shouldn't let him use you like that. Just do the minimum—or show him what you want and then tell him to come back when he's done it."

Sophie knew she'd never have the nerve. She also knew she was incapable of leaving a bad piece of writing uncured. "Will you be late?"

"Uh-uh. Now that I know you're not downtown, I'll come on home. Do you have to work tomorrow?"

"Nope. See you soon."

"Oh, by the way, Harry called. He wants to know what happened to the bribe Filou offered Hiram."

Chapter Twenty-Nine

Because, you see, if the man were an invention—a fabrication—how much easier to make him disappear!
~Agatha Christie

Peveril Hall, Tuesday, May 14

"I thought we were going out to eat." Sophie and Noah were sitting on the front porch watching a gaggle of children ride their bikes down the middle of the road. "It's not fair we have to hang around waiting for Harry." She was bored. *I'm getting tired of the constant harping on mysterious mysteries.*

"I told you, he wants to know where Filou's bribe money went."

"How on earth would *we* know what happened to it? I'm sure it's long gone. Audrey probably spent it all on a new hat or a car."

"Didn't Ian opine she buried it alongside Filou?"

She said crossly, "As I said at the time, that would be crazy. Why not keep it? No one would know."

"It depends on what kind of currency it was. Paper notes could have been traceable. Audrey might have erred on the side of caution and simply thrown the gladstone bag in with the body."

"Gladstone bag?"

"Filou was a salesman. They always carry gladstone

bags."

"That doesn't sound right…" Sophie clicked some keys on her phone. "Aha. Says here gladstone bags are hinged travel cases, invented in England and named in honor of the British prime minister. What you're thinking of is a carpetbag." She read aloud. " 'An American invention, the carpetbag was made of patterned upholstery material, soft-sided so it could hold all one's belongings. The carpetbaggers were the men who flooded the South after the Civil War to help—or if you prefer, exploit—reconstruction efforts.' So…mostly con men." She turned the phone off.

"Just like Filou." Noah grinned.

Sophie cast her mind back to Ian's story of the night Filou was killed. "Ian said Filou had a duffle bag with him."

"A colorful duffle; i.e., a carpetbag." He scratched his head. "But why would he bring the bag with him when he broke in?"

"Because it held the incriminating material he'd threatened to plant—I'm guessing the money he'd intended as a bribe. He planned to accuse Hiram of accepting it."

"Ah."

"Anyway, even if they were paper bills, I don't see why she wouldn't at least hide the carpetbag somewhere so she could reclaim it when the furor died down."

"What furor? No one knew Filou was dead."

"True…" Sophie pinched her lips together. "I've got it. Before Audrey could retrieve it, they were transferred. She never got the chance."

"Except that Ian told us Audrey was behind the transfer application."

Sophie sat up. "Was she? Ian was positive Hiram couldn't hear the confrontation between Audrey and Filou, but maybe he did. Maybe he knew all about it."

"Doesn't fly. Hiram was a law-abiding citizen. He would have gone to the police."

Sophie tried to lasso one of the myriad theories spiraling through her brain and force it to land. "Okay… *Audrey* may not have retrieved the bag, but *James* did. He stayed behind in Bethesda when his sister moved to Baltimore. He knew where the body—and the cash—was buried."

Noah considered this. "You know, if Filou's death was unplanned, you'd think they'd be loath to steal the bribe. It might look bad to the police."

"That's if they confessed. Which they didn't. Or there wouldn't be any mystery."

"And if they didn't come clean about the murder, they'd hardly tell the police about the bribe."

"What about your idea that they were afraid the bills were marked?"

Noah thought it over. "Doesn't compute. It's not like they belonged to the bank—Filou either procured them from a personal account, or from his company."

"We don't know where Filou obtained them. We don't even know how much it was."

"Give me a moment." He stood up and paced across to the wisteria bower. A long tendril of vine snaked down and caught in his hair. In the middle of untangling it, he stopped. "That's it: he must have had a business, and therefore a record of incorporation. Financial statements might pinpoint a large withdrawal from his account. *Ha.*"

"Harry was going to contact some of Filou's colleagues. They'd be able to corroborate that."

"If Audrey returned it, the statements might show that too."

Sophie shook her head. "If Filou withdrew the funds illegally, for a bribe, and then Audrey and James returned it, it would put them in jeopardy."

"If they did it anonymously, there'd be no hint it was ever gone."

"Enough! I'm getting all muddled." Sophie took a deep breath. "We only know about the bribe because Ian and Kendrick told us. We need to authenticate their statement."

"There you go. This is a job for our favorite private dick." Noah got up and pulled his phone from his pocket.

Sophie called after him. "And tell him to get a move on. I'm hungry."

A minute later, Noah came back and sat down on the bench. "Harry thinks it's a good idea. He's been tracking Filou since he left Montreal in 1915."

"Filou was French Canadian?"

"That's what Harry says. He should be able to follow the money trail." He stood up. "By the way, he says he's busy and can't make it."

"Oh really." *I knew we shouldn't have said we'd wait.*

He patted her hand. "Are you up for a road trip tomorrow?"

"Are we going to the Smithsonian?"

"Uh-uh, they're closed. A water main broke under the Natural History Museum. Until they get the water back on, we are unfettered."

"So where do you propose we head?"

He warbled, "Won't you let me take you on a sea cruise?"

"Huh?"

"How about a trek to the last working ferry on the Potomac River, in use since at least 1790?"

"Okay… What's it called?"

"White's Ferry."

"That's where Filou's car was found, wasn't it?" Sophie was surprised to find she was happy to forgo the museum in favor of more sleuthing. "Sounds like fun."

"Not as much fun as what I plan to do this evening."

"What's that?" But Sophie quickly gleaned the meaning in Noah's eyes. She held her hand out. "I'm game."

****

White's Ferry, Wednesday morning

Sophie zoomed in on her phone. "Okay, you go left here on Darnestown Road. It should say Route 28."

"Got it."

"*Brr*. I'm glad I remembered to bring a sweater."

Noah turned the heater on. "The air's chilly for this time of year, isn't it?" They drove through countryside speckled with hamlets and villages until they reached Poolesville. Sophie hoped they'd stop to admire the several historic buildings, but Noah pressed on. "How much farther?"

She checked the map. "This road turns into White's Ferry Road. The river's a little over six miles from here."

Precisely at the six-mile mark, their way was blocked by a five-barred gate. "What's this?"

"The river should be just over that hill. Does this mean the ferry's closed?"

"Why don't you hop out and see?"

"Okay." Sophie bypassed the barrier and walked down the hill. At the water's edge, wooden posts reared out of the water, a few splintery planks of decking still hanging from them. Tied to one of the pilings was a one-car ferry. She turned and yelled, "The boat's here. Maybe it doesn't run on Wednesdays." She hiked back to the car.

Noah pointed at a blue building a few hundred feet away. "That's a restaurant. Maybe they'll know."

Unfortunately it was closed too. "Didn't we pass a country store a mile or so back? Let's try there."

The store was little more than a wooden shack whose outer walls were decorated with cigarette posters and license plates. A huge green inflatable dinosaur gazed down at them from the tin roof. Noah pointed at two decrepit gas pumps, their nozzle-less hoses hanging limply. "This must have been a Sinclair station. Cool."

An old man rocked on the front porch, the chair creaking loudly. His white, frizzy hair stood in stark contrast to his smooth ebony skin. He directed them inside. "Curly'll help you."

Curly proved to be a seventy-year-old the size of a Pittsburgh Steeler. Sophie was not surprised that he was as bald as a worn-out football. He wiped his hands on an apron whose original color was long forgotten and led them back outside. "Beautiful day, eh?"

"Yes, it is. We were wondering what the schedule is for the ferry."

"Ain't one."

"What do you mean?"

"Stopped runnin' in 2021." His face took on an angry scowl that looked like it was used so often it was on retainer. "Goddamn city people. Decided we couldn't have a ferry 'cause the boat was named after a Confederate general. Racist they said. Even took the monument away." He ground his teeth. "Man's been dead hunnerd fifty years. You'd think the libs would have somethin' better to go after."

"Now, Curly." The man in the rocking chair spoke up. "Don't go misleadin' these nice folks. You know Dagwood Burns claimed the ferry dock was trespassin' on his land. Lawyers huddled, and sure 'nough one of 'em found this plat that showed Dagwood's property line. They tole Jackson—he used to pilot the barge—he had to quit."

"So some dirtbag lawyer"—Curly made air quotes—"finds a plat, Moe. So what? The crossing was there long before Dagwood. Long before the farm, for that matter." His voice rose. "This was the only ferry left on the Potomac. How're people supposed to get over to Leesburg now? They have to slog all the way up to Point of Rocks and back down. That's an extra thirty, thirty-five miles." He waved his hand toward the road. "Use'ta see some eight hundred cars pass here every day. This store did bang-up business back then. Sure did." He wiped his nose on his apron. "Even Darnestown's near a ghost town. People don't wanna live in the country no more."

Sophie felt sorry for him. "The barge is still tied up at that little pier. Is there any chance the ferry will start up again?"

Both men shook their heads. Moe's head continued to shake a few minutes after Curly's had stopped. "Old man Burns is adamant. He says he wants to plant an orchard there at the landing."

Moe spat in the dust at his feet. "Ever since his old lady kicked the bucket, he's been ornery as shi—er, a goat."

Noah had been tapping his foot. "Actually, we were looking for information on a crime."

Curly and his friend jerked to attention. "Crime?"

"It happened right here in 1920."

To Sophie's astonishment, neither looked awestruck. "Uh-huh. Kidnapping? Murder? Arson?" Moe glanced at Curly. "Espionage?"

Sophie had a fleeting image of a tiny hamlet wracked with Sodom- and Gomorrah-like violence—flames engulfing buildings and people rioting at the single stoplight, while apocalyptic horsemen rampaged through the yards and pirates lobbed fireballs from their corsair on the river. She gulped.

Noah said. "We're not sure. An empty Hispano-Suiza sedan was found by the side of the road near the ferry. That's a luxury sedan—"

"We know what a Hispano-Suiza is, young man. My granddaddy had an H6."

Moe recited: "Hispano-Suiza, founded 1898 in Spain. Produced the 45 CR, considered the first sports car ever built."

Curly took up the thread. "They began making the H6 after World War One, featuring an inline six-cylinder overhead camshaft engine modeled on its aircraft engines. Most of the luxury market was in France, and some operations moved there in 1911. Trucks, cars, and plane engines continued to be manufactured in Spain until 1946."

"You know your cars, sir." Noah was impressed. "I work for the Smithsonian. I might suggest a show to the folks at the Air and Space Museum." He looked at Moe. "So how many H6s were sold in the US?"

"Not many. The H6 was built in France and

exported to England."

Curly chimed in. "They loved them in Great Britain. Remember, Moe, when we was readin' P. G. Wodehouse in our book club?"

Moe chuckled. "Oh, yeah. Didn't Bertie Wooster's aunt tool around in one? There's one featured in an Agatha Christie book too."

Noah started. "It wouldn't have been *The Mysterious Affair at Styles*, would it?"

Moe furrowed his brow. "Nope. I recollect it was *The Seven Dials Mystery*. Right, Curly?"

"Right. Only a rare few of the elite owned the car in America."

Sophie saw her chance. "So if one were to appear here, it would have caused a sensation, even in 1920."

"Sure did," Moe said proudly. "Written up in all the local papers. Had some sharks circling—swearing it were theirs but didn' have no papers to prove it. Police finally came and hauled it away."

"What happened to it?"

Curly answered. "Stayed on the police lot for a year. When no one claimed it, Grandpa bought it at auction for a hunnerd dollars." He ogled Noah. "You got any idee what happened to the driver?"

"That's what we're here to find out. It was owned by a Charles Filou, a French Canadian who disappeared in April 1920."

"You think he was killed?"

"Maybe."

"*Hmm.* Lemme go check my files." He went inside.

Moe sniggered. "Curly's got boxes an' boxes of clippings. He's collected 'em on every newsworthy event in Montgomery County going back to Colonial times. We call him the Archivist."

Sophie and Noah eyed each other. "I see we came to the right place."

A few minutes later, Curly came out with a folder. Inside were newspaper articles inserted into clear plastic sleeves. "This is all I have on the car. It was discovered the afternoon of April 19, 1920, stowed behind a brush pile at the top of the hill."

"Did the car show any signs of having been in an accident?"

"Nope."

"They didn't find any…er…money?"

Curly looked at Sophie sharply. "You insinuatin' this Filou robbed a bank or somethin'?"

"No." She hesitated. "Well, to be honest, we don't know."

Curly turned a clipping over. "Says here nothing was found in the car except some old clothes." He added gratuitously, "No corpse."

Moe nodded wisely. "I'm guessin' they would have reported that."

"A'course, back then they didn't have all the high tech to pick up latents and such."

Noah asked, "Does your grandfather still have the car?"

"Grandpa? He passed twenty years ago. Mebbe twenty-five. I forget."

"And the car?"

Curly shrugged. "He sold it years ago to a junk dealer. Why?"

Noah made a wry face. "I don't know. It would be nice to examine it—maybe the police missed a clue."

Curly didn't have to say what he was obviously

thinking. *Amateurs*.

"Well, thank you for the information."

"No problem. Sorry about the ferry." He started inside, grousing. "Bloody libs, demolishin' our history…"

As they left, they could hear Moe shouting after him, "It's damned Dagwood, Curly!"

Noah waited until they were in the car to burst out laughing.

"What's so funny?"

"Those guys. Moe and Curly. Would you have said when we stopped at a country store straight out of *Deliverance* that we'd meet two of the most erudite men in North America?"

Sophie presumed it was a rhetorical question.

They had been driving for a few miles when Noah slammed his hands on the steering wheel. "Damn! We're so close. We know who killed Filou and why—"

"But we don't have a body, and we don't have a treasure… *Hmm*, treasure…" Sophie stuck her chin in her hand.

Noah made a sharp turn off the road at the entrance to a roadhouse. The sign said Beagle's Food and Drink. "Hungry?"

"Do you have to ask?"

"I've heard this place has good old-fashioned home-cooking."

"As long as they have wine I'm happy."

"Sure they do. They got red; they got white." He grinned.

"You're saying I'm better off ordering beer." She followed him inside.

The place was empty of customers. A waitress in a

pink-striped uniform drifted over and dropped hand-written menus on the table. "Hep you?"

"Two of your finest lagers please."

"Two PBRs, coming up."

He scanned the menu. "Looks like chicken is their specialty."

"Well, Maryland is famous for its fried chicken. I'll have that."

"Me too." He closed the menu and ordered for them both. When the waitress had brought their beers, he said, "So what do we do now?"

"We're at an impasse. Unless Harry finds something."

"What's his task again?"

"I forget. Tracing Filou, I think. Locating his colleagues? Or a body?"

"Yes, but whose body is he looking for? Filou's or Harry Senior's?"

Before she could answer, Noah's phone buzzed. "Hey, Harry. We were just talking about you. We hit a dead end here at White's Ferry—literally... You do? Swell. Come by tonight? Oh. All right, we'll wait for your call."

"What did he say?"

"He's onto something, but he has to follow up on a lead. He says he'll get back to us when he's run it to ground."

"Run what to ground?"

"He didn't say."

Sophie's mood dipped.

Chapter Thirty

Good advice is always certain to be ignored, but that's no reason not to give it.

~Agatha Christie

Smithsonian Museum, Thursday, May 16

Noah closed the last drawer. "Okay, those were the Aurignacian hand axes."

Sophie put on a brave face. "They were riveting."

"Yes, well, they're more stimulating than the pottery shards from Tepe Yahya, as I'm sure you'll agree. Come on, I've got something a little more engaging for you." He stopped at a door. "This is one of our conservation rooms. Most of the work is done at our facility in Suitland, but when we're preparing a show we need labs on site."

Two women sat across from each other at a long table. Between them lay a dazzling yellow silk robe. "Ladies, may I introduce my friend Sophie Childress." The older woman, wearing a tartan smock, her hair pulled back in a severe bun, gave Noah a half bow. "Mrs. Tetweiler is our senior seamstress. They're getting our stock of Chinese Imperial robes ready for a new exhibition." Noah indicated the younger woman. "And this is Laura. She's our intern."

Sophie watched as Laura laid very fine netting over

a section of the material and began to tack it down with tiny stitches. Mrs. Tetweiler explained. "This robe was worn by a member of the imperial family in the Qing Dynasty. It is over two hundred years old. While it's been carefully preserved, some of the silk is disintegrating. The netting will hold it together so we don't have to use modern silk. We want to keep it as close to its original condition as is feasible."

"It's stunning." Sophie admired the gown. The wide sleeves were embroidered with birds and planets. A large blue dragon, its mouth spewing fire, ranged across the chest.

"It's called a dragon robe or *long pao*. In Chinese mythology, the dragon helped to create the world. The emperor was deemed its earthly incarnation."

"Are the colors significant?"

"Oh yes, everything has a meaning. The colors relate to the elements: wood, fire, earth, metal, and water. Yellow symbolizes earth, or the center." She pointed at images of a pheasant and mountains. "The mountains represent stability; the pheasant stands for harmony. They are two of the twelve auspicious elements of imperial authority."

Noah thanked the ladies and led Sophie out of the room. "So what do you think?"

"It's certainly not dull." She gazed at him. "You're lucky to be in the midst of all this history."

He gazed back. "I'm glad I could show it to you."

It took Sophie a minute to realize that they were surrounded by a large group of elementary school children. The teacher tried to make herself heard above the squeals and yelps. "Children, please don't jostle these nice people. Come along. Next stop is the Hope

Diamond!"

The crowd ebbed and flowed around them as though they were a tree fallen into a rushing river. When the hubbub died down, Noah took Sophie's arm. "Let's go home."

The words jolted her. *Home*? It struck her that she and Noah had kind of skipped the getting-to-know-each-other part. Alarm bells jingled. *It's too much, too soon.* "Um, I think I need to go back to my apartment."

"Oh? Okay. But remember Harry may be coming by. You don't want to miss that."

"He didn't say when, though, did he? I thought he was pursuing some lead?"

Noah grudgingly agreed. "All right. Where's your car?"

"Oh dear, I left it at the Hall."

"I can take you to your apartment, then we'll drive back to Marmion Grove together."

"No!" Sophie suddenly needed space. Except during the sale, she'd spent almost every waking moment with Noah. She had to think this through before things went too far. *Haven't they already, my dear?* It didn't matter; she felt an urgent desire to be alone. "I'll figure out a way to get up there tomorrow, okay?"

He gave her a long, speculative look. "No problem." He didn't say another word on the way to her apartment. When he let her off, he solemnly shook her hand.

She watched him drive away. *What have I done?* Fear shot through her like a hollow-point bullet. *Is he simply complying with my request…or is this goodbye? Is the damage irreparable?* She trudged up the steps and buzzed herself in. *Does he understand?*

Her apartment felt sad, as though it reckoned she

had forsaken it. *When was the last time I slept here?* It had to be days ago. "Hello, home. I'm back." She fed Jelly the goldfish. *I swear he's grown another inch.* Then she plopped on the sofa and sorted through her mail. Nothing but catalogues and solicitations. Wait—a card from her mother. Cloth-draped cross and Easter lilies.

"Dear Sophie, Reverend Pfister asked after you at the service. He wondered when you were going to move west to be with us. Ha-ha. Everyone says hello. I hope all is well. He is Risen!"

Oh my God I forgot to call them on Easter!

She spent a productive hour feeling guilty. By six o'clock, hunger overruled the shame. She opened the refrigerator. A carton of moo shu pork and half a cucumber were its sole occupants. She sliced the cucumber and warmed the noodles up in the microwave. "I shall pair it with a plucky little rosé." Setting the food and bottle on the coffee table, she watched several different news shows, switching channels whenever one went to a commercial, and deliberately kept her mind empty of thoughts of Noah. When her eyes closed for the fourth time, she went to bed and slept for a solid eight hours.

The telephone woke her. "Hello?"

"I think you need to get up here right away."

****

Peveril Hall, Friday morning

In the end, Noah came down and fetched Sophie back to Marmion Grove. "It would take hours by bus and you've missed the nine twenty commuter train."

On the drive up, Sophie searched in vain for a way to bring up her behavior of the day before. Noah studiously avoided the subject. They arrived to find

Harry making a cup of coffee.

"Your coffee machine only makes single servings," he complained.

"Sorry. Mother only drank one cup a day."

He grumbled. "I would have filled a carafe if I could find one." He held up his mug. "Mind if I warm this up?"

"Not at all." Noah filled two more mugs while Harry reheated his in the microwave. "All set? Let's go into the living room."

Harry indicated the sofa. Noah and Sophie sat down together. "Okay, now Sophie's here, I can tell you my news."

By this time, Sophie had relapsed into dwelling on her love life. Harry bleated impatiently, "Are you listening?"

She straightened. "I am. What is it?"

"I think I made a breakthrough. Or at least I have a strong lead."

"To Filou?"

"Maybe. And to the bribe money."

They both sat forward.

"I had a nice chat with Oscar Northcutt."

"So? We already talked to him."

"Well, he was a little more loquacious with me." He tapped the bulge in his pocket.

Sophie gasped. "You didn't threaten him, did you? He's just an old man!"

"I didn't threaten him; I just made it clear that I needed the truth. Even though he never lived here, he did oversee the demolition of the old railroad station."

"Yes, we know that. He told us. In fact, *you* told us the same thing." Noah began to rise. "Is that it?"

"No." Harry turned crafty. "Did you know about the

rumored treasure?"

Sophie answered. "You mean in the station? Oscar told us they found nothing."

"Right, but it made me think. Audrey and James wouldn't have risked taking Filou's body far. It could be buried somewhere in the Grove."

Noah thought this over. "Ian and Kendrick intimated James had dumped the corpse near the car."

"Too risky. Someone might have seen them on the long ride—or near the ferry."

Sophie stared at Harry. "Oscar told you where Filou is?"

"I wish." Harry wrinkled his nose. "Either he's a really good liar, or he has no clue. But—"

Noah stood up. "So all this hoopla is to tell us you don't have any news?" He started to stomp out of the living room.

An idea presented itself to Sophie. "Wait! Oscar mentioned that his mother was the head of the Marmion Grove Garden Club."

Noah shook his head. "No, it was Ian who told us that."

"Oops, yeah. Anyway, she was in charge of the beautification of town public areas. The ladies planted shrubberies around the Post Office."

Harry grinned. "Now you're cooking."

Noah almost knocked his coffee cup over. "Are you saying what I think you're saying?"

He nodded. "The plants are still there. I propose we check them out."

Noah was dubious. "I can't see Peggy Dane letting us dig up her gardens."

Harry said impatiently, "A metal detector might do

the trick."

Sophie put her hands on her hips. "What good would that do? It wouldn't ping on cloth. Or bones."

Harry barked, "Work with me. It *would* ping on metal."

"Metal?"

"Metal, as in coin. Treasure's more important than the hundred-year-old corpse of a scuzzy flim-flam man."

She began to bluster when Noah interrupted. "Never mind that. I'm betting Filou was fully clothed when he went in the ground."

Sophie almost blushed. "I doubt that Mrs. Northcutt would strip the man she'd just killed."

Noah ignored her. "A gentleman of the nineteen twenties would surely have metal somewhere on his person. When were zippers invented?" He started to type into his phone.

Sophie finished off her coffee. "I—"

"1913!" Noah's eyes shone. "Plenty of time for Monsieur Filou—a man of progressive tastes—to acquire a 'universal fastener.' " He looked at Harry.

Harry rose on his toes. "Brilliant! I'll secure the detector and we'll meet back here… Shall we say midnight?"

The others were less euphoric. Noah's voice held a touch of whine. "Does it have to be midnight again? How about, say, ten o'clock? Closer to my bedtime?"

Harry shook his head. "The restaurant in the building doesn't stop serving until nine thirty. There will be stragglers. We can't go until we're sure the place is empty."

"Mrs. Dane lives in the apartment above."

"She does?"

"Yeah. Alan Dane bought it in 1920. His granddaughter Peggy runs the post office." Noah smiled reminiscently. "I grew up with Rusty Dane—Peggy's son."

"Nineteen twenty seems to be a popular year around here."

Harry's remark was offhand, but it brought Sophie up short. "You don't suppose Mr. Dane…"

"What?"

"Could he have observed Audrey and James with Filou's body?"

Noah's brow crinkled. "Surely if he'd seen someone rolling a corpse into a hole in the middle of the night, he would have notified the police."

Harry shook his head. "I checked all the police records around the time. There was no mention of a citizen reporting sketchy activity."

"Maybe he didn't then, but if we wake Peggy up she's sure to call the cops."

"Then we'd better be very quiet."

When Harry had left, the two sat, each absorbed by his own thoughts. Noah spoke first. "You okay?"

"Yes. Why?" She was playing for time.

"I…uh… Sophie, am I…am I pressing too hard? Did I scare you?"

The rush of relief that he understood was overwhelming. "Oh Noah, it's just that we've been on this roller coaster trying to solve all these mysteries. I don't think we've had time to focus on how we feel about each other."

He took her in his arms. "Sweetheart, we have plenty of time. Once we sort through this mare's nest, we can relax and take it slow. Would that be acceptable?"

He looked at her anxiously. "I don't want to lose you."

The pressure off, Sophie managed to give Noah a taste of what would come when she was *really* sure.

****

Dane Circle, Saturday, wee hours

Sophie whispered, "The lights have gone out in the building."

Noah whispered back, "Did you check all the way around the house? The bedroom is in the back."

"You mean upstairs? Yes. All is dark."

"Shall we proceed then?"

Harry held up the metal detector. "Let's start on the side away from the circle, by the tracks."

"Why? It's kind of spooky over there." Sophie shivered. "And what happens if a train comes through?"

"It's not like we're going to be *on* the tracks. You don't want to be noticed by someone out walking their dog, do you?"

Noah touched her shoulder. "Come on, let's get started."

Sophie kept her flashlight pointed at the ground, lighting the way. Noah toted a shovel, and Harry shuffled behind them with the metal detector. They had gone a few yards when the machine started beeping. Sophie held the flashlight over the spot while Noah dug into a bed of azaleas. He groused, "Peggy's going to kill me."

"*Shh.*"

They heard a clunk. "I think I hit something." He tugged a large pebble out.

"Keep going."

Another five inches down and he struck paydirt. He rose off his knees and held an object up. "It's only a trowel."

Harry wasn't deterred. "Coulda been used to dig the grave."

Noah shook his head. "It would have taken forever, and I'm fairly certain Audrey and James would have been in a hurry. Besides, this looks fairly new." He rubbed some of the dirt off. The stainless steel shimmered in the moonlight.

"All right, let's move on. I think we should try the annual beds—it'll be quicker and the ground will be softer."

Sophie objected. "Annual beds would be replaced every year—hence the name. No, Audrey would choose a spot which she knew wouldn't be disturbed for a long time—like a hedge or shrubs."

Harry huffed. "Well, the azaleas were a bust. How about the backyard?"

"There's no yard—only a paved parking lot and a dumpster." Noah walked past the entrance. "Let's try the other side, next to the tennis courts."

Harry squinted in the gloom. "They need a street light here."

"Yes indeedy." Noah's voice held both amusement and a touch of contempt. "Because, naturally, we *want* to be visible to everyone while we excavate Mrs. Dane's flower beds looking for cadavers."

"All right, all right."

Sophie wasn't sure if Harry sounded so gruff because he was nettled or because he was out of breath. She noted the oversized outline of the man against the faint light. *He's clearly not in the best of shape.*

"How about this?" Noah stopped at a low boxwood hedge. "It's been here since I was a little boy. Boxwood is very slow-growing and can live for hundreds of years."

"Worth testing." Harry swung the metal detector over the bush. It beeped. "Aha."

Noah began to trench along the edging. He'd gotten down about a foot when the shovel clanged. "Ooh, this could be it."

Sophie knelt beside him, using the trowel to scrape the earth off. A minute later she yanked a leather pouch from the soil. When she shook it, it jingled.

Harry snatched it from her.

"Hey!"

He loosened the tie and several shiny coins fell onto the ground. "Well, well. Silver dollars."

Chapter Thirty-One

Where large sums of money are concerned, it is advisable to trust nobody.

~Agatha Christie

Dane Circle, Saturday, May 18

The three gazed at the coins lying on the grass. Harry bent down and scooped them up. He counted them out. "Twenty-two silver dollars."

Silver dollars. Sophie brooded. *Where did I hear about silver dollars?*

Noah measured the stack. "Doesn't seem like much for a bribe. Maybe they're some special issue, or the product of a minting error. I hear those can be worth a lot."

"We'll see." Harry didn't sound convinced. He tucked them in his jacket pocket.

"Hey! We should at least share them."

"We'll divvy them up when we get back to the house. Let's not stop now." He turned the metal detector on again. "That's odd. It's still beeping on the same spot."

Noah picked up the shovel. "Maybe there's something buried deeper down."

A few minutes later he struck mud. "Damn. We've hit the water table."

Harry peered into the hole. "Something's down there. Looks like the corner of a box. Grab it, Noah."

Noah glared at Harry. "Funny, I don't remember anyone giving *you* the authority to delegate the dirty jobs." When Harry continued to stand, he spat out, "Kneel down and help me. Now."

Harry snorted but laid down the metal detector. "These are my best pants."

I'd hate to see his worst pants.

"And your point?"

"*Hmph.*" Harry slowly bent forward, bracing himself on the edge of the hole across from Noah.

Noah tugged at the box. "It won't budge."

"Get your hand under it and pry it up." He ducked at Noah's menacing look, and gingerly slipped one hand into the muck and under the metal. It made a squishy, sucking sound. "Gross."

Noah took hold of the other corner. "Do you have a purchase on it? Now heave!"

The two men huffed and puffed, alternating curses with groans, before finally freeing a large metal box from its bed. Noah dragged it onto the grass.

Sophie wiped the sticky goo off the latch with the edge of her sweatshirt. "It's pretty rusty." She tried to open it. "Locked."

"Jimmy it, will you?" Harry's voice was sharp with suppressed excitement.

"With what?" Noah sat back on his haunches. "Say, what constituted a decent bribe in 1920 anyway?"

"Bribe? No, it's…" Harry shut his mouth with a snap. "You think this could be the money Filou offered Hiram?"

"What else could it be?" Noah looked at Sophie.

"Ian was convinced Audrey buried it with the body."

"But he had no proof."

"Wait a minute… The body." Noah gazed down at the hole and rose to his feet. He picked up his shovel.

Harry said quickly, "Let's get the box open first. If Filou's skeleton is down there, it can wait." He hurried off into the night.

Noah called, "Where are you going?"

Harry's voice wafted from out of the mist. "Gotta get some tools."

While they waited, Sophie tried to lift the box and dropped it. "It's awful heavy for paper."

A voice came from behind them. "That's because it's filled with gold bars."

Noah spun around toward Harry, who stood just outside the circle of light. "What are you talking about, Harry?"

Sophie turned the flashlight on their companion. "What's that in your hand?"

Harry waved the gun—a long-barreled Colt revolver—at them. "Step over there, would you?" They retreated to the front porch. "That's better." He rolled a dolly over to the box. "I'll just be taking this off your hands. You can find your way home, can't you?"

Noah blurted, "So you were after treasure all along. So much for filial loyalty. I should have known."

Harry was unruffled. "Not true. I was following my grandfather's trail."

"What does he have to do with the box?"

"On the night of April 17, 1920, the mail train heading from the DC Armory to Frederick, Maryland, was carrying a hundred thousand dollars' worth of gold. My grandfather was the boss of the gang that stole it."

He said it proudly. "The gold was never found. I'm betting this is it."

"Wait a minute. I thought you said the police recovered the loot?"

"I said they recovered the *payroll*. I…um…forgot to mention the train was also carrying gold bullion." His voice was positively jaunty.

Sophie noticed a light go on upstairs in the post office building. *Did we wake Mrs. Dane?* She regarded Harry. *Keep him focused.* "What made you determine it was buried here?"

"The holdup took place as the train left Kensington station. Next stop is Marmion Grove. It's not rocket science."

Noah interrupted. "You say Harry Senior robbed the train. What happened to him? Why didn't he come back for the swag?"

"He and his cronies planned to stash it here, then wait a year before coming back for it. They had a hideout in Harper's Ferry. They holed up there."

"And?"

"The gang…uh…had a difference of opinion. They cut Harry out of the deal."

"They killed him?"

"So I gather. All they ever found was a wallet and a finger."

Sophie concentrated on squelching the image that immediately rose to mind.

Harry was still talking. "However, in that wallet was a slip of paper with the names Peveril Hall and Agnes Reilly. I figure Harry Senior had already laid the groundwork—schmoozing Agnes and scoping out the best place to bury the haul."

Noah cocked an eyebrow. "The wallet is in your possession?"

Harry smirked. "It's a family heirloom."

This doesn't add up. "How do you know the gang didn't just take the gold with them?"

For the first time, Harry didn't sound as confident. "Because the...parts were found up in Harper's Ferry." He rallied. "That means they stuck to the original plan."

"What makes you think he was the gang leader? Seems strange they'd take *him* out rather than the other way around." Noah's eyes drifted to the post office building. Sophie hoped he'd noticed the light too.

"Actually, the police had lifted fingerprints on the door to the mail car. They couldn't identify them back in 1920, but I got hold of their files. By then the case had long been closed, and I was free to follow up all the clues without anyone suspecting my motives. I'd saved a set of my grandfather's prints from a book he left behind." He beamed. "They matched."

Sophie was reproachful. "Noah's right. You never wanted to exonerate Harry. It was all about the treasure."

"You catch on quick."

"So you've known all along the stuff was in Marmion Grove. How come you sent us on those wild goose chases then? To White's Ferry and to the various Northcutts?"

"It gave me time to search the house." He snickered. "It rapidly became clear that I could use you to ferret out information instead of killing you."

Sophie gasped. "The elderberry wine. You poisoned it. You tried to knock Noah off." Fury surged through her.

Harry contrived to look offended. "Hey, it didn't kill

293

him, did it? That's because I only added enough to incapacitate him." He winked. "I thought it was a nice touch to use rat poison—reminded you of Agnes and her suspicions. Put you off the scent." He splayed his fingers. "Turns out it's pretty hard to find. Cost me an arm and a leg."

Noah seemed confused. "But we hadn't yet met you when I drank the wine."

"I told you, I'd been watching you for days. I knew all about the letter to the constable."

"You beast!"

"Hey, I'd like to think I contributed some meaning to your petty lives in the form of a mystery to occupy you. Although"—he leered—"I take it you found other types of recreation along the way. Now, if you don't mind, I'll take my prize and vamoose."

He tried to lift the box with one hand while keeping the revolver aimed at Sophie and Noah. "Ooph. This might take two hands." He waved the gun at them. "You two, move all the way over to the shelter." Once they'd obeyed, he put the gun down and fumbled with the box.

Sophie was desperately trying to come up with a way to tackle him before he had time to pick up the gun and shoot when a voice called from the darkness. "And what might you be doing, Mr. Quayle?"

The voice was familiar. Before she could put a finger on its owner's identity, Oscar Northcutt emerged into the light. He held a vicious-looking SIG Sauer and was pointing it at Harry. "Well?"

Harry didn't turn a hair. "Hello, Oscar. We were following up on your idea." He managed a weak grin. "Looking for buried treasure."

"Oh yeah? I don't care about any treasure. You're

trespassing on private property. Now, kick the pistol over here."

Harry did so.

Sophie's voice was faint. "Are you going to call the police?"

"I will in good time. First I want to make something plain to Mr. Quayle here." He pointed the gun at his chest. "I know who you are, Harry. And I know what you're up to. I won't let you get away with it, see? You leave Marmion Grove alone. There's no treasure here. It's all an old wives' tale."

"Oh, yeah? Then what's in the box?" Harry shoved it with his toe.

Oscar glanced quickly at it. "It's nothing. Just some old junk. Peggy says Rusty used to bury mouse skeletons and snake skins in her garden."

"You're out to lunch, you are!" Harry was miffed. "My grandfather robbed the B&O in 1920 and buried the plunder here." He turned suddenly sly. "If you help us, we'll cut you in."

Oscar's eyes narrowed. "How do I know you're telling the truth?"

"Why else would we be digging here?"

"I don't know. But I want you to stop. You show me what information you have, and maybe we'll talk. Until then, no more digging."

Sophie was perplexed. "Why do you care so much about Mrs. Dane's garden?"

Noah added, "And how did you know we were here?"

Harry chimed in. "Yeah, it's the middle of the night. Shouldn't you be tucked up in bed in Glen Echo?"

"Never you mind. You're the ones in trouble." But

Oscar's voice faltered and his hand began to shake. "Beat it before I shoot."

Harry sighed. "It's your show. But—" He indicated the box. "What if we've already found it?" He began to wheedle. "Don't tell me you don't want to take a peek?"

Oscar was clearly in a quandary. "Okay, move away from the box." Harry joined Noah and Sophie. Oscar stood, shifting from one foot to the other. "I...uh..."

"Step aside, Oscar. We'll take it from here." All four whirled around. Ian and Kendrick appeared out of the shadows. Kendrick said, "Put the gun down, Dad. What on earth were you thinking?"

Oscar's face went pale in the light of the huge tactical flashlight Ian held. "I...uh... I was going to make a citizen's arrest. Peggy and I... Peggy Dane called me and said she heard someone clattering around outside. I promised to check it out for her."

"You came all the way from Cabin John?" Ian was incredulous.

"Um. No. I was"—his eyelashes fluttered— "visiting the Gardiners up the hill."

"Then how did Peggy know to call you?"

"We...uh...we're old friends. She called my cell phone. I told her I was in Marmion Grove, and she...begged me to help."

Ian gave him a hard stare, then gestured at the little trio standing a few feet away. "And these are the intruders?"

Oscar looked sheepish. "Uh-huh. Once I recognized Noah and his girl, I was going to tell Peggy who they were." He scuffed his feet. "But the fact remains they were mutilating her shrubbery."

"Us!" Harry exploded, startling everyone. "No way.

We caught Northcutt here with the shovel." He jabbed at said tool, propelling it a little closer to Oscar. "He's got some bee in his bonnet about buried treasure."

Sophie started to say something, but Noah poked her. "*Shh*. This is fascinating."

"But…"

He whispered, "There's a lot going on here. I want to see it play out."

Ian shone the light on the box. "Is this what Oscar was looking for?"

"We don't know. But when we happened on him, he drew his gun and held us up."

Oscar sputtered. "He's lying! I caught *them*! Ian, Kendrick. You've got to believe me."

The squeal of police sirens rent the air. Sophie sighed in relief. Oscar gulped and dropped the Sig Sauer. Noah picked up both guns and threw them in the trash can. Harry took a step back as though about to turn and run, but Kendrick's arm shot out and grasped his elbow. "Where do you think *you're* going?"

Ian was furious. "All right. Who called the police?"

"I did." Peggy Dane stood on the porch, hugging her pink flannel bathrobe closed. Beside her a tiny white dog growled.

Chapter Thirty-Two

To rush into explanations is always a sign of weakness.
~Agatha Christie

Dane Circle, Saturday, May 18

The little group stood frozen on the pavement. Harry—Kendrick still clinging to his arm—faced Oscar, while Ian stood on one side and Noah and Sophie on the other. Peggy loomed like an avenging angel above them, her pink robe flapping in the morning breeze.

The sirens continued to wail. Ian observed, "There's no shortcut into the Grove. They have to come down Rockville Pike and along Strathmore, so it should take another fifteen, twenty minutes to get here. What do you propose we do?"

Peggy called, her voice high and passionate. "Don't any of you dare leave. Max here is straining at his leash. He'd dearly love to take his pound of your flesh." The fluffy little dog at her feet yipped ferociously.

Noah held up a hand. "Before the cops descend on us, I'd like to hear from each of you."

Out of the corner of her eye, Sophie glimpsed Peggy cocking an eyebrow at Oscar. He gave an infinitesimal shake of his head. She motioned them inside. "Come on in where I can see you."

Sophie gestured at the box. "What about that?"

"We'll bring it with us." Noah took hold of the dolly. When Harry's face spasmed, he said firmly, "Ian will help me."

They trooped into the lobby, Max nipping at their heels. Two long tables lined the side walls, with a couple of wooden chairs grouped in a corner. An old-fashioned gumball machine stood to the right of the entrance.

Noah pushed the box under one of the tables. Oscar and Kendrick took the chairs; across from them were arrayed Harry, Noah, and Sophie. Ian perched on a table, and Peggy hovered by the steps to the mail room.

Harry spoke first. "Like I said, Oscar was looking for the treasure."

"What treasure?"

"The dough from a 1920 train heist. I had foolishly mentioned it to him, and my suspicion that it was buried somewhere close by. My grandfather Harry had a girlfriend in Marmion Grove. I found a note—"

"The note in the wallet with Harry's finger?"

Harry gaped at Sophie. "I don't know what you're talking about." Sophie stared back at him in disbelief. He went on blithely. "It was among my father's things. Harry Senior stated he was on the train when the robbers came through the cars. They got off at Marmion Grove, and he went after them."

"To demand a share?"

"No, *sir*. He was acting as a good Samaritan. He planned to inform the police."

Sophie marveled at his ability to look righteous while lying through his teeth. Noah gurgled. *Trying not to explode in gales of laughter?*

Harry, unruffled, continued smoothly. "See, my grandfather was engaged to be married. He was hoping to receive a reward for his actions."

Really?

Kendrick asked, "Did he see what they did with the box?"

"No. He lost them in the dark. But I figure it had to be close by the tracks. They wouldn't have taken it far." He glowered at Oscar. "Oscar here tried to horn in on our discovery, and he was willing to kill us for it."

Sophie stirred. "How can he horn in on the discovery if he was the one digging?"

Noah put a hand on her arm. "Shush. Wait."

Ian said, "Okay. Oscar? Your turn."

Oscar took several quick breaths. "That is a pack of disgusting lies. Yes, Harry told me about the train robbery. He claimed his grandfather participated in it, but he swore the haul had been recovered."

Sophie felt it necessary to elucidate. "He neglected to mention that the *banknotes* were recovered; the gold was not."

Oscar suddenly shifted his feet. Noah gave him a long look. "He didn't tell us about the gold. Did he tell you?"

"No! I stand by what I said before. I knew nothing about any treasure. The kids' stories were just that…stories. I didn't find anything here."

They all turned to Harry. "All right, which script are you going to stick with?"

Harry's face remained remarkably expressionless. "I told you the truth as far as I knew it. That was before I read the note."

Noah stirred. "So you're claiming that your grandfather was an innocent bystander now? He wasn't the gang's leader?"

Harry blinked. "Um. Well, I may have exaggerated his role just a tad before. To be perfectly frank—"

Frank?

"—he confessed to taking part—against his will—in the stickup. He said the confederates buried the gold and then marooned him, locked in a warehouse. He freed himself but was afraid for his life and escaped to California. He died a year ago."

Sophie's jaw fell open. *This man has a true gift!*

Oscar was staring bug-eyed at Harry. "You're kidding."

At this point, Noah decided to take a hand. "I'm sorry, Harry, but all three stories can't be true. Harry Senior can't at the same time have been an upstanding citizen, a gang lord, and a kidnapping victim. Nope, I'm going with your grandfather being the ringleader. They killed him in a dispute over division of the spoils."

Harry cackled loudly. "You bought that? It was the only way I could entice you into helping me."

"Well, why did you tell Oscar Harry was an accessory to the holdup?"

"I thought he had an idea where the stash was. I wanted to draw him out." He beamed. "Mission accomplished."

Oscar sputtered, "I have no interest in hot money. I'm an honest man."

Ian said gently, "Then why were you aiming a gun at them?"

"I…I…" Oscar's eyes strayed to Peggy. She raised a finger to her nose.

What is going on between them?

"I had to protect Audrey. I didn't want… I didn't want them to find…" He broke down and put his head in his hands.

The answer flashed in Sophie's brain. "You weren't looking for treasure. You know where Filou is buried, don't you?"

Noah took Oscar by the elbow. "Show us."

Kendrick opened the door. As they filed out, the bright light nearly blinded Sophie. *My God, we've been at this all night!* The sun peeked through a layer of grayish clouds. Down Rokeby Avenue a clutch of dog walkers stared toward them. The sirens, which unconsciously she'd tuned out, stopped suddenly as two patrol cars braked in front of them, their cherry lights revolving. A cop got out of the first one. "We got a 9-1-1 call? A prowler?"

Mrs. Dane stepped around the others. "It was from me, Officer."

The policeman looked over the little band bunched together on the front step. "Are these the perps?"

Ian extricated himself. "No. Mrs. Dane was mistaken. There were no intruders, Officer. She saw our flashlights and was worried." He shaded his eyes. "The one street lamp here is out."

"So there's no problem?"

"Actually…" Noah stepped forward. "We may have uncovered a crime."

The policeman's eyes opened wide. "What kind of crime?"

"Murder."

He turned and yelled. "Hey, Murray!"

The other cop rolled down his window. "What is it, Fred?"

"Come on over here. You gotta hear this."

Harry must have been edging toward his car,

because Kendrick grabbed him again. "Really, Quayle? Stick around for the show. It could be amusing."

Harry made a half-hearted attempt to wriggle out of Kendrick's grasp, then sighed deeply and followed the rest.

Sophie thought the second cop looked familiar. "Officer Kent? Weren't you staked out at Peveril Hall last month?"

The cheerful fellow, the beginnings of a pot belly straining the buttons on his uniform shirt, grinned. "Yes, ma'am. You can call me Murray." He tugged at his belt. "By the way, thanks for the double-stuffed. My favorite."

Fred took charge. "Okay…" He pivoted to Noah and pretended to lick the tip of his pencil. "What's your name, sir?"

"Noah Pennyman."

"Pennyman? You Vivian's boy?"

Sophie thought it was cute that everyone still referred to Noah as a "boy."

Noah didn't seem to appreciate it though. "Uh-huh."

Murray leaned in. "Okay, Mr. Pennyman. What did you want to show us?"

Noah's eyes bulged. "I…er…"

Sophie stepped up. "This is Oscar Northcutt." She pointed at the cowering man. "He knows where the body is."

"Body."

"Of Charles Filou, a French Canadian businessman."

Fred turned to Oscar. "Well?"

Oscar's face closed down. In the stubborn silence, Sophie's eyes roamed around Dane Circle. *It must be here somewhere.* Her gaze descended on the railroad shelter. It was nothing more than a covered bench, with a newspaper dispenser and a laminated sign displaying the train schedule. Surrounding it on three sides were golden-leaved Japanese spirea shrubs, with clumps of pink sweet william and royal blue petunias tucked into the empty spaces.

The cop remarked, "Nice garden. Who maintains it?"

Peggy answered. "The Women's Garden Club."

Sophie blinked. *That's it!*

Noah must have come to the same conclusion, for he spun around to Ian. "Audrey Northcutt was head of the garden club in 1920, wasn't she?"

Ian shrugged. "Yeah. So?"

"The club maintained landscaping on all public property. That would include Dane Circle." Noah pointed. "Not just the post office, but the railroad station."

"But Oscar destroyed the landscaping along with the station."

Oscar nodded. "I bulldozed the whole thing."

Sophie gave him a long look. "Did you now?" She turned to Murray. "Oscar told us he hadn't found anything in the debris, but I'll venture that was a lie."

Harry said eagerly, "You mean he found the cache?"

"No. A skeleton."

Peggy sucked in a noisy breath.

They stood staring at the bushes. Finally, Noah said, "We should dig."

Ian agreed reluctantly. "I reckon we have to."

Peggy Dane held up a hand. "We need permission from George first."

"Who's George?"

"George Weatherby. Our mayor. This whole circle belongs to the town. You can't just excavate anywhere you want."

The men shuffled their feet. Finally, Fred said, "Look here, we have probable cause to consider this a crime scene. Murray, get Captain Hinckley on the horn—see if we need a warrant. If he thinks the mayor should be informed, he can contact him."

Murray returned after a minute, clicking his phone off. "He says we don't require a search warrant since it's on public property, but to get permission from the mayor to be on the safe side. If we find anything, we're to secure the scene."

There was a moment of uncertainty. The dog walkers closed in. "Hey, Peggy, what's going on?"

"Never you mind, Matthew Crockett. You neither, Angela."

They sauntered by, casting inquiring looks. Noah turned to Mrs. Dane. "We could use another shovel. Do you have an extra?"

"Certainly. I'll get it."

"And maybe a tarp to hold the plants and soil."

"I'll help you." Sophie followed Peggy around the back of the building. Peggy unlocked a shed and drew out a long-handled spade and a folded tarp. Sophie asked tentatively, "Do you think they'll find anything?"

Peggy chortled. "You'd be astounded how many bodies are buried in a small town. This wouldn't be the first."

Bodies. "Um, Mrs. Dane? Oscar said you and he were old friends. That's why you called him. Has he…has he told you anything he's not telling us?"

Peggy's response was sudden and dramatic. She flushed as pink as her bathrobe and stood stock still. Eyes glittering, she snapped, "I don't know what you're talking about."

Sophie plunged on. "I noticed you two exchanging…um…signals."

The older woman fingered the top button of her robe nervously. "This can't go beyond these walls."

Sophie refrained from pointing out they were outdoors. "I understand."

Peggy's voice dropped. "Oscar and I… We are… We were…"

Sophie saw the light. "You two are—"

She cut her off. "That's all you need to know."

"So Oscar didn't just happen to be in the neighborhood."

"No." Peggy's color gradually returned to normal. "Here, take this tarp, and I'll bring the spade."

When they returned, Noah and Ian had their jackets off. "George says go for it."

Oscar lurched forward. "No!"

Kendrick held him back. "It's for the best, Dad. We've kept the secret long enough."

The policeman looked at them in consternation. "Secret?"

"A family tragedy."

Sophie wondered if they were going to come up with yet another whopper. *This family is the slickest bunch of dissemblers I've ever seen. Aside from Harry, that is.*

Noah and Ian set to, Noah on the south side and Ian on the north. "Let's hope it's not under the shelter itself."

The mound of dirt on the tarp rose higher and higher. The sun was reaching its zenith when Ian's spade struck something. "Help me here, Noah."

They scrabbled in the dirt. "Wait—stop! It looks like a hand."

Peggy turned her face away. The others looked on. "Be careful! That's the arm bone. Oh, and a leg. Is that a hat?"

Murray got a whisk broom from his patrol car. "Brush away the soil from its head. Be careful!" Noah did so. They stood back.

"Huh."

"Huh."

The skeleton that lay exposed still wore the tattered remains of denim overalls. A ball cap covered its skull. "Pretty sure it's a male."

Ian said, "He's not dressed like a businessman. Can't be Filou."

Kendrick contemplated the figure. "Blue collar. Laborer."

"Wait, there's a patch on his shirt." Murray bent down. It says 'B&O.' He must have worked for the railroad."

"But who the hell *is* he?"

Chapter Thirty-Three

I admit, I said, that a second murder in a book often cheers things up.

~Agatha Christie

Dane Circle, Saturday, May 18

Fred took out his phone. "Right. I'm calling in the crime scene unit. We have to secure this area. None of you touch anything." He moved off.

Murray stumped after him. "And I'll call the captain. We need a detective on site to start the process."

The others continued to stare at the body. Finally Noah muttered, "Do you think he's the only one?"

Kendrick twitched. "Only one what?"

"Only one"—he gestured at the hole—"in there?"

Sophie gasped. "You mean… You mean Filou could be buried there too?"

All eyes swiveled back to the corpse.

Ian protested. "There isn't enough room for another one."

"We don't know how deep the hole is."

Oscar croaked nervously. "I can't see someone just dumping a body in on top of another one. It's not like this was an old Indian burial ground or something."

"They could be associated."

"They?" Kendrick gestured at the body. "How? This

guy is clearly a working stiff." He caught himself. "Sorry—no pun intended."

No one laughed.

Ian threw his arms out. "We don't even know how old the cadaver is. No, it's out of the question that he could have anything to do with…you know."

Noah barked, "I tell you what: how about we wait for the experts to do their magic before we discard any theories?"

Murray came back. "We should be able to identify this fellow pretty quick, what with the uniform."

"So the doctor—or the medical examiner—can tell how old this guy is? Or rather, how long he's been dead?"

"Easy peasy."

Noah kicked at a rock. "If he turns out to be the only one, it would mean we were on the wrong track."

Ian sighed. "I sure hope so."

"We still haven't found Filou's body." He shot Oscar an eloquent glance.

Kendrick said heavily, "Should we keep looking?"

Oscar sucked in a breath. "No!"

Sophie secretly agreed with the old man. *Enough is enough.*

Fred came up to them, waving his arms. "All right, all of you. The professionals will take over from here. You can go home."

His peremptory tone changed Sophie's mind. "We found him; we stay." Everyone but Oscar nodded.

"All right, but you'll have to stand over there." He gestured toward the post office building.

There followed an intense, extremely frustrating two hours. The first half hour was consumed in waiting for the crew to arrive. Sophie, checking out the faces in various stages of anxiety, figured no one wanted to risk saying something that could be misconstrued. *Or in Harry's case, come up with a fresh lie.*

Finally, a white van marked Crime Scene Unit–Montgomery County Police arrived and two men got out. Sophie recognized the forensics agents who had investigated the elderberry wine poisoning. Fred introduced them as Ethan and Pete. Ethan smiled at her and doffed an imaginary hat. "We meet again. Miss Childress, isn't it?"

Despite the situation, she was flattered. "Yes."

"No more run-ins with arsenic, I trust?"

"No. And just the one body. So far."

Ethan did a double-take, then grinned. "We'll have to see, won't we?"

The agents immediately set to work. After an initial perambulation around the carcass, Ethan began taking photographs. Pete scanned the ground with a pen light—which struck Sophie as rather pointless given the brilliant morning sun.

Noah was the first to crack. "Aren't you going to remove him?"

Pete scratched his head. "See, we in the CSI like what we call 'procedure.' There's a process we follow. Otherwise we might miss crucial evidence."

"Oh."

As if to assuage their concerns, Pete called to Ethan. "Burrow under the guy—see if anything else pops up, but don't move him yet."

"Will do." A few long minutes later, Ethan approached. "Pete?"

"What is it?"

"I think we need to look around some more."

"Oh? Find something?"

"Yup." Ethan held up tweezers. Clenched in them was a round, ivory-colored object about half an inch in diameter. "This button doesn't belong to the vic's overalls."

Fred studied it. "Could it have fallen off a commuter or pedestrian and worked its way into the soil?"

"Nope. It was down too deep. It was actually *under* the body."

Ian remarked, "The railway has been here since the 1880s. The original station was built in 1893, so it could belong to a passenger as far back as then."

Ethan nodded. "True. So I checked it under the portable microscope. It's made of celluloid. They stopped manufacturing celluloid buttons in the 1940s, but they were most closely associated with clothing of the 1920s. I'd estimate this button to be a hundred years old."

"What is celluloid?" Noah was interested.

Ethan grew animated. "Celluloid is the first pseudo-plastic product ever made. It's primarily manufactured from cellulose—a wood by-product."

Ian took a close look. "It looks exactly like plastic. How can you tell it's not?"

"When you soak it in hot water, it gives off a distinct smell, like mothballs."

Ian was still unsatisfied. "So it's old. That doesn't mean it belongs to the victim of a crime."

Noah turned back to Ethan. "Where did you say you found it?"

"Underneath the skeleton."

Kendrick whistled. "That's gotta date it."

"It'll help; that is, when and if we get an identification for this poor fellow."

"How are you going to do that?"

Pete called one of the policemen over. "Murray, are you ready to let us remove the vic?"

Murray picked up the phone. "Lemme call Chief Duncan. He said he was sending Captain Hinckley." He dialed. "Chief? Where's the captain? Oh, he is. Yeah, Crime Scene's here. Yes, we're still investigating… Why? Because our kibitzers are crossing their fingers there's another vic." He chuckled at something the chief said. "I'm with you, but since we have to wait for the captain anyway, we might as well humor them. Okay." He clicked Off.

Pete huffed. "Well?"

"Hinckley's doing some background before he comes down. Since the vic's wearing a B&O uniform shirt, he might be able to track him down in the missing persons notices or the company's personnel records." He turned to Ethan. "He says to go ahead."

"You think there may be more than a button under there?"

"Only one way to find out."

"We're going to have to move the body."

Murray thought this over. "The medical examiner should see it in situ if possible. Let's poke around the perimeter first."

There followed another hour of both breathless and boring observation while the agents did their thing.

Peggy brought out sandwiches and sodas and they sat on the shelter's bench to wait. A train rumbled to a stop, and the commuters—who had been kept down by the P.O.—were allowed to board. Locals gawked from behind the yellow tape. George arrived and tried to bluster his way in but was turned back. Every few minutes, Harry would make a break for it and fail. As the agents dug deeper and deeper, Oscar grew increasingly agitated. Sophie patted his knee. "What's done is done, Oscar. You shielded her for more than thirty years. It's time the truth came out."

Ian nodded. "She's right, Oscar. It was going to surface one way or another eventually."

Pete yelled, "Got something!"

Noah jumped up. "What is it? Clothes? A skull?"

Sophie shivered at the ghoulish questions.

Pete sat back on his haunches. "It's a hand."

Fred leaned over Pete's shoulder. He straightened and waved at the ambulance. "Okay, it looks like we're going to have to move the first vic to get at the second one." He took out his phone. "Any word on the ME? Not for another hour? Damn." He explained their predicament. "Okay." He put the phone away. "Banks says to take him back to the lab."

The EMTs transferred the skeleton to a stretcher and set it in the ambulance. "Shall we wait for the other one?"

"Might as well."

It took forty-five minutes to clear the dirt from a hand and forearm. Pete was unhappy. "It looks like the body is twisted, as though it was thrown into the grave. The torso is about a foot that way."

"So?"

"So, it's under the concrete slab."

Ian gazed at the policeman. "Does that mean…?"

"Yes. We'll have to jackhammer it up to get at the skeleton."

Kendrick caught Oscar as he pitched forward. Ethan

cleared the bench and laid him down. The tech was concerned. "Is he okay? Maybe you should take him home."

"He'll be fine. It's been a long day—he's just dehydrated." Kendrick cast a glance at Ian. "I'll get him some water."

"Seriously, you should get him out of here. It's going to get pretty gruesome."

"No!" Oscar sat up, panting heavily. "I'll stay."

Noah came over. When the techs had moved off, he said gravely, "You built the shelter, Oscar. Come clean. Did you find Filou? Did you pour concrete over him?"

Oscar said nothing. He sat looking at his hands. Noah turned on his heel and strode away, his expression furious.

Sophie knew she shouldn't feel sorry for Oscar, but he looked so pathetic. *He was just trying to defend his family.*

A crew arrived with a dump truck. Murray directed them to start breaking up the slab. An hour later, they had cleaned off enough of the second body to see that it was a male, dressed in an old-fashioned tweed herringbone suit and polka dot bow tie. The remains of a gray fedora were crushed beneath him. Ethan pointed at his coat. "Celluloid buttons. It's a match."

Pete gazed at the corpse. "So anyone care to hazard a guess who *this* one is?"

The onlookers remained mute. Finally, Kendrick spoke. "We believe this is what's left of Charles Filou, a businessman."

"And how do you know that?"

"Because my great-grandmother killed him."

There was a moment of profound silence. The police

and crime scene agents stared at Kendrick. The others writhed uncomfortably. Finally Fred stirred. "I'd better call this in." He walked away.

When he came back he announced, "Gather up what's left of this one and cart it back to the lab as well."

"We need more time to process the scene, Sarge."

"How much more?"

Pete looked up at the sky. It was getting toward mid-afternoon, and the sun was slanting through the trees. "Another couple hours at least."

"Okay." Fred turned to Oscar. The others gathered around him protectively. The old man asked in a quavering voice, "Are you going to arrest me?"

"Huh? Why would I do that?"

Oscar looked suddenly confused. "Because I knew my grandmother had killed a person and didn't tip off the police?"

Fred cast a glance at Ian and Kendrick. "Neither did they." He tapped his lip. "There's no statute of limitations on homicide."

Kendrick and Ian chorused, "It wasn't murder! It was self-defense. She didn't mean to kill him!"

"She hid the body. That's tampering with evidence—a felony." In the face of their outcry he said quickly, "But you people aren't responsible, and I expect your ancestor is long gone."

"Yes. She died in 1965."

"Then I can't see that we can do much besides close the cold case—if it was ever on file."

Harry offered helpfully, "I haven't found any record of one; we were only going on newspaper accounts of the time. Filou disappeared in 1920."

"*Hmm.* Well, I want you all to go home now. The

techs will cordon off the area. I'll set a couple of uniforms on guard here overnight."

The party reluctantly broke up. Harry immediately lit out for his car. Sophie whispered to Noah. "What about Harry?"

Noah shaded his eyes. "What about him? He's a low life, but do we want to make a stink?"

"He held a gun on us!"

"So did Ian."

"If we let him go, we'll never see him again."

"And that's a bad thing?"

"He's got our silver dollars."

Ian's ears pricked up, and he approached. In a low voice, he said, "Did you say silver dollars? You found some? Where?"

Noah gestured toward the boxwood hedge. "They were buried over there."

"What did you do with them?" His gaze was intense.

"Harry made off with them."

"Really. *Hmm*." He walked away and joined Kendrick and Oscar.

Sophie watched him go. "We should force Harry to pony them up."

"Forget it. They're not ours. I believe the law of salvage applies here. You know, finders, keepers."

Sophie was too tired to debate the point. "Fine."

Noah took her hand and led her up the hill. Later that evening, Sophie was surprised to discover new wells of energy, which she put to good use, or so Noah averred.

****

Peveril Hall, Sunday morning

The phone woke them up. Noah took the call. He turned to Sophie. "That was the crime scene guy—Pete.

He wants us to come down to Dane Circle right away."

"Can't we have breakfast first?" Sophie hadn't had anything to eat since the sandwiches Peggy had made the day before. "I'm starved."

"No time." He stopped with one foot hovering over his pant leg. "All right, stop mewling. I'll make some instant coffee."

He was waiting at the door when she came down. He handed her a waxed cup and a wrapped honeybun. "It was all I could find that was portable."

She ate it hungrily as they headed down the hill. "What do you suppose they want us for? The only mystery left is the identity of the railroad employee."

"Could be that. Could be something new about Filou. Maybe they found the bribe money." He increased his pace. "Hurry."

By the time they reached Dane Circle, Kendrick, Ian, and Oscar were already gathered. Kendrick volunteered, "Dad stayed with me last night." He gave his father a tentative smile.

Noah looked around. "Where's Harry?"

"No idea. Where'd he go last night?"

No one seemed to know. Sophie wondered if he had taken the opportunity to fly the coop. *Well, he* is *twenty-two dollars richer.*

Noah sucked in a breath. "The box." He loped into the post office. A moment later he shuffled out. "It's gone."

"Harry?"

"Who else?"

So...a lot richer.

The van was already parked and the crew deployed around the site. Fred and Murray roared up in their squad

317

car. A slight man in jeans, a white shirt, navy blazer, and bright red tie emerged from the back seat. Murray introduced him as Captain Hinckley.

Sophie recognized him. She nudged Noah. "He was at the station when I gave my statement about your arsenic poisoning."

The detective surveyed the assemblage. "Which one of you is Oscar Northcutt?"

Oscar cringed. "I am."

"Huh." He wrote something down on a note pad. Oscar watched him, terror etched in his face.

Instead of asking more questions, he addressed everyone. "Thanks for coming. We have a development."

Kendrick leaned forward eagerly. "Have you identified the first body we found?"

"Not yet. I have a sergeant working on that. No, we have a new…er…issue." He led them to the open grave. "We found a third body."

Chapter Thirty-Four

If you confront anyone who has lied with the truth, he will usually admit it—often out of sheer surprise. It is only necessary to guess right to produce your effect.

~Agatha Christie

Dane Circle, Sunday, May 19

Noah clasped Sophie's hand and squeezed. "Could you repeat that, Captain Hinckley? You're saying you found a *third* corpse?"

Ian, Kendrick, and Oscar all looked bewildered. Ian finally stammered, "Sorry, but our family can only take credit for the one."

Hinckley held up a hand. "We have no leads so far on the third victim's identity, but I can say with certitude he's more recent than the second guy."

"More recent, as in, he died not long ago?"

Ian asked delicately, "Is he still…fleshy?"

Hinckley laughed. "I didn't ask if the techs actually *pressed the flesh*. The ME will be able to get a fix on an approximate date of decease."

Oscar asked curiously, "So where did this one crop up?"

"Ethan and Pete had started refilling the holes when they noticed a dog rooting around in the debris. Pete tried to shoo him away, but the mutt had hold of a piece of cloth and wouldn't let go."

Murray appeared, leading a shaggy black dog on a leash. "He's not a stray—he's got a collar. I put a call into the owner, a Matthew Crockett. He's coming to get him." He scratched the dog's ears. "Mrs. Dane lent me a leash."

Noah turned back to the detective. "So, was the cloth attached to anything?"

"We couldn't tell until Pete and Ethan scooped out more soil. It was a little to the side of the other two bodies, over there." He gestured toward a grassy area between the tracks and the shelter. On a tarp next to a load of sod and gravel lay a skeleton, still partially covered with soil. A madras jacket hung in tatters from its shoulders. Leather loafers appeared to have survived intact, but when Sophie cautiously drew near she saw that the soles had disintegrated. A few tufts of yellowish hair covered the skull.

Kendrick spoke first. "We dismissed the idea before, but could this be an old Indian graveyard that was paved over in the 1890s?"

Hinckley shook his head. "I doubt the local Indians wore work clothes or had blond hair. And anyway, why would anyone bury a guy in his uniform? And not in a coffin?"

"*Hmm.*"

Kendrick didn't give up. He said hopefully, "We could be looking at a mass grave. Maybe someone killed a whole family."

"A serial killer."

Murray snorted. "A serial killer who thought it was a good idea to bury all his victims in the same spot?"

Noah was inspecting the body. "You think it's

modern?"

"Definitely. We were hoping you guys might recognize the clothes. His coat? The shoes?"

They all shook their heads. "The only one we can identify for sure is Filou. The other two are strangers."

Ian had been twiddling his thumbs. Finally he rapped out, "Oscar, you've always insisted you found nothing when you leveled the station. I'm beginning to find that a little hard to swallow." He glanced at Sophie. "I have to agree with Sophie. You lied to us."

Oscar burst into tears, surprising everyone. Sophie touched his arm. "There, there." She helped him to the bench in the shelter. He sat, quietly sobbing.

Kendrick turned on Ian. "There's no call to accuse my father. Hasn't he been through enough?"

Ian stood his ground. "I just don't see how he could have knocked down a building and cleared away the rubble without finding at least the first two corpses. They weren't down that deep."

"Deep enough. Filou was partially under the trainman."

"Which means the trainman was killed after Filou." Sophie hoped no one noticed the non sequitur. She was watching Oscar. He sat twisting his hands, his face screwed into a frozen rictus. *He's this close to falling apart.*

"And whoever buried him didn't spot another skeleton in the hole before he dropped his own cadaver in?" Ian was indignant.

Hinckley intervened. "Let's hold off on speculation till we get the autopsy results. They'll tell us when and how they died."

Oscar jumped up, his eyes wild. He screamed,

"Wait, no! Stop. I'll tell the truth." He clicked his teeth and abruptly sat down again.

They stopped arguing.

His head in his hands, Oscar took several deep breaths. Finally he spoke, his voice jittery. "First off, I did find Filou's body. The crew had gone home for the day, and I was working the backhoe myself. I didn't have a clue at first but later figured out who it must be."

"How?" Sophie was curious.

"The hat. James had described how nattily Filou dressed. Fancy bow ties and an expensive gray wool fedora. He sneered that the man put on airs to confound his victims." He glanced surreptitiously at Kendrick. "I also found a note in his pocket."

"A note?" It was Noah's turn to be curious. "From whom?"

"What did it say?"

He extracted a stained and wrinkled piece of card stock from his wallet. "It was an invitation from Audrey asking him to dinner."

"*She* invited *him*?"

"He didn't ask to come?"

"Hiram didn't know about it?"

Oscar raised a hand and lowered it. "Quiet. I—"

Noah burst out, "Are you about to confess that she *planned* to kill him?"

"What? No. Nothing of the sort." Oscar began to look rattled.

Kendrick pushed to the front and faced the others. His face red, he shouted, "Leave my father alone! Can't you see he's at a breaking point?"

Out of the hubbub came a low, deep voice speaking slowly. It had the immediate effect of forcing people to listen. Once quiet descended, Captain Hinckley resumed. "Why don't you tell us what you know, Mr. Northcutt?"

"That's it. Audrey asked Filou to come to dinner on April seventeenth. She wrote, 'You and my husband have things to discuss.' "

"Things to discuss…" Noah rubbed his chin. "That doesn't rule out premeditation."

Hinckley held up a hand. "Premeditation?"

Ian pressed his lips together. "Audrey Northcutt, my great aunt, killed Filou." He added hastily, "But it was an accident. It was not, I repeat, *not*"—he glared at Noah—"premeditated. He attacked her, and she clubbed him with a rolling pin."

Hinckley's face cleared. "Ah, right. The sergeant described something along those lines."

Sophie had been casting her mind back to the tale Ian had originally told. "Wait. Ian—it was your father who told you what happened that night, right?"

"Devon, yes. James confessed it to him."

"He said she came upon Filou—disguised—in the office, attempting to plant derogatory material on Hiram."

"Correct."

Noah stirred. "I see where you're going with this, Sophie. When he snuck back to the house after Hiram had thrown him out, he was dressed all in black." He waved a hand at the shelter. "So how did he come to be wearing his good suit and fedora when she put him in the ground?"

No one breathed. Finally, the detective shook himself. "I don't see that it's all that important." When Noah opened his mouth, he raised his voice. "So, Mr. Northcutt? Oscar. What did you do when you found the body?"

"I spread the soil back over him and smoothed it out." He blew out his cheeks. "I'm almost relieved to get that off my chest."

Kendrick patted his shoulder. "It's been hanging over you for years."

The captain asked, "When exactly did this occur?"

His gaze shifted to the sky. "I'll have to check my records—sometime in the late 1980s I think. Could have been 1990."

Kendrick said gently, "It was 1990, Pa. Don't you remember?"

"I…uh…"

Noah said abruptly, "So the other two bodies must have been deposited after that."

Hinckley asked, "How do you come up with that?"

"Oscar would have found them, and I'm certain he wouldn't have left *them* buried. He'd have told the police."

Oscar nodded. "True. I was prepared to keep Audrey's actions secret, but I draw the line at covering for other people's offenses." The ghost of a smile touched his lips.

Hinckley said heavily, "I am not yet prepared to conclude all three are murder victims." He called to the crime scene tech. "Ethan. Get the ambulance down here. He goes to the lab along with the others."

Sophie asked, "How long will the autopsies take?"

"Who knows? We'll need to bring in a forensic anthropologist. I gather they can determine a lot even from a skeleton."

"Age? Sex? Ethnicity?"

"I think so. Look, when we get the results I'll get

back to you." He went off to supervise the exhumation.

"Now what?"

Sophie started to march up the hill. "Breakfast." Noah gave his phone number to the officer and loped after her.

****

Montgomery County Medical Examiner, Monday morning

Captain Hinckley pushed open the gray double doors. His guests—Noah, Sophie, Ian, and Kendrick— beheld a spotless room of steel and ceramic tile. Sophie felt a blast of icy air shoot up her skirt. "*Brr*."

Noah kneaded her shoulder and whispered, "Just think what this place would smell like if it *weren't* so cold."

The detective beckoned them in. "I've invited you all down today to hear from our medical examiner, Benedict Banks, as well as from the forensic anthropologist he's enlisted."

Banks—a florid man with a prominent hooked nose—finished washing his hands in the huge steel sink. Wiping them dry, he indicated the door Noah and Sophie had just walked through. "Let's talk in my office."

He led them down the hall to a cramped, untidy room. Coffee mugs acted as paperweights holding down stacks of folders heaped on every surface. Banks picked up a stack from the desk chair and sat down. Sophie wasn't sure if there even *were* other chairs, so she remained standing. The others did likewise.

A gangly, emaciated man in a three-piece suit detached himself from the bookcase. He coughed into a slightly soiled handkerchief. "Good afternoon."

Banks twitched. "Oh sorry, Jared." He fluttered a

hand. "Allow me to introduce Dr. Jared Shapiro, professor of Physical Anthropology at Columbia University and retired curator at the American Museum of Natural History in New York."

Sophie was captivated by Shapiro's resemblance to one of his own examination subjects. "Professor, if I may ask, why are you here?"

His smile was both unpretentious and ironic. "I am often called in by the NYPD to assist in autopsies of extremely old corpses. This is the first time I've been invited to attend one in Maryland." He bowed his head to the ME. "Banksie and I were roommates at Princeton, and I was happy to help out a fellow tiger."

For the first time Sophie noticed the banners on the wall and the black-and-orange helmet sitting on the filing cabinet.

Captain Hinckley cleared his throat. "Well, gentlemen. May we hear your assessment?"

"Let's start with some background." Banks picked up a clipboard. "You sent us three bodies."

"Uh-huh."

"One was in an advanced state of deterioration as a result of having been left in the ground for a long time—best estimate is a hundred years. It is not an American Indian."

"Well, we knew *that*. Filou was French Canadian."

From Banks's expression, Sophie divined that the statement had been meant as a joke. "I heard there was some discussion of the site being an old cemetery. I wanted to quash the rumor before we had some local tribe slapping us with a lawsuit." He paused. "That was also a joke."

When this had no effect, he mumbled, "Tough

audience" and went on. "From the state of the remains and the remnants of clothes, we estimate he was a well-to-do adult male, approximately thirty-five, six feet tall, and overweight."

"How could you tell that?"

"The extent of wear on the pelvis and feet indicated that they were stressed by carrying excess pounds."

Shapiro added, "He had three gold teeth—typical of the period." He glanced at Banks. "He did suffer from one health issue: congenital syphilis. The disease was transmitted from his mother during pregnancy. It manifests in the long bones—the femora—giving them what we call a celery stalk appearance."

Sophie was shocked. "Was that unusual in 1920?"

"Not really. Syphilis has been with us since at least the fifteenth century. However, its cause and treatment weren't discovered until the first decade of the twentieth century. Often, after the initial infection, symptoms disappear, so the mother may not have known she was infected."

"Oh."

Kendrick asked suddenly, "Did the crime scene investigators find anything with him? A suitcase, for example?"

Ian chimed in. "Or money?"

Hinckley checked his notes and shook his head. "The only thing not still attached to the corpse was the celluloid button."

Sophie observed Ian and Kendrick exchanging looks.

Banks stood. "On second thought, I suggest we go back to the morgue. It will be easier to demonstrate our findings."

When they came out in the corridor, Hinckley called one of the crime scene agents over. "Come along, Ethan."

The rather unwieldy troop of eight crowded into the autopsy room. The medical examiner indicated a table. "Here is the first body you brought in."

Ethan added helpfully, "He was the one on top of Filou, only a couple of feet below the surface."

Banks raised his voice. "We can infer from the striped denim overalls with the B&O logo that he was an employee of the railroad. Approximately twenty-four years old, he had two broken fingers, which appear to pre-date decease by a year or so. Bad teeth, indicating a youth in poverty. Oh, and he was Hispanic."

There was a knock at the door. Ethan opened it and took a slip of paper from someone. He handed it to Hinckley.

The captain read it. "Aha. We've found a promising identification for him. One Miguel Vasquez, assigned to the DC-Martinsburg route, did not report for work on June 9, 1990, and was never heard from again. No indication that B&O followed up, and Vasquez isn't listed on any further employment rolls."

"That's weird. They made no effort to locate him?"

Hinckley winked. "The *railroad* didn't admit it in so many words, but the implication is that he was illegally in the country. They wouldn't want to draw attention to their hiring practices by filing a missing persons report."

"Poor guy."

Ian snorted. "Your solicitude is wasted, Kendrick. If he broke the law to get into the US, he was a criminal. And he took a good job away from a citizen."

"Nobody deserves to be murdered."

Sophie looked down at the skull. *The name is so familiar...how?* Suddenly it came to her. "You said his name was Miguel Vasquez?"

"Uh-huh."

She looked at Noah. "Wasn't he the railroad worker from Guatemala who went missing in 1990?"

His face cleared. "Yes! It was in the Marmion *Bugle*, wasn't it? Did the article say anything else about him?"

She thought back. "I don't think so. It was just a line or two. I'll see if I can find it again."

Hinckley held up the paper. "Don't bother, I have the reference here. It was in the June 12 edition."

Ian pursed his lips. "How did he die, anyway? Can you tell?"

Shapiro answered. "Heavy trauma to the back of the head. His skull was shattered."

"If he was an illegal alien, could it have been gang-related?"

"Ordinarily I wouldn't rule it out...except for one thing."

"What?"

"The third man was executed by the same method."

"Aha. Maybe they were involved in a gunfight—a gang war?"

Sophie couldn't quite picture bands of hoodlums marauding in stately Marmion Grove.

"Allow me to finish. Considering the third man's clothes and other physical traits, I think we can rule out gang membership. Anyway, the two men weren't shot— they were both dispatched by a blunt metal instrument."

"Metal, you say?"

"Uh-huh." He waited while his audience groped for an answer.

"We give up. What is blunt and metal that would be sitting in a railroad station?"

"Methinks a shovel."

Chapter Thirty-Five

The saddest thing in life and the hardest to live through, is the knowledge that there is someone you love very much whom you cannot save from suffering.

~Agatha Christie

Montgomery County morgue, Monday, May 20

"A shovel you say? He was killed with a shovel?" Noah looked meaningfully at Sophie. He mouthed, "Our shovel?"

Kendrick's expression was one of bewilderment. "You're saying the third guy was *also* murdered?"

Banks nodded. "Yup. Hit from behind, just like Miguel."

"Was he Hispanic as well?"

Shapiro answered. "No, he was Caucasian. About thirty, medium build. His left leg had been broken in early youth." He checked his notebook. "Teeth in poor shape for a man of his age. One implant, and a *lot* of fillings." He shook his head in disapproval.

Ian spoke tentatively. "What about the scrap of jacket? Kind of gaudy. Could he have been a salesman—a commuter?"

The medical examiner shrugged. "There's no way to tell from the evidence. It does appear that he and Mr. Vasquez were killed within a very short time of each other."

Sophie opened her mouth to speak, but Ethan interrupted. "I see it like this. Body Three disembarks the train and is jumped by a mugger. Miguel sees it happen and goes to help. Mugger picks up the shovel and wallops Vasquez, distracting Body Three long enough for said mugger to knock him off too."

"But according to the *Bugle* article, Miguel hadn't clocked in. What would he be doing on the train?"

"He could have been hitching a ride home."

"Or playing hooky."

"*Hmm.*" Shapiro shifted his jaw from side to side. "If Miguel was indeed on the train and got off here, then we have a pretty good idea when he was killed—and by extension, Body Three."

"When?"

"Sometime between June 8 and June 9, 1990."

"Well, that should be a big help. I'll get started on the paperwork." Ethan left.

Ian gestured to Kendrick. "We have to go, too. I have a doctor's appointment and Kenny's my ride."

Once they'd gone, Noah turned to Captain Hinckley. "Did you find anything that could have been the weapon?"

He shook his head. "Not in the vicinity, but it's been thirty years."

Noah glanced at Sophie. "We may know where it is."

"Really?" Hinckley's hand hovered over his phone. "Where?"

"Harry Quayle has it."

"Who's Harry Quayle?"

"He was with us when you were exhuming the

332

bodies. Older guy. Balding. On the porky side?"

"Oh, yeah. So what makes you think he has the murder weapon?"

"If Dr. Shapiro is right that it was a shovel, he stole it from us and never brought it back."

The detective's eyes opened wide. "Oh, really. How did *you* come by it?"

"It's a long story. It's best if we have it in hand."

"Can you get in touch with him?"

"I wish we could. He took off last Saturday, and we haven't heard from him since."

Hinckley was concerned. "Is there any reason to suspect he's concealing important information?"

Noah and Sophie exchanged glances. "We…uh… We don't know."

He tapped his phone. "Sergeant? I want an APB on one Harry Quayle. Q-U-A-Y-L-E." He gave the officer the description and flipped the phone off. "Dr. Banks, did you have anything to add?"

"Yes. An item was clutched in the third man's hand."

A tingling sensation ran up Sophie's spine. *This is what always happens in Agatha Christie's books—the single clue that unravels the mystery.* "A train ticket?"

"A name scribbled on a torn sheet of paper?"

"An unique signet ring?"

The medical examiner waited patiently for the clamor to die down. "Nothing so useful. A zippered plastic tote bag. Inside was a honey-do list."

"Honeydew? You mean fruit?"

"No, no. A honey-*do* list. The set of chores the lady of the house wants her husband to do."

Sophie was still hopeful. "What did it say?"

Banks flipped a paper on his clipboard. " 'Library: poisons and Christie bibliography. Garden center: insecticide. Geddes: maps of early train routes, circus venues.' "

Noah cocked his head. "Those don't sound like things he had to do around the house. It's a shopping list."

"And what exactly was he going to buy at the library?"

"Well, then an errand list. Whatever, it rules out the idea that he was just passing through—a salesman."

A commotion started up out in the hall. Oscar burst through the double doors, Ian and Kendrick in hot pursuit.

Hinckley turned. "Can I help you gentlemen?"

Oscar stood before the detective, panting. "I meant to come with the boys, but they left me behind." He glared at Kendrick.

Ian and Kendrick skidded to a stop behind him. Kendrick said angrily, "He doesn't need to be here. Come on, Dad."

Oscar ignored him and dropped into a chair, hand on his chest. "You have the autopsy results?"

Kendrick threw up his hands, defeated. Hinckley calmly brought Oscar up to speed.

Noah turned to Shapiro. "The honey-do list. Let me see it again, please." He studied it a minute, then looked up. "When did you say he was killed?"

"Indications are that he's been buried about thirty years. If he was killed at the same time as Miguel, that would make it June of 1990."

Noah pushed his hair back from his forehead. "I think I know who he is."

Sophie had a flash of understanding. *Of course.* "Who?"

"My father, Roger Pennyworth."

"Your father! What on earth leads you to that conclusion?"

He pointed at the list. "For one thing, my father was a high school history teacher. Geddes is a school supply store."

Hinckley's brow furrowed. "Did you know how he died?"

Noah froze at the words. "I...I..."

Sophie came to his rescue. "Noah's father deserted them when Noah was five years old. That was in 1990."

"Did they live in Marmion Grove?"

"Yes—in Peveril Hall on Waverley Avenue."

"Do you remember the exact date?"

With a herculean effort, Noah pulled himself together. "No. I was too young to pay attention—"

"Or your mother didn't discuss it with you." Ian nodded.

Noah shrugged. "My mother is gone now, but my sister Gretchen was ten years old at the time. I could contact her."

Captain Hinckley was grim. "If it *is* Roger Pennyman, then he met his end only a few blocks from his home."

"But why? *Why* was he murdered? He was a simple teacher with a young family. He had no vices"—here he studiously avoided Kendrick's face—"or shady companions. Who could have wanted him dead?" The anguish on Noah's face physically hurt Sophie. She yearned to go to him, comfort him, make it go away.

The detective said calmly, "You tell me. Are you

aware of anything that might have put him in harm's way? A feud with a colleague? A clandestine relationship?"

"There was one thing." Noah took a deep breath. "My father was obsessed with cold case crimes. Sophie and I found a box in his study filled with the possessions of one Agnes Reilly, who worked as a maid for Hiram and Audrey Northcutt."

Sophie leaned in. "Audrey was the one who killed Filou."

"Yes. About six weeks ago Sophie came across a letter in which Agnes wrote that she may have witnessed a murder on the night of April 17, 1920."

Hinckley said impatiently, "And you think Pennyman's death is somehow connected to what she saw?"

Sophie answered. "We didn't until now."

The captain crossed his arms. "Why don't you begin at the beginning?"

"Okay. As I said, Sophie found this letter."

"And where is it now?"

Noah spoke up. "I have it locked in my desk."

"We'll need it for evidence. What did the letter say?"

"Agnes wrote that she saw a man carrying a body in the Peveril backyard."

"She didn't see his face?"

"No."

"And no member of the household was missing—or looked guilty?"

"Not according to her."

"Why write a letter? Why not contact the police?"

Sophie answered. "Marmion Grove didn't have a

local police force. The letter was addressed to a Constable Bustwick of the Montgomery County police, but it was never mailed." She hesitated. "She *did* worry that she had imagined the whole thing."

"You think she had second thoughts?"

"Could be, but at any rate, she was fired soon after the event."

"Fired!"

"Yes. Audrey Northcutt accused her of stealing a ring. Agnes insisted it was given her by her fiancé. We now know that Audrey killed Filou, so it may have been a ploy to get rid of Agnes before she could tell anyone."

"And what does this have to do with your father?"

Noah said heavily, "Roger must have gotten too close to the truth and had to be eliminated."

"But the so-called murder occurred seventy years earlier! Surely Mrs. Northcutt had expired. What difference would it make if Roger solved it?" Shapiro was genuinely curious.

Noah's eyes widened. He looked at Sophie. She said slowly, "It would make a difference to a family who wanted to safeguard their reputation and the name of their ancestor."

The three men clustered at the side—until now silently listening—tensed. Kendrick faltered, "Are you accusing one of us of killing Noah's father?"

Ian added, "Are you bonkers?"

"You were willing to shoot *us* if we didn't leave it alone."

"Yes, but—"

Oscar put an arm across Ian's chest. "Enough." He turned to Captain Hinckley. "I killed him."

Hinckley went to the door. "Let's go to my office."

Sergeant Kent loitered in the hall. "Follow me, Murray." When they were all settled and the officer was ready, he said, "Please repeat what you said, Mr. Northcutt. You are confessing to the murder of Roger Pennyman?"

Oscar's eyebrows shot up. "Roger Pennyman? Why would I do that? No. I killed the trainman."

****

Peveril Hall, Tuesday morning

"More coffee?"

"Yes, please."

"Have you heard from Ian or Kendrick?"

"No. I sent a text to Ian saying we'd like to meet—I really think we should apologize—but he didn't answer." Noah stirred his coffee listlessly.

Sophie didn't know what to say. Noah had been despondent ever since they'd learned his father's fate. All these years he'd hated Roger for leaving them, only to find out he was the victim of an unknown assailant.

Oscar had confessed that he had come down to Dane Circle late one evening to inspect the site when he saw Miguel standing by a large hole in the rubble left from razing the old railroad station. He was fiddling with something. A shovel lay on the ground beside him. Oscar recognized the spot and realized that the man was about to blow the lid off his deadly secret. When Miguel knelt down beside the hole, Oscar seized the shovel and whumped him over the head.

Hinckley sat him down in the desk chair and stood over him. "Did you know you'd killed him?"

"Oh yes. His whole skull was cracked open like an egg, and his brains were spilling out."

Sophie couldn't tell if Oscar relished reliving the scene or was inured to the grisly details after so many years.

"Then what did you do?"

"I scooped the dirt back over him and left. The next day I had the crew grade the area and pour the concrete slab."

"The slab didn't cover Vasquez though, did it?"

Oscar grimaced. "It was supposed to—the crew screwed it up. At least they got part of the slab over Filou. That was critical."

"That's it? You didn't see Roger Pennyman?"

He was emphatic. "No."

Ian stirred. "You said Vasquez was fiddling with something. Was it a case of some kind? A bag filled with cash perhaps?"

Kendrick joined in. "Filou's bribe?"

Oscar shook his head. "I was so distraught after the…the…incident that I went home. I'm…I'm afraid I imbibed rather a lot."

At that point, Hinckley had the sergeant read Oscar his rights and take him into custody. Ian and Kendrick didn't say a word until they reached the parking garage. Ian murmured, "I'm sorry for all the trouble we caused."

Kendrick's eyes filled with tears. "I can't believe it. We were so close to reconciling and this happens. Now it's too late."

Before Noah could respond, the two cousins had driven away.

Sophie sipped her coffee and regarded Noah with compassion. *It's bad enough for Kendrick, but what about Noah? He has to reorder his thinking about his own father. I so wish Oscar had the answer to Roger's fate.* She thought about the old man. He had seemed such a nice person when they met him in Glen Echo. *Normal.*

And yet he had killed a person in cold blood all to cover up his grandmother's misdeeds.

The phone rang. "Hello?" She put her hand over the receiver. "Captain Hinckley has news." She listened. "Thanks for letting us know."

"What did he say?"

"They searched Oscar's house in Cabin John."

"And?"

"They found what looked like old bills. They're putting it through the system to see if they can trace them."

Noah put down his mug and stared at Sophie. "Do you think they're from the bribe Filou tried to give Hiram?"

"No idea."

"It's conceivable that Oscar *did* find the carpetbag when he uncovered Filou's skeleton."

"*Hmm*. Now I recall, he didn't directly answer Ian's question about a suitcase, did he?"

Sophie was mulling this over when Noah burst out, "That would be crazy. If he found it, Oscar would have taken the bag with him."

She thought she knew the answer. "He planned to. Oscar had only just discovered the body that afternoon. He didn't want to be seen with the bag in daylight. That was his real reason for returning to Dane Circle that night."

"Where he confronted Miguel by the grave."

"Miguel attacked him, and Oscar killed him. Self-defense." Sophie made another cup of coffee. "Is there any more pastry?"

"I wish." Noah rose and started to pace. "We're forgetting one thing. Roger."

"What about him?"

"How did he end up dead in the same spot? Oscar didn't see him."

"He must have come down shortly after Oscar left and found the disturbed earth."

"But what was he *doing* there?"

Sophie cupped her chin in her hands. "He'd been gathering materials on Agnes and the Northcutts."

Noah jerked. "Are you suggesting that during his research into the cold case, Roger came across a clue to the whereabouts of the body?"

Sophie dropped her hands. "No, I wasn't, but the idea has merit. How about this? Roger was there first. Maybe *he* found the bribe money before Oscar or Miguel even got there."

"What would he do with it?"

"Hide it." She nodded with conviction.

"My father was not a crook."

"I'm not saying that, but if *you* found a bag full of notes, you'd do the same thing." She appealed to him. "Wouldn't you?"

"I dare say I would." Noah was clearly wrestling with the idea. "That could mean…"

They looked at each other. "It could be…"

"In Peveril Hall."

Chapter Thirty-Six

The impossible cannot have happened, therefore the impossible must be possible in spite of appearances.
~Agatha Christie

Peveril Hall, Tuesday, May 21

"Should we take our new theory to the police?"

Noah shook his head. "Telling them we suspect Filou's bribe is somewhere in this house would implicate my father."

"How?"

"He's the only one who could have brought it here."

"Maybe so, but…" Sophie was on a roll. "*Maybe* it never left the premises. Kendrick and Ian asserted Audrey got rid of it, but she might have hidden it in the stable or cellar."

"Oh, for heaven's sake, *somebody* would have come across it by now. No, the Northcutts moved out of Peveril Hall shortly after the event. Audrey took it with her. It's the only explanation."

"*Hmm*." Sophie thought this over. "Okay, then how did the bills get into Oscar's house?"

"We don't know yet if they were part of the hoard. The police are still examining them." Noah stopped pacing. "One more strike against the Roger theory. He was killed—or at least found—down by the tracks. If he'd gone up to the house, how did he end up back at the shelter?"

Sophie wiped her forehead. "I suppose you're right. We shouldn't take this to the police. None of it fits."

Noah breathed a relieved sigh. "Agreed. It's their job. We can get on with our lives."

"Unless..." Her anxious eyes sought his out. "Roger *did* have a hand in it."

"Stop! Just stop. I want to savor my new image of a father who wasn't a deadbeat, if only for a little while."

Sophie kissed him. "All right. I have to finish that editing job by Friday. We can chill out on Saturday if you like."

He picked up the newspaper. "There's a peach festival in Germantown on Saturday. Want to go?"

"Sounds peachy."

****

Peveril Hall, Saturday evening

"So what does one *do* with a peck of peaches?"

Sophie dropped a sackful of fruit into a colander. "Well, there's peach pie, and peach cobbler. Peach jam and pickled peaches. Peach chutney and—"

"I get it," Noah said hastily. "And peach gumbo and peach creole and fried peaches. Are we talking *Forrest Gump: the Sequel*?"

"It's the dessert cart at Bubba Gump Shrimp Company. Here." She handed him a fuzzy pink orb redolent of sun and dew. "Let's eat this one and refrigerate the rest for now."

"Agreed." He took it and put his arm around Sophie's waist. "I have another recipe for peaches. Come on."

Sophie had a feeling where he was headed and

stopped at the refrigerator. "I'll bring the champagne and whipped cream."

****

Sophie's apartment, Monday afternoon

"What are you working on?"

Sophie sat back from the laptop and held the phone to her ear. "That man's horrendous manuscript. I told you about Mr. Spofford. He's written this agonizing memoir about his prostate cancer."

"Well, cancer *can* be agonizing."

"Yes, but that's not why it's so painful. The…er…colorful detail is pretty hard to take, yes. The trouble is, he can barely put a coherent sentence together. I keep trying to teach him about grammar and punctuation. You know, so the product is actually *his*. But he refuses to listen and just hands me this jumble and expects me to fix it."

"I hope you're charging him enough for that Caribbean cruise I've been eyeing."

"Full fare." She got up and went to the kitchen to warm up her coffee. "So what are you doing?"

"I had to come into the museum to take care of a few things. As I was finishing up, Captain Hinckley called. We're to meet him at the police station at six. Want me to pick you up?"

"Sure."

They reached the station in Gaithersburg at 6:05. "Glad you could make it." The detective motioned them into the office. A man with a buzz cut and taut neck, wearing a uniform bristling with medals, sat at the desk. "Noah, Sophie. This is Assistant Chief of Police, Lester Duncan. He's in charge of the Investigative Services Bureau. Chief? These are the two I told you about, Noah

Pennyman and Sophie Childress. Noah is the son of one of our victims."

The chief did not rise but gestured toward the two chairs before him. "Sit down. I have a few questions for you."

Noah interrupted. "Captain Hinckley told me you had some news."

Duncan looked momentarily put out. "Um, yes. About the bills that were found in Oscar Northcutt's home. They were marked."

"Ah. So Filou planned to claw back the bribe once he'd gotten Hiram to approve his project." Noah hissed. "What a grifter."

Captain Hinckley did a double take. "What are you talking about?"

"Aren't the bills part of the bribe money?"

"What bribe money?"

"Filou's. That's why Audrey Northcutt killed him, isn't it?"

Hinckley's jaw dropped. "She killed him for *money*?"

"No, no!" Noah ran his fingers through his hair. "Sophie had better do the honors."

She took a minute to put the facts in some semblance of order. "Charles Filou wanted to purchase land from the B&O Railroad, but Hiram Northcutt refused. Filou went to Peveril Hall to try and change Hiram's mind. First, he tried to bribe him, and when that didn't work, he threatened him. According to our…sources, Filou had the funds with him, but it's unclear what happened to them. We surmised the bills in Oscar's house came from those funds."

"And who are your sources?"

Sophie hesitated, then at a nod from Noah, she blurted, "Kendrick Northcutt and Ian Surry."

Hinckley checked his notes. "They were with us at the morgue, right? Relatives of the man who confessed?" He turned thoughtful. "That's why they were asking if we found anything with Filou's body. Huh."

Chief Duncan fixed his visitors with a frigid glare. "Your sources are in error. The notes have in fact been traced to a robbery. The Capitol Limited passenger train left Union Station at eleven thirty p.m. on June 8, 1990. It was robbed somewhere along the line between Kensington and Gaithersburg. The loot was never found."

Noah looked at Sophie. "Didn't Harry tell us it was recovered?" He frowned. "Except for the gold, that is."

"No, Harry was talking about the *1920* job. The one his grandfather took part in."

He bobbed his head. "I stand corrected. Say, have you guys picked him up yet?"

Hinckley bristled. "No."

Duncan was tapping a finger. "Never mind that. The 1990 heist netted a hundred thousand dollars, worth almost two hundred fifty thousand in today's currency."

"Did they at least catch the thieves?"

"Unfortunately, no, but the investigation centered on an inside man who police believe let them onto the train. His name was Miguel Vasquez."

"The victim? Really? Wow. So he was a bad guy!"

Noah cried, "So Oscar should be given credit for bringing down a criminal! You'll have to let him go."

Hinckley replied, "Oscar is still responsible for Miguel's death, whether or not he knew he was a hoodlum."

Sophie conjured up the image of the little man who loved the band organ. "I still have trouble believing Oscar's confession was real. I mean, you only found a few bills in his house. Maybe the robbers dropped them. He could have simply stumbled over them."

"Well, *somebody* killed Vasquez."

"I think I have the answer to that."

They all turned to the door, where Harry Quayle stood grinning. In one hand was a familiar-looking shape wrapped in brown paper.

The shovel.

"What the hell, Harry. Where have you been?"

"Me? Investigating. That's my job, last I checked."

The captain crooked a finger at him. "Come in... Mister?"

"Harry Quayle, at your service." He flipped open his wallet, displaying a photo ID. "I'm a licensed private investigator."

The captain's voice was low and lethal. "I have an all-points bulletin out on you, Mr. Quayle. We have reason to believe you're withholding evidence in this case."

Harry held up the shovel. "You mean this? I was only keeping it safe. Pennyman here left it lying around where anyone—even a suspect—could have nicked it." He handed it to Hinckley.

Hinckley was not mollified. "What exactly have you been doing since Saturday?"

He glanced at Noah and Sophie. "Had to make myself scarce. These two amateurs were holding me back."

Sophie could tell his tone riled Noah. He spat out, "Are you aware we found the bodies of my father and a bank robber along with that of Charles Filou where the old railroad station stood?"

"Of course!"

Sophie said mildly, "You ran off before Roger Pennyman's corpse was exhumed. Were you spying on us?"

"I've been kept in the loop by a…friend."

Chief Duncan stared at him. "And who might that friend be?"

Harry smiled unpleasantly. "You're aware I don't have to divulge my sources…*sir*."

Hinckley interrupted. "That's Chief to you, Quayle. This is Assistant Chief of Police Duncan."

A period of silence followed while people scrambled to pick up the dropped thread of discussion. Noah nabbed it first. "So tell us your news."

"I followed a lead." His eyes flickered, and Sophie wondered if perhaps that lead was not exactly legally obtained. "It took me to an informant with rock solid evidence."

"Evidence of what?"

"That Oscar Northcutt killed Miguel Vasquez."

Hinckley let out a breath. "He's already confessed."

"Oh, yeah?" Harry looked more interested than humbled. "What exactly did he confess to?"

"That he caught Miguel at Filou's grave site and in a fit of hysteria hit him over the head with a shovel."

"And his justification?" Harry's eyes twinkled at some secret joke.

"Miguel had discovered the body. Northcutt didn't want his grandmother's sins to come to light."

Sophie said firmly, "He's really sorry now."

Duncan's tone was patronizing. "We have since

learned that Vasquez was a member of the gang that robbed the mail train."

"But Oscar had no part in that." Noah looked hopefully toward Hinckley.

Harry's snicker became a titter, which morphed into a cackle, finally erupting in raucous laughter. His reaction was not received well.

"What are you on about?"

He wiped his nose. "What a crock. No, your sweet little old Oscar murdered Miguel Vasquez in cold blood for the oldest motive in the world. Money."

Chapter Thirty-Seven

But what does it matter which? If one of your parents killed the other, would it really matter to the mother of the boy you were going to marry, which way round it was?

~Agatha Christie

Montgomery County police station, Monday, May 27

Harry looked around the room. "Why are you all so shocked? It's not like people don't kill for money every day."

The captain recovered first. "Hang on a minute." He opened the door to the hall. "Sergeant Kent? Can you come in? I need you to record Mr. Quayle's statement."

The portly officer bustled in. "Oh, hi, Miss Childress. Mr. Pennyman." His eyes passed over Harry and landed on Chief Duncan. He gulped. "Chief." He opened his notebook.

Hinckley nodded at Harry. "All right, why don't you sit down and spell it out for us."

Noah vacated his seat, and Harry plunked down on it, wheezing slightly.

Duncan prompted, "Well?"

"Just hold on there a minute." Harry stuck his hands in his pockets and leaned back on the rear legs of his chair. "This information doesn't come cheap. I don't have a paying client, so I want compensation."

The chief shrugged. "We haven't offered any reward. I see no benefit in remunerating you for dope on a cold case."

"What if I can show you where the money is?"

"What money?"

"The money Filou used to bribe Northcutt."

"What about the train robbery?"

"The 1990 heist? I may have information on that too."

"Dammit, Harry," Noah burst out. "Just tell us."

Harry finally realized he was playing to a hostile crowd. "Okay, okay. Miguel Vasquez was a member of MS-13."

"MS-13?" Sophie was flummoxed. "It sounds like a book club."

Hinckley answered. "I only wish it were. It's an extremely violent Salvadoran gang."

Duncan tapped a pencil on the desk. "It's actually American-based. MS-13 was formed in Los Angeles in the 1980s to safeguard Salvadoran refugees, but it quickly devolved into the most vicious, bloodthirsty organization in the country. It's now in all fifty states and rapidly expanding."

"Captain Hinckley said Vasquez was recruited to be the inside man."

Harry shook a finger. "Not recruited, no. He was the equivalent of a fully fledged 'made man,' in Mafia parlance. And illegal to boot. He got a job with the railroad in order to help his cronies get on board the train." He paused. "B&O might want to revisit their employee screening. Just sayin'."

"It's lucky B&O is no longer hiring then, isn't it?"

Noah's tone was dry.

Duncan pretended to write something down. "Go on."

"So in the wee hours of June 9 they hit the Capitol Limited. After bashing in the conductor's head, Miguel broke into the RPO—that's the Railway Post Office."

Hinckley whispered, "The mail car."

"Yeah. He raked up the payrolls and checks while his colleagues—being scabby little creeps—hit on the crew and the few passengers for their watches and cash. They were still on the train when it rolled into Marmion Grove. The other gang members scattered before the engineer could sound the alarm, leaving Miguel to stow the goods. He noticed the gardens around the railroad shelter had recently been dug up, so he decided to deposit them right there. And that's where Oscar bumped him off."

Chief Duncan interrupted. "What was Northcutt doing out at midnight so far from home?"

"What do you *think* he was doing? He was about to disinter Filou."

"Why?"

"For the bribe money. Duh."

"Yes, well, chances are he wasn't there to give Filou last rites. The question is, why didn't he remove the bag when he first uncovered the body?"

Sophie answered. "He found Filou in the afternoon, when people were still about. He waited until dark to come back for it."

Harry clucked. "Wrong-o. He actually found the skeleton a week earlier. At the time his only thought was to hide it. He had no idea who it was, but he didn't want the hassle of police trampling all over his construction site, so he covered it up. A few days later, circumstances changed."

"Circumstances? Dogs worrying the corpse? Rain in the forecast?"

Harry glared at Noah. "I'd ix-nay on the sass—I haven't finished the story yet."

Noah drew a line across his throat and smirked.

The PI went on. "Something triggered his memory of the story of Audrey and Filou he'd heard from his uncle Devon. He drew the obvious inference."

"And returned to the scene to retrieve the money?"

"Yessir."

Noah crowed suddenly. "We were right, Sophie! Filou *did* carry a carpetbag!" He halted. "Could the bag itself be valuable? As a historical artifact?"

The others gave this speech the attention it deserved.

"But"—Sophie was puzzled—"Oscar told us that he didn't find anything except the corpse in the grave."

"He lied."

The detective leaned forward. "On the record, are you claiming that Oscar Northcutt killed Vasquez to get both the train money *and* the bribe money?"

"No, no. See, Oscar was just starting to dig when he saw the train slowing. Vasquez jumped off and approached the shelter. Oscar was terrified that he'd be caught. He dropped the shovel and hid behind a hedge. Vasquez stopped right next to where Filou lay. He noticed the top of the case and bent down to get a better look. Oscar snuck up behind him and wham!" He simulated smashing something over Noah's head.

"Hey!"

Harry ignored Noah's yelp. "He dumped Vasquez into the hole, nipped the carpetbag, and hightailed it out of there."

"What about the train swag? Did he take it too?"

Harry blinked. "Um… My source wasn't specific on that score." He looked up at the ceiling, then said brightly, "My guess is Oscar wasn't aware what Vasquez was doing there."

Noah said slowly, "Do you believe the shovel we found in the garage is the murder weapon?"

"What else could it be?"

The chief was looking more and more bemused. "Shovel?"

Hinckley explained. "They found a shovel hidden at Pennyman's house."

Chief Duncan pointed at the package. "Would that be it?"

"It sure is." Harry unwrapped it and laid it on the desk.

Sophie was thinking hard. "Noah. Do you remember which substances the lab detected on it?"

"*Hmm*. Not really. Construction dirt? What else?"

"Blood…and creosote."

Noah looked bewildered. "What's creosote?"

"It's used to treat railroad ties." She looked at Hinckley. "That means the shovel was at the station site. It has to be the one Oscar used to knock Vasquez out."

Hinckley checked his notes. "Let's see, shovel…shovel. Here it is. Yup, creosote, construction sand, asbestos, formaldehyde—"

"All consistent with a demolition site like the railroad station."

"Yes. Also blood—unidentified." He bore down on Harry. "Since you have deigned to return it to the police, perhaps we can find a match."

"Maybe you could start with Vasquez."

The police chief had been reading Hinckley's notes. "Wait a minute. The creosote extracted from the soil sample was very old—maybe turn of the century."

Sophie hiccupped. Duncan tilted his head. "You have something to say, young lady?"

"Forensics said the shovel was manufactured in 1918."

Duncan grunted. "So the same shovel was used for both the 1920 and the 1990 homicides. Nothing like recycling. The Sierra Club would be proud."

Hinckley hesitated. "Um, Chief? The 1920 vic was in fact killed by a rolling pin."

Duncan didn't bat an eye. "Yeah, yeah."

The sergeant piped up. "Maybe it wasn't the murder weapon, but it could have been used to bury Filou."

Noah wasn't convinced. "There's another little issue. The shovel was behind wallboard at Peveril Hall that had been there since the twenties. How could it have been used for a murder in 1990?"

Harry rolled his eyes. "Tell me, how did *you* find the shovel?"

Noah pursed his lips. "I pulled one of the panels out."

"It was pretty easy to do, right? Almost as though it had been detached before."

"Huh. All right, how did it get to Peveril Hall?" As the words left his lips, Noah's eyes grew wide and a retching sound issued from his throat. He turned to Sophie. "M...mother?"

Sophie's heart stopped. *Vivian? Did she kill Roger after all? Was Harry right all along?*

Hinckley took the hint from his chief, who was

exhibiting signs of impatience. "All right. Let's finish this up. We found a few bucks from the 1990 robbery at Oscar's house. If he didn't take Vasquez's sack, where did he get them?"

Harry scuffed his shoes on the floor. "I dunno— mebbe they'd fallen out of the bag and were lying on the ground."

Duncan leaned forward. "I want to know one thing, Quayle. How did you find all this out?"

Harry started to squirm. "That's proprietary information."

The captain straightened. "Well, none of this will stand up in a court of law. It's merely hearsay, unless you can provide sources and documentation."

"Ah, that's where the compensation comes in."

The captain towered over him. "You are aware you can be arrested for obstructing an investigation?"

"Wait a minute… Compensation." Sophie stared at Harry. "That night we dug up the box in Peggy's hedge, you told us it was from the train your grandfather robbed in 1920."

Noah piped up. "You swiped it from the post office."

Sophie put her hands on her hips. "So you must already have your reward."

Harry turned beet red. "You've no call telling the cops about that."

"Why not? It doesn't belong to you."

"Yeah." Noah chimed in. "You're going to have to return it anyway."

Hinckley rubbed his hands together gleefully. "Harry Quayle, you're under arrest for grand larceny. Murray, read him his rights."

Harry shrank back. "Hold on a minute."

"What?"

"I'm…um…innocent. Cross my heart."

At a word from Duncan, Hinckley settled down. Harry—a wary eye glued to the captain, resumed. "It wasn't the gold. In the box, I mean." He looked abashed. "Turns out it was one of those whatchamacallits—time capsules. Just a bunch of crap inside—letters and a flag, some seeds…and this toy grenade labeled Nuclear Weapon. What on God's green earth does that signify?"

Noah gave a delighted snuffle. "I can answer that. Marmion Grove was the first town in the country to declare itself a nuclear-free zone." Noah grinned at Sophie. "No one ever accused us of not being progressive enough."

"I think the word you're looking for is 'eccentric.' "

Harry gave them a blank stare. "There was a card inside that stated the town buried it for their demi-sesquicentennial. You wanna explain that too?"

"Seventy-fifth anniversary. I remember my father talked about it. He was thirteen at the time." He reached out to pat Sophie's knee. "I forgot to tell you that he grew up in the Grove. They held a full week of events. He showed us photos. Must've been a hoot." Noah smiled reminiscently.

"Well, at any rate, it wasn't the wampum I was looking for." Harry was glum. "I'm beginning to wonder if old Harry Senior lied to his son."

"You mean, he wasn't the dashing highwayman he claimed to be?"

Chapter Thirty-Eight

No innocent person ever has an alibi.

~Agatha Christie

Peveril Hall, Wednesday, May 29

"So the captain let Harry go?" Sophie poured a tot of bourbon into her tumbler.

"Yeah. He didn't actually steal anything." Noah held out his glass. "Hit me."

She did. Then she poured whiskey into his glass. She set the bottle down and sat next to him at the kitchen counter. "I know the time capsule didn't yield any treasure, but doesn't absconding with it count? And what about his attempt to poison you? That's at least a misdemeanor."

"The police have bigger fish to fry. They've been going over Oscar's house with a fine-toothed comb. They still haven't found any sign of the bribe money. Since the marked bills belonged to the 1990 stickup, they could trace them. But the bulk of the haul is as yet undiscovered."

Sophie sipped from her glass. "They didn't find any of the 1920 gold either, did they?"

"No. We still don't know where that was buried."

Noah's phone rang. "Oh, hi, Harry. I thought you'd be long gone by now... Sure, come on over." He hung up. "I presume Harry wants to express his remorse for his behavior."

"As well he should. Slipping arsenic into your mother's elderberry wine—most disrespectful."

"Don't forget he held us at gunpoint as well."

She cracked, "Yeah, over a pecan pie recipe and a toy grenade."

"Still…"

Harry knocked on the back door. "Hey, folks!" he said cheerily.

"What makes you so chipper?"

He grinned. "I'm happy to announce that my grandfather was not a loser."

Knowing Harry, Sophie had to ask. "How do you define loser?"

"Excellent question." When Harry eyed her glass thirstily, she filled another tumbler and handed it to him. He belted the alcohol down. "Ooh, that hits the spot. Thanks."

"You were saying?"

"Harry Senior did in fact commit a crime."

"And in your universe that rehabilitates him?"

"Absolutely. Every family should have a black sheep, a ne'er-do-well, an outlaw. Otherwise, what stories do you tell around the campfire?"

Noah said grumpily, "Why do you need a relative? You're a natural."

"Nah, I couldn't have done it without a role model— or at least genes I could use to justify my iniquitous tendencies." Harry was irrepressible.

Sophie had had enough. "So what did Harry Senior do?"

"He stole the bribe money!"

She mentally listed all the sources of lolly attested to so far. "Okay, at least the cash from the 1920 holdup has been recovered. Some of the banknotes from the 1990 have been found. Am I good so far?"

"Yes."

"But you're saying the money Filou offered to Hiram Northcutt to let him buy the land—that *Harry* took it? Didn't you tell us Oscar was the thief?"

"I was misinformed." Harry sobered. "Well, to be precise, he told the truth to a point. He *did* smoke Vasquez. And he *did* find the carpetbag—" He squinted at them. "But it was empty."

Noah stirred. "Where did you learn this?"

He beamed. "I had a little chat with Oscar."

"In prison?"

"No, no. He's out on bail. The charge is second-degree homicide, and the judge didn't deem him a flight risk. I caught him at home. He was packing his bags."

"Did you call the police?"

"Me? No. I offered him a deal if he'd come clean to me."

"Oscar told you things he didn't tell the police?" Sophie was flabbergasted.

"Oh, yeah. He gave me a whole slew of material—including what I relayed to the cops at our little chinwag last Monday."

"So Oscar *himself* was your source?"

"Yup."

Sophie whistled. "Question: why would he tell *you* anything?"

"I offered to give him an alibi."

"An alibi! He'd already confessed. Why would he need an alibi?"

Harry winked. "He doesn't."

"But—"

He took out a small tape recorder. "How about we get it from the horse's mouth?"

Sophie glanced at it. "Oscar allowed you to record him?"

Harry gaped at her. "Are you kidding?"

Noah put his elbows on the counter. "Never mind, Sophie. Play it, Sam."

Harry pressed the button. Oscar's voice came out jangly and shrill.

"I was by the grave. The carpetbag was stuck in the soil. I was trying to wrest it loose when the train whistle blew. As the train pulled in, I saw shadowy figures in the back of the caboose. Some of them jumped off and ran into the woods on the far side of the tracks. Vasquez jumped last and started toward me. He had a big sack slung over his shoulder. He saw the open pit and..." They heard some rustling and heavy breathing, then Oscar came on again. "He clapped me on the back and said, 'Gracias.' I think he aimed to use the hole to stash his sack. When he leaned over it, I brained him with the shovel, then toppled him in."

Harry's voice prompted, "What did you do then?"

"I grabbed the sack and the suitcase and took them to my car."

Noah smacked his hand on the counter. "I *knew* it. He took them both! Why didn't you tell this to the police?"

Harry stopped the recorder. "I had to withhold some juicy bits or I'd never get paid."

"But—"

Sophie grumbled, "Let's just hear the rest."

Harry clicked the button again.

"When I came back to bury Vasquez, Pennyman was standing near the shelter."

Noah gasped. "So Oscar *did* see Roger."

Sophie spluttered, "Why the hell was *Roger* at Dane Circle in the middle of the night?"

Harry pressed pause. "He'd dug up—if you'll pardon the expression—a clue that Audrey had buried Filou there. He'd come down to scope it out."

"What did Oscar do?"

"He asked Roger what he was doing there. Roger excitedly told him that he was on track to solve a long-dormant mystery—a homicide right here in Marmion Grove. He spoke of Agnes's letter and how it led him to Charles Filou. He had tracked down the Hispano-Suiza sedan." Harry sneered, "Some desiccated redneck in western Maryland had it in his barn. He said he'd picked it up in a junkyard but never even took it for a spin. It had been gathering dust for decades."

Noah gave Sophie a knowing look.

"Anyway, he showed Oscar a circus poster he'd found stuck between the cushions in the back seat. It was wrapped around a rolling pin. A bloody rolling pin. And I'm not swearing."

Sophie gasped. "That's how the blood got on the poster!"

Noah fidgeted. "Odd the police didn't find it."

Harry shrugged. "They had no cause to suspect a crime had been committed. Why bother to search for anything beyond ownership papers?"

He turned the machine on again. "I thought I'd successfully headed Pennyman off when—"

"Wait a minute." Sophie held up a hand. "Did they

know each other?"

"What difference would that make?"

"Roger would hardly have divulged his discoveries to Oscar if he was aware of the family connection."

"Ah, but he wasn't. He'd only solved the mystery of Filou's disappearance. He hadn't yet identified a perpetrator."

"But how—"

"And who—"

As they seemed about to settle in for a longish debate, Harry interrupted impatiently, "Do you want to hear the rest of the recording or not?"

"Please." Sophie locked her lips.

"I'd successfully headed Pennyman off when he noticed the shovel. He walked over to the hole. I knew he'd see the body and figure out what had happened. I had to think fast. 'Oh,' I said, 'I was about to tell you. I stumbled upon this fellow. I think he's dead, but I have no idea who he is. Would you mind going for the police?' Instead of leaving, Roger bent down to examine Vasquez. So I said, 'Okay, I'll go' and pretended to head to the post office building. Instead I picked up the shovel and beaned him too."

There was a short silence, then Noah burst out, "Oscar killed my *father*?"

Harry gave Noah a sympathetic look. "It wasn't planned." He pressed stop on the machine.

"Wait a minute." Sophie clicked her tongue. "How did the shovel end up in the carriage house at Peveril Hall?"

The question roused Noah out of his funk. "Don't forget the poster. That came from the garage too, not from the hoard Roger confiscated from us."

"If you'll stop interrupting, I'll explain. After Oscar knocked Roger off, he figured the safest place to stow everything was at Peveril Hall. There would be no way to trace it back to Oscar Northcutt of Glen Echo."

"But what about Filou's carpetbag? What happened to his money?"

Noah poked Sophie. "He told you. Oscar took it along with Vasquez's sack."

"Not exactly." Harry chuckled. "This is where my sainted grandpa comes in. See, the night of Filou's demise in April of 1920, Harry was on his way to see Agnes. He walked up the drive around one in the morning and found the ring in the courtyard where Audrey had dropped it. Harry was still standing in the yard when she returned with James."

Noah stirred. "Funny, we all assumed that Audrey had toddled off to bed by then."

"No. See, she first drove Filou's car to Bethesda to pick James up. When they arrived back at the Hall right on Harry's heels, he jumped in the bushes and watched."

"That's how Filou's car came to be in the courtyard."

Sophie cried, "Why did Harry hide? He wasn't planning to burgle the place, was he?"

Harry contrived to look offended. "My grandfather? A burglar? Nothing so mundane. No, Agnes had told him that Audrey disapproved of their relationship. He didn't want her to find out they were secretly meeting."

"So what did he see?"

"Audrey and James stood in the courtyard arguing—the bits he overheard seemed to be about what to do with the body. Finally, Audrey went back inside the house and James disappeared behind the building. He reappeared carrying Filou over his shoulder."

"That's when Agnes glimpsed the shadow with the bundle."

"Right. After Agnes went back to her quarters, Harry decided to follow James, who took the car down to Dane Circle. He buried Filou next to a freshly planted hedge. Before he refilled the hole, James tossed a carpetbag in on top. Harry waited until he left, then quick like a bunny hopped over and tugged the bag out."

Sophie—who was by now used to Harry's embellishing the truth, took exception. "But you said the suitcase was still in the grave when Oscar found it."

Harry giggled. "This is where it gets funny. See, my grandfather was afraid someone might recognize the bag, so he emptied the contents into a knapsack and threw the carpetbag back in."

Noah didn't buy it. "You're telling us that when Oscar hooked it out of the grave, he didn't check *inside*?"

Harry leveled a solemn gaze at Noah. "He'd just killed a man. Do you think he'd take a few minutes to inspect his trophy? No, he lugged it back to his car on the double."

Sophie refilled her glass. "Back to Harry Senior. He is now endowed with a boatload of cash. What was his next step?"

"Oh, this is the best part. Harry was so cocky he went right back to Peveril Hall, proposed to Agnes, and gave her the ring."

Noah's lip curled. "I take it he didn't tell her about the money."

For a moment, Harry shifted on his stool. "Uh, no."

"But *she* told *him* what she'd seen that night."

Sophie had an inspiration. "He was the one who

helped her write the letter to the constable!"

"Yup. He figured he'd do a good deed by exposing a crime."

"No, he didn't." Noah put his empty glass in the sink. "He wanted to make sure the police would be distracted from any evidence he might have left at the scene."

Sophie pondered the new revelations. "She must have also told him she was pregnant that night. So he took his pot of gold and hit the road. What a..." She caught Noah's expression and kept her adjective to herself. "Where did he go?"

Harry sobered. "That's the thing. I know I told you before that he planned the 1920 train heist."

"Yeah, and then you admitted he was dumped by the robbers."

"No, no," cried Sophie. "First he said they'd killed him in Harpers Ferry—or was it California? At any rate, you only found a...a...body part."

Noah pointed an accusing finger at him. "Which, if any, of your yarns is true?"

Harry reddened. "None of them. Grandpa simply decided to take his jackpot and bug out. He wasn't the gang leader—or even a minion. Just a thief."

Noah muttered something.

"What was that?"

"But not a burglar."

Harry grinned. "Heavens, no."

Sophie tried to clear her head. "So *was* there a train robbery in 1920 or was that a lie too?"

"No, no. It really happened. A gang halted the train in the woods just north of Kensington and snatched the mail bag. Got away with some ten thousand dollars in checks and cash."

"But it was recovered."

"Like I told you."

"What about the gold?"

"There was never any gold." He scowled. "My grandfather made it up to look good."

Sophie leaned forward. "How on earth do you know all this?"

"FBI records. They had a list of what was taken. No gold."

"Yeah, but how did you learn all this about Harry?"

"Ah. That's pretty cool. I told you I tracked down my father, Harry Junior, in Florida, right?"

"Right, but he didn't remember anything about his father."

"That's not entirely true. Harry Senior came to see him."

"You're kidding! When? Where had he been?"

"Whoa, slow down. I told you my parents divorced in 1970, right?"

"When you were ten."

"Yes. My father moved to Florida. Well, one day who should turn up but Harry Senior." He spoke quickly to stem the mounting questions. "He told him essentially what I've told you—"

"And which version was that?" Noah's sarcasm was lost on Harry.

"That he—that is, Harry Senior—had nothing to do with the 1920 job, but he did witness Audrey's disposal of the body. And stole Filou's money."

"Why did he jump ship?"

Harry hunched his shoulders. "You were right, Sophie. He didn't want to be encumbered with a wife and child, and he sure as hell didn't want to squander his new-found wealth on diapers and furniture. So he hitched his way out to California."

"And?"

"With Filou's cash as seed money, he founded a company that made zippers. Turned it into a million-dollar clothing franchise."

"Huh."

Sophie was dubious. "Why did Harry Senior bother to confess to his son? I mean, he turned his back on him all those years ago."

Harry shifted on his seat. "Dunno. I guess he wanted to get it off his chest. He left after that and never got back in touch."

"And your father? What was his reaction?"

"Dad? He was fine with it." He smirked. "His girlfriend wasn't. She kept agitating to petition Harry Senior for some kind of stipend or bequest. She even threatened to go to the police, but Dad was adamant. He wanted no part of 'unethical' behavior." He grimaced. "I must say I'm rather ashamed of him. Didn't follow in the family tradition. Ethics. Pah!"

Noah took his glass out of the sink and poured more whiskey in it. He didn't offer any to Harry.

Sophie decided to let it go. "What happened when you told Oscar you knew Filou's bag was empty?"

"What could he do? He admitted it." Harry's mouth twisted. "He expected me to use that to get him off the hook. Ha."

"You didn't tell him Harry Senior took it?"

Harry put a hand to his breast. "And despoil my ancestor's reputation?"

"What about the alibi you promised him?"

"I lied." Harry's smile was serene.

The whole affair left Sophie feeling very cross. "Let me get this straight. The lie you told us to conceal another lie, which papered over another lie…is also a lie?" She counted on her fingers. "Have I missed one?"

Apparently, Harry didn't think this required an answer.

Chapter Thirty-Nine

Too much mercy…often resulted in further crimes which were fatal to innocent victims who need not have been victims if justice had been put first and mercy second.
~Agatha Christie

Smithsonian, Atrium Café, Sunday, June 2

Noah blew the foam off his beer. "This is nice. I'm glad you could come over for lunch."

"I'm looking forward to seeing your exhibit."

"Well, you're in luck. I wangled a private tour." His eyes sparkled. "I happen to know the one in charge."

Sophie—who had known all along but found his little subterfuge too entertaining to dispel, said in a shocked voice, "That would be you?"

He preened. "The one and only. Eat up and we'll sneak in the back way."

She took a bite of her burger. "This is scrumptious."

"Yes, and I want you to know I'm proud of you. The other museum restaurant is pushing plant-based protein. It's like Chinese food; you're hungry an hour later."

Sophie decided it was time to bring up her purpose for visiting. "You said Captain Hinckley had given you an update. I want to hear it."

"Oh, yeah." He put his burger down. "Oscar has admitted that the bribe money wasn't in Filou's grave."

"That's not news. It only lends further credence to Harry's claim that his grandfather took it."

"Right. I briefed the good detective on Harry's latest revision. He somewhat less than cheerfully added it to the file. I have a feeling he won't balk at closing this phase of the investigation."

Sophie agreed. "At least one good thing came out of all this."

"What's that?"

"It puts to bed forever the notion that your mother killed your father."

Noah choked. "You never really bought into that, did you?"

"Of course not." She sipped her iced tea. "What about the train money?"

"From the 1920 robbery?"

"No, from 1990. The one Miguel and his gang pulled off."

Noah nodded. "Once they played Harry's tape recording for Oscar, he made a full confession. Guess what he'd done with the spoils?"

"I give up."

"Poured it into the upkeep of his beloved Wurlitzer."

Sophie put down her glass. "You're kidding! How much cash did it involve? Tens of thousands, as I recall. That band organ must be a money pit!"

Noah shook his head. "Madman."

"Who is?"

"Oscar. He's certifiable."

"Well, duh. He murdered two people."

"It's not that. He was seduced by filthy lucre—but only so he could maintain a musical instrument. Bizarre."

She dunked her burger in the pool of ketchup. "It must run in the family."

"Why do you say that?"

"I had a call from Peggy Dane. She told me that the bag of silver dollars we found in her hedge was part of a thirty-year-old burglary."

"The coins belonged to Peggy?"

"To her late husband."

Noah frowned. "How did she even hear about it? They disappeared into Harry's pocket and with any luck he spent them on a new pair of pants."

"Yesterday Ian presented himself at her front door and confessed that when he was a teenager he and a couple of pals broke into Peggy's apartment. The Danes were away for spring break, but according to her, none of you Marmion Grovers ever bother to lock your doors."

"It's true." Noah munched on a French fry.

"The boys purloined the coins and some books they thought might be valuable, and drank a couple of beers."

"A prank. *Hmm*. Why bring it up now?"

"Ian was required to get a higher security clearance for his new job at State. Part of his 'penitence' was to admit his guilt and ask his victim for forgiveness."

"So did Peggy forgive him?"

"She was inclined to let it go. It wasn't a lot of money, plus she'd only bought the books at a yard sale a month before." She chuckled. "Evidently the gang cleaned up after themselves—even recapped the beers they didn't finish. She appreciated that."

"So young... How come Ian didn't return the silver dollars before this?"

"One of the other boys had buried them, Ian didn't know where until the night we dug them up."

"What did they do with the books?"

"The paperbacks were discovered in a heap by the tracks a few days after the crime was reported. Only one old hardback was missing."

Noah brooded over the news. "Thirty years… When was the break-in?"

"I don't remember… Oh, wait." She gazed at Noah. "The spring of 1990."

"The year my father died." He sucked in a breath. "Yard sale. Did she say where it was?"

"As a matter of fact, it was at Peveril Hall."

"Oh my God. I remember it. My parents had a great row over some book that Mother had sold. Dad was yelling about it's being super rare and very valuable. He said he'd discovered it in a cupboard. Mother sent him down to the P.O. to see if he could buy it back."

Sophie nodded. "Peggy tells Roger it's been stolen, but he stumbles across a pile of books near the tracks. Finds the book. Opens it. The letter falls out."

"And the rest is tragedy."

Noah sighed. "It's still unclear how it ended up in the bottom of a box of his books. Wouldn't he have kept it out—or put it with Agnes's things?"

"Maybe he was killed before he had decided what to do with it." Sophie saw a silver lining. "At least now we can return the book to its rightful owner."

"Yes. Aren't you glad you didn't let Eudora sell it at the book sale?"

"It would have fetched a pretty penny, though." She finished her drink. "Shall we?"

As they rose from the table, Noah's phone buzzed. "Hello? Oh, hello, Blanche." He whispered, "It's Blanche Prine, Agnes's daughter… Whoa, slow down.

What? She did *what*? How did you find out?" He listened for a long time, his face going through multiple contortions while Sophie tapped a foot nervously.

What could she be telling him that's so earth-shattering?

Finally Noah hung up. He stood there, his eyes vacant, the phone dangling from his fingers. Sophie had to poke him twice before he reacted.

"What did Blanche say?"

He sat down abruptly. "You'd better sit down for this."

She did as she was told. *Anything to make him talk.*

He took a deep breath, then gripped his mug and drained the last drops of beer. He sat back, still panting.

"Noah…"

"Remember way back when we weren't sure what role—if any—Agnes actually played in the mystery?"

"She was a witness—happened to be there at the right time."

"She didn't just *happen* to be there."

"What do you mean?"

"The night Audrey killed Filou and Harry Senior came a-calling, Agnes was outside."

"I know. To shoo away the raccoons."

"No, to meet Harry. They were…um…messing around in the stable when Audrey came back with James."

Sophie sucked in a breath. "So they were in flagrante delicto while James and Audrey were dealing with Filou's corpse?"

"At first. They stopped when James came around the corner with the body. She and Harry watched as James stripped off the black clothes and put Filou's suit back on him."

"Ah, that's when the hat fell out." The pieces were falling into place. "What did they do with the discarded pants and shirt?"

"She didn't see. James must have pitched them."

"Pitched… No, he left them in the car. Remember Curly's news clipping? They found a bundle of clothes in the Hispano-Suiza."

"Ah. An oversight."

Sophie shook her head. "I'm sure they didn't constitute a clue. Filou wouldn't have kept any identification in the pockets. Then what happened?"

"Like our Harry said, his grandfather followed James to Dane Circle. He saw him dig the grave and throw the carpetbag in alongside the corpse."

"Okay. So why are you so discombobulated?"

"Because what we didn't know was that *Agnes* followed *Harry*."

"To Dane Circle?"

"To Dane Circle. After she saw Harry empty the carpetbag, she hightailed it back to Peveril Hall. When he returned, he proposed and gave her the ring. But she had seen him pick it up off the ground."

Sophie yelped. "I'd forgotten. Agnes told her son about that. I didn't put two and two together. That could only mean she knew he was a liar."

"Right. Then, when Harry didn't say a word about the money, she finally saw him for the bounder he was."

"She broke off the engagement?"

"Nothing so timid. She offered him a celebratory toast of elderberry wine. *Doctored* elderberry wine."

Sophie's hand went to her mouth. "The rat poison?"

Noah nodded. "Agnes murdered Harry."

"*Agnes*? Oh my God!"

Noah warmed to his narration. "Then our mercenary little maid took it upon herself to relieve Harry of his bankroll."

"What did she do with the body?"

"She dragged it into the woods." He wrinkled his nose. "In 1920 there were still foxes, coyotes, even black bears, roaming the neighborhood. It was never found."

For the first time Sophie felt a touch of pity for a Quayle. "I don't understand. Why not admit she knew about the money and tell him he'd have to take her with him or she'd spill the beans?"

"Nobody could accuse Harry Senior of being smart. No, he was bent on taking a powder, leaving her in the lurch."

"Her letter." Sophie said slowly, "The letter to her mother announcing her engagement. Remember? She said that once they had a nest egg she could quit her job and be a real housewife. She had been working since she was fourteen, supporting her family. The sight of all that dough must have been irresistible."

"And when she realized Harry was going to keep it for himself…"

"She did what she had to do."

Sophie knew it would take more than a minute to absorb the news. Finally she managed, "How did Blanche learn this?"

"As she lay dying, Agnes confessed to killing Harry. Blanche wasn't about to rat out her own mother. Until the money appeared, that is."

"The money?"

"Uh-huh. Agnes told Blanche everything, except what happened to the bribe."

"So how did she—I mean, Blanche—find out?"

"A few weeks ago, she received a check from the Eden State Bank in Delaware for fifty thousand dollars. She called the bank to ask what it was for, and they told her Agnes had opened a savings account in late April of 1920 and deposited a substantial amount of currency. She had left instructions that it was to be liquidated twenty years after her death and the accumulated funds sent to Blanche. When Blanche asked to see the original documentation of the deposit, they sent her a certified letter from Agnes and a canvas bag—the kind armored cars use to transport deposits. Inside was a large envelope stamped with the return address of Charles Filou Development Company. It was empty. She reached the obvious conclusion."

"The certified letter—how did Agnes manage that?"

"It was a form letter. She only had to sign it."

"Huh." Sophie mulled over these new disclosures. "It begs the initial question, doesn't it? The question that brought us all here: why did Agnes write the letter to the constable?"

Noah shrugged. "To give herself an alibi?"

"But if the letter to the police was her alibi, why not send it?"

"Well, for one, she had been terminated. She could just leave the scene. And two, no one knew or cared what happened to Filou, and most people—including her family—were just as happy to write Harry Senior off as a bum. She didn't need the letter."

"Her family." Sophie stared at Noah. "Agnes did make one mistake though. She lied to her mother about her marriage plans."

"How so?"

"The letter to her mother was dated April 20—*after* she'd done away with Harry."

"She kept her ill-gotten gains secret from her family as well."

"And why not? Her mother had disowned her."

"So it wasn't actually a mistake." Noah sat back. "She was a lot smarter than we gave her credit for."

"And had a real knack for self-preservation."

He pushed away from the table. "Oh, one more thing. You want to know how the opal ring got into Roger's box?"

"Was Ian right? Audrey simply forgot it when they moved?"

"Nope."

"Audrey gave the ring back to Agnes?"

"Also nope. Agnes stole it back when she left the Northcutt employ. Apparently she hid it in the house, intending to return for it, but the Northcutts moved before she had the chance, and the new owners refused her entrance."

"And Roger found it. He put it together with her letter to Constable Bustwick and the other evidence." Sophie crumpled up her napkin. "He solved the crime but never got the chance to present his evidence to the police."

Noah grunted. "Maybe it was karma that we came along." He slapped a twenty on the table and rose. "Ready?"

As they walked out of the café, Sophie halted and cried, "Poor Harry!"

"Harry Senior?"

"No, Harry III. Our Harry. He was so proud of his villainous ancestor. How crushed he'll be to learn he was done in by a mere slip of a girl."

"Although perhaps buoyed to discover that his sainted father wasn't a saint after all. Harry Junior must have made the whole thing up about Harry Senior and his zipper business."

"You're saying Harry Two is just as prone to embellish his family name as Harry Three?"

Noah burst into laughter. "So for once our Harry was hoist by his own petard. Delicious."

Sophie giggled. "Harry wanted so much to have a famously degenerate family and they all turn out to be petty con artists."

"I don't know. Harry Senior *did* steal the bribe money."

"Yes. Well, there's that."

They were both quiet, thinking over the last few days. Sophie felt numb. *Despite the red herrings, the conflicting clues, the misrepresentations—it all comes back to little Agnes.* "I'd like to go home for a while, Noah. I need a break to sort through my feelings."

Noah looked shaken as well. "Sure. Do you still want to see the exhibit?"

"Oh yes." She took a deep breath. "I'll meet you back here…when?"

"How about five? The museum closes at four thirty, but I have a key card. We can sneak in."

His puckish expression cheered her up. "Okay."

****

Smithsonian, Sunday, 5:00 p.m.

Sophie met Noah at the mall entrance. He flashed an ID at the security guard and led her to a staff elevator that took them up to the second floor. They hiked through a series of darkened, empty hallways. "These circle behind the galleries so we can move shows in and out with minimum disruption. Ah, here we are." He opened a door.

They entered a pitch black room. "Uh-oh, I forgot. We locked the main doors until the grand opening gala tomorrow night. Wait here." He crossed a large hall, his footsteps echoing on the marble floor. Suddenly, banks of track lights illuminated a barn-like space. Small alcoves wound around the hall. A large banner proclaimed The Story of the Book. Noah returned to her side. "I hope you won't be too distressed to learn that we're not featuring antique cars."

"Not me, but I'll bet Moe and Curly will be."

"No worries. We're in the planning stages, but the projected date for Classic Cars and the Crimes Committed in Them is next December. I have brought them in as consultants."

"Excellent."

They passed by presentations on paper making, the Silk Route, early manuscript creation, and illuminated manuscripts. Noah pointed at an exquisite miniature illustration depicting horsemen and hounds. "This is a page from the *Shahnameh*, the great book of the kings of Persia. Note the orangey-red hue? Its vibrancy is derived from lead. The artists were forever ailing, and no one knew why."

"Were other pigments toxic too?"

"Some." He moved on to a display on book binding. "For example, the vivid green of this book's cover is due to arsenic. Back in 1775, a man named Scheele mixed arsenic and copper to produce a gorgeous emerald green. Victorians loved it and used it in everything from journal illustrations to wallpaper and clothing. Even toys were painted with it. Those who worked with the stuff died at an alarming rate, covered in hideous sores."

Sophie gazed at Noah. "The Christie book. You don't suppose—"

"No, thank God. By 1920, manufacturers understood the lethal effects of arsenic and discontinued its use."

She wasn't entirely reassured. "You said they used it for wallpaper. Peveril Hall's a Victorian house."

Noah turned to her with a grin. "Perhaps we should lick the dining room wall and see if it upsets our tummies."

"Ha-ha. Say…the elderberry wine. Maybe it already contained enough arsenic to sicken you before Harry tampered with it."

"Well, that would be one less thing he can be indicted for." Noah took her hand. "I almost forgot. Gertrude telephoned."

"Your sister?"

"Uh-huh. I asked her about our book."

"The Christie?"

"Yup. Mother was cleaning out Roger's study a month after he disappeared and found it on his desk. She packed it in a box along with a bunch of his other books."

"I thought she locked the tower?"

"Not until a year later, when she finally acknowledged he wasn't going to return." He came to a glass case. A sign on the wall above it said Identifying First Editions. "Ah, here we are. This is what I wanted to show you."

Sophie drew in a breath. "*The Mysterious Affair at Styles*! I thought you gave it back to Peggy."

"I did. She sold it to an anonymous buyer, who lent

it to the museum." He pointed at a square sign underneath the display. "In return, he gets a shiny brass plaque."

"Oh, Noah." She gazed at it rapturously. "I'm so glad it didn't end up on a dusty shelf in some dusty bookshop, never to be read."

"Well, the masses will only have until the end of the year to admire it. It's a private loan."

Her eyes welled up. "That's too bad. So the buyer wants it back?"

"Afraid so." He looked down at her. His mouth twitched nervously. "But once the exhibit's over, you'll be able to read it whenever you want. That is, if you're living at the Hall." He fumbled with something in his pocket.

Silence.

He looked up. "Sophie? I meant with me. At the Hall. I decided not to sell the house. We could live there."

Continued silence.

"You and me. Peveril Hall. Sophie? Hello?"

She roused herself. "I'm here."

He relaxed slightly. "I was thinking we could have the ceremony in the townhall on Grace E. D. Sprigg Day. The Grove already springs for fireworks, so we could save some serious coin there. Of course they're left over from the Fourth of July. The fireworks, I mean."

She could only nod.

After a minute, he said shyly, "Here." He opened a little velvet box.

She stared at the beautiful emerald ring. Words stuck in her throat.

His voice cracking slightly, Noah whispered, "It was

Mother's."

"I…uh…remember. We found it in her box of mementos."

"Turns out she left it to me in her will. She wrote a little note that said, 'May it bring you the same joy your father brought me.' " He pressed his lips together. "I wish I could tell her that he didn't…didn't…"

Sophie touched the ring. "I think she knew."

After another silent minute, he said, "Sophie? Maybe I'm not being clear enough. Will you marry me?"

"I…" She didn't know how to tell him she couldn't respond because she was concentrating all her faculties on the throbbing in her chest.

"Sophie? Talk to me!" He held up the ring and said anxiously, "If you're worried about arsenic, emeralds don't contain anything toxic. I looked it up." He gazed at her. "What do you think?"

The dam broke.

The night watchman found them later, holding hands and taking turns reading to each other from *The Mysterious Affair at Styles*.

Thank you for purchasing
this publication of The Wild Rose Press, Inc.

For questions or more information
contact us at
info@thewildrosepress.com.

The Wild Rose Press, Inc.
www.thewildrosepress.com